The Last

of How

It Was

A NOVEL BY

T. R. PEARSON

For

Marian B. S. Young Orblike

One

She said it was a blood thing, Aunt Sister did, and not even
from Great-granddaddy really but likely Great-uncle Jack that
would be Great-uncle Cyrus Barnard Yount who got called
Jack everywhere but the front of the Bible, and Aunt Sister
insisted it was down from him with Great-granddaddy just a
conduit to Granddaddy himself who got the whole of it, and
Momma asked her the whole of what like she always asked her
the whole of what and Aunt Sister waved her hand in the air
like usual and like usual told her back, "You know," which
Momma said did not tell her anything so she got waved at and
You knowed all over again and Daddy suggested
Temperament? and Daddy suggested Passion? but Aunt Sister
stuck with foolishness like always, just plain foolishness she
guessed with maybe some passion to it somewhere but
foolishness mostly. Momma would have preferred
temperament and would have preferred passion, would have
preferred anything to plain foolishness as it was her own
daddy and him dead and in the ground and still spoke ill of,
but Aunt Sister insisted it was the fact of the thing and not
even his doing anyhow but down from Great-uncle Jack
primarily and maybe down somewhat from Great-aunt Della
too, but Momma objected to Great-aunt Della straightoff as
Aunt Della had not been but married in and Momma defied
Aunt Sister to say just how it was a blood thing when it was not
even blood really but pure matrimony instead and Aunt Sister
told her, "Maybe," and told her, "Somewhat," in that sweet
high voice that let Momma know she had told her both of them
before.

They killed an indian in Oklahoma which was not hardly the thing they'd done the most of but was near about entirely what they got recollected for whenever they did get recollected and they did get recollected with some regularity since nobody else much roundabout had ever killed an indian but just Germans and Japanese almost exclusively. And while they had in fact killed him together, there was a general agreement locally that Aunt Della had killed the most of him since Aunt Della had been the one with the rifle and had shot him the first time and the second time too which would be once in Oklahoma and once in Arkansas because truly they had only begun to kill him in Oklahoma and had not pursued him exactly but had run up on him anyhow outside Osceola and so had finished killing him there. But as Aunt Sister told it, Great-uncle Jack had been the one that wanted to kill him straightoff, had been the one that tried to kill him straightoff with his own eight fingers and two thumbs, but he was a mean in-dian, Aunt Sister said and a big strapping indian too with fingers and thumbs himself and a bonehandled knife in his boot that he went for straightoff which Aunt Sister said was just like an indian, just precisely exactly the sort of thing an indian would do, especially against a man with just fingers and just thumbs but just Aunt Della too. And they chased him directly, or anyhow Uncle Jack caught up the knife and chased him with it but he was old then and already short-winded and so could not overtake even a wounded indian who ran gripping his shoulder with his fingers over the hole in the back and his thumb over the hole in the front, and Uncle Jack swore at him with what breath he could get and cursed him and waved the bonehandled knife in the air like a wild man, and Aunt Sister told Momma, "Blood thing," and told Momma, "Foolishness mostly."

Daddy was the best one to hear it from because Daddy was what Momma called indelicate and so did not leave out what Aunt Sister left out and what Momma left out too but told all of it, even some of it that never happened, and he said what got done and said what got said just like it had got done and just like it had got said or worse sometimes which was what Momma objected to specifically though she did not care for the truth of the thing either on account of it was rough and on account of it was vulgar and on account of Daddy liked it that way. He said they had lived in a shack, Great-aunt Della and Great-uncle Jack that nobody called Cyrus Barnard or even plain Jack really but always Mr. Jack like they called Granddaddy always Mr. Buck, and while they had tried to improve it into something not so shacklike, had worked and labored to make it something neat and regular, it would not ever yield to them as they did not have the touch for neat and the touch for regular which Daddy said was what had drawn them to each other in the first place.

She'd come from the Wolf Island Creek Cottens who'd commenced as farmers but did not have much talent for it and so sold their property and bought into a drygoods and wares business in Stacy which was where Uncle Jack first feasted on Aunt Della, or anyhow Daddy said that was what Uncle Jack had called it, feasting, and not just laying eyes on or looking at but sometimes even exchanging longing glances with as Uncle Jack had a kind of mysterious verbosity to him that he'd cultivated and refined somewhere and somehow but nobody knew just where and just how really only that he had not cultivated and refined it off his own daddy who did not ever but grunt for a thing to get it. Of course he won her, Daddy said, won her with the feasting and the glancing and whatnot, and as Daddy told it Uncle Jack had always insisted that on his wedding day she seemed to him a vision come down from the heavenly orb what with the baby's breath all roundabout her head and the lacy frills on her dress starched and standing up most everywhere, but truly there was not anything heavenly orblike about Aunt Della except for maybe just the baby's breath and maybe just the lace since Aunt Della looked the image of her two sisters who looked the image of their Granddaddy Cotten who had been notoriously unsavory and unappealing, unsavory through his own exploits and enterprises mainly, but unappealing by way of his daddy who carried the Cotten ears and the high Cotten forehead into a union with a Ruffin Tate, which would be one of your hooked-nosed, tiny-little-chinned Tates, and together they produced such pure and untainted homeliness that it had not been noticeably diluted and dissolved away even three generations later when Aunt Della got born with the ears and the forehead and the nose and the tiny little chin too that still then were not your divine and ethereal items and did not grow to be heavenly orblike except for Uncle Jack who was all they needed to be heavenly orblike for.

We own a photograph of them that Momma keeps in the endtable drawer and Aunt Sister claims she's got one just like it and two others not so much just like it but she cannot ever recollect what drawers she keeps hers in so we look at Momma's whenever we look at one which is bent and broken at the corners and had a cup sat on it one time or another judging from the ring but you can still see Uncle Jack plain enough and can still see Aunt Della and the hindquarters of Uncle Jack's mule, little Spud, and the most of his wagon which would be the one with the roof on it and the sides to it that him and Aunt Della traveled in and traded out of once they had give up farming and sold off their acreage but for the little piece their house sat on, and notwithstanding the bent corners or the ring either you can tell just precisely exactly how unheavenly orblike Aunt Della was with her hair cut in bangs across her forehead and her nose and her chin and the little wiry rest of her and you can tell as well just precisely exactly how unheavenly orblike Uncle Jack was too which is not anything Momma and Aunt Sister tend to discuss much as him and them go back in the same direction.

She had no talent for farming, of course, since she had not been raised to farm while Uncle Jack, who had been raised to farm, had no talent for it either so while he sowed corn and alfalfa and cotton and started tobacco too, the fields came up primarily in quartzstones and shale and consequently he did not harvest much corn or alfalfa and did not pick much cotton or pull much tobacco but just grubbed rocks mostly, or anyhow when he was not wishing milk from his cow or eggs from his chickens or nursing his pigs that annually contracted a sickness and annually died of it. His only unmitigated success was likely in the area of tomatoes as he had planted enough vines for a boatload of Italians and so had more than plenty even after the worms got what they got and the groundhogs got what they got which left Uncle Jack to get what he got that would be stewed tomatoes and sliced tomatoes and tomatoes all mashed and pureed in sauces in addition to the sores in his mouth and the hives between his shoulders along with his entirely reformed opinion of pulpy food in general.

But aside from the tomatoes not much of what was supposed to come up came up and most everything that was supposed to stay up fell down commencing with the chickenhouse that lost its roof in a wind and as the roof had been supporting the walls they collapsed atop each other mortally wounding one of the occupants who consequently got stewed and seasoned and served up with a red sauce. Along about the second anniversary of its construction the pigpen came all to pieces, due to gravity primarily, and likely the pigs would have escaped and lit out for the new territory if they had not been so ill and feeble, so Uncle Jack just patched the thing with tin and wire and what rubbish he could find and then turned his attention somewhat to the lean-to out back of the house that kept the weather off his stovewood as the top of it had come loose from the posts on the one end and the clapboard on the other and so was supported exclusively by the woodpile itself and adjusted up and adjusted down whenever the wood came and went so Uncle Jack turned his attention to it only somewhat since he could not decide was it troublesome or maybe just revolutionary.

Naturally the house itself was a matter of some persistent concern to Uncle Jack and Aunt Della too since they did not know but they might wake up one night not so much in it as underneath it, figured they'd probably wake up one night not so much in it as underneath it judging from the muleshed which had been fashioned after the main dwelling and had been quite sturdy and serviceable right up to the very moment it became just slabpile and so not sturdy anymore and not really serviceable either except as kindling. Surely the mule would have been killed what with the rafters and the planks and the shingles falling in all around him but Uncle Jack had already killed the mule previously and so spared him in a manner of speaking. Of course it had been accidental and unintentional, Daddy said, and probably did not bear mentioning except so as to illustrate a point that Daddy insisted needed illustrating notwithstanding Momma's objections and Aunt Sister's objections too which they voiced altogether and at once since they both had a notion of the point and an idea of the illustration and did not want to hear the one make the other on account of how it might be unflattering, Aunt Sister suggested like she did not know would it be unflattering or not and Momma said unflattering too like she did not know either.

So Daddy said there was this mule prior to little Spud that had been just plain Spud and bore no relation to little Spud except as his predecessor and namesake and him and Uncle Jack had got on like no-body'd believe, but then Daddy said Uncle Jack was always one to charm a mule, possessed a pure talent for mule charming, which was not Daddy's chief point but he dwelled on it anyhow until Momma looked at him that way she had of looking at him that worked like words only better, and Daddy said, "Anyway," and set back in partly with the mule but mostly with Uncle Jack who took up his axe out from the muleshed and took up his snaking chain and fitted out plain Spud in his harness and then led him out between the cornfield and the tobacco field which were both just commencing to sprout and come up in rocks as it was spring. They headed on across the level ground and then up a slight rise to a wood at the western edge of Uncle Jack's property where Uncle Jack intended to lay over some trees and so season them for the winter. Naturally, Daddy said, Uncle Jack carried the axe and the chain and walked along in the front and Spud followed behind him unreined and untethered and solely of his own accord which Daddy said fairly much confirmed Uncle Jack's mysterious and near about miraculous hold over mules, or anyhow he observed it to me primarily and then repeated "Mysterious" and repeated "Near about miraculous" somewhat to me and somewhat to himself and somewhat to Momma and Aunt Sister too since Daddy was not one to let a thing lie no matter how he got looked at.

He had in mind several hickories and two loblolly pines and he set in with one of the hickories straightoff as it was slight and slender and Uncle Jack was not one to tax himself at the outset of any sort of undertaking or actually at the middle or the end of it either but especially not at the outset, so he hacked at the slightest and slenderest of the hickories and brought it down without hardly breaking a sweat after which he cut off what limbs might be a hindrance and secured one end of the snaking chain to the treetrunk and fastened the other to the mule prior to suggesting that perhaps plain Spud would oblige him in dragging the entire tree on out from the woods to a nearby grassy place where Uncle Jack figured to prop it on rocks he guessed since he could bend over most anywhere and raise up with one. Naturally plain Spud commenced to drag the thing straightoff once it had been only just suggested to him, Daddy said, that he go ahead and commence to drag it, and though he strained and faltered at first he proceeded to build himself up a head of steam and fairly much yanked that entire tree on out of the woods, yanked it almost exactly like he yanked the second one, which was bigger, and yanked it almost exactly like he yanked the third one too, which was bigger still and lay at the far limits of just what plain Spud could yank. So a loblolly pine was not even a remotely yankable item which meant Uncle Jack would not have to just cut down the loblollies but would need to halve them and third them and quarter them too and once Uncle Jack set in to figuring and speculating how many hacks it might take to fell and halve the third and quarter a loblolly he grew distraught and exasperated since he did not believe he had that many hacks left in him, and as was his way when he got distraught and exasperated over such a thing as felling and halving and thirding and quartering a loblolly Uncle Jack set about pondering a way around it all which Daddy decided was part of his point and part of his illustration though not by any means the most of the one or the most of the other either, but just a germane factor, Daddy called it, and then took some rebuttal from Aunt Sister who could not see as it was a failing to be curious about a thing, could not see as it was but daring and adventuresome to which Momma amended inventive herself and Daddy told the both of them, "Alright," that way he said Alright which had nothing whatsoever to do with approval.

Uncle Jack figured they might could pull the thing over, figured they might cut it maybe halfway and then draw it on down with him naturally the one to do the cutting and plain Spud naturally the one to do the drawing on down, so he chose the smaller of the loblollies saving the bigger tree for the last just in case he never did get to it and he laid into the little one working like he usually did in wild and fairly misdirected bursts which tended to start well enough with a true lick but straightaway fell off to a general beating delivered partly by the actual axeblade and partly by the pole and every now and again by the helve too when the burst was especially wild and especially misdirected, so Uncle Jack cut into the loblolly some but just mauled it primarily while plain Spud looked on with what Uncle Jack took for a haughty expression as he was not in the proper frame and passio'ft to judge an expression really. And Daddy said Uncle Jack grew peevish right off, grew peevish almost exclusively with the mule since he could not see the profit in growing peevish with the tree, and he told plain Spud, "Alright then, you bring it down," and looped the snaking chain around the loblolly trunk one time as high up as he could manage prior to fastening the opposite end on the harness and then he smacked plain Spud on the rump once and told him, "Go on, go on, pull it over" and smacked plain Spud on the rump a second time and while he did not stride forward, not even so much as to draw the chain taut, plain Spud brought his head around and looked at Uncle Jack that way an animal has of looking at a human once he has sensed idiocy with whatever it is they sense idiocy with.

Daddy indicated that was part of his point, not so much the idiocy really but Passion, he said, and Temperament and Aunt Sister added, Foolishness mostly, but Daddy told her just usually foolishness in the end and insisted on Passion and insisted on Temperament as it was his point and his illustration anyhow. Momma wanted to know was that the most of it, the passion and the temperament and even the foolishness too, since they did not any of them seem much of a revelation to her, but Daddy told her back it was likely only the half of it and maybe not that and Momma blew a breath like Momma can and wedged her chin between her thumb and forefinger and asked him, "Germane factors?" which Daddy did not say yes to exactly but did not say no to either.

Naturally plain Spud could not pull over the loblolly even once he'd drawn the chain taut and been actually driven some by Uncle Jack who Daddy said could drive a mule near about as well as he could charm one, so Uncle Jack, who had exhausted the bulk of his peevishness on plain Spud's hindquarters, took up the axe again and commenced to chew on the pine trunk with it as a means of aiding and assisting the mule who brought his head around at the sound of the axe so as to look at Uncle Jack almost precisely like he had looked at him before, and Daddy said Uncle Jack hacked and beat and beat and hacked and took time off to slap every now and again at plain Spud's backside until eventually plain Spud actually pressed forward ever so slightly and then inched some more and then inched some more after that before the significance of the pressing and the inching too struck Uncle Jack all at once and he lapsed into a hacking and beating frenzy so as to compound the pressing and compound the inching and only when they had become full striding did the true and earnest nature of Uncle Jack's predicament, which was actually plain Spud's predicament mostly, make itself clear and apparent to Uncle Jack who was the only one left for it to become clear and apparent to since plain Spud had got a grip on the thing previously. Daddy said the trunk had commenced to crack and had commenced to pop and splinter at the cut and then had set to pitching over and rotating somewhat when Uncle Jack hollered, "No!" which was hardly enough to undo everything the axe and the mule had jointly accomplished, but Uncle Jack hollered, "No!" again anyhow and "No!" after that too but could not hold up the tree even a little and it gathered some considerable velocity and sailed on down towards the underbrush which was essentially the direction of the mule too but Daddy did not let it get to the mule straightoff as he had a point to derive from his illustration and Momma asked him was it the other half of it altogether and Daddy told her back, "Yes ma'am."

He called it just a general blindness to consequences and called it pure shortsightedness and called it even foolishness mostly too and said it was in fact his main point and his main illustration at least until Oklahoma and until the indian which would still be the same point primarily itself, but Daddy said he felt obliged to establish the tendency beforehand, the tendency in Uncle Jack, that is, so as to imply and lead to the tendency in Great-granddaddy and naturally Granddaddy too, which was where it was all going anyhow, but Aunt Sister insisted it was a male tendency almost exclusively, insisted Daddy say as much outright and indicated me as the reason for it since Granddaddy was her own brother and Momma's own daddy and she did not want it let out that her and Momma too had inherited the shortsightedness and the general blindness as well as the foolishness and she indicated me as what might let it out otherwise, so Daddy announced how it was a male tendency, how it was a male tendency exclusively at least almost, and he lit his first Tarey-ton of the halfhour which was how he smoked them whenever Aunt Sister came to sit with us on account of her constitution which Aunt Sister made out to be fragile and delicate though her doctor Mr. Shackleford, who was Mamma's doctor too, said she could whip most men he'd ever come up on, and she held her powderblue Kleenex up to her nose like always and looked at Daddy overtop it in that disgusted way she had of looking at Daddy which was just precisely the way Momma had of looking at him too and so seemed to indicate and establish another tendency altogether.

Daddy had left plain Spud under the falling loblolly for an appreciable time and had left Uncle Jack employing his vocal cords to no good effect really, and seemed to me the lapse and the pause had served to heighten the drama of the predicament and the drama got heightened further still once Aunt Sister set about telling Daddy how vile a thing tobacco was and then allowed Momma to throw in with her own opinion which ran towards vileness itself and Daddy dipped his ash in the scallop shell he always dipped his ashes in and listened to more of what he had to listen to most every time he struck a match. So the drama was at somewhat of a frightful pitch by the time Daddy got back to the tree and the mule and Uncle Jack too or anyhow seemed to me at a frightful pitch until I recollected how the mule had not got killed in the muleshed but prior to it in the woods by a tree and as these seemed to be the woods and this seemed to be the tree the drama fell away precipitously and straightoff.

Daddy said it hit him a glancing blow and then yanked him on down not completely beneath it but beneath it enough so as to finish what the glancing blow had commenced, and Daddy said it was not a pretty thing, the coming together of the mule and the loblolly, but not so extraordinarily gruesome either since plain Spud did not look anything but asleep mostly and only pulverized here and there. Of course Uncle Jack ran to him straightaway still hollering "No!" with remarkable regularity notwithstanding how utterly fruitless even the entire bulk of "No!"s together had proved to be and he pushed at the loblolly with his arms and kicked at it with his feet and laid his back to it as well but could not move it off plain Spud who was dead already even then, and Daddy said Uncle Jack got wild and frantic and tried to prize at the tree with a stick that broke and tried to prize at the tree with the axehandle that broke too and so he just blubbered instead, blubbered like a child, Daddy said, and laid his face atop an unpulverized portion of plain Spud and wailed and moaned and still said "No" when he could get the breath for it, and Daddy said it all suggested a point he'd like to make, a point about the passions and emotions in Uncle Jack and Uncle Jack's people which would be Great-granddaddy and Granddaddy and Aunt Sister and Momma too but Momma told him he'd used up his point already, had expended both halves of it and so did not have even any piece of a point left to him, and Daddy told her back, "Alright then," that way he had that meant something otherwise.

He said they were a passionate, were an emotional people, Younts that is, said it direct to me and announced to Momma and Aunt Sister how he figured it was a thing I ought to know, a thing I ought to bear in mind much like a point if not precisely a point exactly, and then he proceeded to something else directly, the something else in this case being Aunt Della who was home ignorant of the loblolly and the dead mule beneath it and so had not got worked up into a froth just yet which gave Daddy the opportunity to explain and expand upon Aunt Della's frothiness as it was a trait with her just like the passion and emotion and foolishness and general blindness too were traits with Uncle Jack. Aunt Della derived from a frothy people, and even Momma and Aunt Sister agreed to it once Daddy had said it, and Aunt Sister herself recollected how a Ruffin Tate, maybe even Aunt Della's own momma's brother, had got asked by a Danville McGehee if perhaps he wasn't a Dunleavy on account of how he put the McGehee in mind of a Dunleavy, and Aunt Sister believed it was likely the chin mostly and maybe the nose somewhat too since present-day Tates looked like present-day Dunleavys to her because of the chin mostly and because of the nose somewhat, but the Ruffin Tate told the McGehee straight out, "Hell no!" and even Aunt Sister told it Hell no! so as to be historically accurate though she was not a profane woman and like Momma took a dim view of all manner of swearing, and she said the Ruffin Tate had not hardly got his mouth shut when he went ahead and knocked the McGehee down with his right hand and then removed a sizeable portion of the McGehee's remaining teeth with his left boot and he did not explain why at the time even though the McGehee hollered and wailed and wondered why, did not explain why really until he got picked up by the sheriff that was a Perkins and by the sheriff's brother and the sheriff's brother's boy and even then did not say but, "Them Dunleavys's from Connecticut. I ain't like them not anyhow," which Aunt Sister said had some reason to it though not hardly ponderous amounts and while Daddy explained it as a clash of ideologies Momma just said, "Yankees" which seemed to address the thing well enough and so Daddy went ahead and said "Yankees" too.

Aunt Sister wanted to know wasn't that pure frothiness if anything was and though we all figured yes, we guessed it was pure frothiness exactly, Aunt Sister felt obliged to supply us with a frothy moment from the Wolf Island Creek Cotten side of the family too but she could not come up with one straightaway and so Daddy set in on the frothy moment chief in his mind which was actually the frothy moment chief in Aunt Sister's mind as well that she had in fact come up with straightaway but had kept to herself as it had seemed an indelicate frothy moment ill-suited for mixed company. So Daddy said there'd been this gang of Cottens and Momma told him, "Louis," bending it upwards like she was prone to, and Aunt Sister told him, "Louis," bending it some herself, and Daddy said there'd been this gang of Cottens that were all nephews and cousins and brothers to Mr. Robert Cotten, one of the prominent elder Cottens of the home-place, and they had thrown together to be a gang on behalf of Mr. Robert Earl himself who was having what Daddy called difficulties and got told "Louis" again by Momma and by Aunt Sister too and so Daddy called them "Acute difficulties" and lit a Tareyton.

Daddy said Mr. Robert Earl Cotten liked a taste every now and again which just meant most all the time for Mr. Robert Earl Cotten who only called it every now and again to appease Mrs. Robert Earl Cotten, a firm Christian woman who did not believe anybody should do anything most all the time, especially drink which she did not believe anybody should do even every now and again so Mr. Robert Earl Cotten called it every now and again actually implying rarely and only once in a while and he kept his bottle out back of the house in the toolshed behind a plank and did not visit it but every day which was his every now and again and once in a while too. Now Daddy said Mr. Robert Earl Cotten had a womanfriend, which would be a womanfriend aside from Mrs. Robert Earl Cotten, who lived through the woods towards Oregon Hill and operated what Daddy called a cottage industry, and he liked it so much he said it again and got a rise out of Aunt Sister who squirted some air out between her lips before she lay her fingers atop them. Daddy said this womanfriend of Mr. Robert Earl Cotten's did not manufacture any palpable item, not so as you'd notice anyhow, but instead she provided what Daddy called services and provided what Daddy called favors and charged what Daddy called a fee, and Daddy said business was extraordinarily good most all the time primarily on account of the vast array of Cottens in what Daddy called the private sector, Cottens being more naturally attentive to their servicing than your ordinary people, and Daddy said Mr. Robert Earl Cotten was certainly not the exception though likely not the rule either since Mr. Robert Earl Cotten struck out through the woods near about as often as he struck out to the toolshed and weren't any Cottens otherwise that could keep pace with him.

But there came to be some trouble, Daddy said, and he indicated the frothy moment was fairly much at hand. Seems Mr. Robert Earl Cotten grew incapable, or anyhow Daddy called it incapable and explained to me primarily how there was a serviceable condition and an unserviceable condition and Mr. Robert Earl Cotten grew incapable of everything but the latter which he was not generally capable of but only half the time if that much, and consequently he could strike out through the woods well enough but could not participate in any sort of transaction once he got to where he was going, or anyhow could not participate in hardly any of the usual transactions on account of he was not himself, Daddy called it, and Momma told him, "Alright," just about the same way he tended to tell it to her. Daddy said Mr. Robert Earl Cotten's persistent unserviceable condition troubled him considerably and he wondered at the why of it and the how of it and did some wishing and even did some praying too which Mrs. Robert Earl Cotten caught him in at the bedside and she became ecstatic and rapturous straightoff. However, did not anything improve matters much and Mr. Robert Earl Cotten had come to believe he might not ever transact again and so was casting around to find something to blame for it when he came upon the jar behind the plank in the toolshed and held it up in the light to study and hypothesize over and naturally it seemed to him rightoff that if such a potion could render people blind and dead and variously afflicted it could almost surely render a solitary Cotten incapable. Of course it was all theory and all hypothesis at the outset but once Mr. Robert Earl Cotten had explained his predicament and had explained his views to his nephews and cousins and brothers they threw in together and elected the liquor the guilty element outright since they were not any of them of a hypothetical and theoretical bent, at least not so as you'd remark it straightoff, Daddy said. Of course they decided directly to do something, they did not know what something exactly, but something wild and ganglike and frothy too, and they pretty much figured as they could not render Mr. Robert Earl Cotten any less incapable than he was they would go ahead and render some capable somebody else incapable too and they figured it might as well be the Sadler Montgomery that had brewed and sold the liquor or if not the Sadler Montgomery then some one of his relations who might be so unfortunate as to get handy and available.

So they set out to Sadler still wild and still ganglike and increasingly frothy and the most of them walked except for Mr. Robert Earl Cotten himself and his brother James Pugh and James Pugh's boy, James Pugh jr., that drove the wagon his uncle and daddy sat in the back of, or actually just his daddy sat in the back of while his uncle lay stretched out atop a quilt and under a blanket with a sack beneath his head and got tended to and seen after by James Pugh sr. who had decided, along with the rest of his brothers and his nephews and his cousins, that incapability was likely the kind of thing that needed tending to and seeing after, was surely the kind of thing that would not benefit much from a brisk walk, so Mr. Robert Earl Cotten got nursed by his next least brother who was not much acquainted with nursing practices except for the laying of wet rags and so he laid one wherever he could find a place to though not anywhere near the source of the incapacity itself since Mr. Robert Earl Cotten and James Pugh together did not see as that would improve things much, the rag being wet and the water being cold and the problem being what it was anyhow.

The Sadler Montgomery lived back off a dirt road off an oiled road and kept his still and his liquor under a ledge down by the

Wolf Island Creek which was where the gang of Cottens headed straightoff so as to bust up the still and pour out the liquor. They followed two old ruts down to the ruined gristmill and then headed upstream along the creekbank beating back the brush for the elder afflicted Cotten who got helped along by his brothers sometimes and sometimes by his nephews and cousins as well and they fairly much held him up and propelled him also since the tending to and the seeing after had pretty completely weakened and diminished his resolve to be fit and his resolve to be well and he so utterly gave himself over to his incapability that he could not but drag his feet and gasp and wheeze and such as that. Naturally the gang of Cottens found the gasping and the wheezing and such what Daddy called inspirational, and once they had reached the ledge with the still and the liquor beneath it they set about venting themselves rightoff. The cousins primarily stomped the vats and the tubing and the paraphernalia while the nephews dumped the grain and the sugar into the creek and the brothers commenced to pour out the finished and refined product from the various jars and jugs roundabout, or anyhow poured out the finished and refined product until Mr. Robert Earl Cotten himself, who had been propped against a hickory tree, suggested that perhaps they should not pour out all the finished and refined product, suggested that perhaps they should reserve some few pints and maybe some few quarts too, suggested that perhaps they might want to keep a taste of the medicine to give to the doctor himself, and Daddy said the Cotten brothers and nephews and cousins too pondered Mr. Robert Earl Cotten all perplexed and squinty and then pondered each other some as well since aside from not being hypothetically and theoretically bent not any of them were bent much figuratively either and so they wanted to know from each other what doctor and medicine where as they could not comprehend which was the one and what was the other.

Naturally Mr. Robert Earl Cotten generated considerable enthusiasm with his plan to introduce the pints and quarts too direct into the Sadler Montgomery thereby rendering him somewhat incapable himself though maybe just stricken and nauseated which was not the sort of discomforture they were after exactly but all the Cottens together decided they would settle for and feel gratified by just stricken and just nauseated also if they could not produce any manner of true incapability, so they came up out of the creekbottom by way of the gristmill ruts all agitated and purposeful with Mr. Robert Earl Cotten hauled along at the forefront by two of his brothers followed up by his nephews with the pints and his cousins with the quarts of what they were all calling medicine anymore and with James Pugh and James Pugh's boy, James Pugh jr., bringing up the rear as their draft horse could not get the wagon up the ruts like he had got it down them.

The Sadler Montgomery had dropped off to sleep in a stuffed chair in the front room and had left the kerosene lamp to burn beside him on the table since he had not much intended to drop off to sleep but had pretty completely medicated himself throughout the course of the evening and so did drop off anyway which left the kerosene lamp to burn unattended beside him and it did burn with quite a handsome flame that eased on down the wick and into the basin and so the lamp was most thoroughly lit by the time Mr. Robert Earl Cotten got propped up on the front porch from where he banged on the door with his fist. Of course the Sadler Montgomery did not know it was the banging that had woke him up and figured straightaway it was the inferno instead or anyhow what looked to him like an inferno at the outset since he generally roused up from a sleep all squinty and perplexed himself and he leapt up from his stuffed chair right sharply and got his naked feet all wrapped and tangled in his loose galluses but managed to snatch the lamp up off the table anyhow and stumble with it to the door which he flung open direct into the propped-up and afflicted Cotten who had not expected the front door to open out since his own front door at his own house did not open out and as best as he could recollect did not any of his brothers' doors at their own houses open out either, so understandably once the thing hit him flush he pitched off the porch backwards partly from the force of it but partly from surprise and incapability too and the Sadler Montgomery pulled up short at the lip of the porch and hurled the flaming lamp on out into the front yard which he did not know was full of relations of the Cotten he had knocked off his front porch that he did not know yet he had knocked off his front porch. Consequently then, the Sadler Montgomery was verily astounded to discover just what company he had and where, or anyhow Daddy called it verily astounded straightoff until Momma and Aunt Sister threw in together and objected to verily astounded as it did not seem to them a thing a Sadler Montgomery could be, especially not to Aunt Sister who endeavored to picture verily astounded on the face of a Sadler Montgomery but announced how she could not on account of what she called the disharmonious elements involved, the Sadler Montgomery being the one of them and the verily astounded being the other. Aunt Sister insisted there were rules and properties to the telling of a thing, rules and properties which Daddy was taxing mightily due to his blending and mingling of the verily astounded, which Aunt Sister felt to be a fitting and near about imperial expression, with the lowly Sadler Montgomery who could not have been any more unfitting and unimperial and stayed human, or that's how Aunt Sister saw it anyhow and she asked Momma did she see it just precisely the same and Momma told her, "Just precisely," and then looked at Daddy the way Aunt Sister was already looking at him and Daddy chewed his lip and drew a Tareyton out from his shirt-pocket.

So he said the Sadler Montgomery flung the lamp on out into the yard where the chimney broke and the flames spread thereby illuminating the majority of the Cottens which the whole fiery business had landed in the midst of, and Daddy observed how the Sadler Montgomery was straightoff struck plumb shitless by what company he had and where, and though Daddy paused to accommodate critical appraisal, critical appraisal did not ensue. They set on him, Daddy said, set on him in a wild and frothy fit all but for Mr. Robert Earl Cotten himself who had landed on his back atop the packed dirt Mrs. Sadler Montgomery called her flowerbed and was just commencing to touch and feel all roundabout himself so as to determine what of his parts and pieces that had not been incapable previously were maybe incapable now at least partly and somewhat anyway, so it was just the healthy dozen and a half of them that set on the Sadler Montgomery all wild and all frothy and naturally the thing was not fair and not just either as it was the sole and solitary Sadler Montgomery that got set on and him all tangled up in his galluses and still perplexed and still squinty too. So the ones without the pints and the quarts commenced to beat him and the ones with the pints and quarts commenced to kick him and in the course of the fray, which was not one of your more hotly contested frays since there was only the one side to it, the Sadler Montgomery's trousers slipped off his hips and dropped down around his ankles while his undershirt just deteriorated to the point of absolute invisibility. Consequently, he got pummeled into near about pure nakedness but for his trousers which he was only wearing somewhat, and the Cottens with the pints and the quarts gathered roundabout the Sadler Montgomery and began to pour what liquid they had into him which seemed to the Sadler Montgomery a reprieve of sorts from the beating and the pummeling and he did not mind so much that they banged his teeth every now and again with the jar rims since they'd left off banging anything else otherwise.

Mr. Robert Early Cotten was desirous to pour a little of the liquor himself, and Daddy observed how in the symbolical way of things it would only be proper for him to do at least a part of the pouring and he asked Aunt Sister didn't she see it just precisely the same but Aunt Sister did not let on she did exactly, maybe on account of the desirous and likely on account of the symbolical too. So Mr. Robert Earl Cotten got helped up by a brother on one arm and by a cousin on the other and once he was on his feet he discovered he had not afterall rendered anything incapable in addition to the original incapable thing and he found as well he felt up to pummeling the Sadler Montgomery a little himself and so he did pummel him a little and naturally the Sadler Montgomery, who was getting fairly much fed up with the beating and the pummeling and the pouring, wondered at the elder Cotten how come for all of it though not in so many words exactly but just said, "Hey!" so as to reveal the thoroughgoing incomprehensibility of it all, and Daddy paused and asked Aunt Sister, "Just precisely?" but Aunt Sister did not tell him just precisely then either.

Daddy did not know was it the naked flesh or was it the pummeling or was it the sweatstink in combination with the liquorstink and the pummeling and only partly the naked flesh on account of whose naked flesh it was anyhow, the who in this case being the Sadler Montgomery and the flesh in this case being all over the place, and Daddy asked me had I heard of the Greek gods and such, asked me had I ever seen a picture of one, Zeus maybe, with his muscles all wavy along his stomach and the rest of himself all wavy too, and I told him, "Yes sir," and Daddy told me back this had not been Zeus exactly. "Not wavy," Daddy said. "Not anywhere." As Daddy figured it, to view the naked Sadler Montgomery was to come to grips with the laws of physics as the Sadler Montgomery was primarily gravity on parade. "Everything falling," Daddy told it, and Aunt Sister added, "Just precisely," without even being asked to.

So Daddy did not suspect it was the naked flesh but maybe only slightly somewhat, and instead he indicated the sweatstink and the liquorstink and especially the pummeling which altogether constituted what Daddy called the vigor of the moment, and as Daddy saw it the vigor of the moment itself had brought about the stirring that did get brought about down deep in the very heart of Mr. Robert Earl Cotten's incapability. Daddy said the one manner of excitement had just got translated and transformed to another manner of excitement and he wondered did we understand the logic of it and Momma told him quick and hard just how well we comprehended the whole business. Apparently Mr. Robert Earl Cotten comprehended the whole business some himself right straightaway and he commenced to ponder the various sorts of things that would likely prod and cultivate the stirring still further, and the sorts of things he did ponder, which Daddy gave out just as your general commerce mostly, did in fact prod and did in fact cultivate the stirring into something more elaborate than a stirring really and the relative novelty of the sensation struck the elder Cotten dumb at least momentarily, momentarily enough anyhow for James Pugh jr. to fetch his jackknife up out from his shirt where the strap round his neck let it dangle and then open the thing and suggest to his uncle how outright incapability was not hardly anything the liquor and the pummeling too seemed entirely able to render without assistance anyhow, and he rotated the assistance in the air so as to let the moonlight glint off the blade of it, but Mr. Robert Earl Cotten did not hear the suggesting and did not see the assistance either and only intended the "Alright" that he did in fact say as a means of approval and congratulations for those parts of his own self that had got noticeably lively of a sudden but of course the Alright applied otherwise as well and James Pugh jr. took it otherwise straightoff as did the rest of the nephews and the cousins and the uncles too, the majority of whom closed in tight around the Sadler Montgomery and attempted to restrain at least some little piece of him as the Sadler Montgomery had commenced to object most strenuously to his predicament and had commenced to argue against it and wonder at it or had set in with a "Hey!" or two anyhow which was an expression of great utility to him.

Daddy supposed they'd have gone ahead and removed from the Sadler Montgomery that part of him they were threatening to remove since heat and frothiness generally produce in people a zeal for things they would not have a zeal for otherwise, but what the Cottens were all worked up and zealous about did not have much to do with any actual cutting or any actual whacking, which surely would have brought about some extraordinarily actual bleeding and instead they were utterly caught up in the justice of the thing and the general rightness of it on account of how they were your basic and fundamental eyes for eyes and teeth for teeth and incapabilities for incapabilities sort of people, Daddy called it. So while they stayed hot and stayed frothy to do what fit and do what suited did not anybody want to take up in their fingers that part of the Sadler Montgomery somebody would have to take up in his fingers if it was to be shorn away, and anyhow did not anybody want to shear away that part of the Sadler Montgomery that had to get taken up in somebody's fingers if it ever did in fact get taken up, not even James Pugh jr. who'd fetched up his knife well enough and shown off the blade of it but had not ever before stuck it in a human and so had only figured he would out loud but not anywhere else really.

That was the dilemma then, Daddy said, that was the predicament and the circumstance. You had your Sadler Montgomery all naked and quizzical, Daddy called it, and the bulk of your Cottens latched onto some little piece of him though not any of them even in the general vicinity of that little piece of him that the solitary nephew had his knife out to cut and whack on which he did not intend to cut and whack on anyhow but just had announced he would and so felt compelled to seem about to, and Daddy said it was a scene of some considerable weight and complexity like on an antique canvas, some sort of framed and galleryhung antique canvas with some sort of framed and galleryhung antique canvas title. "The Money Lenders Cast Out from the Temple," he said. "Or The Calling of St. Matthew," he said. "Or Jacob," he said, "Wrestling with the Angel," and then Daddy pondered the thing, taking into account the weight and taking into account the complexity prior to laying his chin onto the heel of his hand and telling Momma and telling Aunt Sister and telling even me too, "The Peril of the Sadler Montgomery's Organ," and Momma would have told Daddy herself it was pure blasphemy all of it every bit but Aunt Sister beat her to it as Aunt Sister could get offended and draw a responsive breath all at once while Momma could not do but the one thing at a time.

Daddy said they were simply stuck between solutions, the one being to forge ahead and the other being to back away, and as he figured it they were likely on a line to the former not because any particular and specific Cotten out of all the Cottens together wanted to see the thing whacked on and cut but mostly because it was all the Cottens together and not just particular and specific Cottens apart, a whole gang of Cottens actually, near about a mob of them, and Daddy said gangs and Daddy said mobs too did not much care for the particular and for the specific. So likely things were pretty much up with that Sadler Montgomery or anyhow one item was pretty much up with him in a manner of speaking, or would have been pretty much up with him if another similar item on the elder Cotten had not suddenly got pretty much up itself in another manner of speaking entirely, and the elder Cotten that had been still and silent and utterly transfixed flared up into some genuine liveliness and raised both his arms over his head and capered round in a circle one time and hooted and yelped and hollered, "Alright!" hollered, "GodAlmighty!" too but not until he'd leapt clean off the Sadler Montgomery's front porch and struck out across the yard towards the treeline and Oregon Hill.

Naturally the rest of the Cottens grew astounded straightoff and all of them together watched Mr. Robert Earl for as far as they could watch him and then listened to him after, listened to him beating himself a path through the thick woods in the dark with nothing but his paraphernalia to guide him which Daddy said was compass and sextant and bloodhound too. Of course he did not appear distraught any longer and did not appear afflicted, leastways not afflicted in the burdened and encumbered sense of the thing, or anyhow had not appeared afflicted to the gang of his relations for that brief lively moment when he had capered and stomped and hooted and yelped and hollered prior to leaping too and then bolting even, and it was suggested by a nephew and then by an uncle after that maybe he was cured, that maybe he was not incapable any longer, and the rest of the relations decided together that likely it was in fact a miracle along with the Sadler Montgomery who insisted it was purely miraculous to him as he was looking to be agreeable anyway, and Daddy said it did indeed have all the trappings of a miracle and was somewhat like the loaves and the fishes but more truly akin to the wellspring in the desert and while it did not feed the hordes or quench the parched multitudes it did in fact prevent the Sadler Montgomery from toting his organ off in his pocket which was just what he'd resigned himself to toting his organ off in, so he was most noticeably struck with wonderment and with awe but the bulk of the Cottens were struck some themselves and Daddy said the heat and the frothiness dissipated and fell away directly like heat and like frothiness will and all the Cottens and the Sadler Montgomery too looked off to the treeline towards Oregon Hill where they could not see Mr. Robert Earl any longer but could hear him well enough, could hear him snapping off twigs and stomping brush underfoot in route to his purgation and his relief which would be the bed and which would be the woman-friend atop it and which would especially be the ensuing commerce once him and her had got together so as to "Transact," I told him, and Daddy said back, "Yes sir," and Daddy said back, "Just precisely."

Uncle Jack could not ever tell a thing direct and outright partly due to his native faculties which had not ever developed sufficiently so as to allow him to see all of an item without traveling roundabout it and partly due to his mysterious verbosity which would be that same mysterious verbosity he had refined and cultivated somewhere and somehow. Consequently, then, Uncle Jack did not tear out of the woods and across the tobacco patch and through the yard so as to burst into the shack and share with Aunt Della news of the mule and news of the loblolly, but instead Uncle Jack tore out of the woods and across the tobacco patch and down through the yard so as to burst into the shack and ask after Aunt Della's morning which he professed to be curious in the course of and wanted to know had it gone to suit her. Now Aunt Della was quite well enough acquainted with Uncle Jack to know he did not ever ask after her morning or her afternoon or her evening either except to preface something else entirely, usually some unfortunate and disastrous something else which was their predominant brand of happenstance, so Aunt Della laid her hands to her hips and asked Uncle Jack, "Which and how come?" and Uncle Jack slapped his kneejoint and howled and guffawed and told Aunt Della how it just tickled him inside out to see the way she got down to the bottom of things so direct and straightoff and then he howled some more and guffawed some more too so as maybe to infect Aunt Della with a dose of general levity but Aunt Della did not possess much of a riotous disposition or anyhow did not love a good laugh like Uncle Jack but only tittered every now and again when the occasion seemed to merit a titter and as she'd already laid her hands to her hips and already took on her usual severe expression, tittering did not seem much of a possibility. "What?" she wanted to know. "And where was it?" And Uncle Jack rolled his hatbrim up in his hands and watched himself do it. "Well, it seems that," Uncle Jack said commencing with his favorite expression since if a thing just seemed to up and happen that did not imply guilt or blame or irresponsibility or even idiocy either but just ill luck and misfortune and so suggested that maybe the guilty or the blameworthy or the irresponsible or even the idiotic party had been near about as thoroughly victimized as whatever it was that had got ruined or destroyed or just generally annihilated which was what things usually had got whenever Uncle Jack commenced, "It seems that," so Aunt Della asked him, "Which?" and asked him, "Just how?"

"Well," Uncle Jack said and unrolled what of his hatbrim he'd rolled up, "it seems we have before us a most grave and sober circumstance."

And Aunt Della said "Alright," which was just the way Daddy said Alright to Momma sometimes and just the way Momma sometimes said Alright to Daddy but was probably mostly the way Daddy said it since it was Daddy telling the thing anyhow.

"It's Mr. Spud," Uncle Jack said and watched his fingertips on his hatbrim though they were not rolling or unrolling either but just laying atop it. "Seems he's been struck dead."

"What by?" Aunt Della wanted to know.

"A paroxysm likely."

"A which?"

"A fit," Uncle Jack said, "a seizure, palpitations I do believe, a burst vessel most surely, I mean just your general paroxysm."

And Aunt Della lifted her hands off her hips and crossed her arms over herself. "Alright," she said. "Go on."

"It hit him of a sudden," Uncle Jack told her. "I mean one minute he was just plain Spud and the next minute he was all tight and rigid with his eyes rolled back some."

"A paroxysm," Aunt Della said.

"Yes ma'm," Uncle Jack told her. "Triggered somewhat by the tree just maybe."

"What tree?" Aunt Della wanted to know and cut her eyes at Uncle Jack that way that made his blood rise up into his follicles.

"Weren't awful much of a tree now but just made a racket coming over and I do believe the noise of it set off the whole business, or maybe partly the noise anyhow and partly the snaking chain."

"Snaking chain," Aunt Della said.

And Uncle Jack told her, "Yes ma'm," and recommenced the rolling and the unrolling of his hatbrim.

Daddy said it was Uncle Jack's practice to set off with an outright lie and then gradually introduce the truth into it so that what had begun all lie would then drop off to lie mostly followed by half lie and then lie just somewhat prior to no lie whatsoever, so to get at the truth Aunt Della did not have to do anything really but say everything Uncle Jack said right behind him and cut her eyes and generally make herself as unheavenly orblike as possible which was not truly much of a chore for Aunt Della. The facts then did come to light but only in little spurts and gushes and Aunt Della just stood where she'd been standing with her arms crossed over herself like she had crossed them and allowed the facts and verifiable circumstances to wash over her until she had absorbed quite enough of them to become fully irate immediately afterwhich she got particularly undivine and particularly un-ethereal which was how she usually got whenever she pitched a fit and naturally that was what she did pitch straightaway along with a few additional items one of them being an enameled serving plate that did not break out but a part of the window and another of them being an iron pothook that did not break out but the rest of it and the last one being a sealed jar of stewed tomatoes that sailed on out into the yard and busted on a quartzstone which was not so calamitous a thing as far as Uncle Jack could tell.

They gave plain Spud a truly apostolic sendoff, Daddy said, or anyhow bid him a most thoroughly unmulelike farewell. Uncle Jack dug the grave himself and made it square and plumb and almost three feet deep which was near the same as tunneling to China anywhere else considering the rock roundabout, and him and his neighbor to the east, Mr. Dale Pittman, who Daddy said was cousin twice removed to the icehouse Pittmans in town, together dragged plain Spud out from the woods or anyhow drove and encouraged Mr. Dale Pittman's draft horse, Eloise, that had been named for Mr. Pittman's mother while she was still alive to know it and Daddy said she never seemed to appreciate it much. They rolled plain Spud on into his grave with fence-posts but did not cover him over straightaway, did not cover him over with dirt that is but he did get bedecked with violet peach blossoms that had come out on the tree behind the barn and with daisies too that had come out all along the hedgerow on the hillside and eventually even with dirt as well once Uncle Jack had hired out the preacher Mr. Tilley to perform a Christian ceremony though not so much for the mule really and not so much for himself either but primarily for Aunt Della who Daddy said possessed the bulk of the Christian leanings between them, but naturally Momma and Aunt Sister threw in together and insisted Uncle Jack had possessed just as much of the bulk of the Christian leanings as Aunt Della if not more of it. They said he'd been righteous and kind and goodhearted and Aunt Sister announced how he'd lived and prospered in the ways of Jesus just like her daddy had lived and prospered and just like Granddaddy her brother and just like Momma and just like her own self had lived and had prospered in the ways of Jesus Christ Almighty, and Momma went ahead and suggested, just like she always went ahead and suggested most every time it came up and it came up plenty, that Daddy might just could stand to live and could stand to prosper in the ways of Jesus his own self and then she looked at Daddy that fierce and holy way that Christians look at people, especially heathen people like Daddy who had commenced a Baptist but converted, and Daddy looked at her back in that way, I suppose, that heathens look at Christians, or anyhow that way Daddy looks at Momma whenever Momma gets fierce and whenever Momma gets holy, and with an unlit cigarette hanging out from the corner of his mouth Daddy said, "Ja HEE zus," and Daddy said, "CRYst uh," and then waved his hand in the air so as to make a blessing at Momma and at Aunt Sister too who drew back together like he'd doused the both of them with ditchwater.

Naturally Daddy could not recommence directly with the story of the mule and Uncle Jack and Aunt Della and the bulk of their leanings as Momma and Aunt Sister had to get unincensed first which was not the sort of thing that could be rushed or hurried along but had to unfold and had to evolve and did unfold and did evolve but ever so gradually on account of how Momma and on account of how Aunt Sister were not your cheekturning kind, Daddy told it, told it to me primarily but in front of Momma and in front of Aunt Sister too and thereby did not but hinder the unfolding and hinder the evolving as well. However, Momma and Aunt Sister did get unincensed once they had discussed the thing and had decided they would be sweet and kind to Daddy no matter what sort of jackass he was to them as it was in the spirit of Jesus Christ to be sweet and to be kind, Aunt Sister announced saying it "Ja HEE zus CRYst uh" herself which was how she always said it and which was even how Momma said it too sometimes once she'd got infected, Daddy called it, and Aunt Sister forgave Daddy and Momma forgave Daddy too and Aunt Sister blessed Daddy with her finger and Momma blessed Daddy with her finger after and Daddy slid about and fidgeted and adjusted himself in his chair like maybe he'd have preferred the ditchwater.

So he got on with the thing shortly once he'd been forgiven and blessed and once he'd lit his Tareyton and once he'd been told how vile a thing tobacco was by Aunt Sister who asked Momma wasn't it vile and got told herself, "Indeed." And he said it was not exactly a proper and sanctified service since Mr. Tilley was not exactly a proper and sanctified preacher but in his middle years had just been called and touched and moved and agitated somewhat in the spirit, most especially touched, Daddy said, which always confounded the proper and confounded the sanctified and insisted on something else entirely. There was only the three of them at the outset, Uncle Jack and Aunt Della and the Reverend Mr. Tilley, gathered roundabout the plumb and square and three-foot-deep open hole with the mule and the daisies and the peach blossoms inside it, but before the whole business got well underway they were joined by colored Uncle Lucas from the Graham property up the road and Uncle Lucas took up a place across the open grave from Mr. Tilley and Uncle Jack and Aunt Della too and stood there all sober and grim in his black broadcloth suit and his boiled shirt and string tie and with both his hands clasped roundabout his Bible that did not have much cover left on the frontside or the backside either one, due to some excessive and extraordinary fingering and speculating and thumbing about. Daddy said colored Uncle Lucas was a devoted student of the entire funereal process with a concentration in the graveside ceremony as he intended to be the chief element at one someday and wanted to see what it was like beforehand since he imagined he would be otherwise disposed once the time came, and Daddy said colored Uncle Lucas was a chief element after a bit and was otherwise disposed too.

The Reverend Mr. Tilley commenced with a general history of the mule as a manner of livestock which did not have much at all to do with the actual history of the mule as a manner of livestock but then the Reverend Mr. Tilley was not acquainted with the actual history of the mule and so had to call upon the general history instead, which he concocted outright. An anecdote followed, an anecdote concerning plain Spud, quite naturally, and concerning Aunt Della and Uncle Jack too and told in fact by Uncle Jack to the Reverend Mr. Tilley who did not concoct and fabricate but a slight portion of it in the retelling afterwhich there was a moment or two of silence not expressly intended for contemplation but employed for contemplation anyhow by Uncle Jack and Aunt Della who considered their loss and by colored Uncle Lucas who considered his prospects and by the Reverend Mr. Tilley as well who wondered should he pray or should he sing and at last decided on praying since he did not have much talent for singing anyway. He did not know just what he would pray for but set out nonetheless with a kind of all-purpose petition followed by more silence while the Reverend Mr. Tilley endeavored to settle in his own mind whether it was proper and prudent to pray for the deliverance of a mule into the kingdom of heaven and since he knew from Uncle Jack it had not been a wicked or ill-tempered creature he decided likely it was proper and likely it was prudent in this instance at least somewhat and so he did pray for the deliverance of plain Spud into the kingdom of heaven and got Amened twice by colored Uncle Lucas and then Amened once apiece by Aunt Della and Uncle Jack who did not usually Amen in the course of a prayer but figured since Uncle Lucas had they would too. Mr. Tilley drew from his general history of the mule throughout his prayer so as to illustrate various qualities and characteristics that seemed to him bore illustrating even a second time over and though Uncle Lucas Amened in the midst of several of the Reverend Tilley's more impassioned moments and even Lawd Lawded one time when the reverend paused to draw breath, Aunt Della and Uncle Jack did not contribute further partly from grief, Daddy supposed, and partly from their own natural inclination not to Amen or Lawd Lawd either, and partly too, Daddy figured, on account of the scent roundabout which rose up from the hole all thick and putrid and malingered in the air so as to prevent a man from knowing just what might come out his mouth if he opened it. Seems that plain Spud had not got buried straightoff on account of how the hole had not got dug straightoff so it was not just the usual mulestink but the mulestink and the rotstink together that the peach blossoms and the daisies too did not but make worse somehow and they all had to breathe it, even the Reverend Mr. Tilley who seemed to inhale every now and again himself prior to praying and invoking and actually singing a little too, all of it a means of fretting over plain Spud's everlasting soul which Daddy said did not seem to call for any fretting over as plain Spud had already commenced to get resurrected aroma foremost.

So he was not in the muleshed when it fell in on itself and Uncle Jack admired the planks and the rubble and announced to Aunt Della how it had been a merciful, how it had been a fortuitous thing since he would have got maimed and would have got mutilated and so would have got shot too if he had not got killed already, and Uncle Jack suggested and implied that there was a mystery to the universe that he could not even begin to get a grip on and Aunt Della pondered him with one of her unethereal and undivine expressions that was not much mysterious itself. They did not have a mule then, Daddy said, and did not have a muleshed to put it in but just the sick pigs and the eggless chickens and the rocks and the weeds and the scantling corn and the paltry tobacco and the plow with the empty traces before it, so they needed a new mule to put them near about back where they'd been before which was not anywhere to be really but was about the only place they figured they could get to until Uncle Jack met up with Mr. Nunnely the mule trader and together they admired what mules Mr. Nunnely had to offer which led to some talk of mules as a breed and a species followed by a bandying about of several mule-related items, and Daddy said Mr. Nunnely, an expert in such matters, recognized straightaway Uncle Jack's talent for charming mules and then Daddy stopped himself to wonder had he mentioned Uncle Jack's talent for mule charming and Momma and Aunt Sister both indicated Yes, he had, without saying as much really.

Mr. Nunnely had a mind to retire from the mule trading business and told Uncle Jack how he had a mind to retire from it which Uncle Jack grew perplexed over as retiring was a novel concept to him since he did not figure but a man quit his labor when he died from it. But Mr. Nunnely said he had realized somewhat of a profit in mule trading and when Uncle Jack asked him was it actual cash money Mr. Nunnely took out from his pocket a roll of just what he'd realized somewhat of, a girthsome roll, Uncle Jack told Aunt Della and then showed her girthsome precisely with his thumb and his forefinger. Money was not anything Uncle Jack ever saw much of and naturally a profit was not anything Uncle Jack ever realized even somewhat of. Consequently, then, the girthsome roll of actual cash money impressed him in an inordinate sort of way and Uncle Jack and Mr. Nunnely laid their forearms across the top rail of Mr. Nunnely's corral fence and set about wondering just who might trade mules in Mr. Nunnely's place when Mr. Nunnely took his retirement and so was not trading mules any longer, or anyhow Daddy said it might have sounded like wondering and may have looked like wondering too but was not wondering really, was not even figuring or pondering either but was actually the settling and concluding of a thing that had not even been spoken outright but had got mutually understood anyhow and mutually agreed upon without ever needing to get spoken, without ever needing a signature or a handshake or any manner of ceremony except for the spitting and except for the forearms across the fencerail which Daddy said was how most things got settled and which Daddy said was where too.

So Uncle Jack wasn't a dirt farmer when he got back home like he'd been a dirt farmer when he set out and was not actually a mule trader yet either but figured he was just partly the one anymore on his way to becoming the other as he had spat and had laid up against the corral fence which seemed to him as good as his word and his bond though it did not strike Aunt

Della hardly the same since spitting and fence-leaning do not hold for women the sanctity and credence they hold for men and Daddy said Aunt Della was the careful one anyhow and the prudent one too and naturally did not want to surrender even their shabby and altogether insubstantial existence for something only maybe less shabby and maybe more substantial, but once a thing got hold of Uncle Jack there was not any shaking it loose from him or him from it and Daddy said this mule trading business had the grip on him right from the start.

Of course, Daddy said, he had a talent for mule charming, and Daddy stopped himself to wonder had he mentioned the mule charming previously but Momma and Aunt Sister did not indicate anything this time, and Daddy told how Uncle Jack had got charmed a little himself by the girthsome roll primarily and the idea of profits if even only somewhat, so while he still seemed undecided and unconvinced and maybe a little bit willing to hear out Aunt Della whenever she objected or made herself contrary he was actually completely decided and convinced and deaf too and did not know anything but mules and did not know anything but profits and could not open his mouth without the one or the other coming out from it. Consequently, then, Uncle Jack did not figure he would ever again cultivate the quartzstones or nurse the pigs or swear the chickens, and though she was reluctant and unwilling at the outset, soon enough Aunt Della commenced to figure that she would not ever again cultivate quartzstones or nurse pigs or swear chickens either and she began to open her mouth and let out Mules and let out Profits too.

They struck a deal, Daddy said, not just a spitting and fenceleaning agreement but a verifiable arrangement in true and actual ink on an uncontestable leaf of paper and Uncle Jack and Aunt Della got a wagon and a mule to pull it and a little piece of money for a stake in exchange for property primarily which would be all their timber and all their pasture and all their fields, everything in fact but the house and the barnyard which they insisted on keeping the deed to out of sentimentality mostly and which Mr. Nunnely did not much want anyhow since he would have to finish collapsing everything that had not finished collapsing on its own which, aside from the muleshed, was everything. And they packed the wagon, Daddy said, which would be the wagon with the roof and the sides to it, packed it full with their clothes and their blankets and their rifle and their tomatoes too, and they harnessed the mule, Daddy said, which would be their new mule, little Spud, that would get bigger than plain Spud eventually but was not then anyhow, and Aunt Della said goodbye to the Tates and said goodbye to the Cottens and Uncle Jack said goodbye to what Younts he could hunt up which would be almost exclusively Great-granddaddy, and then Daddy said, in that air of frivolity and utter carelessness that generally distinguishes the outset of a grand adventure— and as Aunt Sister was especially taken with the grand adventure part of it she had Daddy repeat it to her so she could savor and relish the appropriateness and suitability of such an elegant phrase in conjunction with her relations, so Daddy told her Grand Adventure again and told her Carelessness and told her Frivolity too as he was quite taken with them himself and so savored and relished some on his own until Momma encouraged him with a noise in her throat—and Daddy said it was a Jemison that took the picture as Jemisons were in the picture-taking business then and only the insurance business later, and Daddy said it was Uncle Jack that squandered and frittered away the little piece of the piece of money on it, which Daddy indicated to Aunt Sister was the careless and the frivolous part of the thing since the money was for mules primarily and not for poses really, and naturally Momma fetched the photograph out from the endtable drawer and we all took a turn pondering the bent corner and the watermark and the flank of the mule and the bulk of the wagon with Uncle Jack before it, his arm across himself and his hat upright atop it, and beside him Aunt Della with her bangs and her nose and her chin and all her little wiry parts otherwise.

ii

Daddy said they did not ever shut him up in it, did not ever close and bolt the door, but did not ever need to, Daddy said, since he was in his first and in his already well before they even knew to put him in theirs too with its steel bars and its steel bed and its plain white sink and plain white toilet along with the open and unbolted steel door that his did not even have one of, so was no call to close him away, Daddy said, as he was closed away likely even before the very moment he watched himself do it, likely even as soon as he knew he could do it, would do it, and thereby could not be prevented from it even if they'd held his arm like they'd tried to hold his arm and even if they'd wrenched loose the pine knot like they'd tried to wrench loose the pine knot since it was not truly the blow and was not truly the consequences that sealed him off and shut him away like he got sealed off and got shut away but just the knowing that he could and the knowing that he would and of course, after, somewhat the knowing that he had which Daddy said was like steel bars and steel doors and steel bolts too only worse.

Sheriff Browner didn't worry much over it and thought the sofa was alright for him or maybe the straightchair in the corner and told the deputy just exactly that, not ever looking at the parts of him that were his eyes but near about at everything else otherwise like Sheriff Browner always looked at everything else otherwise, but Deputy Burton insisted not the sofa and not the straightchair either on account of protocol, he said, on account of standard procedure, which was what caused Granddaddy to go where he went though with the door not shut and not bolted because while the sheriff most always gave way he did not ever give way but partly. Daddy got allowed to go with him as far as the corridor anyhow and got allowed to loiter at the bars and pass cigarettes through to Granddaddy who sat on the bed holding with his left hand to the near support chain like maybe he would drop off onto the floor otherwise, and Daddy said Granddaddy did not seem much inclined to talk about it or even much inclined to pass the time of day, which was something Granddaddy generally stayed inclined to do, so Daddy passed the time of day for himself and for Granddaddy too and wondered out loud would it rain and decided out loud it likely wouldn't and wondered out loud would it cool off but figured it would not cool off until it rained and since he'd already decided it likely would not rain he went ahead and decided it likely would not cool off either. Granddaddy just raked his mustache, Daddy said, that way Granddaddy had of raking his mustache which was not with his fingertips like most mustaches get raked but instead with the flap of skin between his thumb and forefinger which he would drag from his nose to his bottom lip always five times exactly as that was his grooming procedure though the flap of skin between his thumb and forefinger did not actually do any grooming to speak of on account of how Granddaddy did not ever grow one of your groomable mustaches but just the thick, bristly variety that did not ever get long enough to be much affected by wax or a comb or a skinflap either.

They had Mr. Clay Weathers on the straightchair in the office with the doors shut and the windows raised ever so slightly and Deputy Burton circled round him with his thumbs hooked in his belt and the various parts of his paraphernalia creaking and groaning and jingling somewhat, and Mr. Clay Weathers wiped himself all about the face and neck with a yellow handkerchief that had previously been a white handkerchief prior to telling the deputy, "No sir," just like he'd told the sheriff, "No sir," on account of how Deputy Burton insisted he had not made out just what it was Mr. Clay Weathers had told the sheriff, so Mr. Clay Weathers wiped himself and told the deputy just precisely what he'd told the sheriff and then wondered couldn't they prop open the door so as to stir up a draft but got told No sir back by Deputy Burton who creaked and groaned and jingled somewhat.

Sheriff Browner watched himself bounce the eraser end of a pencil off his desktop and without ever not watching himself bouncing the eraser end of the pencil he opened his mouth and said, "Did you know him by sight?"

"Hadn't never laid eyes on him," Mr. Weathers said one time to the sheriff and one time to the deputy who could not seem to hear and comprehend a thing unless it got repeated directly at him.

"Not never?" Deputy Burton wanted to know and grabbed on to the arms of Mr. Weathers's chair so as to bring himself into full listening range and Mr. Weathers grew ill and put out of a sudden and asked the deputy back, "Didn't I just say I hadn't never laid eyes on him?" and then him and Deputy Burton exchanged spiteful expressions and as the deputy was not the sort to abide a sharp reply, not with any detectable grace anyhow, he laid his face up snug to Mr. Clay Weathers's face and told Mr. Clay Weathers, "I'll be the one asking the questions here," and Mr. Clay Weathers appeared to be on the verge of a Yes sir, which was just the kind of response the deputy liked to inspire, when Sheriff Browner wondered why didn't Deputy Burton prop open the door so as to stir up a draft and consequently the Yes sir did not ever come about since Mr. Clay Weathers of a sudden employed his lips otherwise and managed to render up a slight but utterly triumphant smirk. "Thank you, Sheriff," he said still with his face in the deputy's face and still with his mouth laid out and turned up and with his voice saying "Sheriff" like it would not ever say "Deputy" no matter what encouragement he had to suffer.

Sheriff Browner wanted to know how they'd got onto him, wanted to know had they just hunted him up or had they collected clues roundabout or had they got put on him by somebody somewhere, and Mr. Clay Weathers said they scoured the countryside straightoff but would not any of the niggers say who it was and did not any of the whitefolks know who it was and so did not any of the niggers say anything and the whitefolks just figured it was likely their least favorite nigger and so said him which Mr. Clay Weathers said left him and Daddy and Granddaddy too with still the one stole car and near about five hundred niggers that stole it. So he did not suppose they had collected clues to any good effect and did not suppose they would have hunted him up as quick as they did hunt him up if they had not got legitimately put onto him by what Mr. Clay Weathers called an actual eyewitness, and the sheriff asked him, "Eyewitness to what?" and got told, "To the Bel Air with the thieving nigger at the wheel of it," and the sheriff asked him, "Going where?" and got told, "Down the road, I guess," and Deputy Burton already had five of his fingers wrapped around one chairarm and was reaching towards the other when Mr. Clay Weathers reconsidered and decided it had not been down the road but had been up the road instead as they had caught him midway to Stacy and he bent himself around the deputy's bulk and announced his change of opinion invoking several local geographical considerations so as to corroborate his notion that Stacy, being to the north of Neely, could not get arrived at from there by driving down the road, and wondered did the sheriff see the logic of it and got told, "Yes sir," and he wondered did the deputy see the logic of it too and got told, "Christ."

The sheriff wanted to know just who it was that had seen the Bel Air and the victim, he called him, driving up the road, and Mr. Weathers said it had been Mrs. Gilchrist's boy, Teddy, and the sheriff told Mr. Weathers back, "1 see," but did not exactly get heard saying I see on account of the deputy who said Christ again overtop him and then hooked his thumbs on his belt and blew out a breath in a wholly exasperated sort of way prior to adding, "That boy's retarded," and then sucked some air with appreciable passion.

"He ain't," Mr. Weathers told him.

And the deputy said, "Well he's afflicted somehow."

"He's just slow," Mr. Weathers told him.

"He ain't even moving," the deputy said and took hold of both chairarms at once. "Look it, Teddy Gilchrist's going on thirty-two years old, can't be five feet tall, don't know which end of himself to put his pants on, hadn't never run two sentences together that had a thing in the world to do with each other and all of it on account of that little tiny head that you'd have seen for yourself if you could get him out from under that duckhunting cap long enough to look at it. It's a sad thing," the deputy said though not sounding at all grievous and sorrowful, "but that boy was born afflicted and hadn't never got over it."

"Sees well enough," Mr. Weathers said.

"But he can't ever recollect what he sees," Deputy Burton told him, "can't ever remember what he's seeing while he's looking at it."

And Mr. Weathers said, "All I know is we went where he said go and found what he said he'd seen which was that Bel Air and which was that nigger inside it."

"Blind luck," Deputy Burton insisted and was making for the chair-arms when the sheriff asked Mr. Weathers, "The Gilliam?" and got asked back, "The who?"

"Inside the Bel Air," the sheriff said. "A Gilliam, a Pelham Gilliam we figure."

And Mr. Clay Weathers told him, "I guess. Weren't no hellos."
"Well what was there then?" Deputy Burton wanted to know
and laid his face direct up into Mr. Weathers's face so as to
find out straightaway. "What was there if there weren't no
hellos?"

"He run," Mr. Weathers told him and then peered out around
the bulk of the deputy and said, "He run," to Sheriff Browner
who had set back in to bouncing the pencil off his desktop and
so had set back in to watching himself do it.

"Seen you coming and just run," the deputy said prior to
drawing himself off from Mr. Weathers's face and off from Mr.
Weathers's chair and then hooking his thumbs where he
usually hooked them and carrying himself roundabout the
office with his ordinary insufferable splendor. "Peculiar thing,"
the deputy observed. "A colored Gilliam sees three crazed
white men coming after him and he just up and runs off. Awful
mysterious."

"Ain't so peculiar," Mr. Weathers said. "Ain't so mysterious.
Man steals a car and gets caught at it he goddamwellbetter
run."

And the deputy left off his tour momentarily so as to not get
interrupted by the creaking and the groaning and the jingling
too. "Didn't get caught stealing it," he said. "Got caught riding
in it."

And Mr. Weathers said back, "It was him. He had them lye
scars on his cheek Miss Addie saw and that green shirt and
them brown pants and those black sneakers with the laces out
and the tongues flapping."

"And you caught him on the roadside?" Sheriff Browner
wanted to know, still bouncing his pencil and still watching
himself do it.

"No sir," Mr. Weathers said. "Come up on him in the road."

"And just run him on into the ditch I guess," Deputy Burton announced amid some creaking and some groaning and some jingling too. "I mean him in a Chevrolet and him being black." And Deputy Burton crossed his arms over himself and pondered Mr. Clay Weathers who thought of a thing to call the deputy just as the deputy thought of a thing he was risking to get called and so they did not need but to look at each other and communicated all of it well enough.

"Louis blowed the horn at him," Mr. Weathers said not at all to the deputy, "and we rode up alongside him and Mr. Buck and me too tried to wave him on into the ditch but he would not get waved and just sped up some so we sped up some with him and blowed at him and waved at him again and likely he'd have sped up all over but with him in a Bel Air and us in Inez's Buick wasn't but so much speeding up we could manage, so we rode behind him when we couldn't ride alongside him and followed him on up through Ruffin towards Stacy until Mr. Buck saw he'd wrecked it already, saw he'd backed the right fender into one thing and backed the left fender into another, and Mr. Buck got hot and got fiery and told Louis, 'Ram the son-of-a-bitch,' and Louis told him back, 'But Chief,' on account of the Buick," Mr. Weathers explained, "on account of Inez, and Mr. Buck pointed up the road a ways and said, 'Put him in that daybank yonder,' and naturally Louis wanted to know how exactly, as running Chevrolets into claybanks was not truly anything he did much of and as it was not truly anything Mr. Buck did much of either he told him back, 'Anyhow you can,' which Louis didn't find all that extraordinarily helpful so I explained to him just when to pull up," Mr. Weathers said, "and just how to pull over so as to squeeze the Bel Air off the pavement and into the ditch but that boy got wild once we commenced to close in on him and once we commenced to ease over and he yanked the wheel and bounced his front fender off our front fender and of a sudden Louis got wild some himself and he said a thing to that Gilliam out the window and that Gilliam said a thing back and Louis hooted one time like Louis does every now and again and then yanked the wheel himself and run that Gilliam on into the ditch and run us on into the ditch too and that Gilliam hadn't hardly plowed into the daybank when we plowed into it just beyond him."

"Naturally he run," Mr. Weathers said, "had his legs going before he ever hit the ground and shot on around the Bel Air and scooted direct up the daybank like a lizard, and it weren't no slight daybank either, I mean it had some pitch to it. You seen it yourself," he said to Sheriff Browner almost exclusively and the sheriff told the eraser end of his pencil, "Yes sir," which was both a yes sir for the pitch and a yes sir for the seeing it too and Deputy Burton threw in with a "We seen it," out the side of his mouth as he simply could not not throw in with something. "I mean it was steep," Mr. Weathers said, "and soft to boot and that boy just flew up it but old Mr. Buck had lit out just behind him and lord if he didn't make like a lizard his own self and near about caught him at the peak of the thing but couldn't find a part of that bastard to hold firm to and he slipped on over the lip and out of sight and Mr. Buck slipped on over the lip behind him."

"And you and Louis?" Sheriff Browner wondered not in any snide and pointed sort of way but just as a matter of general curiosity, that is general curiosity until the deputy added his "Yeah" which implied the snide and implied the pointed and so Mr. Clay Weathers exclaimed ever so demonstratively, "I got the crooked spine, ain't hardly able to make like a lizard. Dr. Shackleford says I am in a grave condition. You ask him and see doesn't he. And Louis, well the man had already wrecked his aunt's car and his wife's car in one morning so likely he didn't feel up to climbing a claybank and I won't be the one to hold it against him."

"Wait up now," Sheriff Browner said. "I just wondered how you ended up where you ended up and didn't mean anything otherwise," which soothed Mr. Weathers appreciably, or anyhow had set in to soothing him appreciably until Deputy Burton hooked his thumbs on his belt and creaked and groaned and jingled somewhat prior to dropping his chin and saying, "Yeah."

"Well we went after him too," Mr. Weathers insisted, bending the whole business upwards like Momma does to "Louis" sometimes, "just circled round so as to flank him, and we would have caught up straightoff on account of they had veered in our direction anyhow but Louis got his pantsleg all tangled in a thorny bush and would not yank it loose since he had wrecked his aunt's car and had wrecked his wife's car already and did not want to add his trousers to it. We caught up anyway, though not as straightoff as we might have caught up otherwise, but we did gain on them directly and I seen Mr. Buck's white shirt through the trees and Mr. Buck's white hair and that nigger on out in front of him just beating it through the underbrush and Mr. Buck gaining looked like, Mr. Buck near about so close as to reach out and touch that nigger with his fingertips, and I guess he did reach out and I guess he did touch him too since by the time we got to where they'd arrived at that nigger looked touched what with his nose bloodied and his lip laid open, looked considerably touched and likely four knuckles at a time."

"Took a beating did he?" the deputy asked, and as that was the brand of thing to naturally call for some creaking and groaning and jingling, it got some.

And Mr. Weathers said back, "Had one coming to him, I figure, and anyhow weren't no terrible thrashing exactly but just a poke in the nose or a poke in the mouth whenever Mr. Buck would ask to know a thing and wouldn't get told it."

"A thing like what?" the deputy wanted to know.

"Just your ordinary sorts of things," Mr. Weathers said, "like how come he'd stole it and how come he'd knocked Miss Addie over and how come he was such a sorry son-of-a-bitch in the first place."

"And he resisted?" the deputy wanted to know.

And Mr. Weathers commenced with, "Well," and then stopped himself prior to recommencing with, "Well," and then adding to it, "it wasn't so much that he resisted but mostly that he was not so exceedingly quick and lively of tongue while Mr. Buck was maybe a little too exceedingly quick and lively himself."

"So he got beat," Deputy Burton said.

"No sir," Mr. Weathers told him, "not beat, just hit some. I mean Mr. Buck would ask to know a thing and that nigger would lay his tongue out his mouth and then draw it back in so as to maybe set about making a word with it but by then, of course, Mr. Buck would have give up on an answer and so would poke that nigger one time and ask him another thing and out would come the tongue again and that was pretty much how it went for a spell."

"And that don't seem to you like getting beat?" Deputy Burton wanted to know.

"No sir," Mr. Weathers told him, "just hit some."

And Deputy Burton blew out a breath in that expressive and telling fashion that suited him to blow out breaths sometimes and he looked sideways at the sheriff so as to maybe encourage him into an exhalation but the sheriff did not exhale, not with noticeable flair anyhow but just so as to keep existing and he ran a groove the length of his pencil with his thumbnail. "Now," he said, pondering the groove and pondering the thumbnail somewhat, "what about that pine knot?" "Weren't anything but handy," Mr. Weathers told him. "You seen where it happened there in the grove, place littered all roundabout

with knots and limbs and branches and such so when he stooped over after something stout and firm he came up with that knot straightoff." "Well then how come was it he needed a thing stout and firm in the first place?" the sheriff wondered. "Seems to me he was giving out plenty more than he took already."

"Sheriff," Mr. Weathers said, "It was just that nigger. I mean if he'd have acted right and usual wouldn't none of what happened to him have happened to him, anyhow not the pine knot part of it."

"Right and usual?" the sheriff said back.

"Yes sir," Mr. Weathers told him. "That nigger weren't sorry. I mean he was sorry in a general no count kind of way but he weren't sorry he'd took the Bel Air and weren't sorry he'd knocked Miss Addie over to do it and didn't give a happy shit if the thing was ruint and beat in and buried in a daybank near about up to the doorpanels. That nigger didn't care but just sat on the pine straw touching at his nose and touching at his lips and wouldn't none of what went after have gone after if he'd repented even the least little bit."

"So Mr. Buck hit him with it," the sheriff said.

"Yes sir," Mr. Weathers told him, "Mr. Buck hit him with it but didn't hit him with it straightoff. I mean he would have hit him with it straightoff, or anyhow seemed set to, but Louis caught hold of the one arm and I caught hold of the other and we held him off from it for a spell, likely would have held him off from it for good but for that nigger again that couldn't just sit still and quiet but had to open his mouth and say what he said."

"Say what?" the deputy asked and struck out towards the chairarms which Mr. Weathers grabbed on to himself so as to prevent and discourage him. "I'll have to think on it," he told Deputy Burton. "I'll have to ponder it some," he told Sheriff Browner, "As it was a whole string of things," and he did think on it and did ponder it some and eventually came out with it all slow and deliberate and an item at a time prior to running through it over again for the benefit of the sheriff and for the benefit of the deputy who wanted to hear not just what it was but what it had sounded like too.

"And then he hit him?" Sheriff Browner wanted to know.

"Wouldn't you?" Mr. Weathers asked him. "I'd have hit the son-of-a-bitch my own self if it'd been my sister that had got knocked over and had her Bel Air stole, so Mr. Buck got considerably agitated, and I do mean considerably agitated, I mean wild and feverish, and he just up and busted loose from us."

"From the both of you?" Deputy Burton wanted to know and then revealed somewhat of his sentiments in an exhalation.

"Yes sir," Mr. Weathers told him. "Weren't no man could have held him. I mean the juices were up and it wouldn't do but for him to bust loose and get at that nigger."

"And so he hit him," Sheriff Browner said.

"Yes sir. Hit him." Mr. Weathers told him.

"Along about here," Sheriff Browner said and laid his pointing finger upwards across his forehead.

"Yes sir," Mr. Weathers told him. "Along about there."

"Just swung the thing the one time," the sheriff said, and
though the deputy told him, "Sheriff?" all urgent from across
the room Sheriff Browner just held up at him the flat of his
hand and said, "The one time," again to Mr. Weathers who told
him, "Yes sir," back and then looked himself at Deputy Burton
who was making one of those secret law enforcement hand
signals that quite naturally confounded Mr. Weathers and so
prevented him from explaining it to the sheriff who had
wondered at Mr. Weathers just what it was the deputy might
be attempting to communicate, and as the hand signal failed
him altogether Deputy Burton creaked and groaned and
jingled somewhat across the office so as to hunker down over
the sheriff's desk and have a private word with him which he
did have since Mr. Weathers could not hear anything but the
slight noise of it. The sheriff, however, did not bother to have a
private word back and instead asked the deputy loud and
outright, "Why don't you step on over to Bill Covington's and
bring us back some Pepsi-Colas," to which Deputy Burton
replied all loud and outright himself, "Pepsi-Colas?" and the
sheriff told him, "Yes sir," and then wondered at Mr. Weathers,
"Five of us, isn't it?" and Mr. Weathers said, "Yes sir, they's five
of us, but I'd make it four Pepsi-Colas and a gingerale. Won't
do but for Mr. Buck to have a gingerale," and so the sheriff
said, "Four Pepsi-Colas," and the sheriff said, "One gingerale,"
and the deputy told him back, "Alright," pretty much like it
gets told around our house.

Daddy figured he would set the bottle atop the toilet lid but
there was not but the ring and so he figured he would set the
bottle atop the tank but there was not even a tank to set the
bottle atop of so he tried to hand it direct to Granddaddy but
Granddaddy would not take it into the hand with the cigarette
in it and would not take it into the hand with the bedchain in it
either, did not even look like he'd heard Daddy ask him to take
it into the one hand or the other, so Daddy tried to set it on the

chairseat but could not set it on the chairseat as the chairseat was sloped and slanted which left him only the slab floor to set it on and he set it on the slab floor somewhat away from Granddaddy but somewhat close to him too and then he told Granddaddy just precisely exactly where he'd set it and asked Granddaddy not to kick the thing over if he could at all help it but Granddaddy did not hear that either and so kicked it over almost straightaway and likely would have been peeved and put out with himself for spilling his gingerale all across the cell floor if he had only known he had.

They put Daddy into the chair that they had at last let Mr. Clay Weathers out of and Deputy Burton shut the office door again just like he'd shut the office door before which prompted Daddy to wipe and dab at himself with his shirtsleeve and which prompted Daddy to observe how air would not circulate through a closed door, observe it somewhat to Deputy Burton who had already commenced his creaking and his groaning and his jingling but observe it mostly to Sheriff Browner as he was chiefly plain and regular and so sweated and suffered just like Daddy who was plain and regular too. So the door got set ajar again just like it had got set ajar before which deflated Deputy Burton somewhat just like he had got deflated somewhat before and together him and Sheriff Browner wondered a thing or two in Daddy's direction and asked a thing or two outright and Daddy told them pretty much what he'd seen and pretty much what he'd done and pretty much what Granddaddy had done too all of which had some kinship to what Mr. Weathers had made mention of previously though was not just precisely what Mr. Weathers made mention of previously because, as Daddy explained it to Deputy Burton when at last he got pressed and goaded into explaining it, he himself was not just precisely Mr. Weathers which the sheriff seemed to comprehend and appreciate well enough but which the deputy did not appear to take much stock in.

Daddy said he described everything that happened, described everything that happened two times over, which would be once for the sheriff and which would be twice for the deputy as the deputy did not ever seem to absorb a thing straightoff, and then he got dismissed into the main corridor while the deputy fetched Granddaddy out from his cell so as to ask him everything two times that he had already asked two times of Mr. Weathers and Daddy too. And it was in the corridor, Daddy said, that he ran up on Momma and Grandmomma and straightoff commenced to swear and revile Mrs. Viola Demitt since he figured Mrs. Viola Demitt was the one that had called them, or if not Mrs. Viola Demitt then likely Deputy Burton, so Daddy swore and reviled him some in addition to what swearing and reviling he'd done on the deputy's account previously, but Momma told him it had not been Mrs. Viola Demitt or the deputy either and instead they had got called by the mayor's secretary Mrs. Gresham who did not see but everything and did not know but everything and did not tell but everything too or anyhow did not ever tell but as much of everything as she knew which was not ever everything entirely but always was just enough of everything to flabbergast and agitate whoever it was she was telling it to which in Granddaddy's case would be Grandmomma who got told by Mrs. Gresham that Granddaddy had hunted down somebody, she did not know where, and had outright killed and murdered him, she did not know how, and had got brought in and locked up straightaway, she figured she knew why.

Quite naturally Grandmomma fell to pieces at once and altogether and as she was by nature a woman of considerable passion she commenced to sweat and palpitate rightoff and dropped to the kitchen floor in a fit where she stayed even after the fit had pretty much spent itself out since passion was not the only thing Grandmomma had considerable of. Daddy said she had not ever been a dainty woman but had commenced full-figured and then had proceeded from there to something did not anybody have a seemly word for, especially not Daddy who did not hold seemliness in much esteem. So Grandmomma laid on the linoleum after the fit and after the palpitating on account of she could not get up from it since those parts of herself with muscle to them could not manage those parts of herself without it and though she latched on to two drawerpulls and tugged with her arms and pushed with her legs thereby actually levitating the bulk of herself she did not stay levitated but shortly, due primarily to the drawerpulls themselves which had not been designed with hoisting Grandmomma in mind and so the left one snapped at the screw just as the right one was about to and Grandmomma pitched over backwards carrying the silverware drawer with her and spilling out the insides of it all overtop herself.

She did not know just what to do as she had become, aside from agitated and flabbergasted too, purely wild with exasperation so she went ahead and shrieked which was what she generally did when she did not know what to do and since Grandmomma had herself two lungs that could fuel a shriek for a goodly while she most always stirred some attention roundabout whenever she up and cut loose and had even brought the fire department the time she sat on the chicken-snake but that had been an outside upright shriek and this one was an inside laidout shriek with some restrictions to it on account of the place settings atop Grandmomma's stomach but Mrs. Talton next door heard it anyhow and snatched up Mr. Talton's garden spade off the back porch prior to heading on down the steps and across the sideyard at a dead run, dead run of course being almost exclusively a figure of speech with Mrs. Talton who rivaled Grandmomma in sheer bulk and magnitude and so could just as soon beat her arms and hover as run. She rounded the upper end of the hedge and picked up appreciable momentum down along the side of the house and across the backyard which had somewhat of a slope to it and since she did not commence to brake early on she passed up the back steps and proceeded on into the honeysuckle hedgerow and the wire fence amidst it. Straightoff the spadehandle got all tangled up and confused in the vines and Mrs. Talton, who was somewhat tangled and confused herself, set in to thrashing about in the honeysuckle and yanking at the spadehandle so as to free it and she did free it but not until she'd thrashed and yanked and generally beat around sufficiently to make herself irksome to the bumblebees to the left of her and the bumblebees to the right of her too and an assortment from each side set to work on Mrs. Talton's forearms and on Mrs. Talton's lower legs which Mrs. Talton took notice of almost immediately and grew frantic on account of straightaway but since she did not know just precisely what to do to get clear and free of the bumblebees Mrs. Talton did what Grandmomma always did whenever she did not know just what to do and Grandmomma had not hardly finished listening to the shriek from there on the kitchen floor when she drew off a breath so as to reply.

Now Mr. Cole on the other side of Grandmomma had taken a disability from the cotton mill in 1952 on account of his emphysema and he chose to spend his retirement in a soft chair at the back of the breakfast room where he coughed up phlegm and spat it into a bucket in a recreational sort of way and as coughing and spitting too were for Mr. Cole fairly constant and noisesome undertakings he did not hear much of what went on in the world around him but primarily just what went on in his throat and in his mouth and in his bucket too. However, he did catch a little piece of Mrs. Talton's initial shriek on account of how close by Mrs. Talton had shrieked from and the sound of the thing had near about arrested Mr. Cole in the middle of an expectoration which would be actually at the outset of the expectoration since an expectoration is not the sort of thing that can be arrested in the middle and he sat up straight with his lips pressed tight together and only puckered somewhat and held what little breath he had so as to listen for what he had heard a piece of just previously, and consequently Grandmomma's reply from the kitchen floor got remarked by Mr. Cole as did Mrs. Talton's second full shriek after along with Mrs. Talton's third full shriek as well as the flickering portion of a fourth shriek that Mrs. Talton set in on just as she was busting loose from the honeysuckle which naturally was just as she commenced to run, run here still fairly much in the figurative sense though not so utterly figurative as before due to the bumblebees which were quite thoroughly actual themselves.

Of course Grandmomma got ecstatic straightoff once she heard Mrs. Talton tromping up the wrought iron stairway, or anyhow once she heard the plain tromping which she figured to be originating with Mrs. Talton on account of the general resonance of it and when Grandmomma got ecstatic she generally did the very same thing she did when she did not know just what to do and so she cut loose just as Mrs. Talton laid her fingers on the screen door handle and the sound of an uncontestable shriek so immediate and doseby spurred Mrs. Talton on across the porch decking at a kind of a trot, or anyhow at something less than her full dead run but still with some pace to it, and she burst directly on through the kitchen doorway and raised up the digging end of Mr. Talton's garden spade so as to introduce it to whatever scoundrel had so afflicted and tormented Grandmomma as to bring about the shrieking but Mrs. Talton did not have much chance to cast about for somebody to hit or even flail at one time on account of she stepped directly onto a soupspoon and commenced to fall over straightaway. Grandmomma could not aid her much except maybe as a buffer between Mrs. Talton's fleshy backside and the linoleum and Grandmomma could not see the advantage in that so she slid herself clear of the backside and clear of the shovelblade too and observed how Mrs. Talton dropped to the floor which she did not manage with much velocity or noticeable recklessness but which she did manage nonetheless lurching one time and then sinking much like a punctured frigate. So then it was the two of them and the silverware and the garden spade as well all scattered across the kitchen floor and Grandmomma told Mrs. Talton Hello and got told Hello back by Mrs. Talton who was curious to know how come in a general sort of way but was too polite and neighborly to ask it outright.

Couldn't neither one of them get up and couldn't the both of them climb up each other and so rise together even after Grandmomma explained to Mrs. Talton just why they had to get up and why they had to rise which was also pretty much why they were where they were in the first place and the most they could accomplish was some sliding around from the stove and refrigerator side of the kitchen to the sink side of it and then back again though Mrs. Talton did manage to lift herself somewhat on the oven door until the hinges gave way. So they were still on the floor with the silverware and the garden spade when Grandmomma detected a footstep on the bottom iron stairtread followed by a second on the stairtread above it and a third on the stairtread above that and Grandmomma and Mrs. Talton grew uneasy directly as they were not in any position to defend themselves and did not know but they would have to against whoever it was that had set in to climbing the back stairs which they did not know for certain was Mr. Cole until Grandmomma detected, in addition to the footsteps, a fairly vile and indelicate noise which was the sound of Mr. Cole clearing his throat of what had congregated there and then clearing his mouth of what he'd cleared his throat of. Consequently, then, there was euphoria on the kitchen floor, at least for a spell, and Grandmomma and Mrs. Talton hooted and shrieked together and even called out a time or two in actual English so as to drive and motivate Mr. Cole some but Mr. Cole did not need driving and did not need motivating near as much as he needed resuscitating and he paused midway up the stairs and drew off for himself breaths that rattled in his throat like so much shot in a bucket and then of course he dredged some and spat prior to getting hooted and shrieked at and even called to outright by Grandmomma and Mrs. Talton together whose affliction Mr. Cole had speculated upon all the way from his breakfast room to Grandmomma's back door but as silverware and a garden spade and whelpy bee bites had not figured into his speculations even the least little bit he was not fully prepared for what he stepped into the kitchen and saw which was the silverware and the garden spade and Grandmomma and Mrs. Talton too scattered across the linoleum with the whelpy bee bites scattered across Mrs. Talton.

Naturally Mr. Cole leaned himself against the kitchen doorframe and breathed heavy for a time and naturally Grandmomma and Mrs. Talton simultaneously exploded into fits of agitated graciousness that got all mixed and mingled together and so did not fall upon Mr. Cole's ears in any sort of comprehensible form which did not matter much on account of how Mr. Cole did not ever listen to what fell upon his ears whenever he happened to be particularly breathless and he happened to be particularly breathless most all the time, so the ladies exuded from there on their backs on the linoleum and explained to Mr. Cole just what had befallen the both of them and Mr. Cole laid up against the doorframe and listened to the air beat about in his trachea on its way into him and on its way out of him too while Grandmomma told somewhat of the phonecall and somewhat of the palpitations and somewhat of the drawerpull and somewhat of the screeching as well prior to giving over to Mrs. Talton who told somewhat of the screeching herself and somewhat of the garden spade and somewhat of the bee bites and theorized on the soupspoon since she'd not yet had the leisure to determine if it had been a soupspoon exactly, and then Mrs. Talton and Grandmomma too commenced to look forward to a time when they would not be sprawled atop the linoleum, when they would maybe be upright again and they wondered could Mr. Cole just perhaps help them realize their goals in this respect and Mr. Cole told them back, "Whut?" which was not so much a What as to the last few things they'd said but was more of a general and far-reaching What than that since Mr. Cole had not heard the first of what they'd said or the middle of it either on account of how utterly captivating he'd found the rattle in his throat which told him more than Grandmomma and Mrs. Talton too could ever fix their mouths to say.

But even Mr. Cole had breath sometimes, and he got his back directly and so set about assisting Grandmomma and assisting Mrs. Talton, or anyhow tugged at the one some and then tugged at the other which took most of what breath he'd collected so Mr. Cole laid up against the counter edge and pondered Grandmomma and pondered Mrs. Talton as well and then observed to the both of them, "Lord God, gone need a winch," which hit Mrs. Talton funny even stretched out on the linoleum and she set in to shaking all over and infected Grandmomma who set in to shaking all over herself until she recollected just why she was on the kitchen floor in the first place and so left off shaking straightaway and encouraged Mr. Cole to tug at her some more anyhow and right directly if he could. But the tugging the second time was not any more effective than the tugging the first time and likely Mr. Cole would have needed a winch in fact if not for the garden spade which Mr. Cole studied most intensely as he laid up against the counter edge the second time he laid up against it and he decided in his own mind just where he would put the blade of the thing and just how he would prize up Grandmomma and just how he would prize up Mrs. Talton and as he did not consult Grandmomma or Mrs. Talton either, since he had decided in his own mind already, but just went ahead and attempted what he'd figured he would attempt, Grandmomma was somewhat surprised at the sensation of the shovelblade beneath her posterior and it was mostly the shock and not so much the prizing itself that righted Grandmomma who climbed up the shovelhandle almost unassisted and then threw in with Mr. Cole on the raising of Mrs. Talton thereby rendering what had seemed an impossible undertaking only improbable at the most. And when there was at last nothing on the linoleum but silverware and feetbottoms Mrs. Talton expressed her supreme gratitude to Mr. Cole and

Grandmomma expressed her gratitude just behind her which had commenced supreme itself but had got dwindled and diluted when Mr. Cole turned round and spat into the kitchen sink.

So it was already a calamity, even before Grandmomma knew just who had got hunted down and who had got killed, it was already a calamity for her anyhow, and Daddy said when he ran up on Grandmomma and Momma too in the town hall corridor he was struck straightoff with how extraordinarily frazzled Grandmomma appeared to be as he did not ever see her but in her usual moderately frazzled state. Naturally, then, Daddy took Grandmomma by the elbow and ushered her across the hallway to a bench against the wall figuring as he did that a good sitdown might soothe and relieve Grandmomma somewhat, but once she saw just where her and her elbow were getting led Grandmomma shook loose from Daddy and told him she could stand up on her own two legs if he didn't mind, snapped and hissed at him actually but then apologized for it straightaway once she'd recollected how Daddy could not know she'd got frazzled like she got on account of what extended sitting down she'd done just previously, and Grandmomma patted Daddy on the top of his hand like she always did when she was sorry for some one thing or another and Daddy told her back, "That's alright Miss Alice," like he always did whenever he got patted on the hand.

So Grandmomma did not sit down on the bench and did not lean up against the wall but stood in the middle of the corridor pulling at the fingers of one hand with the fingers of the other while Momma up and took Daddy by the elbow and led him not so much anywhere in particular but just off and away somewhat where Daddy figured he would get asked who had got killed and how come exactly and so pondered both items on his way to wherever it was him and his elbow were going but no matter how he pondered he knew just the Gilliam, which was only the name and not anything otherwise, and had not even admitted to himself yet the how come, let alone commenced to believe it, so Daddy set himself to tell Momma not much of anything but once Momma had got Daddy where she wanted him and had put her face up next to his face she did not want to know exactly what he was all fixed to tell her but instead opened her mouth and said, "Louis, tell me that's not my Buick out front at the curb," and Daddy raised up his eyebrows that way he does that means Oh shit which he raises his eyebrows and says outright to most everybody but Momma who just gets the eyebrows by themselves, and as her face was where it was and his face was where it was Momma saw the eyebrows and knew what the eyebrows meant and so opened her mouth again and said, "Tell me that's not my Buick," with some considerable emphasis on each word of it, but Daddy still did not say anything to her except with his eyebrows and except with his eyes too which he rolled upwards ever so slightly, and by way of encouragement Momma said to him, "Louis," bending it like she can and Daddy obliged her straightoff saying, "Inez, that's not your Buick," and Momma laid her hands to her hips that way Momma can and said back to him, "Well just what is it then?" and though Daddy knew what it was all along, had known what it was ever since the claybank, he wondered to himself if maybe it wasn't perhaps something otherwise if only just possibly but decided it was what he'd figured it was at the outset and so he went ahead and told Momma, "My ass, I guess," and Momma said back to him, "Louis Benfield!" that way she does not ever say it to me no matter what I do.

Even Grandmomma heard it which meant everybody else heard it better on account of Grandmomma's ears did not ever pick up but somewhat of what went by them and Grandmomma left off pulling at her fingers and said to Momma, "What?" and said to Daddy, "What?" and said to the both of them, "What is it?" and then commenced to pull at her fingers again and commenced to fret in a general and thoroughgoing sort of way which brought Momma to her and together they sat on the bench against the wall and held each other's hands and Momma told Grandmomma it would all be alright and encouraged Daddy to tell Grandmomma it would all be alright too which he went ahead and told her even though Daddy said he had already figured then it would not ever be alright exactly, could not ever be purely alright anymore.

They got done with Granddaddy sooner than they'd got done with Mr. Weathers and Daddy mostly because Granddaddy could not seem to recollect much of what had gone on and so mostly got told what had gone on by the deputy and then got asked had that been pretty much what had gone on and Granddaddy usually guessed it had been though he could not seem to recollect what had gone on exactly, so they were done with him near about straightaway but did not turn him out into the corridor rightoff due to the deputy's objections which Sheriff Browner felt obliged to weigh some prior to dismissing altogether. Deputy Burton did not see as it was fitting to turn out a killer and Sheriff Browner wondered why not considering who it was that had done the killing and what it was he'd done the killing to, and the deputy said to him, "You mean a nigger," but the sheriff told him back straightoff, "No sir. I mean a criminal, a car thief." "A nigger criminal," the deputy said. "A nigger car thief." And Sheriff Browner told him, "Alright then, that too, but we gone let him loose from here 'cause he won't go nowhere and he won't kill nobody else." "Likely not," the deputy said back, "but ain't nothing square about it." And Sheriff Browner studied his desktop and studied his fingers upon it and then laughed one time that mirthless way he had of laughing prior to telling Deputy Burton just, "Square," and then just, "Turn him out," and the deputy jerked his chin and spun round on his heels but the sheriff did not see the one and did not see the other either as he was looking not much of anywhere like usual and so saw whatever he always saw whenever he looked where he most always looked.

But still Granddaddy did not get let loose straightoff and Deputy Burton told Grandmomma they'd got mired up some in the documents and the forms and such, and Grandmomma, being a woman of considerable passion, told him to get unmired and directly or she'd see somebody about it, she did not know who exactly, and have a thing done to the deputy, she did not know what exactly either, and Grandmomma shook her leathery pointing finger under the deputy's nose so as to make her vague and nameless threats all the more emphatic and the deputy gave way somewhat most probably on account of the finger almost exclusively and he led Grandmomma and Momma and Daddy too back into the lockup where Granddaddy had got put into the cell he'd been put into previously and sat there on the iron bed studying the same patch of concrete floor he'd studied all along and Grandmomma had not hardly laid eyes on him when she said, "William Elsworth Yount, you come out from there!"

And Granddaddy did not but look at his patch of floor and did not but open his mouth ever so slightly and say, "I can't."

"You most certainly can too," Grandmomma said back and then bore in some on the deputy. "Tell him he most certainly can too," she said.

"Well you see I got these papers," the deputy replied somewhat to Grandmomma but somewhat to Momma and Daddy and even Granddaddy as well. "I got these forms and these documents and there's some typing to be done and some data," Deputy Burton said to Grandmomma, "data," Deputy Burton said to Momma and Daddy and Granddaddy as well, "that needs collecting. You see we're a little mired up just now."

And Grandmomma told him, "Five minutes," and then repeated it not even with her mouth but just her finger and the deputy excused himself to everybody, which would be Granddaddy too, and actually hurried up the hall and through the doorway where he had not hardly disappeared when Grandmomma told Granddaddy again, "Come out from there."

And Granddaddy told her back, "I can't."

"In here with convicts," Grandmomma said and laid her hands to her hips like Momma does.

"Ain't none but me," Granddaddy told her and Grandmomma looked into the one cell down from Granddaddy's and into the two cells up from his which she'd been reluctant to peer into previously on account of who she feared she might see and what she feared they might be doing. "Well you come on out anyhow," Grandmomma insisted and then she turned to Daddy and said, "Tell him to come on out," and her voice got all high and squeaky there at the end and she took up her nose between her fingers and commenced to gasp and suck air which she persisted at no matter how Momma held her roundabout the shoulders and talked to her low and quiet and she did not get regular again until the deputy showed up with what papers and forms and documents that needed signing by Daddy and by Granddaddy too who wrote their names where the deputy told them to write their names and wrote their initials where the deputy told them to write their initials and when the papers had got collected and stacked and neat-ened around the edges Grandmomma said to Deputy Burton, "Tell him he can leave here," and Deputy Burton said to Granddaddy, "You can leave here, Mr. Yount," and Granddaddy lifted his head and looked at Grandmomma and at Daddy and Momma and Deputy Burton too, looked at them in that way that said I can't but without the words.

iii

Daddy said he did not know how they got there. Daddy said they likely did not know how they got there either, and so he figured the mule did it, just went, Daddy said, just went where

he'd gone before and so took them with him, which would be
Uncle Jack and would be

Aunt Della and would be their wagon with the sides and the
roof to it. Straightoff Uncle Jack did not know was Oklahoma
next to Tennessee or farther over and could not Aunt Della tell
him for certain though she had an inkling it was not just
Tennessee with Oklahoma jammed up against it but Tennessee
and then maybe Missouri and then maybe Oklahoma, so they
just went knowing what little they knew and decided they
would find out whatever they might find out when they got to
where they could and they followed Mr. Nunnely's route on out
from Ruffin and southwest across the mountains to Knoxville
and then on from there near about pure west to Dyersburg
where the road branched two times and Uncle Jack managed
to take the wrong branch the first time and the wrong branch
the second time too all on account of the big square house with
the columns and the verbena that Mr. Nunnely had told them
to turn at and which had got lightning struck and had burned
clean down to the underpinnings, columns, verbena, big
square and all. So Uncle Jack and Aunt Della stopped at the
fork and Aunt Della held the reins while Uncle Jack peered
roundabout for any sort of upright item with any sort of
stanchions and any sort of flowers too but did not find but the
rubble and the mortared rock and so told Aunt Della, "This
ain't it," and went off to where he should not have gone which
he discovered was where he should not have gone once he
reached Mayfield Kentucky and the road quit. So they turned
around and spent the following day riding down the road
they'd spent the previous day riding up and Uncle Jack bore off
otherwise at the rubble pile and proceeded on to the second
branch where he stopped the mule and gave over the reins to
Aunt Della and peered roundabout for some sort of nut tree
Mr. Nunnely had told him grew square in the middle of the
fork but weren't any nut tree anywhere, just a sweetgum and
that not precisely square in the middle of the fork but
noticeably off to the south somewhat and Uncle Jack asked

Aunt Della, "Sweetgum make nuts?" and Aunt Della shook her head no and Uncle Jack told her, "This ain't it," and so drove on like he'd come and he stayed gone that way for the most of the afternoon, until near about dark anyhow when Uncle Jack and Aunt Della and the wagon with the sides and the roof to it and little Spud too passed round off the road they'd taken to the one they hadn't yet and Uncle Jack rose up ever so briefly so as to announce, "Sweetgum don't make nuts," telling it not to Aunt Della who already knew it but just out into the general air.

Daddy said they did eventually cross the line into Arkansas and proceeded on into Osceola where Uncle Jack stopped at the general supply so as to lay in a thing or two, chiefly coffee and flour and molasses and corn meal but also chiefly snuff as well, chiefly that is for Aunt Della who was the one that dipped and most generally Aunt Della preferred Railroad Brand which came in a gut instead of a tin but did not the clerk at the general supply know anything about a snuff in a gut and had not the clerk at the general supply even heard tell of a brand called Railroad so he made an inquiry to the customers roundabout and they all said "Railroad Brand" to each other for a time and then observed near about in unison how there weren't no such snuff anywhere. Naturally Aunt Sister had commenced to fidget at the outset of the snuff talk and once Daddy broke off to light a Tareyton Aunt Sister asked Momma didn't she find dipping purely as vile as your regular smoking, and Momma told her, "Viler," straightoff, and Aunt Sister thought for a time and decided viler suited her too on account of the drool and the dribble, Aunt Sister said, and of course the spit as well and the spit can it went into, and Momma and Aunt Sister together decided it was an utterly unbecoming habit not so much in men, who Momma said possess a native crudeness, but particularly in women, even your unheavenly orblike variety, and Aunt Sister told her, "Just precisely," while for his part Daddy sucked off a breath and belched like he can whenever he wants to which Momma and Aunt Sister could not but be astounded and repulsed at and together they told him, "Louis!" that way they said Louis when they were astounded and when they were repulsed but Daddy just dropped his chin and insisted he was being native which he wondered could he be blamed for or not, and Momma drew out her mouth and looked at Daddy that way she looks at him whenever he taxes her.

She laid in a store of Old Henry, Daddy said, which was what the clerk dipped and so recommended and which was what the bulk of the customers dipped and so recommended too, and it did not come in a gut or a tin either but came in a little cloth sack with a drawstring at the neck and a picture of Old Henry dyed right into the sacking, a picture of Old Henry holding by the drawstring a sack of Old Henry, and Aunt Della put it all in a box in the back of the wagon and did not sample even a pinch of it until Morrilton when she turned the Railroad Brand gut inside out and licked it but without much good effect and Aunt Sister told Daddy she guessed not and Momma told Daddy she guessed not too and Aunt Sister said to Momma but for Daddy mostly, "What a vice will do to some people," and Momma said back to Aunt Sister but for Daddy too, "Yes ma'm," and Daddy said to me, "Them that's got one," which was for me only somewhat. And Aunt Sister wondered why it was Daddy had to dwell on such a thing as snuff anyhow, wondered it at Momma mostly who could not but wonder back since it did not strike her that snuff should figure like it seemed to figure, at least so far, but Daddy insisted it was a crucial element and Momma told him, "Uh huh," that way that did not mean but the contrary and Daddy insisted crucial element again and Aunt Sister asked him crucial how and Daddy said just crucial and Momma observed how it did not seem to her but to gum up the progress of the thing, and Aunt Sister squirted air out between her lips and Daddy hooted one time and said, "Gum up," and hooted another time and told Momma she was a regular stitch which Momma did not appreciate rightoff as she had been earnest and so not a stitch but inadvertently.

"So here's how," Daddy said and went back to Morrilton Arkansas where Aunt Della prized open the neck of a sack of Old Henry with her least finger and pinched out some to lay in her cheek and she maneuvered her chin so as to lump it up and let the juices flow roundabout it and Uncle Jack, still in possession of his mysterious verbosity, even in Arkansas, asked Aunt Della was it savory and was it satisfying like the clerk and the customers too had suggested it might be savory and might be satisfying, and Aunt Della dribbled some off into the can she generally dribbled off into and then sampled a fresh dollop, rolled it around some on her tongue and announced how it was not savory and satisfying exactly. "Like sucking sawdust," she told him and spat out the entire lump not even into the can but clean off the wagon and she said to Uncle Jack, "Let's have a piece of it," and Uncle Jack fished around in his coatpocket for his plug and his jack-knife and gave the both of them over to Aunt Della who cut off some of the one with the blade of the other and laid it between her teeth where she gnawed at it and ground it down to a pulpy mass and then spat a stream off her side of the wagon as Uncle Jack spat a stream off his which was along about when little Spud lifted up his tail and laid down an item of his own and Daddy said the bunch of them together looked something like a firehouse pumptruck in an Independence Day parade, though maybe not just precisely, Daddy added once he saw who was looking at him and how.

Aunt Della couldn't chew plug for long. Daddy said that was the crux of the thing and then insisted mostly in my direction but not truly to me really that the thing did have a crux and that the crux of it was that Aunt Della could not chew plug for long which he would be pleased to elaborate upon if he might, Daddy said to me but not for me hardly at all though I told him Alright anyhow on account of Momma and Aunt Sister did not but glare at him like they had been. Daddy said plug churned Aunt Della's stomach so she could not chew it but a little at the time and as Old Henry did not suit whatsoever she could not well satisfy her needs and cravings and consequently grew harsh and testy like women tend to, Daddy said just at me once more, and like women tend to Aunt Della did not see fit to horde up all the suffering for herself but passed a portion of it on to Uncle Jack who was not looking to suffer but got to and passed another portion of it along to the mule who, being a mule, likely expected to suffer anyhow. So it was not just snuff talk for the sake of snuff talk, Daddy said primarily to Momma and primarily to Aunt Sister and not hardly even at all to me, but it was snuff talk prefatory to the repercussions and prefatory to the crux, the one being somewhat of the other and the both together suggesting and implying and insinuating too, Daddy said, the significance of Aunt Della's disposition in what Daddy called the pageant of consequences which Momma objected to straightoff like she usually did when Daddy commenced to wax what Momma called bombastic, and Aunt Sister, who was not one to weigh out an inference and an implication and had not ever in her lifetime bothered to just insinuate a thing, wanted to know square and flatout just what in God's wondrous world it was Daddy was getting at anyhow and Daddy told her, "Causality mostly," and Aunt Sister pondered him back like he'd damned her to perdition.

"You see," Daddy said, "it was the dead mule that led to the live mule and it was the live mule that led to the mule trading and it was the mule trading that led to the Old Henry and it was the Old Henry that led to the plug chew and it was the plug chew that led to the bad temper and it was the bad temper that led to the general suffering and it was the general suffering that eventually led to the indian."

"What indian?" Aunt Sister wanted to know.

"The shot one," Daddy told her.

"Over snuff?" Aunt Sister said.

And Daddy told her, "Well," and told her, "after a fashion," and Aunt Sister looked at Momma and Momma looked at Aunt Sister and the both of them expressed a common sentiment without ever opening their mouths to do it.

Daddy said they traveled on throughout the night on account of Aunt Della was too jumpy and sour to lie still and so did not want the mule and Uncle Jack to either and they had passed through Fort Smith and on across the Oklahoma border into Poteau before the sun had got high enough to see by which put them just shy of Hartshorne to the southwest by midday and as it was just shy of Hartshorne they'd been heading towards all along Uncle Jack gave over the reins to Aunt Della and took out from his jacketpocket the folded scrap of paper which would be the same folded scrap of paper that had given him the columns and the verbena and the nut tree too so quite naturally Uncle Jack did not study it with much the same reverence and attention he'd spent upon it previously but just glanced at the germane parts so as to learn Mr. Nunnely's opinion in this instance and then figure for himself was there any call whatsoever to believe it. Daddy said he found out he was looking for a London, a mule trading London that did not go by but his initials, Mr. Nunnely had not bothered to say what initials exactly, and lived just off the road in a sod-roofed house, and in this particular case the information turned out to be extremely accurate and utterly factual but not altogether discriminating on account of most all the Londons went by initials and lived just off the road in sod-roofed houses, and to make things even more tangled up and confused, most all the Londons got their living trading livestock, as commerce was what usually passed from London to London like ears with Cottens and hooked noses with Tates.

Daddy said Uncle Jack learned straightway that Mr. Nunnely had not cut any sort of remarkable figure in Oklahoma since did not any of the Londons seem to recollect him even vaguely and remotely, did not seem to recollect him at all except for the one time when W. J. London wondered had the Nunnely been that fellow back in November with the cough which stirred up Uncle Jack some since he had heard Mr. Nunnely cough a time or two himself, but Mr. W. J. London's brother, R. H. London, and Mr. W. J. London's brother's boy, R. H. II, both agreed that the man back in November with the cough had been a Norris that was not from the east anyhow but from the west and had not traded in mules but cattle and the two R. H.'s agreed among themselves and then convinced the W. J. too that also it had not been just a cough but had been the consumption mostly which, as the elder R. H. recollected it, the Norris had died from in the hotel in town, and R. H. II along with W. J. recollected it the same way themselves once they'd got prompted to, but W. J., who was reluctant to give up the thing entirely, wanted to know from Uncle Jack had his Mr. Nunnely contracted and died from the consumption anytime lately and Uncle Jack thought on it some and consulted Aunt Della prior to telling W. J. London back, "No sir, not so as you'd notice."

Naturally Aunt Della was not getting less ill and less sour and less jumpy as the morning progressed into the afternoon partly because interviewing Londons did not divert and amuse her near so much as it diverted and amused Uncle Jack who would just as soon work his mouth as any other part of himself, but primarily because by midday Aunt Della was deep in the midst of a violent snuff withdrawal trauma, what Daddy called getting the monkey out from between her cheek and gum, and accordingly her disposition had dropped off from just harsh and just testy and had got purely vicious by the time they came up on Mr. J. T. London who told Uncle Jack straightoff he traded mules and who told Uncle Jack straightoff he'd seen that wagon of his before, the one with the sides and the roof and the windows to it. "Come a fellow in the very one," Mr. J. T. London said, "not but last year now. Little fellow," he told Uncle Jack and raised his hand up level in the air along about his own nose which Uncle Jack commenced to make a contrary face at so J. T. London scratched himself in the nostril and added, "Right big for a little fellow though, and bulky too."

"Bulky where?" Uncle Jack wanted to know.

And J. T. London told him, "All roundabout, primarily."

"In the shoulders?" Uncle Jack asked.

"Most especial in the shoulders," J. T. London told him and laid out his arms some so as to suggest and imply the bulk more precisely. "As fine a little bulky fellow as I ever come across. Said his name wasuh," and J. T. London wrapped his fingers around his chin, lifted his head somewhat, and puckered his face up considerably.

"Nunnely?" Uncle Jack told him, mostly by way of encouragement.

"Yes sir, just exactly," Mr. J. T. London said back. "Never come across a finer little bulky fellow."

"He's a good one," Uncle Jack said and turned round to Aunt Della so as to ask her, "Idn't he?" which she snapped and yipped at.

"And getting along alright?" Mr. J. T. London wondered.

"Good," Uncle Jack told him, "real good."

"And the missus?" Mr. J. T. London wanted to know.

"Still dead," Uncle Jack told him.

"Yes, I do recall how grievous and forlorn he was," Mr. J. T. London said and dropped down his head and clasped his hands before him, "but he was a fine little bulky fellow, as fine as I've ever come across, and you must be that buddy of his he come out with near about every breath, said his name wasuh," and Mr. J. T. London knotted his face all up.

"Yount," Uncle Jack said. "Jack Yount."

"Why the very one," Mr. J. T. London exclaimed. "This is a pleasure, sir," he said and extended his hand to Uncle Jack who took it and pumped it some. "I never known a man spoke so highly of."

"Well, we ain't but acquainted," Uncle Jack told him.

"Now me and you both know Nunnely wasn't one for carrying on much but he did carry on over you," Mr. J. T. London said. "Told me he didn't know nobody more decent and good than his friend Jack Yount. Told me many a time."

"Aw, now," Uncle Jack replied and grinned stupidly first at Mr. J. T. London and then round behind himself at Aunt Della and afterwards at his own shoetops.

"Yes sir, I do recall it, many a time. Said weren't nobody better not anyhow he could think of, and Nunnely weren't one to carry on, so if it's a man like you that's got business here I'd be proud to transact it with you, most proud," Mr. J. T. London said and wandered off from Uncle Jack some so as to admire the wagon with the sides and the top to it. "Ain't she a thing," he told Uncle Jack and circled from the near side around the back and then up the far side where he came up on

Aunt Della and so tipped his hat at her and told her, "Ma'm," but did not get told anything in return, did not even get looked at hardly until he canted himself up against the front left wheel rim and took out from his shirtpocket a tin of Sweet La La, a tiny blue tin with a hinged top which he laid open with ever so much care and Aunt Della grew keenly interested of a sudden and brought herself partway out over the seat arm so as to peer into the tin unobstructed and Daddy said the pungent aroma of pure snuff drifted up towards her and filled her noseholes causing Aunt Della to get agitated and goose pimply straightoff and she drew in some ponderous air and shuddered one time, Daddy said, and Aunt Sister told him, "Near about sinful," which Momma threw in with even before Aunt Sister could ask her did she want to throw in.

Daddy said Mr. J. T. London had pinched him out a goodly portion of Sweet La La and deposited it next to his molars before he ever noticed just precisely how he was getting leered at from the wagonseat and even when he did notice and did stiffen up straightaway he did not know just what to do for it except tip his hat again and say Ma'm again and by way of reply Aunt Della shoved at him all the rest of her Old Henry, which was two full sacks and the most of the used one, and she proposed a trade or actually did not propose a trade clear and outright but simply shoved the Old Henry with one hand and snatched at the Sweet La La with the other which implied and suggested what she had not proposed otherwise and Mr. J. T. London watched the shoving hand do its shoving and watched the snatching hand do its snatching and managed to relieve Aunt Della of what Daddy called the solitary violated sack of Old Henry which he opened at the neck and sniffed at and then let dangle between his fingers by the drawstring. "Ma'm," he told Aunt Della, "I'd just as soon dip ratshit. Whyn't you try a pinch of this here," and he extended the tiny blue tin with the tiny hinged top out towards Aunt Della who had it in her own hand even before he knew he'd give it up and what she did not spill out she got to her mouth somehow and pumped saliva through it straightoff.

Daddy said there is a time in every human life of supreme relief and satisfaction, not your emotional or philosophical or theological variety, Daddy said, but more your primitive and physiological and purely elemental sort of relief and sort of satisfaction, and then he recollected for the benefit of Aunt Sister and me and Momma too a prominent instance in his own lifetime which Daddy said was brought about chiefly by the meatloaf at Mr. Castleberry's Dinette, or actually the chopped red pepper in the meatloaf in combination with a 7-Up and the heat of the day and Daddy said he had not got up from the counter and gone two blocks when his stomach commenced to churn and sputter and little tiny sweat droplets popped out all across his forehead which Daddy said was when it came to him, came to him full and complete and utterly fullblown like a vision in the night and so he could not but know that he would do a thing shortly, a thing he did not have the power to prevent, likely did not have the power to delay but maybe somewhat, and Daddy said he stopped there on the pavement with the sputtering and churning in his stomach and a kind of vague sinking feeling setting in everywhere otherwise on account of how, as Daddy figured it, there is not much worse in this world than having to do the kind of thing he had to do and not being at home to shut the door and do it.

He said he set in to recollecting what toilets there were roundabout and who had charge of them since a man in his condition could not rush into just anybody's house or place of business and do to the toilet there what Daddy was planning to do to a toilet if he could only get to one, but before he could decide precisely where he would deposit what was about to get deposited somewhere his stomach left off churning and left off sputtering too and Daddy said it seemed to him in that one brief and giddy moment that maybe he could get home after all, so he struck out up the boulevard at his usual pace and did not accelerate until two blocks past the post office when the churning and the sputtering kicked in with renewed vigor and by then of course there was nowhere else to go but home and nohow else to get there but afoot so Daddy headed south down Spring Street and then goose-stepped on up Pender Avenue and rounded the corner, which put our house in sight, and

Daddy said he wanted to sprint, wanted to bolt down the road and up the front steps and direct into the bathroom, but could not convince his stomach to sprint with him and so trotted instead, or anyhow Daddy said he would call it trotting as he did not believe there was an actual word for it since there is no regular and ordinary occasion for a man to contract and knot up all the muscles in his body and then try to run and consequently there is no regular and ordinary occasion to call it anything, so Daddy said it was a trot that he went at kind of sideways and bent over and holding himself everywhere he could hold himself and every way available and he made the front walk and scaled the steps and burst on in through the doorway and across the living room and partway down the back hall before Momma intercepted him and attempted to inquire as to just why he was where he was just when he was there since he was supposed to be somewhere else altogether and Daddy said he gave Momma a kind of forearm shiver to the collarbone and then ducked on into the bathroom where he shut himself up so as to perform in private the act itself as well as the ritual preceding it which would be the triumphant lowering of the ring and then of the trousers and then of the posterior too followed hard up, of course, by the general purgation in all its thunderous glory, and Daddy mused briefly while Momma and Aunt Sister squirmed in that unapproving way they have of squirming, afterwhich Daddy observed how he could not recollect a more thoroughly satisfying moment, but once Momma had cleared her throat like she clears it sometimes Daddy announced how that would be satisfying in your primitive and physiological and purely elemental sort of way which put him back to where he'd set out from there with Aunt Della and her first taste of Sweet La La and that after Old Henry and after plug chew and after no suitable substitute otherwise which rendered the Sweet La La all the more savory and appealing and Aunt Della sucked on her fresh lump of it and made all manner of gratified noises and then dribbled off some into the can she had not dribbled off into anytime lately and wondered at Mr. J. T. London just where he'd come across such a thing as Sweet La La in a tiny blue tin, insisted on knowing it straightaway, and Mr. J. T. London told her, "General drygoods."

"Whereabouts?" Aunt Della wanted to know.

"Up the road yonder," Mr. J. T. London said and threw out his arm in a kind of a direction. "Just the other end of town."

"How far?" Aunt Della asked him.

And Mr. J. T. London told her, "Mile or two I guess," and then raised his pointing finger to his hatbrim and poked some underneath it.

And Aunt Della said, "Alright then," to Mr. J. T. London and said, "Alright then," to Uncle Jack and even said, "Alright then," to little Spud too as she loosed him from the wagon traces and climbed onto his back afterwhich she turned him and her both around towards Uncle Jack and towards Mr. J. T. London and said to them, "You go on and transact. I'll get back directly," and she kicked little Spud one time with her heels and set off down the road with her little wirey parts out from her at various angles.

And Mr. J. T. London watched her go for a bit and then told Uncle Jack, "Handsome woman, mister."

And Uncle Jack watched her go for a bit himself and then told him back, "Orblike," and Mr. J. T. London could not decide rightoff was it French or was it German or maybe even Huguenot but knew straightaway it was not regular English.

And Daddy left off talking and fetched out a Tareyton from his shirtpocket and fetched out a kitchen match from between the cushion and the chairarm and struck it on his shoewhelp and then cupped it in his hands and held it there. "Of course that was the road to carry her where she had to end up," Daddy said. "That was the road to carry her right straight to him."

"To who?" Aunt Sister wanted to know.

And Daddy lit his cigarette and shook out his match. "The indian," he said.

"What indian?" Aunt Sister wanted to know.

And Daddy told her slow and deliberate, "Sister, the shot one."

Two

He was not even Granddaddy then, not but Mr. Buck and nothing otherwise that he would get to be once he did it and once it got let out that he did it and how and with what, which did not anybody believe straightaway, which did not anybody want to believe after they could not help but believe it on account of did not seem to anybody Granddaddy could do what he did and how and with what as he was just Mr. Buck and nothing otherwise. They lived down the street from us not even so far as to be out of sight, him and Grandmomma in the house Granddaddy built which is not to say commissioned and contracted out but framed and wired and plumbed and just built altogether himself with nobody but Great-granddaddy to loiter roundabout the lot and indicate every little item that should have got done some otherhow which hardly was an aid and a benefit to Granddaddy as Great-granddaddy did not ever lift and tote and maneuver anything but the finger he indicated with. So he put it up himself since there was no money for help and no help but Great-granddaddy and it was just precisely right all over and square and true and not at all plain and unadorned even if it was Granddaddy making it who did not regularly make houses but would not let himself off just on account of that. So he planed down moldings and cased out the windows and doors with them and cut lacy ornaments for the gable peaks with just his coping saw and turned the pickets himself on Mr. Simpkins's pedal lathe. Then him and Grandmomma painted the whole inside and the whole outside too with Grandmomma painting the bottom parts and Granddaddy painting the top parts and Great-granddaddy loitering in the yard so as to better indicate with his indicating finger what places they'd passed over.

It was a peculiar sort of a house, not on account of how Granddaddy built it but on account of how Granddaddy drew it up, and Granddaddy did draw it up with some suggestions from Grandmomma who knew mostly what she did not want but not what she did want exactly, so Granddaddy weighed out what Grandmomma did not want and then drew fairly much what he wanted figuring it would be what Grand-momma wanted too since it was not what Grandmomma did not want and consequently it turned out peculiar on account of Granddaddy was not regular and ordinary and did not want regular and ordinary things, or anyhow did not exclusively want regular and ordinary things though naturally some of what he ended up with was regular and was ordinary too. The front of the house was not so unusual with the parlor on the one side and the main bedroom on the other but Granddaddy built a closet off the bedroom that you could step full into and there was a rack for clothes on the left side and a rack for clothes on the right side and in between them a fluffy chair and a floorlamp so as to accommodate Granddaddy who needed the closet to take his evening toddy in since Grandmomma would not generally allow whiskey in the bedroom as the vapors of it tended to give her the headache in the night. A door at the back of the bedroom opened into the bathroom which was spacious and tiled most everywhere and had a little window in the wall over the tub that nobody could see in and nobody could barely see out either except to look at the sky which was all Granddaddy ever looked to see when he bathed in the morning so as to discover just what sort of day he was bathing for.

Opposite the lavatory a second bathroom door opened into the back hallway and direct across from it Granddaddy had hung a most extraordinary oak door fashioned as it was from a solitary two-foot-wide plank. He'd salvaged it out from a tumbledown smokehouse on a piece of property up 29 that Great-granddaddy held the deed to and he insisted on hanging it in the house though Grandmomma insisted just as stoutly that it not get hung anywhere she'd have to open it or shut it either partly on account of it was thick and bulky and heavy too and partly on account of Grandmomma did not love an old, plain, natural thing like Granddaddy did and since Granddaddy was weighing off what Granmomma did not want and balancing that out with what he himself required he struck on a place for the oak plank where it would not get much swinging open or swinging shut either which was direct across the hallway from the bathroom door and he finished the thing out with a hammered iron pull and hammered strap hinges and cased it roundabout with an oiled oak frame and I do not recollect that Grandmomma ever pulled it open or swung it shut either and if she did it was not to get out from the hall and into anywhere else since the plank door did not but give onto the plaster behind it. Only Granddaddy opened it regularly and Daddy opened it sometimes since Daddy had a warm place for an old, plain, natural thing like Granddaddy did and nobody else ever bothered with it much but for Mrs. Phillip J. King's mother that was visiting from Burlington and took tea with Grandmomma which gave her occasion to step into the bathroom and get freshened which gave her occasion to step out from the bathroom and across the hall where she tried to go out the plank door like she knew she'd come in through it but got hindered and perplexed by the wall and while Grandmomma got her unhindered she could not get her unperplexed on account of Mrs. Phillip J. King's mother was certain she'd opened the plank door and passed on into the hallway, for some reason was even more certain she'd done it once she saw that she could not have which perplexed Grandmomma somewhat herself but nonetheless did serve to explain and illuminate just where it was Mrs. Phillip J. King had come by her all-consuming pigheadedness, Daddy called it, which apparently had got passed down to her instead of dimples and instead of wavy hair.

There was an extra bedroom next to the bathroom across from the plank door at a diagonal but did not anybody much ever stay in it except for Grandmomma sometimes when Granddaddy pitched about and kicked her in the night and down a ways from that was the back stairs up to the landing at the top of the house which was the only stairs up to it and it was not in any way an extravagant and spacious landing but just a little square one with a door to the left of it that opened onto the attic room where Grandmomma kept her meat in the winter and dried her fruit in the summer and a door to the right of it that opened onto the room where Granddaddy smoked his pipe and chewed his tobacco and picked his guitar, a room Grandmomma and Granddaddy too called the sewing room on account of Grandmomma's machine was in it somewhere. The back hall gave out at the breakfast room that was finished in knotty pine with windows and shelves all roundabout and a frosty louvered door off it to the iron steps and the backyard but just a regular ordinary paneled one off it to the kitchen that had a window over the taps like most kitchens and a window elsewhere like most kitchens too and cabinets up high and cabinets down low and two sinks and a countertop and a Frigidaire and a range with drawers in it for the pots and the saucepans and a can opener with a red crank up high on the wall next to the doorway to the dining room which was not one of your expansive dining rooms, not even one of your ordinary regular-sized dining rooms but just a little closet of a dining room with hardly the space for a hutch, a sideboard, a table, and people too which did not please Grandmomma much, had not ever pleased her much really on account of how she had requested from Granddaddy something more on the scale of one of your regularsized if not expansive dining rooms and so had expected to get it as Granddaddy insisted he was all compassionate and sympathetic to Grandmomma's whims and desires, but Granddaddy could not bring himself to draw in a sizeable dining room and frame it up and finish it out on account of there was the breakfast room and on account of there was the kitchen and on account of there would be the dining room too which meant appreciable square footage squandered just for food almost exclusively and Granddaddy did not ever love a meal like Daddy loves a meal, like most men love a meal really, but just ate to please Grandmomma who was ever suggesting how unharmonious things might be if he did otherwise. So the dining room Granddaddy drew in and framed up was tiny and was cramped and Grandmomma did not complain straightoff because she figured it for a butler's pantry and did not ever get told by Granddaddy that it wasn't until she figured it for a dining room when Granddaddy told her it was and expounded some on the theory of square footage and general utility which Grandmomma did not much believe was a part of the building code though Granddaddy insisted it always had been.

Truly he was conserving his square footage for the room that Grandmomma would not have wanted if she'd known she was going to get it but as Grandmomma figured the dining room for a butler's pantry she figured the one beside it for the dining room when it was in actuality Granddaddy's den, or anyhow Granddaddy intended it for his den where he would smoke his pipe and chew his tobacco and pick his guitar and he paneled it roundabout with beveled cypress and floored it with oak and closed it off from the dining room on the one side and the living room on the other with a pair of railhung carriage doors he'd scrounged up, Grandmomma said, from somewhere though Granddaddy had a more noble word for it that meant pretty much the same thing. Naturally Grandmomma objected to the den straightoff since she'd thought it was a dining room all along, objected of course to the general notion of it but to the particulars of it as well and she informed Granddaddy how she did not much want to dust the oak floor and did not much care for the sight of the cypress walls and could not well slide the carriage doors without strain and suffering as she was not a stable boy anyhow and Granddaddy went ahead and sympathized with her since it was already built and so was past unbuilding or even tampering with to much effect but Grandmomma did tamper with it anyhow and to more effect than Granddaddy ever figured she could tamper with it. First she carpeted the whole thing right overtop the oak, which pierced Granddaddy direct to the heart, and then she painted the whole thing right overtop the cypress, which likely would have done Granddaddy in had he not been still numb from the carpet, and then she propped open the carriage doors in a permanent sort of way, which did not affect Granddaddy much as he was already about as devastated as he could get. Afterwards she hung draperies and pictures and placed dainty furniture roundabout so as to cap off and garnish the whole undertaking and once it was all done Granddaddy attempted to smoke his pipe in the room he'd built to smoke his pipe in but got prevented from it by Grandmomma on account of how the smell lingered, so he attempted to chew and spit in the room he'd built to chew and spit in but got prevented from that by Grandmomma on account of how the whole activity displeased and offended her and clashed outright with the atmosphere roundabout, so he attempted to pick his guitar in the room he'd built to pick his guitar in but got prevented from that too for reasons a little more complicated than just aroma and atmosphere.

Granddaddy was not of a musical disposition like some people which is to say he did not regularly vent himself in song just for the pleasure and satisfaction of it, did not whistle hardly at all, rarely listened to the radio with much attention and did not ever sing the words in church but just gnawed on the melody instead, so he had not shown any inclination to be musical and melodic for the longest time after Grandmomma met him and married him and took up residence with him which was primarily how come she got so dismayed and put out when Granddaddy went off up the street to Mr. Beaumont's on a Saturday in 1948 so as to help him shingle his garage and then came back early on in the evening not with any more dollars and any more cents than he'd departed with as he had not got paid with dollars and with cents but had instead elected to get paid with guitar, six strings' worth and one of them busted. Grandmomma was not pleased and Grandmomma could be not pleased in a notable and demonstrative sort of way and it was partly because Granddaddy had not ever been musical and had not ever been melodic and partly because Granddaddy had not ever been wealthy either and would not get wealthy working for guitars, likely would not stay solvent, so Grandmomma got put out and indignant and Granddaddy got put out back, which he ventured to do only sometimes, and he told Grandmomma how music was his life's blood which was quite naturally a startling bit of information considering what Granddaddy could do to your standard recessional, so Grandmomma got put out still further and told Granddaddy a few things about himself he had not suspected and did not especially hold with and consequently Granddaddy objected outright and told Grandmomma a few things that she was not altogether pleased to hear, and the whole business went back and forth for an appreciable while with Granddaddy suggesting a thing to Grandmomma and Grandmomma suggesting a thing back to him and it carried on through supper and well into the evening and did not get resolved until somewhat later in the night when Grandmomma told Granddaddy he'd damn well better make some music on it and soon and Granddaddy told her back he guessed he would when he was good and ready for it and then Grandmomma pitched over to face west and Granddaddy pitched over to face east and they showed each other their backsides under the covers.

So he commenced to pick at the thing straightaway and not exactly because music was his life's blood, and Daddy said at the time they were in the house Great-granddaddy let out to them which was just around the corner from his and was not much of a house really but only a plain, squat frame structure with two rooms in the front and two rooms in the back and not even a bathroom but for the one in the yard, so Grandmomma could not hardly get away from the picking except to leave the neighborhood and even then she could hear it sometimes when Granddaddy was on the porch and the wind came through just right but still it did not sound like music to her, only noise somewhat diminished and far off but noise anyhow, and it was noise, Daddy said, noise that him and Momma did not have to hear much of as Daddy was with the railroad in Danville at the time and so was subjected to the picking not but two weekends a month. Daddy said he got a book. Mel Bay, Daddy suspected, though he did not know was there Mel Bay books in 1948 even if it did seem like there had been Mel Bay books forever, and Daddy said it was an oversized paper-cover book with pictures throughout of guitar frets with black dots for the fingertips and the instructions not just on how to play but on how to stand up with a guitar and how to sit down with one, as well as a brief history of the instrument and a diagram of all the parts and all the proper names for them which was what Granddaddy commenced with as he would not ever build but atop a worthy foundation, and even afterwards he did not attempt to play straightoff on account of he attempted to tune instead and could not. Mr. Bay, if it was in fact Mr. Bay, suggested a pitch pipe and Granddaddy went downtown and bought one and then blew on it and plucked and blew on it and plucked and blew on it and plucked some more but did not accomplish much except for the dizziness and the nausea, anyhow did not accomplish much in a musical sort of way but he kept at it nonetheless through the dizziness and through the nausea too and tuned the strings up and tuned the strings down again and then up once more after and while he did not ever hit the notes he wanted to hit and would not know he had hit them even if he did, he kept blowing and kept plucking because of Grandmomma primarily who had told him he was not musical and not melodic and whenever Grandmomma told Granddaddy he was not a thing he got determined to become it.

Quite naturally, Granddaddy did not figure he could display to the best advantage his rhapsodic soul with the six notes he'd managed to blow and pluck to and so he consulted Mr. Bay, if it was in fact Mr. Bay, who advised on page seven not just the pitch pipe but a piano also if a piano was handy and while Granddaddy had not figured a piano was handy at first he figured after the pitch pipe that maybe he'd best make one handy somehow and he thought on the subject for a spell and reasoned that as the area roundabout was fairly thick with Baptists, who as a group are quite partial to piano music, then there would likely be a higher incidence of local pianos than he might firstoff have thought, and Granddaddy worked out a formula, Granddaddy being the sort to calculate and formulize, whereby he allowed one piano for every thirty-five Baptists he knew of which yielded overall seventeen pianos somewhere close by and he commenced to seek them out. Of course most all the prominent families in Neely owned pianos, which would be your Pettigrews and your Benbows and your McKinneys and your Ridley-Prices if you asked a Ridley-Price, as most all the prominent children took lessons from Mrs. Hobgood out towards Lawson-ville but Granddaddy was not ever the sort to beat on a door after some one thing or another, especially not a door that he'd find anybody prominent behind on account of Granddaddy grew uneasy around airs and gentility so he calculated and formulized still further and decided he would simply introduce pianos into whatever casual conversation he came up on around town and see if he got anywhere much because of it, but straightoff it was not possible for Granddaddy to introduce pianos into what conversations he came up on since pianos would not suitably fit into most of what Granddaddy ever talked about so he just carried on in his usual sort of way and did not get around to what it was he wanted to get around to until after he'd wandered all up and down the boulevard and gotten around to most everything else there was to get around to when at last he came up on Mr. Phillip J. King who was waiting on the sidewalk for Mrs. Phillip J. King to bring her creams and ointments out from the drugstore and Granddaddy set in directly with pianos and thereby avoided having to introduce them subsequently.

He sucked at his teeth like Grandaddy always sucked at his teeth whenever he was about to observe one thing or another and then observed how piano music just stirred him somewhere inside and wondered did it stir Mr. Phillip J. King if only just somewhat, and while most anybody else would have been struck by the sheer and extraordinary oddness of such a thing as a piano observation passing out from between Granddaddy's lips and into the open air Mr. Phillip J. King did not make much of it primarily because he was fairly completely overcome by the fact that he had got asked his opinion by somebody other than Mrs. Phillip J. King who generally asked his opinion and then told him what it was just after. So Mr. Phillip J. King replied near about straightaway, telling Granddaddy, "Lord yes, same with me, Mr. Buck," and Granddaddy raked his mustache five times with his skinflap and then asked Mr. Phillip J. King was he musical, asked him did he play, and got told, "A little bit," which lifted Granddaddy's spirits considerably, or anyhow lifted Granddaddy's spirits until Mr. Phillip J. King asked him back, "What is it you want to hear?" and drew out from his shirtpocket a Marine Band in the key of G which Mr. Phillip J. King licked the wooden parts of prior to asking Granddaddy again did he want to hear anything in particular as Granddaddy had not suggested a melody and Granddaddy told him, "A piano mostly," which Mr. Phillip J. King apparently took for "Shenandoah" since "Shenandoah" was what he set out with or anyhow he insisted it was "Shenandoah" once he got done with it and Granddaddy took him at his word on account of some few parts of the thing had put him in mind of "Shenandoah" though the melody had altogether seemed like something otherwise since Mr. Phillip J. King had a way with notes and tunes but did not excel much in the rhythm part of the thing, but nonetheless Granddaddy told him it was as fine a rendering as he'd ever heard and naturally Mr. Phillip J. King, in an effort to please Granddaddy further and more completely, graced him straightaway with another selection that had some snap and jump to it and sounded kind of like "Shenandoah" again only frantic this time but turned out to be "Camptown Races" and once he got done with it Mr. Phillip J. King blew and sucked a couple of pairs of Doo Da's by themselves thereby persuading Granddaddy to his view of the thing and Granddaddy told him it was as fine a rendering as he'd ever heard.

Mr. Phillip J. King had already struck in on a third number that was somewhat "Shenandoah" too when Mrs. Phillip J. King emerged from the drugstore with her creams and her ointments and took hold of Mr. Phillip J. King at the elbow which fairly much disrupted the recital and left Granddaddy by himself on the sidewalk where he just stood for a spell all disappointed and downtrodden and then moped off towards the house with his hands shoved down deep in his pants pockets which was where he put his hands and how he made off with them when things went like they'd gone and he was almost home when he heard it and naturally he did not know he had heard it at first as he was not listening to what he was hearing but realized only after a spell what it was he was in fact hearing and then commenced to listen to it in earnest and stopped himself there on the sidewalk direct in front of the Congregationalist church. Granddaddy had always figured Congregationalists purely for organ people and so found himself astounded at the sound of the Doxology, that Granddaddy did not even know Congregationalists made use of, played on a piano, that Granddaddy had not even suspected they'd have played it on, and he stopped dead on the sidewalk still with his hands where he'd put them and still with his head where he'd hung it and let the music wash through the open sanctuary doors and engulf him roundabout or actually not so much wash and not so much engulf but more thunder and tinkle as it is your organs that will wash and will engulf but not hardly ever your upright pianos and surely not the Congregationalists' upright piano as it was third-hand and had not ever truly thundered and tinkled much anytime lately.

So Granddaddy stood there on the sidewalk reveling and basking in the sort of noise he'd been scouring the countryside to revel and bask in and at length he peeked on into the sanctuary to see who it was beating the keyboard which turned out to be Jonellen Marie Hayes, Mr. and Mrs. Jennings W. Hayes's oldest girl that played at the Con-gregationalist church over the objections of her momma and her daddy too who were Presbyterians themselves and so quite naturally considered Congregationalists one of your primitive life forms. Jonellen Marie Hayes had the kind of disposition for music that Mr. Phillip J. King did not possess which is to say she could keep a beat and could keep a rhythm even if she did not always hit the note she reached for but sometimes pulled up shy and sometimes overshot it and consequently provided a kind of variety in her music that was not consistently pleasing but was ever novel and unexpected.

Granddaddy did not tell her, "Hello, Jonellen Marie Hayes," straightoff like he'd figured and planned to once he'd taken occasion there at the doorjamb to figure and plan, did not tell her, "Hello, Jonellen Marie Hayes," on account of he did not know just what he would say after, had not decided how he would introduce the guitar and introduce Mr. Mel Bay, if it was in fact Mr. Mel Bay, so Granddaddy just lurked there in the doorway which was not exactly what he considered he was doing in the doorway but which was what Jonellen Marie Hayes figured he was up to once she felt him back there with her neckhairs and turned round to verify it and she asked him straight-out why it was he was lurking where he was lurking and Granddaddy told her back, "Hello, Jonellen Marie Hayes," even though he had not quite decided about the guitar or Mr. Bay either. But Jonellen Marie Hayes did not consider that a hello explained the lurking much and so she insisted on discovering just who it was in the doorway and why, as she could not see the who on account of the backlight and could not know the why until she got told it, and Granddaddy stepped on into the sanctuary proper where she could see it was just him and then sucked at his teeth ever so briefly prior to observing how piano music stirred him somewhere inside. Of course Jonellen Marie Hayes flushed straightoff since she was not much accustomed to stirring men inside or anywhere else and had not ever got accused of it before and she tinkled some at the upper end of the keyboard in an agitated and embarrassed sort of way and then just sat with her legs twisted roundabout each other while Granddaddy proceeded on up the aisle wondering as he did so just what lilting piece he had heard out there on the street and back there at the doorway and Jonellen Marie Hayes thought for a moment and then decided it must have been the Dox-ology though she had not ever considered the Doxology a truly lilting piece herself.

Granddaddy wondered could he hear something otherwise, laid his near arm atop the piano and wondered could he just linger a spell and listen to whatever it was Jonellen Marie Hayes might see fit to play, and Jonellen Marie Hayes did not tell him he could not but did not exactly tell him he could either and only flushed some more on top of what flushing she'd done already and tinkled some more and worked and twisted her legs some more so that it did not seem she would ever get them untangled. Then she struck direct into "What a Friend We Have in Jesus" with all ten fingers at once and hit pretty much what white keys she aimed for and what black keys she aimed for too and carried through with the refrain three times over and the verse part three times over as well while Granddaddy laid up against the piano-end and fairly much swooned outright on account of the general whipping up his insides were undergoing. He did not get much chance to recover once the final chord died off into the reaches of the sanctuary as Jonellen Marie Hayes was commencing to feel somewhat whipped up herself and so set off straightaway into "God Is Our Help in Ages Past" but served to introduce it to the extent that Granddaddy was not but partly shocked and surprised when what followed the preface followed it, and he tapped his foot and held himself so as to seem generally whipped up and stirred but did not need to really as Jonellen Marie Hayes had got all agitated and lathered herself and had pretty much forgot where she was and who was with her which might explain how come she could jump from "What a Friend We Have in Jesus" and "God Is Our Help in Ages Past" to "Bess You Is My Woman Now" which she did in fact jump to and which did in fact have some sway and beauty to it not to mention considerably more genuine lilt than the Doxology.

Now it happened that the Congregationalist Reverend Mr. Langley lived hard up next door to the sanctuary in the painted block parsonage and as it was not Friday when he wrote his sermons or Saturday either when he read them to Mrs. Langley and got told how to punch them up and where and not Monday too when he rendered matrimonial council or even Tuesday when he visited the sick and infirm but was instead Wednesday which for the reverend was very much like Thursdays when he did not do anything in particular, the Reverend Mr. Langley was not doing anything in particular in an official sort of way but was just crawling roundabout among his irises grubbing up weeds and singing in his deep throaty baritone the words to whatever Jonellen Marie Hayes happened to set in on next door and the reverend knew most all the words to most all the verses to most all the hymns Jonellen Marie Hayes ever had occasion to set in on as the reverend tended to flip through the hymnal quite regularly at bedtime and most nights managed to peruse an actual

selection or two with some attention whenever Mrs. Langley
was not reading to him snatches from the Family Circle. So the
reverend held forth with "What a Friend We Have in Jesus" in
its entirety and mustered up enough of "God Is Our Help in
Ages Past" so as to keep from chewing the air throughout the
most of it and naturally he was in a purely singful mood by the
time the first few chords of "Bess You Is My Woman Now"
commenced to arrive in the iris bed. Consequently then the
Reverend Mr. Langley, who had been a thespian in the
seminary, set in on the third one just like he'd set in on the
previous two and did not even notice it was in your more
nondenominational vein until Mrs. Langley stuck her head out
the door and told him as much and the reverend shut his
mouth straightaway, sat bolt upright on his knees, and peered
off at the sanctuary like maybe he could see through the walls
of it and he did not leave off with his peering and his glaring
and his bolt uprightness until well after Jonellen Marie Hayes
had finished out with a two-fisted crescendo which she did not
hardly pause behind prior to recommencing with "When the
Moon Comes over the Mountain" that not the Reverend
Langley or Mrs. Langley either one could determine the
hymnfulness of for a goodly bit until Mrs. Langley herself
recollected where she had heard it and out from whose mouth.

So the reverend got up onto his feet and brushed the dirt from
his trouser legs still looking at the sanctuary walls and not but
glancing at Mrs. Langley in that way he had of glancing at her
when he wished to share and express his disgruntlement and
she looked at him back that way she had of looking at him back
when disgruntlement was what she wished to share and
express too. "It's not the suitable thing," she said.

And the reverend told her, "No ma'm, it's not."

"It's not the proper thing," she said.

And the reverend told her, "No ma'm, it's not."

"If it was my place to say a thing, I do believe I would," she said.

And the reverend told her, "Yes ma'm, there's a thing that needs saying," and he left off peering through the sanctuary wall long enough to face up to Mrs. Langley and tell her directly, "Excuse me, Momma," which Mrs. Langley jerked her chin at thereby dismissing the reverend who set out towards the front sanctuary doors with resolve but not any velocity to speak of until "When the Moon Comes over the Mountain" gave way to "Fascinating Rhythm" which the reverend recognized straightoff as the sort of number people actually danced to and he glanced ever so briefly over his shoulder at Mrs. Langley in that way he had of glancing at her and got looked at back.

Jonellen Marie Hayes saw him first with her neckhairs even before Granddaddy, who was looking that way anyhow, could see him with his eyes, and her neckhairs told her straightaway just who it was and why while Granddaddy could not but see it was somebody beating it up the aisle at a determined jogtrot like Jesus coming to fetch out the moneylenders, and as Granddaddy did not know it was the reverend beating it up the aisle and so had not puzzled out why, he was fairly stunned when of a sudden "Fascinating Rhythm" turned headlong into "Christ the Lord Is Risen Today" without so much as a halfbar of prefatory fingerwork. Quite naturally the reverend was fairly irate by the time he arrived up at the altar where the piano was as the jogtrotting had not tended but to aggravate what agitation he'd carried through the doors with him and he demanded to know, demanded to know primarily from Jonellen Marie Hayes since it was her fingertips at the source of it, just why it was he had been hearing drifting out from the church such music as he had been hearing drifting out from the church, and Jonellen Marie Hayes slid around sideways on the piano bench and kind of halflooked at the reverend out from under her eyebrows with her neckhairs all upright and prickly and the reverend observed direct at her how it did not seem to him that the church of God was a fitting place for secular melodies, saying secular like it was caught crossways in his throat.

Of course Jonellen Marie Hayes, who was backwards and frail anyhow, tended to require just the minimum of hard words before she deflated entirely, and she was commencing to draw in and fairly much disappear from sight when Granddaddy, who had not said anything just yet on account of he had been figuring and calculating what to say like he generally figured and calculated, intervened at last on behalf of Jonellen Marie Hayes who sat on the edge of the piano bench in a semi-inflated state and watched Granddaddy lay his arm round the reverend's shoulder and gaze into the reverend's face all earnest and perplexed prior to saying to the reverend, "Lo, I am troubled," and the reverend became of a sudden changed and transformed like Granddaddy had figured and calculated he would since there is not a preacher anywhere that lives but to get consulted.

Straightoff the Reverend Mr. Langley laid his hand on the small of Granddaddy's back and said to him, "Tell me, beloved, the manner of your affliction," saying it without any bite or edge to it but in words all slick and lubricated that left a kind of trail in the air like what follows a slug.

And Granddaddy moved his own hand off from the reverend's shoulder and onto the small of the reverend's back. "I am afflicted," he said, "with a general sadness," and Granddaddy drew a breath not so much to get wind but mostly to let the reverend hear it get drawn and hear it get let out too. "Sorely afflicted," Granddaddy said and loosed a trail of his own.

"Sadness of a particular source?" the reverend wanted to know.

And Granddaddy told him back, "Lo," which was not entirely what

Granddaddy had set about to tell him back but was all he came out with except for the gasp afterwards, which would be the first gasp, following which he pinched up in his fingers the piece of nose between his eyes and gasped again, which would be the second gasp.

Daddy has always insisted that Granddaddy himself could manufacture what the horses did and then pile it so high as to cover a man up entirely, and it would seem that after the Lo and the first gasp and the second gasp too there was not much of the reverend left out in the open air except maybe for the parts he breathed through and he took his hand off from the small of Granddaddy's back and laid it up on Granddaddy's bare neck making somewhat of a smudge on account of the dirt from the iris bed. "Beloved, we must help each other in times of pain and despair. How might I soothe your soul and bring balm to your spirit?"

And Granddaddy let loose the piece of nose from between his fingers and laid back his head so as to gaze upwards towards the sanctuary ceiling. "Dear Lord," he said, "I am never so happy as when I hear a melody, any little verse, any little refrain."

And the reverend jerked his finger at Jonellen Marie Hayes and told her, "Play."

"Any little snatch of music," Granddaddy said. "Any little chord, any little bar, any little thing with some snap and some jump to it."

And the reverend wagged his entire hand over the keyboard so as to attract the attention of Jonellen Marie Hayes who had commenced with "Nearer My God to Thee" which did not have much snap or much jump either and of a sudden she transformed it into "Stand Up for Jesus" that near about magical way she had of transforming melodies and the reverend squeezed Granddaddy's neck somewhat with his fingertips and Granddaddy said to the sanctuary ceiling, "Just most any little secular item," which prompted more finger jerking and more hand wagging as the reverend attempted to communicate to Jonellen Marie Hayes just precisely what he wished to communicate to her which he succeeded at partly straightoff judging from how "Stand Up for Jesus" got changed and altered direct into "Glowworm" which Granddaddy did not complain about or gasp on account of but which the reverend still wagged and jerked at as it did not seem snappy or jumpy enough to him so "Glowworm" did not stay "Glowworm" but through the chorus one time before it got punched up and syncopated and changed over entirely into "Fascinating Rhythm" which Jonellen Marie Hayes beat out on the keyboard with special fervor.

Granddaddy blessed the Reverend Mr. Langley straightaway and the reverend thanked him warmly for it and blessed him back and then excused himself and commenced to slip on off down the sanctuary aisle backside foremost so he could observe how the strains and the harmonies purged the sadness and purged the trouble and if the way Granddaddy grinned at Jonellen Marie Hayes and got grinned at back was any indication the sadness and the trouble had got gone along about when the reverend did, and the Reverend Mr. Langley stepped out through the doorway and stretched himself prior to proceeding on around the sanctuary to the block parsonage and the partly weeded iris bed as well as to the openly dismayed and disgruntled Mrs. Reverend Langley who stood where she'd stood all along with her arms crossed over herself and listened to what she heard and looked back at the reverend even before she could get looked at first.

So Jonellen Marie Hayes tuned it and out of gratitude primarily, or anyhow tuned it once Granddaddy had run off home to fetch it and had carried it back and had listened to all the notes themselves and had plucked to match them but could not, and then she strummed it one time and strummed it again and Granddaddy heard it like it was supposed to sound and found himself purely purged and purely soothed and balmed too, and Jonellen Marie Hayes, who knew some guitar, changed her fingers and strummed it again and changed her fingers and strummed it one more time and then gave it over to Granddaddy who strummed it himself and then laid his fingers across the neck of it and strummed it again but as Granddaddy did not know just precisely where to change his fingers to he did not make much in the way of music with his strumming like Jonellen Marie Hayes had made music with hers.

And that was how it commenced with Granddaddy, or anyhow that was the outset of what Daddy called Granddaddy's tuning period which lasted what Daddy called longer than death itself. When Granddaddy got the guitar Momma and Daddy were living in Lynchburg where Daddy kept the books for a furniture store and when Granddaddy got the guitar tuned Momma and Daddy were just moving to Danville where Daddy would keep the charts for the railroad, and as Danville and Neely were not much of any ways apart Momma and Daddy traveled home at least twice every month and Momma and Grandmomma would visit while Daddy got tuned at which was meant to be a variety of entertainment but was not, Daddy said. Granddaddy did not use the pitch pipe but just his ears and just his fingers too, and Daddy said he would twang each string about seventy-five times as he tightened it and loosened it and tightened it again and once he'd adjusted and twanged them all he would go back and fine-tune them and then strum the six together so as to decide which of them needed additional tightening and loosening and fine-tuning as well, afterwhich he would play what actual chords he knew setting his fingertips one at the time on the strings they were to lay atop of.

Mr. Mel Bay, if it was in fact Mr. Mel Bay, was a deliberate sort of teacher and brought his students along at fairly much a glacial pace which was well suited to Granddaddy who did not do anything in a hurry ever which meant learn and which meant tune and which meant strum and which especially meant move his fingertips from one spot on the guitarneck to another, and Daddy said consequently there was something timeless and eternal about the way Granddaddy played a selection as it did not seem but that it was always just beginning. Naturally he prefaced every number with a spell of tuning followed by some general and apparently indiscriminate strumming which preceded the positioning of the guitarbook, a matter of some importance to Granddaddy who did not want whoever he might be playing for to see just what what it was he might be playing as he preferred it be deciphered and guessed at instead, guessed at mostly, Daddy said, guessed at almost exclusively at the outset, near about blindly too. But then at first Granddaddy did not know but the chords for "Oh Susanna" and "Clementine" and "Camptown Races" which made the guessing a fairly probable undertaking, especially since the Doo da's, which was kind of a downstroke and an upstroke right quick together, gave "Camptown Races" dead away and so left just the other two to choose between and Daddy could usually figure out which it was if he acted like he had an itch and stretched and contorted so as to see a piece of the page. He did not have much to go on otherwise, not anything audible anyhow, since Granddaddy simply could not make a chord with much success and could not keep a rhythm at all, but he worked and worked at it, Daddy said, and the astounding thing was he did not get any better, not for what seemed forever anyhow which is plenty long for anybody.

Daddy said him and Momma would come to Neely and then go away and then come back again and then go away and then come another time and the dogwoods would have budded and flowered and the grass roundabout would have got thick and the weeds would have got high and some people would have moved into town and settled into houses that other people would have moved out of or died out of sometimes so that people that had been weren't anymore and every now and again people that had not been were, and Daddy said if there was anything constant about any of it, any one thing that did not bud or flower or sprout up or get laid under, any single item that him and Momma could come back to find just like they'd left it, it was Grand-daddy's guitar playing which was not ever any better and sometimes even seemed worse though likely it could not have been. Daddy said Granddaddy simply could not make his fingers do what fingers need to do on a guitar if the end result is intended to be musical and melodic and Daddy supposed Granddaddy was intending to be musical and was intending to be melodic too, still supposed it and theorized it even those times Granddaddy was something extremely otherwise and he was something extremely otherwise most all the time on account of his strumming was spasmodic and his chords were haphazard and inaccurate and, even after months of unflagging and devoted practice, he still could not change his fingers with even the speed and alacrity that some men change their trousers in the bedroom. Daddy said it simply did not seem to him that Granddaddy was intended to succeed at guitar playing and he admitted he oftentimes wondered when the instrument itself might be laid away in a corner so as to get dusted once a week with all the rest of the furniture, but Granddaddy would not give it up and persisted in the tuning and the strumming and the ponderous finger changing even if he did not get better at any of it, and he worked on through Mr. Mel Bay's book, if it was in fact Mr. Mel Bay, and learned to play so many songs so badly that Daddy could not determine anything much from just a Doo da and he still insists even now that the most trying and rigorous question he has ever been pressed to answer usually followed a spell of tuning when Granddaddy would set his fingers on the guitarneck and lay his pickend on the bass string and hold off from strumming just long enough to ask Daddy, "What's this here?"

Then he built his house, the one he drew up and framed and plumbed and wired and painted too, and in the midst of it built his den that Grandmomma thought was a dining room until Granddaddy told her it wasn't and explained to her just what it was which Grandmomma told him it wasn't either, so he did not even get to smoke or spit or pick in it before he got banished upstairs to the sewing room that Grandmomma did not but keep her machine in and Daddy figured it was the banishment that did it, not so much the banishment that taught him to tune and strum and pluck and change his fingers, but the banishment that made it all seem so miraculous and mystifying when he came out from it into the world again and could play a thing that nobody had to guess at. Momma and Daddy had come back by then, had come back from Lynchburg and from Danville too and had bought the house up the street, from where Daddy could sit on the porch glider and watch Grandmomma lay the chicken manure to her potted ferns and her geraniums and even smell it sometimes which was near about all he had to watch except for the Epperson sisters across the street and Mr. Tiny Aaron's white Impala which would pass at regular intervals with its wheelbearings clicking, or anyhow was most all he had to watch until Granddaddy came out to get watched too, came out in May, Daddy recollected, sometime between supper and nightfall and with his guitar that Daddy had not heard even the first sour note from since the banishment, so he was not particularly looking for Granddaddy and especially was not looking for the guitar which meant he did not see Granddaddy straightaway and did not straightaway notice the music either, and it was music, Daddy said, music rare and pure like music can be most especially in spring just prior to nightfall when the air is right for a melody and Daddy said it was a melody, said it was "Sweet Betsy from Pike" with Granddaddy picking it and

strumming it and singing it all at once and Daddy said he
fetched Momma out from the kitchen and together they
walked down the street not but breathing and listening and
had not hardly got up the steps when Grandmomma herself
pushed open the screen door and stepped outside with her
apronend caught up in both her hands and her chin laying
down where it generally did not lay and they all listened
together, Daddy said, and watched together as Granddaddy
strummed and picked and changed his fingers and sang out
from under his mustache in a voice had not any of them
suspected he could produce and even when he got done they
were still just breathing and just listening and just gaping too
and Granddaddy laid both his finger arm and his strumming
arm overtop the guitar-body and told Momma and Daddy and
Grandmomma as well, "Evening."

And Daddy said that would be the summer Granddaddy
became something otherwise than just Chief and just Mr. Buck
which he had been for Daddy ever since that first night Daddy
stepped up onto the porch planking underneath the yellow
lightbulb with your moths and just your general bugs flapping
and beating all roundabout it and he knocked with his
knuckles on the screendoor frame and got looked at by
Granddaddy who leaned forward some on the sofa to do the
looking but did not hardly begin to get up so Daddy went
ahead and announced how he was Louis Benfield from out
towards Twin Oaks and how he'd come to escort Miss Yount to
the theatre and Daddy said Granddaddy still just looked at him
but not with any interest much and then laid himself back
against the sofa cushion that he'd rose up from and opened up
before his face the Chronicle that he'd shut temporarily and at
last said out from behind it, "Come in if you want," which
Daddy said was about all the invitation he needed as at that
time he was primarily getting led around by his glands which
did not call for much pomp or ceremony or even good will
really. So it was just Chief and just Mr. Buck too for what
Daddy said was the longest while and him and Granddaddy

actually got on some and fished together out at Mr. Tadlock's where they did not catch anything but puny bream that they gave to the colored Carrouthers and hunted squirrel together off beyond the quarry but did not ever shoot much squirrel to speak of and rarely discharged their shotguns truly at anything except for the hornets' nest that one time which Daddy, upon reflection, wished he had not discharged at, and of course they rode the highways as well, rode them in Granddaddy's black Chevrolet halfton but with Daddy behind the wheel of it so as to free Granddaddy to lay partway out the window and admire the countryside, so Daddy said he felt like he knew Granddaddy in a considerable and thorough sort of way by the time Granddaddy got his guitar and commenced to torture folks with it that way he did torture folks for a while which Daddy said he figured would keep up longer than it did in fact keep up since Daddy did not suspect there was a part of Granddaddy all delicate and refined that could turn the noise he made from those six strings into something otherwise, did not suspect there was even the patience to develop what might be delicate and what might be refined, not in a man anyhow who said, "Horseshit!" and spat hard most every time anything went to the contrary for him. But then he did play it and pick it and sing with it too and not so as anyone would ever have to wonder play and pick and sing just what exactly and even did not act like he'd done anything once he'd done it but only laid his arms where he laid them and said what he said.

And Daddy insisted that was how a time commenced, the best time he recollected out of all he could recollect, and he said he would pull the porch glider up snug to the rail that way Momma objected to and would prop his feet against the banister and lay his head back on the cushionedge and blow his Tareyton smoke straight up like a chimney-stack as he listened to whatever it might be Granddaddy picked and strummed and sang sometimes from his own chair on his own porch down the street, and Daddy said while it sounded fine up close it sounded even better off a ways on account of it was not just "Sweet Betsy from Pike" or just "Greensleeves" or just "The Tennessee Waltz" but them and the crickets too and the frogs sometimes and the leaves twisting round along with the traffic and the doorsprings and the voices otherwise, so it was just a part of everything else, just the part that was the best part, Daddy said, the part that made all the rest of it seem better than maybe it was.

However, it did not stay only Granddaddy for long on account of Mr. Phillip J. King initially who lived a house up from Momma and Daddy with Mrs. Phillip J. King and Itty Bit their imported terrier that could not tolerate harmonica music on account of the general pitch of it and consequently Mr. Phillip J. King did not get allowed to play much roundabout his own house as the dog would wail and moan and thereby cause Mr. Phillip J. King to get told by Mrs. Phillip J. King, "Daddy, pack it away," and somehow Mr. Phillip J. King could not ever bring himself to not do what Mrs. Phillip J. King told him he'd best get done, so the King house was not truly a hotbed of harmonica music as Itty Bit was ever ready to wail and ever ready to moan. But Granddaddy did not have a dog and did not have a Mrs. Phillip J. King either which was what drew Mr. Phillip J. King down the street when he did get drawn down the street in addition, of course, to the melodies that Mr. Bay, if it was in fact Mr. Bay, had taught Granddaddy to pick and strum and in addition too to the melodies that Granddaddy had found out for himself which came to be the most of the melodies he played after a spell. And Granddaddy would always start in with some elaborate picking that would lead to a strum or two and then a steady beat afterwhich Mr. Phillip J. King would jump in with his marine band and blow and suck some in a general kind of way on account of Mr. Phillip J. King did not possess so agile a tongue that he could play just a solitary note or even two notes blended but tended to call up whole conglomerations of notes together with enough of them to the same purpose so as to suggest some manner of harmony.

Daddy said it all sounded fine from the glider, sounded sweet and pure even though he knew at least half of it was not, and he recollected how at the outset they tended to play "Shenandoah" considerably more than they played anything else since that was what Mr. Phillip J. King tended to play most regularly himself and so knew just precisely when to blow where and when to suck where else which was the kind of thing Mr. Phillip J. King felt compelled to know before he commenced to play as he was not improvisational by nature and did not have a feel for what notes grated side by side and what notes did not. And Daddy said it stayed just Mr. Phillip J. King and just Granddaddy playing "Shenandoah" mostly but not "Shenandoah" all the time until Granddaddy ran up on Mr. Wyatt Benbow of the Big Apple Benbows who played the guitar himself and invited him down to the porch too where him and Granddaddy and Mr. Phillip J. King all played "Shenandoah" together punctuated by various other selections that Mr. Phillip J. King would blow on every now and again but would primarily just sit idly by and listen to while he waited for "Shenandoah" to come round once more.

Naturally word got out of who was doing what on Granddaddy's porch after supper and Mr. Peahead Boyette's daddy, Emory Boyette, grew interested enough to carry his fiddle with him down the road to Granddaddy's in search of some accompaniment since his regular guitar picking friends had all died off and of course Granddaddy and

Wyatt Benbow and Mr. Phillip J. King too made him welcome straightaway and commenced to play just what they had been playing for a while with Mr. Emory Boyette sawing some up above the melody and some down below it on the fiddle that had been his own daddy's and would be Peahead's after it had finished being his and it was not any homegrown contraption but a regular Italian fiddle, Daddy said, with a genuine ring to it and not hardly any varnish left anywhere to speak of. But of course they got away from "Shenandoah" and the like after a bit on account of Mr. Emory Boyette knew mostly Irish jigs and your regular hoedown music which left Mr. Phillip J. King with relatively little to blow and suck to except every now and again when he would set out on a chorus of "Camptown Races" and him and Granddaddy together would show off their Doo da's.

Mr. Wiley Gant got invited by once it was determined just precisely how inadequate Mr. Phillip J. King was proving to be and Mr. Wiley Gant brought with him all halfdozen of his marine bands that were the little kind he could cup and hold in one hand since one hand was all he had to cup and hold them in and just his empty sleeve otherwise that he did not bother to pin up but only buttoned the cuff of and then let hang just however it would. He could play anything and all the parts to it at once and could even manage to sing it too sometimes, sing it in that high metallic voice just like the one he talked in and rightoff could not the rest of them hardly play for listening to Wiley Gant who Daddy said did not need the halfblock of crickets and frogs and wheelbearings and doorsprings and general voices to enhance and perfect what in his case was flawless up close, and not even Mr. Phillip J. King could but get swept up in it hearing coming out from Mr. Wiley Gant's mouth organ what he wanted to come out from his own but could not manage somehow, at least could not manage until Mr. Wiley Gant showed him just how to lay his tongue and where on "Turkey in the Straw" and Mr. Phillip J. King blew and sucked and made pretty much some actual music.

Of course they all knew who it was they were missing and they all knew what it was they were missing too and they all knew why it was they were missing who and what they were missing which would be Mr. Emmet Dabb and which would be Mr. Emmet Dabb's banjo that Mr. Emmet Dabb had a way with like Wiley Gant and his mouth organs and his high metallic voice, but Granddaddy and Mr. Emmet

Dabb did not geehaw and everybody knew they did not and knew as well that their daddies before them had not geehawed either but did not anybody know how come exactly as it was a thing that had a history and longevity all its own and so did not seem to need explaining, but Daddy said it was not just your vague bad blood that had rose up for no good reason like most bad blood that does in fact rise up but was instead some fairly legitimate ill will brought about primarily by Mr. Emmet Dabb's great-granddaddy, that had been a Seymour, along with Granddaddy's daddy's oldest brother, Henry Justin Yount, that had traveled with Emmet Dabb's great-granddaddy Seymour just prior to the war up north to Danville where the two of them together got on with the railroad and they cleared the right-of-way and leveled the lines and rode the trains that carried troops in and out of Richmond and just all roundabout the state to wherever there was someplace to go and skirmish. So they heard about most all of it, not just in the papers but straight from who'd been there and who'd seen it, heard it near about like it'd happened though not quite really and then told it again themselves to whoever hadn't but read of it which would be First Bull Run and Cedar Mountain and Antietam and Mechanicsville and Savage's Station and Malvern Hill and Second Bull Run too, and it sounded good to them when they got told it and sounded extraordinarily grand when they heard themselves turn around and tell it again to whoever it might be that had not but read of it and so did not and could not know what they believed they knew upon having just ridden the same train with men who may have even been where they said they'd been and may have even seen what they said they saw.

And they wanted some of it, Daddy said, wanted some of it not just to tell but to see and to know because they did not ever ride the train with the dead ones and so had not learned what it was truly, and Daddy said they enlisted together in Altavista around the middle of January 1863 and got shipped off to the Army of Northern Virginia in Richmond where they drilled and marched for weeks and fell into ranks and fell out of them and pointed their rifles and even fired them sometimes but did not do anything much extraordinarily grand, not at first anyhow as there was not anything extraordinarily grand that needed doing in Richmond just then, and so they waited, which Daddy said an army does the most of anyway, waited for the cold to give way and waited for the rain to give way and waited for the mud to give way too which made it April when they got sent north out of Richmond to Fredericksburg all of them in a gang that Henry Justin Yount and Emmet Dabb's great-granddaddy Seymour neither one knew to call a brigade or a division or just a unit either but only a gang that walked the roads some and rode the rails some and joined up with General Lee's regular troops in Fredericksburg where they waited some more. And Daddy said then there were the yankees come south out from Washington that camped just the far side of the Rappahannock close enough to see plain but not hardly near enough to shoot at which left just the spying with glasses and with naked eyes too at the white canvas tents and the blue-clad soldiers all roundabout them and the horses and the field pieces and the supply wagons and the smoke that rose up from everywhere and massed together overhead like foul weather, and Daddy said it must have looked like a hundred thousand men all spread out there in the river valley, must have looked twice everything Lee could muster, maybe even more than twice on account of it was, which did not anybody with the glasses and with the naked eyes too bother to indicate to anybody else.

Then they moved, Daddy said, not the yankees but Henry Justin Yount and Emmet Dabb's great-granddaddy Seymour and all their bunch up from Richmond along with every bit of three quarters of what Lee had and they withdrew to the south and then swung round westward and advanced to the north somewhat all of them marching together not so much in a gang this time but in rank like an actual army with Lee up at the front of it and J. E. B. Stuart on ahead of him and with the officers swarming all about them on horseback shouting down whoever it might be that needed shouting down and bracing up most everybody else, and Daddy said aside from Lee and aside from Stuart it was Rodes and Mahone and Hoke and Gorden and Hall and Early and Kershaw and Heth and McLaws and then him too that the ones that could read had read of and the ones that could not had heard about, him on his chestnut with his back all stiff and set and his oily black beard laying down across his coatfront, him that even the lowliest private called Mister Stonewall Sir and right at him too as it was a name and designation that transcended rank altogether. And when they split there in the road with Lee going the one way and Jackson going the other Henry Justin Yount and Emmet Dabb's great-granddaddy Seymour fell in with their corps up from Richmond that fell in with Mr. Stonewall who wheeled around one time on his horse and then raised up his arm and indicated just where it was he intended to go.

They were after Hooker, Daddy said, after Hooker and that piece of his army he'd drawn off from the riverbank to maneuver with and they caught up with him at a place called Chancellorsville, Daddy said, caught up with him from two directions at once on account of Lee came the one way and Jackson came the other and Daddy said it was near about dark when they hit, dusky anyhow, and Jackson drove into Hooker's flank from the woods with his men all spread and cast about in the thickets and the scrub and Daddy said as the light was low and the proceedings were somewhat at a pitch anyway, things got considerably jumbled up and confused what with the rifle shots and the hooting and the yelping and the muzzlesmoke floating thick in the air so Daddy said it was understandable that what did happen could happen and Granddaddy, whenever he had a thing to say about it, which was not any considerable portion of the time, always insisted it was not just understandable really but inevitable and thereby blameless, especially blameless he would say though he did not ever begin to subscribe to just who Mr. Emmet Dabb suggested it had to be blameless for on account of he did not ever begin to subscribe to what Mr. Emmet Dabb said he'd got told by his daddy who'd got told it by his momma who'd got told it by her daddy before her who had not needed to get told it himself as he'd been there to see it and had seen it, Mr. Emmet Dabb insisted, or would not have told it, but Daddy said it was dusky and smoky and confused all roundabout everywhere so maybe he had not truly seen plain what he thought he'd seen clear enough which would be Henry Justin Yount raising up his rifle and firing into a clump of bramble that Mr. Stonewall Jackson himself pitched out of.

Now it is a hard and ponderous thing to tell a man that his own relation distinguished himself in battle by shooting his own general out from a stand of scrub like Mr. Emmet Dabb and Mr. Emmet Dabb's daddy before him told Granddaddy and told Great-granddaddy too but it is a harder and far more ponderous thing to tell a man that on account of his own relation shooting his own general out from a stand of scrub not just the general got killed but the entire war effort got pretty much given over to the other side which was also what Mr. Emmet Dabb and Mr. Emmet Dabb's daddy before him told Granddaddy and told Great-granddaddy too since as they figured it with Mr. Stonewall Jackson dead at Chancellorsville that did not leave but just Long-street and Ewell and Pickett at Gettysburg who were just Longstreet and just Ewell and just Pickett and not Jackson any of them which was why what happened did happen and that coupled with Vicksburg had to lead where it led which was Lookout Mountain and the Wilderness and Spotsylvania and Cold Harbor and Petersburg and Appomattox at last and all of it on account of that one rifle shot in the bushes that Mr. Emmet Dabb had got told about by his daddy who'd got told about it by his momma who'd got told about it by her daddy who'd said he'd seen where it came from and seen where it went though Daddy said things were dusky and smoky and considerably confused.

Naturally a sort of a rift had developed between Younts and
Dabbs what with the Dabbs insisting it was a Yount that had
lost the war and the Younts, although a fairly tolerant people,
finding themselves pressed to insist back a few things about
Dabbs in return, and it was Great-granddaddy that insisted the
chief thing on account of it was Great-granddaddy that
reasoned out how if Henry Justin Yount was dead at Cold
Harbor, which was where Henry Justin Yount came to be dead
at last, then he did not ever get the opportunity tc deny what
all got put on him which made him just the fellow to put it all
on since he never was able to tell how maybe it was the
Seymour that raised the rifle and fired it causing General
Stonewall to pitch out wounded like he did pitch out, how
surely it must have been the Seymour that aimed and fired and
hit square on the general since what kind of a man but a liar
and a fraud would tell such of the dead. Of course now the
Dabbs would have as soon believed in evolution as Great-
granddaddy's Chancellorsville theory and they reacted to it
straightaway telling Great-granddaddy he was a pigheaded
shitass if there ever was one which seemed to the Dabbs to
answer the thing well enough, and Great-granddaddy, not the
sort to get bested in an exchange, made a similar assessment of
Dabbs as a general variety of upright beings and then emended
a brief and altogether pointed appreciation of Emmet Dabb's
daddy's wife who Great-granddaddy said he'd always figured
for livestock, and Daddy said the Dabbs told him back an
unseemly thing or two about Great-grandmomma and matters
just proceeded on from there.

So things got pretty completely away from Stonewall Jackson
and

Chancellorsville after just a little while and the Dabbs and the
Younts commenced to feud in a general and far-reaching sort
of way for as long as they were still able to be snide and
spiteful with each other outright, afterwhich they did not feud

directly but just spoke ill of each other whenever the opportunity came around with the Dabbs letting it be known how, if it was in their power to do so, they would dispatch all the Younts they'd ever heard tell of straight to perdition and with the Younts broadcasting a similar kind of item themselves. So they did not speak at each other much after the first several barrages but just of each other mostly, and the Dabbs laid low the Younts and the Younts laid low the Dabbs for a considerable few years until at last circumstances altered dramatically with the death of Emmet Dabb's daddy that Great-granddaddy insisted had been brought about by deceit primarily, though Dr. Shackleford held with the liver, followed hard up by the death of Emmet Dabb's momma who Great-granddaddy insisted had got took by the pinkeye which Dr. Shackleford did not see fit to honor with an alternative. And that left just Emmet, Daddy said, who did not ever have much hand in the whole business anyhow but just did what his Daddy said do and told what his daddy said tell, and could not even Great-granddaddy, that could revile and vilify most anybody anytime, revile and vilify Emmet Dabb with much enthusiasm to speak of on account of there was so much revilable and so much vilifiable to him that the sport kind of departed from the thing even for Great-granddaddy who did not require much sport really, so he did not say a hard thing against Emmet Dabb but on a seasonal basis so as to keep himself honed and fit, and then when Great-granddaddy passed on that winter he did in fact pass on Emmet Dabb did not bother to make even one vicious observation in return but instead had sent to the Heavenly Rest mums in a pot with a card in amongst them, a card Grandmomma read as she was the one that read all the cards and then showed to Granddaddy on account of it just said Sympathy— Emmet Dabb, which struck her as honest and sincere, but Granddaddy told her, "Horseshit," and threw it on the floor and stomped it and Grandmomma did not but let him since it was his daddy dead and his hurt to get out somehow.

And then it was just not anything, not anything between Dabbs and between Younts, not anything rude and mean but not anything otherwise either somewhat because Granddaddy was not exactly his daddy but mostly because Emmet Dabb was surely not his. Likely he was his momma primarily as he did not ever have much to say like she never did and would not ever do but what he got told like she always would which together fairly much made him the cipher she had been herself except for Emmet's distinctive personal habits or more actually the utter void thereof. Daddy said he had the hygiene of a roothog and it did not take but somewhat of a nostril to detect him most anywhere he was or soon intended to be or had departed from either since he traveled in his own special funk that apparently everybody but him could smell. He did not seem to have any sort of philosophical objection to soap and to water and to the use of the two in combination; he had been quizzed on the topic in an indirect and wayward manner and had not disclosed any variety of grievance against washing as a general practice, but yet he did not wash his own self, simply elected to keep from it, and so owned and implemented his bathtub much like the man that owns a rifle but does not shoot his supper with it.

Naturally the sensitive and thoughtful people in town got somewhat agitated on account of Emmet Dabb and commenced to impress upon the unsensitive and thoughtless people in town how his need for assistance was considerable which is to say that the ladies of the Flower Society told the rest of us Emmet needed a bath and straightaway. It was late autumn so there was not anything going with your plants and your shrubs anywhere local which left the Flower Society just to meet on Tuesdays and talk about other people without the pretense and inconvenience of discussing your plants and your shrubs, and as Mrs. Tullock's turn had come up they were all collected together in her front parlor drinking coffee, except of course for Mrs. Anna Victoria Hewitt Sulley who took tea with milk in it on account of her momma had come over on a boat as a child and had instilled, Mrs. Anna Victoria Hewitt Sulley called it, certain tastes and penchants, Mrs. Anna Victoria Hewitt Sulley called them, in her own children which she said was why she had such a natural instinct for tea though she did not ever seem but to leave most of it in the cup, and then Mrs. Tullock came round with cookies on a tray and all the ladies took one, even Mrs. Anna Victoria Hewitt Sulley who called them biscuits, and quite understandably a silence and a stillness fell upon the room as the ladies chewed and savored and worked up some manner of exclamation over what it was they were about to swallow and Daddy said it was just Emmet Dabb's misfortune to wander by out front in the middle of all the silence and the stillness and the chewing too which meant he got looked at and studied like he would not have got looked at and studied if anybody had been saying anything whatsoever.

Mrs. Estelle Singletary, who was closest to the window and so felt compelled to comment firstoff, washed down her piece of cookie and announced, "Repulsive," that loud irritating way she has of saying things, and her sister, Miss Bernice Fay Frazier added, "Disgusting," and then harrumphed one time in undisguised indignation, and Mrs. Tullock from across the room at the serving table stiffened some and told the both of them how she had followed the recipe exactly and she was sorry but she had eaten two out of the oven and they had tasted fine to her and then she set down the cookieplate so that it bounced one time on the tabletop and crossed her arms over herself and looked injured. Of course the ladies all cooed and wheezed and soothed things out straightaway, even Mrs. Estelle Singletary who was not extraordinarily soothing and balmlike by nature, and once the entire society had found out just what was repulsive and what was disgusting they all crowded together around the front windows before he could get full away and watched how he went and exclaimed little things about him until he had rounded the corner out of sight when Mrs. Ira Penn set in to telling how she had got closed up with him in the elevator at the Belk-Legett on her way to the housewares in the basement which she would have walked down the steps to except for the handrail was not at a height to suit her and so she did not feel safe walking down the steps at the Belk-Legett and several of the attendant ladies who rode the elevator their own selves agreed with Mrs. Ira Penn that she had hit upon just exactly why. Mrs. Ira Penn said he got on just as the doors were commencing to shut otherwise it would have been only her and the operator Mr. Claudell Jones but ended up being the three of them together, or anyhow the three of them together and Mr. Emmet Dabb's aroma too which Mrs. Ira Penn said had a kind of presence to it and straightoff expanded clear up to the ceiling and clear down to the floor and out every way sideways it could expand to, and Mrs. Ira Penn said she got weak and bilious about the stomach in an instantaneous sort of way and felt like she would just fall out right there between floors, could feel herself sliding somewhat down the wall, and knew she was right at fainting dead away and likely would have fainted dead away if she had not considered how it would be when the doors opened in the basement and there she was sprawled out on the elevator floor likely with her skirt tugged up indecently and a spot of shoegrit on her cheek and her hat flopped out backwards and a whole crowd there to look at her all sprawled out and indecent, especially Sophia Greely come over from the sewing center and Mrs. Ira Penn wondered didn't everybody know how Sophia Greely liked to wag her tongue and all the ladies together said My yes or something kin to it.

So she held on, Mrs. Ira Penn told it, held on to the rail roundabout the elevator wall until the doors opened and Mr. Emmet Dabb hauled his aroma out onto the selling floor and Mrs. Ira Penn said the exhaust fan tried to suck what was left on up into the elevator shaft but could not entirely so she stepped out through the doors herself in hopes of drawing off an untainted breath but shortly discovered that following Mr. Emmet Dabb was somewhat worse than standing next to him and she grew weak and balky all over, so weak and so balky in fact that she could not recollect what she had come out to the Belk-Legett to fetch home anyhow which Mrs. Ira Penn told the ladies had been a garlic press for the sake of Mr. Ira Penn who had accidentally got hold of half a clove in his spaghetti sauce and had suffered on account of it, had suffered so acutely as to persuade Mrs. Ira Penn to use just the juice in the future and not ever the whole item again. But she said she could not recollect it was a garlic press she had come after and so lingered outside the elevator in a state of befuddlement until somewhat of Mr. Emmet Dabb came wafting up to her from off her blousefront and brought her around sufficiently to impress upon her just how offensive she had become, and Mrs. Ira Penn said she could not get home and out from her clothes fast enough and did not even try to clean them, she said, did not see but that they could not be made right again so she gave them to Columbia, her cleaning woman, except for the hat that Mrs. Ira Penn said had not been affected much.

Several of the ladies said they had smelled Mr. Emmet Dabb themselves and told where they had smelled him and to what effect as a means of sympathizing with Mrs. Ira Penn who had obviously smelled him under the crudest and most confining circumstances and Mrs. Doris Lancaster from out on the highway told how she'd got hold of a clove of garlic herself once and had got turned all inside out on account of it. Mrs. Tullock wondered why it was Mr. Emmet Dabb went around unwashed when his momma and his daddy had not gone around particularly dirty themselves as best as she could recall and while several theories on the matter got aired out and fretted over were not any of them satisfying in a logical sort of way and to cap things off Mrs. Anna Victoria Hewitt Sulley announced how some people in Europe did not bathe but on St. Elfin's Day which not any of the ladies were acquainted with, there being no Catholics present except for Mrs. W. P. McKinney who had an aunt that had married a Catholic which she felt rendered her Catholic at least somewhat but not

Catholic enough anyhow to have heard tell of St. Elfin or his day either which Mrs. Anna Victoria Hewitt Sulley said fell sometime in April she thought. Of course they all wanted to know what was Elfin the saint of, wanted to know was it soap or was it water or was it maybe hygiene in general but Mrs. Anna Victoria Hewitt Sulley said she did not know what Elfin was the saint of exactly, said did not anybody know as best as she could recollect, said it was just one of those unknowable things which was why she did not know it, and Miss Bernice Fay Frazier wished aloud in a general sort of way that some people would not bring things up if they could not carry them through as that irritated her most completely, and Mrs. Anna Victoria Hewitt Sulley told her back, "Well I am truly sorry to be the source and wellspring of your irritation," and then humphed one time and got humphed at back and so laid her nose up where she liked to lay it and left it there until Mrs. Tullock brought round the cookies and brought round the coffee and brought round the water to heat up what tea Mrs. Anna Victoria Hewitt Sulley had left in her cup.

They all agreed Mr. Emmet Dabb should be clean and wholesome like normal people, all agreed he was a blight and an affliction roundabout town with his stench and his filth especially as he tended to walk and circulate and so made himself what Mrs. Ira Penn called accessible and it was Mrs. Ira Penn herself that suggested how maybe the Flower Society could take an interest in Mr. Dabb, could endeavor to change and augment him since changing and augmenting was what the Flower Society tended to have a talent for, but the ladies as a body seemed to view the notion with considerable indifference and did not truly get stirred and truly get agitated over it until Mrs. Dwight

Mobley, who did not hardly ever suggest anything but most usually just sat somewhere out of the way with her purse in her lap, wondered if maybe they couldn't work up a St. Elfin's Day so as to manufacture an excuse to get Mr. Emmet Dabb into the bathtub, and the idea took hold straightaway. The ladies were all for any brand of new festivity as they were generally your festive sort of people and since it was Mrs. Anna Victoria Hewitt Sulley that had brought up St. Elfin in the first place several of the ladies commenced to quiz her so as to discover just what it was that everybody was washing for. Right off they wanted to know was it religious or was it social since half of the members present were Baptists and did not want to tamper with anything they should not tamper with, but Mrs. Anna Victoria Hewitt Sulley did not recollect that it was a particularly religious sort of thing, not churchly anyhow with your Latin and your wafers and your wine and whatnot though she did seem to recall how the whole business set out with an invocation and a prayer, and the ladies wanted to know what whole business exactly, wanted to know was it a parade or was it an indoor ceremony or was it a luncheon with maybe a speaker and coffee after or was it a dinner on the ground or was it some kind of grand ball maybe, and Mrs. Anna Victoria Hewitt Sulley considered her alternatives and without seeming to pick and choose went ahead and picked and chose selecting straightoff the grand ball which appealed to her in a prodigious sort of way and coupling with it the dinner on the ground so as not to offend and exclude those ladies that did not possess much in the way of your continental and grand ball-like sensibilities.

Of course the whole business was so extraordinarily novel that it took hold of everybody directly and the thing got discussed and bandied roundabout and naturally came to be changed some and came to be augmented and once it all got settled and once it all got decided it was not truly a grand ball anymore and not exactly a dinner on the ground but had come to be the St. Elfin's Day Potluck Dinner Dance at the armory with Mr. Emmet Dabb as the honorary keeper of the basin once the ladies had decided he should keep something and once the ladies had decided a basin was what it would be which was after they consulted Mrs. Anna Victoria Hewitt Sulley who seemed to recollect how St. Elfin had stopped at a country farmhouse so as to take his rest and had got offered a basin of water to wash his neck in on account of his neck had got unduly grimy somehow and he was so touched and moved by the hospitality of the poor farmer and the poor farmer's wife that he blessed their harvest and thereby swelled it threefold, or maybe fourfold, Mrs. Anna Victoria Hewitt Sulley could not remember which exactly.

So Mr. Emmet Dabb was to get a basin to be the keeper of and was to get prior to it a ceremonial cake of soap and a ceremonial bristle brush and a ceremonial bath towel and a ceremonial little squat jar of cream deodorant and of course a ceremonial suit of clothes too if the ladies could get him sized in time without him knowing that sizing was what he was getting and for what since they did not want to give Mr. Emmet Dabb the opportunity to decline to be what they were going to make him. They put Mr. W. P. McKinney on it, or anyhow Mrs. W. P. McKinney put Mr. W. P. McKinney on it which would be Mr. W. P. McKinney of the block and mortar McKinneys who was the loudest and friendliest of the three McKinneys altogether and could not talk to anybody without laying his hands on him somewhere and so when he did at last run up on Mr. Emmet Dabb in what appeared to be a haphazard and coincidental sort of way he took hold of him at the neck and took hold of him at the elbow too and then talked at him all loud and friendly like he talked to everybody. Mr. Emmet Dabb did not ever have much in the way of social intercourse considering how he emanated, Daddy called it, so he was not much practiced at turning phrases and such which meant he listened mostly and made noises every now and again but did not truly converse in the accepted sense which naturally had no bearing on what Mr. W. P. McKinney did as he was entirely a one-man production that squeezed and slapped and poked Mr. Emmet Dabb fairly much all over before arriving at his neck and arriving at his forearm which Mr. W. P. McKinney took hold of and held to while he got earnest and got sincere and he said to Mr. Emmet Dabb, "Emmet, you know what I am?" and straightaway Emmet Dabb made his noise that meant no. "Then I'll tell you what I am, Emmet," Mr. W. P. McKinney said and squeezed Emmet Dabb's neck and Emmet Dabb's elbow too. "I'm a 38 regular."

And Emmet Dabb looked at Mr. W. P. McKinney and then made a slight and altogether futile attempt to get loose at the neck and get loose at the elbow and then he looked at Mr. W. P. McKinney all over again and contemplated a noise but did not know which one to make.

"Have been ever since I was twenty-seven," Mr. W. P. McKinney said. "Thirty-eight regular," and he squeezed Emmet Dabb a little on the thirty-eight and a little on the regular too. "I'll bet you're a thirty-eight yourself, aren't you? Maybe a long but sure enough a thirty-eight," and Emmet Dabb made his noise that meant he did not truly know or give a happy horseshit either which Mr. W. P. McKinney took for a Yes sir and he told Emmet Dabb back, "I figured it. It's not hardly ever that I'm off but maybe one size and that's not hardly ever, and you know what?" and Mr. W. P. McKinney squeezed the one part of Emmet Dabb prefatory to squeezing the other, "I'll bet you're not more than thirty-six roundabout the beltloops. Tell me that's so," and Mr. Emmet Dabb made a noise that Mr. W. P. McKinney judged to be wholly noncommittal. "Alright, maybe thirty-eight," Mr. W. P. McKinney said and Mr. Emmet Dabb made an additional noise that struck Mr. W. P. McKinney as a brand of affirmation though it was actually his happy horseshit noise all over again but with a fresh bend to it there at the end. "And that inseam," Mr. W. P. McKinney said and let loose of the neck entirely so he could step back off as far as his elbowholding arm would allow, "I'll give it thirty-one inches, thirty-one if it's an inch," and he waited for whatever sort of noise might follow but not any did which Mr. W. P. McKinney did not know how to take exactly so he said "Thirty-one" all over again and squeezed some on the thirty and squeezed some on the one too which got him the noise he'd been hoping to get and Mr. W. P. McKinney told Emmet Dabb, "I figured it. Thirty-one and thirty-eight and thirty-eight regular. I figured it," he said and he let his neckholding hand loose from Emmet Dabb's neck so as to slap him on the back with it and then let his elbowholding hand loose from Emmet Dabb's elbow but did not use it against Emmet Dabb otherwise and he looked up into the various treelimbs overhead and asked Emmet Dabb didn't he think the leaves had turned off all pretty and bright and Emmet Dabb made a noise at him that did not even Emmet Dabb quite comprehend.

Daddy said the ladies of the Flower Society agreed not to let it out just precisely why they were putting on a St. Elfin's Day Potluck Dinner Dance at the armory in the first place so did not the news of just why and just who for get broadcasted and circulated for near about a week as those things the ladies kept secret generally tended to get loosed about a week behind the regular items, so everybody found out what it was and why, maybe even Emmet Dabb too though he did not ever let on if he did know, or anyhow did not ever make the kind of noise that could be deciphered as knowing and apprehensive but just went around like he usually went around and emanated like he usually emanated. Daddy said as it was not to be a private function the ladies hired out Mrs. Alice Covington that mostly painted rocks for paperweights and such to draw them up a St. Elfin's Day Potluck Dinner Dance poster with maybe, aside from the pertinent information, a picture of St. Elfin on it but Mrs. Alice Covington was not well acquainted with St. Elfin and could not find him anywhere in her illustrated New Testament, not even in the print of it, so she probed Mrs. Anna Victoria Hewitt Sulley for a description once the ladies had indicated to her that Mrs. Anna Victoria Hewitt Sulley was the one of them she'd best probe and she considered the grimy neck and the threefold and maybe even fourfold blessing and imagined what sort of saint it might be that would do what St.

Elfin did where and when St. Elfin did it, which Mrs. Anna Victoria Hewitt Sulley was not extraordinarily clear on, and Daddy said the St. Elfin Mrs. Alice Covington eventually drew for the ladies of the Flower Society seemed to him part Jesus and maybe part Grumpy too, or anyhow part something with some dwarf to it and he was dressed altogether casually for a saint in what looked to be a bathrobe and with a synthetic sponge in one hand and a bristle brush in the other. Mrs. Alice Covington had reasoned that if she could not get all the details of the thing in a solitary picture then she would settle for the spirit of the whole business which she was satisfied she had settled for and the ladies of the Flower Society decided they were satisfied too once they had voted to be, so the posters got printed and went up all roundabout town thereby exposing otherwise Christian people to a saint they had not ever heard tell of who they learned they were to pay fifty cents and cook a dish to honor on a Saturday night in the armory where they would dance to the melodious strains of Jarvis Boyd and the Jarvis Boyd Five of which there were actually eight altogether not counting Jarvis Boyd but which there had been five of not counting Jarvis Boyd when the front drumskin got painted and lettered.

Daddy said rightoff people took to the idea of a dance even if it was in part for a saint they were not well acquainted with because most everybody had found out that it was also in part for an aroma they all knew well enough and the ladies let out early on that ticket sales were brisk, they called it, even though they had voted not to let it out at all and straightaway they told how many they'd sold and how much they'd made once they decided not to tell it and a committee of three was se-credy dispatched to Greensboro to fetch back Mr. Emmet Dabb a proper suit of clothes and did not anybody know where they'd gone or why until they were near about out of town. The ladies had rented out the armory for the evening of Saturday December the twelfth which had struck them as a fitting time for an exotic activity on account of it fell midway between

Thanksgiving and Christmas which were not ever truly exotic for most people, and tickets selling like they were and money coming in like it had been the ladies found they had sufficient funds not just for Mr. Emmet Dabb's suit and for Mr. Jarvis Boyd and the Jarvis Boyd Five and for punch and for crepe too but money for cut flowers on top of it and money for the little red Spanish nuts in the can and money as well for the lifesized picture of St. Elfin that Mrs. Alice Covington drew at a discount.

Of course there was still the problem of getting Mr. Emmet Dabb to come to the Potluck Dinner Dance that was just as much his as it was St. Elfin's since there was not hardly the chance that just an invitation would bring him, so the ladies formulated and figured and otherwise schemed in a general sort of way and voted on a particular method to induce Mr. Emmet Dabb to do what he apparently had no desire to do whatsover, and as the ladies had all done some considerable inducing previously they had little trouble with the formulating and the figuring and the scheming but could not well pare the methods down since there was such a preponderance of them to choose from. However, they did at last settle on just the one plan and decided not to tell it out but only to those people that needed to know it which meant everybody else did not find out but just after and did not anybody object to it except for the Lions somewhat and the Moose somewhat and the Elks somewhat and the Knights of Pythias somewhat too on account of how the plan called for Rotarians instead of any of them otherwise so they all went ahead and objected but not with much fervor to speak of.

The ladies had Mrs. Alice Covington manufacture an official-looking keeper of the basin certificate with your Latin motto at the top and your gold seal at the bottom and your herewiths and whereofs and therefores all thick in between and they rolled it up and tied it with a ribbon and on the very afternoon of the Potluck Dinner Dance itself gave the thing over to Mr.

Ira Penn and Mr. Estelle Singletary along with the official St. Elfin's Day soapcake and the official St. Elfin's Day bristle brush and the official St. Elfin's Day bath towel and the official St. Elfin's Day little squat jar of cream deodorant and of course the box too from J. C. Penney in Greensboro with the blue suit in it and the white shirt and the spotted tie and the sheer stretch socks that the ladies did not call a suit and shirt and tie and socks but called Raiments instead and then instructed Mr. Ira Penn and Mr. Estelle Singletary on just how to call them Raiments too and seem to mean it, and Mr. Ira Penn said, "Here sir are your Raiments," to Mrs. Sue Beth Aldred who'd got picked to play Emmet Dabb though not for any reason truly all the ladies insisted when they picked her, and Mr. Estelle Singletary told her, "Here sir are your Raiments," too and then told it again on account of how he grinned the first time which Mrs. Estelle Singletary corrected straightaway. Then the ladies showed Mr. Ira Penn and Mr. Estelle Singletary what was to get done with the certificate which straightaway was the loosening of the ribbon around it and the unrolling of the thing followed by the reading aloud of the part between the motto and the gold seal which the ladies called the Dictum and which they had Mr. Ira Penn and Mr. Estelle Singletary call the Dictum too to Mrs. Sue Beth Aldred who stood and listened to the whole business get read to her like she figured Mr. Emmet Dabb might stand and might listen and which was fairly close to just precisely how Mr. Emmet Dabb did stand and did listen once he'd managed to yank open the front door that did not hardly ever get knocked on and so did not hardly ever get opened.

They had on their green Rotarian blazers with the little round insignia on the pocket that the handkerchief stood up in and their blue Rotarian trousers and their striped Rotarian ties with their silver Rotarian tieclips midway up them, and Mr. Emmet Dabb was impressed quite immediately on account of he did not ordinarily run up on many Rotarians dressed so that you'd know what they were but he did not know what they were anyhow even with the blazers and the trousers and the ties and the clips too since he did not ordinarily run up on many Rotarians dressed so that you'd know what they were. He figured instead that they were maybe Rosicrucians judging from the letters roundabout the emblems but then he did not know what Rosicru-cians were either and anyhow he was quite certain that Mr. Estelle Singletary, who seemed to be the one of them on the left, was a Free Will Baptist and he did not suspect a man could be a Rosicrucian and a Free Will Baptist at the same time.

From there on the front porch Mr. Estelle Singletary loosed the ribbon off from around the manufactured certificate, unrolled the thing, and set about the reading of the Dictum of it in the voice Mrs. Estelle Singletary had suggested that he read the Dictum in which was not the voice he truly ever did anything much else in and so it startled Mr. Emmet Dabb somewhat to hear what was coming out from Mr. Estelle Singletary's mouth the way it was coming out from it and he got so agitated and so distracted that he did not well hear and comprehend the actual gist of the Dictum but instead just absorbed the spirit and pomposity of the thing and quite naturally figured it straight-off for a subpoena likely from the tax office for that time in 1946 when he did not report the sixty-two dollars he'd earned from Mr. Jemison baling hay. So he was ready to give himself up, in fact was wholly resigned to it, when Mr. Ira Penn opened up the J. C. Penney box like he'd been told to and said to Mr. Emmet Dabb, "Here sir are your Raiments," like he'd practiced, and Emmet Dabb eyed the suit and the shirt and the tie and the socks too that he'd always figured you had to leave the bighouse to get and Mr. Estelle Singletary repeated to him the part of the Dictum about the Ablutions that Emmet Dabb had not understood the first time and had not learned about since.

They wanted to know could they step into the house, could they step maybe just into the foyer, wanted to know it not in the voices they had said Ablutions and had said Raiments in but just in the regular sort of way anybody would want to know a thing, so Mr. Emmet Dabb let them on into the foyer where Mr. Ira Penn and Mr. Estelle Singletary together translated and paraphrased the Dictum and explained to Emmet Dabb just precisely what sort of honor was getting bestowed upon him as well as just precisely what his end of it would be and Mr. Ira Penn lifted up the Raiments so as to reveal beneath them the soap and the bristle brush and the bath towel and the little squat jar of cream deodorant all of which Mr. Emmet Dabb studied and perused like maybe they'd just been hauled out from the pyramids. He found he was not entirely enthusiastic about Ablutions once he discovered what they were and after he'd confessed to Mr. Ira Penn and Mr. Estelle Singletary how he did not keep up with his saints and his apostles and such, he wondered would this Elfin likely send him to hell if he said no to all of it, and Mr. Ira Penn and Mr. Estelle Singletary decided together they were afraid that he would which caused Mr. Emmet Dabb to roll his lips up in his mouth that way he always did when faced with conundrums, Daddy called them.

So he went ahead and agreed to it on account of he had not learned awful much from his momma and his daddy but that hell was not the sort of place he wanted to be and Mr. Estelle Singletary read the Dictum another time thereby raising things back up to the proper tone and spirit afterwhich him and Mr. Ira Penn followed Mr. Emmet Dabb on into the bathroom like they had got instructed and told to and as Emmet Dabb was not up on his rituals in addition to his saints and his apostles he did not object to the company. So they watched him draw his bath and watched him strip naked and climb into the tub where he got handed the soapcake and the bristle brush and got told how to use the one in combination with the other and they watched him scrub and watched him rinse off and then gave over the bath towel and watched him dry with it prior to receiving the little squat jar of deodorant that he screwed off the lid of and sniffed at, and Daddy said all of it together was probably how come Mr. Estelle Singletary and Mr. Ira Penn did not ever go through the buffet at the armory like everybody else, not even for Mrs. Jennings W. Hayes's baked beans that she put the onions and the bacon and the molasses in and always made a tub of on account of how they got eaten up. Daddy said an Ablution is simply not the kind of thing that bears much observing, most especially if it is the Ablution of a man who does not customarily ablute.

Naturally the crowd at the armory was ripe and anxious with anticipation as they awaited the arrival of the keeper of the basin and his Rotarian entourage. Daddy said him and Momma were there and Momma's waxed bean salad that Momma likes to make for potluck and Grandmomma and even Granddaddy were there too with chicken and with deviled eggs and overtop of Granddaddy's objections on account of Grandmomma had that way with Granddaddy that Momma had with Daddy though would not any of the four of them ever admit to it. Jarvis Boyd and the Jarvis Boyd Five, which would be the nine of them altogether, set up in the back corner that Jarvis Boyd had stood in and shouted out of so as to test the acoustics which Jarvis Boyd told Daddy were middling at best and Daddy went ahead and apologized to him on behalf of the national guard who Daddy explained were not much up on acoustics and Jarvis Boyd said that was quite apparent to him. Jarvis Boyd played the trombone in addition to conducting the Jarvis Boyd Five which he did not use a stick for but just his fingers that he pointed with and snapped sometimes too, and as it was Jarvis Boyd that selected what got played and how, Jarvis Boyd and the Jarvis Boyd Five tended to be noticeably trombone-oriented which is to say most everything they set out on had at least some trombone in it. Even if it was not a number that generally called for trombone some little snatch of it would get played on trombone anyhow and every now and again big snatches as well, big snatches that mostly had not been meant for trombone like the little snatches that usually had not been meant for trombone either, so Daddy said they did things to a melody and did things to a beat that he did not truly have words for and consequently could not explain except to say that no matter what Jarvis Boyd a-oned and a-twoed and then snapped his fingers and set in on, it all came out sounding like the marine hymn.

So Daddy said there was some actual dancing going on but mostly your marching and your stomping and such when Emmet Dabb finally did arrive flanked by Mr. Ira Penn on his one side and Mr. Estelle Singletary on his other, and Daddy said he made a most striking entrance defined and articulated as he was by the green blazers to his left and to his right and the striped ties and the blue trousers too as well as getting somewhat defined and somewhat articulated on top of it by his own outfit which Daddy said was not nearly so handsome as the Rotarian getup but had some flair to it primarily on account of did not anything fit but the socks and the tie which left Mr. Emmet Dabb to protrude, Daddy called it, from most every little protrudable place which meant your legholes and your armholes but meant other places too, places that generally do not get protruded out of, or anyhow not so much as Mr. Emmet Dabb protruded out of them on account of the pieces of him had to go somewhere and could not hardly the majority fit inside the blue suit except partly which was almost exclusively because it was Mr. W. P. McKinney that wore the thirty-eight regular and Mr. Emmet Dabb that wore the forty-two long or anyhow fitted in a forty-two long very nearly entirely. So Mr. Emmet Dabb stood there in the armory doorway with a Rotarian to his left and a Rotarian to his right and his own self leaking out from his suit in a liberal and unexpected sort of way and the ladies of the Flower Society noticed him directly, as they had been looking for him, while everybody else noticed him directly too since a spectacle is the kind of thing that gets noticed directly, and Daddy said all at once the crowd that had been eating left off eating and the crowd that had been stomping roundabout the linoleum left off stomping and the Jarvis Boyd Five, anyhow the eight of them that had been carrying the beat, left off carrying the beat, while Jarvis Boyd himself persevered a spell on his trombone on account of he did not ever play but with his eyes shut and naturally did not see what there was to see as straightoff as everybody else saw it. And Daddy said it was not just the suit that bore looking at, or anyhow not just the parts that stuck out from it, but only happened to be the suit and the parts too that were most arresting, Daddy called them, and so got the bulk of the initial attention but gave way soon enough to the various other aspects and circumstances of Emmet Dabb's person that were mightily altered and changed over which Daddy said was his hair mostly that previously had always looked sort of laminated onto his skull but had got scrubbed with the soapcake and dried with the towel and so had puffed up and swelled out and swirled and drooped into places it did not ordinarily swirl and droop into, and then of course there was Emmet Dabb's face underneath it scraped clean of the stubble that it did not hardly ever seem scraped clean of, and Daddy said he did not know was it aftershave or cologne or just sweat and regular face-grease but Emmet Dabb's cheeks and his nose and his forehead and his chin too had a kind of low-grade sheen to them that they did not usually have and that with the hair and with the suit and of course with the little white pieces of shin that the socks did not stretch up to and the trousers did not fall down over altogether rendered Emmet Dabb somewhat worth contemplating.

He did not seem much at ease, Daddy said, partly on account of how he was getting constricted and especially where which would be at all the places you can't touch in front of people and most of the other places too, and partly on account of how he was getting contemplated, contemplated from everywhere by everybody, and then not just contemplated and not just constricted but talked at too, firstoff by Mrs. Tullock who had been voted the official greeter and so delivered the official greeting which was a kind of a Dictum only there was not so much of it, and then, in her capacity as official greeter, Mrs. Tullock offered Mr. Emmet Dabb her fingers and he went ahead and took them and squeezed them and laid them all together in a bunch. But Daddy said not the contemplating and not the greeting and not the fingersqueezing either seemed to soothe Emmet Dabb appreciably and he stood like he had stood between his Rotarians looking misplaced and ill about it and took up in turn all the fingers that got laid out in front of him to get squeezed, which Daddy said was more fingers than any man needed to shake and squeeze and lay together in one place, so straightoff he did not get the cape that the ladies called the Grand Cowl and did not get the stick that the ladies called the Grand Scepter but just got contemplated and just got constricted primarily until he ran out of fingers to shake and to squeeze and to lay together when he did in fact get draped across his shoulders the Grand Cowl that Miss Bernice Fay Frazier had sewed herself from a red velour housecoat and got put into his hand the Grand Scepter that Mrs. Anna Victoria Hewitt Sulley's husband, Duncan Sulley, had made from a piece of broomhandle and a Styrofoam Christmas ornament and then had painted with the paint he'd used on his fueloil tank.

But Daddy said somehow Mr. Emmet Dabb did not look any more regal with the housecoat and the broom handle than he had with just the tight suit, maybe on account of he did not seem pleased to be trailing the one and did not seem pleased to be holding the other and had not yet managed much enthusiasm over the fit of the third, which Daddy said did not make for your beneficent and goodly expression on the face of Emmet Dabb as he got escorted across the armory floor by Mrs. Estelle Singletary herself in the direction of what some of the ladies called the Grand Throne and some of the ladies called the Place of Honor which was what Daddy called the folding chair with the quilt on it, and as it was a processional of sorts Jarvis Boyd and the Jarvis Boyd Five struck in with "Pomp and Circumstance" like they had been told and instructed to do and Daddy said while it sounded mostly like the marine hymn it did sound in fact somewhat like "Pomp and Circumstance" and so contributed to the atmosphere and managed to inflate just your regular walking across the linoleum into something like proceeding even though it was just Mrs. Estelle Singletary and even though it was just Mr. Emmet Dabb who got fairly much deposited onto the folding chair with the quilt atop it which Daddy said could not have been a pleasurable thing considering what grip the blue suit had on him and where.

The ladies of the Flower Society had not quite figured what they would do with Emmet Dabb once they got him and his stick and his robe into the folding chair so mostly they just looked at him and mostly everybody else just looked at him too and he looked back somewhat though not at all in a bold and regal sort of way on account of Daddy said a housecoat and a broomhandle and a folding chair are not the sorts of things to make a man bold and regal if he is by nature not the one and not the other either and Daddy said Emmet Dabb had not ever been both, not hardly bold and not hardly regal but just dirty and foulsmelling which even then was not anything he had calculated to be but just something he was, or anyhow just something he had been until the ablution and until the cream deodorant and something he would be again after but something he wasn't for a time anyhow which was what got him looked at and what got him contemplated and, eventually, what got him talked at too not just by the ladies but by most everybody, who congratulated Emmet Dabb like the ladies had congratulated him without ever wondering how come it was they could bathe every day themselves and not ever get praised and honored for it. And then they brought him a plate, Daddy said, which would be the ladies this time and not anybody otherwise, and they brought him iced tea in a cup, and he balanced the plate on one knee and held the tea between his legs and ate a biscuit firstoff and ate some chicken after and attempted two forkfuls of macaroni salad but dropped the bulk of both of them down his shirtfront and Mrs. Tul-lock licked her napkin and got off what she could for him. Then there was music again, Daddy said, trombone music primarily, and there was dancing and stomping roundabout to it, even dancing and stomping roundabout on the part of Mr. Emmet Dabb who left his housecoat and his stick on the Place of Honor and took his turn doing whatever it is people do to the marine hymn which the people that were doing it did not seem to comprehend entirely, and Daddy said Mr. Emmet Dabb twirled round various of the ladies and various of the ladies twirled round Mr. Emmet Dabb who did not seem to possess much natural rhythm or much natural grace either which Daddy said were not the sorts of things a bath would instill in a man if he did not have them already or even enhance much if he did. And then the ladies brought him molded Jell-o, Daddy said, and more iced tea and he did not spill on himself but a little of both which Mrs. Tul-lock made a show of wiping at though she failed to lick her napkin like she had licked it before.

And Daddy said it just gave out after a while, the agitation and the enthusiasm, even the passing curiosity on the part of those people that had not got agitated or enthusiastic. Daddy said all of it gave out and went back to being whatever it had been, anyhow whatever it had been in reference to Mr. Emmet Dabb which, as best as Daddy figured it, was civility mostly, so Mr. Emmet Dabb sat on the Grand Throne with his robe over his shoulders and his stick in his hand and Mrs. Alice Covington's lifesized picture of St. Elfin taped to the wall behind him and he jerked his chin back at the people that jerked their chins at him and wagged his finger back at people that wagged at him their fingers but did not get any more food brought to him and did not get any more food dabbed off him and did not twirl or get twirled roundabout the linoleum like he had but just sat jerking and wagging and with his stick and his robe and his constricting blue suit for company. Daddy said the novelty of a clean Emmet Dabb just wore off and eroded with a kind of velocity that the ladies of the Flower Society had not quite anticipated and interest waned palpably, Mrs. Estelle Singletary called it once Momma asked her how come things had gone like they went, so it was just Momma that danced with Mr. Emmet Dabb after nobody else would anymore and just Momma that communicated with him other than by means of her chin and her fingers and just Momma that seemed to get hurt and get bothered by how he got left off to himself once things waned like they waned and wore off like they wore off and eroded like they eroded which left Mr. Emmet Dabb to loiter at the buffet or loiter at the throne or take a turn on the floor with Momma whenever Momma got to aching on account of it, Daddy called it, and he said Granddaddy watched the whole business with some scrutiny and some interest as it was his daughter doing with a Dabb whatever it was everybody else was doing which Granddaddy did not any more have a word for than

Daddy did as could not either one of them figure just what it was people might do to the marine hymn but for stomping and marching and Granddaddy and Daddy had both of them seen stomping and marching before and so knew this was not it.

Consequently, then, after the Dictum and the Ablutions and the Raiments and the Cowl and the Scepter and the Throne it was just Emmet Dabb again though Granddaddy insisted it had just been Emmet Dabb all along and he said to Daddy over the trombone but not so loud as to get heard by Grandmomma, "Horseshit, pure and plain," and as it was not in response to anything in particular that Daddy could recollect he wondered back at Granddaddy, "What, Chief?" and Granddaddy crossed his arms over himself and told Daddy out from the side of his mouth, "You can put a hat on a jackass and call it the pope," and Daddy looked at Granddaddy that slantwise way he sometimes looks at people but Granddaddy did not see him do it on account of Granddaddy had peered off like he did whenever he figured he'd truly said a thing and he

told himself, "Yep," one time and then told himself, "Yep,"
again behind it.

Daddy said as best as he could tell, Mr. Emmet Dabb did not
take to ablutions in any regular sort of way maybe on account
of he had not been much impressed with soap and with water
and with cream deodorant, but Daddy said he did take to his
blue suit, notwithstanding the general grip of it, and he wore it
on through December and January and February and well into
March which somewhat perturbed the ladies of the Flower
Society who objected to what Daddy called Mr. Emmet Dabb's
fashion statement as it seemed to them your basic four-letter
word and there they were the cause and source of it, so they
discussed their dilemma and debated with and snapped at
each other and then came out for a civil action but did not even
get to file the papers, had not got so far as figuring who would
do it, since they all wanted to, when Mr. Emmet Dabb bent
over at the waist to pick up a dime and so prompted the left
side of his pantseat and the right side of his pantseat to retract
from each other in a drastic and altogether irreversible sort of
way that could not be corrected but with dungarees which
would be the dungarees he'd stepped out of before to put on
the trousers he'd backed out of at last.

So things pretty much got settled on their own, Daddy said,
and went back to what they had been before Mrs. Anna
Victoria Hewitt

Sulley ever brought up and suggested St. Elfin, which the
ladies of the Flower Society would not allow her to forget she
had brought up and to forget she had suggested. Of course
Emmet Dabb had not got changed and had not got altered
much and had commenced to go back to what he was almost as
soon as he'd come to be what he wasn't, but the dungarees
were in fact the true conclusion to it, and the first time
Granddaddy saw him in them after the suit and after the
dinner dance he told Daddy just what he had seen and just

where and then said again very nearly the same thing he'd said before about the jackass and about the pope, though it did not seem to Daddy quite precisely the same thing, and Daddy wondered out loud how come Granddaddy and Mr. Emmet Dabb did not make it up, wanted to know from Granddaddy exactly why it was they did not make it up, and Granddaddy said back at him, "Make it up?" and Daddy told him, "Yes sir," and promptly got told back, "Horseshit," which for Granddaddy was an expression of considerable application.

So they did not make it up then and likely would not ever have made it up later but for the guitar that Granddaddy took instead of regular money and but for the way he learned to pick it and to strum it and but for the men he came to pick it and to strum it with who all knew what they needed as much as Granddaddy knew it and who all knew where to find it as much as Granddaddy did, but naturally they did not ask Granddaddy could they bring him since Granddaddy would not say but no, could not say but no, and naturally they did not tell Granddaddy they were bringing him when they did but just brought him anyhow which would be Mr. Wyatt Benbow and which would be Mr. Emory Boyette who escorted between them Mr. Emmet Dabb with his banjo strung across his back on bailing rope. Daddy said he saw them go by, saw them from the glider and dropped his feet from the porchrail so as to lay his arms across it and watch what might happen since he did not know would it just be an assault or a murder outright, and he said Granddaddy was tuning and playing some with Mr. Wiley Gant and tuning and playing some with Mr. Phillip J. King and so was engaged and was occupied when Mr. Wyatt Benbow and Mr. Emory Boyette and Mr. Emmet Dabb too arrived at the porch steps and stopped there on the walk, and Granddaddy said, "Evening," before he saw exactly who he was saying Evening to and got told the same back by not just the two men he'd figured to hear it from but by them and somebody else on top of it which was why he looked up from his tuning and from his playing and which was when he saw

not Mr. Wyatt Benbow or Mr. Emory Boyette either but just
Mr. Emmet Dabb in his dungarees and his cotton shirt and
with his hair all slicked and stuck to his head, and Daddy said
Granddaddy did not but look at him and then did not but spit
one time and look at him again while Emmet Dabb twitched
and squirmed and edged about a little and at last told
Granddaddy, "Nice night."

And Granddaddy strummed a chord one time and changed
over and strummed another and then said back, primarily into
his guitar hole,

(i T _ »»

I guess.

Then Mr. Wyatt Benbow, who'd come to be near about as
twitchy and squirmy and edgy as Mr. Emmet Dabb himself,
commenced to talk just in a loose and general sort of way
about most everything all at once which brought him round
eventually to Mr. Emmet Dabb's banjo and he poked at Mr.
Emmet Dabb and said to him, "Show it to Buck. Show it to
Buck. 19 and 10, Buck," he said to Granddaddy, "stamped right
there on the butt of it. Show him the 19 and 10, Emmet," and
Emmet Dabb swung the banjo around to his frontside and
jabbed it thickend foremost towards Granddaddy who looked
at it with his face all blank and empty and then told Emmet
Dabb, "Alright," and not anything otherwise.

"And he can pick that thing," Mr. Wyatt Benbow said. "Can't
he pick it?" he asked Emory Boyette who shook his head yes.
"Can pick it sure enough," Mr. Wyatt Benbow said. "Go on,
Emmet, play a thing for us. Go on now." And Mr. Wyatt
Benbow told Granddaddy, "Listen," and told Wiley Gant and
Mr. Phillip J. King, "Listen," and then told Mr. Emmet Dabb,
"Go on. Go on. Pick us a tune now." And Daddy said Mr.
Emmet Dabb laid his right foot atop a stairtread and rested the

banjo on his thigh and then strummed it one time and covered the strings and strummed it one time again and then commenced to pick with just his fingernails, and Daddy said straightoff he could not hear what it was exactly but could see well enough how Granddaddy stiffened all over and could see well enough how Granddaddy set his teeth and he still could not himself hear but little snatches of it and not an entire run of melody until the traffic quit and the breeze quit and all at once the crickets quit too like crickets will sometimes which was when he heard enough of it to lay his chin atop his hands atop the porchrail and tell himself, "Oh shit," on account of it was "Dixie."

Daddy said Granddaddy did not move not anywhere even though he was all pitched forward in his chair a way that most people don't stay at least not hardly the way that Granddaddy stayed it and Emmet Dabb played the whole thing through one time and then set about playing it through again to accommodate Mr. Wyatt Benbow who had struck in to singing on the second verse and got joined up at the refrain by everybody but Emmet Dabb who watched his own fingers and everybody but Granddaddy who watched Emmet Dabb and did not move, Daddy said, not anywhere even after they'd got done with it and even after they'd all praised the fingerwork and praised the picking, all except for Granddaddy who did not move even the trifling bit it would have taken to do that but only sat, Daddy said, all pitched forward like nobody ever sat much and looked, Daddy said, all roundabout Emmet Dabb's person like he did not get looked at hardly ever. Then Mr. Wyatt Benbow whewed one time and humphed one time in his throat after. "Lord, makes me hurt to hear it," he said. "Just makes me ache in the heart." And Mr. Phillip J. King, who was not nearly so old as Mr. Wyatt Benbow or Granddaddy or any of the rest of them either, wondered why it was nobody much grew cotton anymore anyhow, wondered why it was you couldn't drive out into the country and see it all along the roadsides like previous times, and Wyatt Benbow considered the thing, but talk of cotton and talk of old times made him ache in the heart too, and recollected how he'd lost cousins twice removed at Guilford battleground and how his great-uncle Cuthbert had got shot all to pieces during the siege of Atlanta and at the thought of it all Mr. Wyatt Benbow grew somewhat touched and weepy and he said to Mr. Phillip J. King, who was still wondering about cotton mostly, "Lord, they were good men."

And Daddy said he could see it from there at the porchrail, could see Mr. Emmet Dabb lift his banjo off from his thigh and set down on the stairtread the thick end, the end with the 19 and 10 stamped into it, and Daddy said he could even hear him too, hear him reply to Mr. Wyatt Benbow, or anyhow seem to say to Mr. Wyatt Benbow what he was not saying to Mr. Wyatt Benbow at all. "They was all good men," he told him and did not look but at Granddaddy and but at his own feet after.

"Lord, I guess," Mr. Wyatt Benbow said back not knowing just who it was Emmet Dabb had been talking at anyhow and not knowing just why. "Such fine men. Makes me ache. Makes me ache here," he said and laid his hand atop his chest. "I don't but hear a name and throb all roundabout." And then Mr. Wyatt Benbow stiffened his old self, Daddy said, and drew up straight and proper and opened his mouth and intoned, Daddy called it, "Mr. Robert E. Lee," which was met with some grave and prayerful mumbling on the part of most everybody and Mr. Emory Boyette come in right behind it all with Braxton Bragg that produced some noticeable wincing and flinching all across Mr. Wyatt Benbow's person, and as he did not figure anybody else would say them Mr. Wiley Gant threw in with Quantrill and threw in with Mosby too which set Mr. Emory Boyette onto Ma-gruder and then Pickett after and Wiley Gant had Jubal Early by then and had Bedford Forrest as well and Mr. Phillip J. King gave out Longstreet as that was most of what he knew aside from Lee, and Emory Boyette got onto J. E. B. Stuart after him and Joe Johnston too, and Mr. Wyatt

Benbow tormented his own self with P. G. T. Beauregard before they all gave out for a spell which was when Grandmomma said it, said it from behind the screendoor that had not any of them noticed her behind, said it with her apronend caught up in her fingers and her shoulder against the jamb, said it so loud and so clear that even Daddy heard it plain. "Stonewall," she told them, "Jackson," and Daddy said Mr. Emmet Dabb that had not been stiff got stiff of a sudden and Granddaddy that was still all pitched forward with his teeth set stayed it.

"Lord yes, Stonewall," Mr. Wyatt Benbow said and laid his hand back up where he'd laid it previously. "As good a man as there's ever been."

"They was all good men," Mr. Emmet Dabb told him and did not but look at Granddaddy square and direct like Granddaddy was looking at him.

"Yes sir, yes sir," Mr. Wyatt Benbow said. "I guess that's the truth of it. Even some yankees that was worth something. Grant," he said. "Hooker," he said. "Thomas," he said.

And Wiley Gant told him, "Shitfire," and then excused himself to Grandmomma straightaway. "Don't tell me about no yankees," he said to Wyatt Benbow. "Not me." And he whipped himself around one time fast so that his empty sleeve could not hardly keep up with him. "Grant," he said. "Hooker," he said. "Thomas," he said. "Pilfering plundering sorry bastards," and again he apologized straightaway to Grandmomma who allowed it. "What about Sheridan that did what he done?" Wiley Gant wanted to know but did not anybody dare to answer to it and Wiley Gant set in again with "What about " but he did not finish the thing out as he could not even say the other and did not anybody else tell it for him as they could not hardly say it themselves, and Wiley Gant stalked across the planking with his empty sleeve trailing out behind him. "That blackhearted son-of-a-bitch," he said and did not even begin to be sorry for it on account of he knew and they knew and she knew too that it was what suited best and they all hated and despised him there together as thoroughly and completely as a thing could be hated and despised, and Wiley Gant said, not so much to Wyatt Benbow but just out loud and to nobody, "Don't tell me about no yankees," and then laid his open hand across his eyes and stood very still and quiet.

Daddy said he did not know for certain but believed it was in fact Granddaddy that struck in with "Dixie" this time that Emmet Dabb picked up on and then Wyatt Benbow and Emory Boyette and Mr. Phillip J. King as well who blew on what parts he knew to blow on and just listened to the rest of it which was solely the strumming and sawing and the fingerwork in addition to the blowing sometimes until well into the second refrain when Daddy said Mr. Wiley Gant commenced to sing it in his sweet high voice and got joined by Grandmomma who carried the harmony underneath him and did not anybody else put in but to pick and to strum and to blow some straight through to the end of it which Daddy said had not full well died off and away when Mr. Wyatt Benbow, still with his hurt and his ache, set in with "Tenting Tonight on the Old Campground" that Granddaddy and Emory Boyette and Emmet Dabb endeavored to play with him once they figured out what it was he was playing but that did not anybody sing but Mr. Wyatt Benbow himself on account of Grandmomma was not much acquainted with the words and Wiley Gant said it was a yankee song, said he was purely convinced it was a yankee song, and insisted he would not sing a yankee song any more than he would marry a yankee woman, and Daddy said that kind of took some of the feeling out of the thing for Mr. Wyatt Benbow who was not much acquainted with the words himself and so finished in the middle and quit. And Daddy said they went direct to the "St. James Infirmary" after and on to the "Cumberland Gap" after that and ended up at "Hard Times Come Again No More" with the whole slew of them singing at every conceivable pitch and range and pace too but at a common volume, what Daddy called flatout, and when they got done Mr. Wyatt Benbow whewed one time and humphed too and wondered if that had been a thing or hadn't it, and everybody agreed it had been, agreed it had purely been a thing indeed.

Daddy said he laid out over the rail and watched Mr. Wyatt Benbow head up the porch stairs to his usual seat with Mr. Emory Boyette just behind him which left Emmet Dabb by himself with his one foot on the sidewalk and his other on the stairtread above it and his banjo caught up in his arms and he did not make out to go up and did not make out to back off but just stood where he'd been standing until Granddaddy asked Mr. Phillip J. King wasn't there an extra chair around the corner somewhere and once Mr. Phillip J. King had hunted it up and brought it back with him Granddaddy said he had figured there had been one which was all the invitation Mr. Emmet Dabb got but was all he needed too. So they played, Daddy said, all six of them together with Grandmomma watching from the doorjamb and Daddy himself watching from the glider, and they played everything they could play and some things they couldn't and sang everything they could sing and some things they couldn't too, and Daddy said they did "Fox on the Run" and "Rockytop" and "The Tennessee Waltz" and "Rank Strangers" and "Up a Lazy River" and Mr. Emory Boyette sang a song his daddy had taught him about a lady that drownded herself in a mill pond and Mr. Wyatt Benbow figured it was on account of love though did not any of the words tell exactly what it was on account of but Mr. Wyatt Benbow went ahead and figured love anyhow and got all achy in his heart and attempted to sing a song he'd heard about love and about death and about pain and suffering but he could not recollect how it started off and could not recollect how it finished up and only recollected some little snatch of the middle of it and so sang that and quit and when nobody set in on something otherwise Mr. Phillip J. King played

"Shenandoah" on his own and got complimented on it by Grandmomma who was put in mind of "Red River Valley" which she commenced to sing with nobody but Granddaddy to strum it and Mr. Wyatt Benbow gasped and clutched at himself when she got done with it on account of the sheer beauty of the thing and then Mr. Emmet Dabb struck in straightaway with a song about cowpies that Wiley Gant sang the words to and all throughout it Emory Boyette gasped and clutched and made out to be in raptures himself.

Daddy said they played on later than normal, on past the dusk of the day and into the full dark and had not left off when he got up from the glider and flicked his last Tareyton over the porchrail and into the yard, and he said he stretched himself and yanked his shorts down some and yanked his trousers up some and then pulled the glider back from the rail where Momma does not like for it to be prior to lingering a spell there at the door with his fingers wrapped around the screenpull and Daddy said he sucked a breath and held it and listened through the crickets and the scant frogs and the traffic too at the voices all mixed and blended together with Mr. Wiley Gant's up there at the top and Mr. Emory Boyette's down there at the bottom and everybody else's all spread out in between and, as Daddy recollected, it was "I'll Fly Away" that had some picking to it and some strumming and some blowing and some sawing as well and then gave out of a sudden and as Mr. Wyatt Benbow whewed and humphed and wondered hadn't that been a thing, Daddy stepped on into the house and latched the door behind him.

ii

He said she come out onto the plank sidewalk with a little blue hinged tin in her left hand and a little blue hinged tin in her right hand too and as she did not have any actual pockets and did not carry anything in the way of a purse, she could not but catch the one up under her arm while she fetched a pinchful out from the other and Daddy said she had her mouth full open and her fingers near about in it when she first got talked at, got talked at by what turned out to be a Williford that had his backside all laid up against the storefront and his arms crossed over himself, and Aunt Sister wondered if maybe that wasn't some manner of Williford like what's local and indigenous roundabout on account of what Willifords she'd ever seen most generally stayed sprawled up against some one thing or another, but Daddy told her Hartshorne and told her Oklahoma and though Aunt Sister told him back, "Maybe so," Daddy said it was most extraordinarily unlikely as Willifords did not seem to him the sort to spread and migrate.

And she turned around, Daddy said, on account of the Williford was behind her mostly and only beside her somewhat and she said to him, "What's that?" since she had not heard just precisely what he had said to her, or had not absorbed and took hold of it anyhow, and the Williford pulled at the skinflap between his noseholes with his thumb and his forefinger and then asked Aunt Della a second time just precisely what he'd asked her straightoff. "Lady," he said, "you looking an injun?"

And Aunt Della told him, "No sir," and dabbed at her snuff with a snuffmop she'd cut off a birch tree and then she turned back around to loose little Spud from the hitching post at the street but was not anything there to loose, no reins, no mule, nothing but the rail all slick and leatherstained and Aunt Della looked up the road a ways to see was she at the post she'd been at previously and then looked down the road a ways afterwhich she got all squinty and puckered up about the face and attempted to recollect for certain how she had come to be where she was anyhow and she did seem to recall arriving on a mule and did seem to recall tying the mule up to where it was not tied up any longer and she studied the rail a second time and determined to her own satisfaction that there was not any little trace of reins around it and not any little bit of mule nowhere close by, and Daddy said the Williford, still all sprawled and crossarmed, made a noise down in his throat so as to remind Aunt Della how he was where he was and knew what he knew and Aunt Della left the rail and stepped on across the plank sidewalk direct up to him and aimed square at him her pointy nose and parted her thin little lips and told him, "Go on."

And Daddy said the Williford spat straightoff which Momma went ahead and objected to outright on account of she figured her and Aunt Sister had already been subjected to enough saliva to float a boat and it simply did not seem to her that everybody Daddy made mention of had to go and spit, but Daddy insisted it had been a time of considerable spitting, a time of ponderous and widespread chewing and dipping and just your general hocking up of things so he felt compelled to put it in so as to be at least reasonably accurate, and he said he could not be more than reasonably accurate anyhow since he was having to leave out most all the pissing in the street and of a sudden Momma and Aunt Sister both got a little stiff and frosty together and Momma observed to Aunt Sister but loud enough for all of us to benefit from it how she did not wholly appreciate Daddy's discretion in some things and Aunt Sister told her, "Just precisely," back and Daddy waited for Momma and Aunt Sister to lay their hands in their laps like women will and then proceeded, recommencing with the Williford spitting like he had not ever got stopped on account of it.

Daddy said it was a scraggly Williford with long yellowwhite hair and roundabout his face in patches scantling whiskers that maybe would have made up a mustache if he could have gotten them all under his nose at once. He had on a kind of a hat with a brim that drooped and laid down most everywhere and a wool shirt and galluses overtop it and thickweave trousers tucked down into his boots and Daddy said he had not moved from wallowing against the storefront and had not uncrossed and dropped his arms on account of they were ledged up atop his stomach and so did not cause him any

exertion to speak of, and Daddy said he lowered his head down
and sideways some and raised his shoulder up and over a little
and wiped his mouth on his shirt and then said to Aunt Della,
"Lady, you hunting a mule?"

"That's right," Aunt Della told him.

"Then you hunting an injun," he said and spat for the general
drama of the expectoration, Daddy called it.

"What injun where?" Aunt Della wanted to know.

"Don't matter what injun," the Williford said. "They's all just
like the rest on account of they's just your thieving kind of
injun and your dead kind of injun and it ain't but the one that
comes to be the other, so don't matter what injun exactly." And
Daddy said the Williford spat with a kind of a punctuational
effect.

"Alright," Aunt Della told him, "where then?"

And the Williford kind of raised himself off from the wall and
stood all independent and upright which let the air blow
roundabout him and so circulate his scent which Daddy said
was dank and was loamy and altogether human in a low and
unimproved sort of way. "Up the road not awful far they's a
house," he said and raised his finger so as to indicate up the
road but without pointing south or west or north or east either
but just overhead somewhat. "And next to it they's a kind of a
lowslung sort a place where injuns take their liquor. Mostly
ain't no animals tied up out front except today. They's a mule
there along about now." And Daddy said the Williford spat
after a fashion that was a blending of the punctuational and
the dramatical all together.

"Where now?" Aunt Della wanted to know and peered up the
main road and down the main road and off along the solitary

cross street she could see off along in preparation for what pointing and indicating she expected to come but did not the Williford point and did not the Williford indicate, did not the Williford so much as raise his finger like previously, and once Aunt Della had peered everywhere she could peer and see anything much she looked back at the Williford himself and asked him, "Where now?" just like she'd asked him it before.

"Up the road not awful far," he said and Aunt Della watched him raise his pointing finger and followed it up to his nose where the pointing finger itself, in conjunction with the thumb, took hold of the little skinflap between the nostrils. "A course ain't no straight and easy way to get to it. A person's liable to need some leading and some guiding first time out."

"Leading and guiding?" Aunt Della said.

And the Williford told her, "That's right."

"Who from?" Aunt Della wanted to know.

And the Williford crossed his arms atop his stomach and worked his face and turned his lips up under and then out again. "Now I could do it my own self," he said, "but I got some gainful work coming to me in a bit now and don't seem quite square I should give over what wages I'd have from it so as to take you down the road. Don't strike me like the smart thing."

"I'd give you money," Aunt Della said, "but I ain't got but these three pennies left from this snuff," and she opened up her hands to show the tin of Sweet La La in her left one and the tin of Sweet La La in her right and prized up the hinged lid on the one tin so as to exhibit the three pennies laying in with the snuff. "I'll give you these," she said, "and I'll give you a tin too."

And Daddy said the Williford told her, "Don't dip," and then spat hard out the side of his mouth in a manner that Daddy

145

insisted was not just dramatical and punctuational but emphatical too. "Liable to be trouble," he said. "Injun's full of meanness sober, damn near wild with it drunk. Three pennies and snuff I don't dip ain't gone put me nowhere you want me to be."

"What then?" Aunt Della wanted to know.

And Daddy said the Williford took hold of his chin with the same fingers he'd used on his skinflap and grew squinty of a sudden while he weighed off and pondered the various elements of the undertaking, and once he'd arrived at what he arrived at he turned his lips up under and then turned them out again and spat one time in what Daddy said was just your noncommittal and habitual sort of way. "15 cent," he said at last. "That's how I figure it."

And Aunt Della told him, "I'll have to fetch my Jack."

"Fetch him," the Williford said, "and fetch his gun along with him."

"He ain't close by," Aunt Della told him.

And the Williford said Alright that way that Daddy does.

"You'll be here?" Aunt Della wanted to know.

And the Williford told her, "Yes ma'm," and then laid and sprawled himself back up against the storefront with his arms ledged atop his stomach and his legs crossed like he meant not to ever be anywhere else.

So she walked back, Daddy said, carried her own little wiry self and her three pennies and her two tins of Sweet La La back the way she'd come that Mr. J. T. London said was maybe two miles but had not seemed it even on the mule and had instead seemed twice it or three times it and struck her like maybe four times that now that she did not have the mule underneath her but just her own feet and the rock and the dust and the dirt otherwise, and Daddy said Uncle Jack and Mr. J. T. London that were in the corral by the road transacting did not either one see her straightoff on account of they had mules to ponder and look at instead, not mules of any bulk and magnitude much, Daddy said, but tiny scrawny mules mostly that Mr. J. T. London called specially formulated and called hybrids and called sleek too instead of tiny and instead of scrawny, and Daddy said Uncle Jack stuck his fingers in the mules' mouths and studied their teeth on account of he had a notion that's what people did with mules and he rubbed his hands along their undersides and down their legs and peeked in their ears every now and again and then nodded and made noises at himself so as to appear to have learned something from it all, but the more he pondered and looked and studied and peeked and rubbed the tinier and scrawnier the mules seemed to get on him and he wondered at Mr. J. T. London which would do the pulling, the mule or the plow, but Mr. J. T. London told him it was just breeding and was just sleekness and then set himself to reveal a thing to Uncle Jack, set himself tight and close to him so as to tell to Uncle Jack what appeared to be a piece of private and specialized information, and Mr. J. T. London parted his lips somewhat and said, "Vigor," alone and by itself and Uncle Jack pondered him and studied him and peeked at him and said, "Vigor?" his own self back and got told, "Yes sir," and got told, "actual and inbred," and got told, "Vigor," again which was commencing to strike Uncle Jack as not just specialized and private but mystifying too the more he heard it said and he nodded and made a noise at himself and Mr. J. T. London laid his arm across Uncle Jack's shoulder and set about recollecting a thing their good friend Mr. Nunnely had said to him one time, a thing which did not turn out to have much to do with vigor or breeding or even mules as a general item but was just a sort of a comment about nothing much in particular following which Mr. J. T. London asked after the health of Mrs. Nunnely who still did not have much health to speak of as she continued to stay dead no matter how solicitous he grew on account of her.

And Daddy said they still did not see Aunt Della, who was almost at the corral fence and had expected to get seen previous to arriving there but did not and she laid herself up against it much after the fashion of the Williford but frontwards and still did not get seen straightoff by Uncle Jack who was studying mules or by Mr. J. T. London either who was studying Uncle Jack and as she was give out and winded from the walk Aunt Della just stayed there against the fence for a spell tired and ignored, or tired and ignored anyhow until one of Mr. J. T. London's special bred mules wandered over towards her, stuck a part of his snout somewhat through the fencerails, and bit Aunt Della on the stomach, when she grew lively of a sudden and jumped upright and hooted one time and got noticed very nearly straightaway partly on account of how she hooted but partly on account of how high she yanked her dress and how low she yanked her bloomers so as to get a look at the mulebite that had grown purply already, and Daddy said the dark teethmarks on the creamy white stomach was likely the first thing Uncle Jack and Mr. J. T. London noticed after the hoot and Uncle Jack, who did not ever exclaim much, exclaimed directly, "Lord, what is it?"

"I been bit," Aunt Della told him still with her dressend up high and her bloomerbottoms down low.

"What by?" Uncle Jack wanted to know.

And Aunt Della told him, "Mule," and touched the teethmarks with her fingertip.

"What mule?" Uncle Jack said.

And Aunt Della said back, "That there," and indicated with her finger much in the Williford style of indicating.

And Daddy said Mr. J. T. London, who had not yet entirely removed his arm from Uncle Jack's shoulders, pinched up a piece of skin in his fingers and said to Uncle Jack, "Spunk too. Bred and cultivated."

Daddy figured it was on account of there was so many of your tiny scrawny and spunky mules circulating roundabout the corral that Uncle Jack failed to notice straightaway how his own standard and regular-sized one was not anywhere in sight in a run of country so flat and treeless that a mule could not get hid and vanished except maybe in a hole dug for it, and as her mulebite pained and troubled her acutely, Aunt Della did not recollect to tell Uncle Jack about little Spud rightoff which allowed him to muse some on his own and once he'd grown weary of the mulebite and grown weary of the tiny scrawny mules and grown weary of the talk about the cultivating and the breeding of them he set about casting around to see whatever he might be able to see otherwise and after a minute or two of just your aimless peering about he attempted to hunt up his own animal so as to measure the regular item against Mr. J. T. London's Oklahoma hybrid which would be along about when Uncle Jack discovered how there were not any mules roundabout but for the tiny scrawny and spunky kind and directly, troublesome mulebite or not, he insisted of Aunt Della, "Where's ours?"

"Our what?" she asked him back and brought her bloomerbottoms up and laid her dressend down as her fingertips did not seem to have much curative effect.

"Mule," he said to her.

And Aunt Della told him, "Stole."

"Who by?" Uncle Jack wanted to know.

"Some injun," Aunt Della said.

"Whereabouts?" Uncle Jack asked her.

And Aunt Della flicked out her indicating finger and told him, "Town."

And Daddy said Uncle Jack swore in a kind of vile and unrepeatable sort of way which was how most people did in fact swear back then, Daddy told it, even your Christian people which Uncle Jack undoubtedly was and Aunt Sister said, "Bless him yes," and Momma nodded just behind her and Daddy himself said, "Bless him," and Daddy himself said, "Yes," too and then commenced to fish around for his matchpack.

Mr. J. T. London told them, "Cherokees," told them, "Cherokees come from the Blue Ridge," and swore some himself as Uncle Jack had established the precedent for it, and then Aunt Della set in to explaining about the Williford and what he'd said and what he'd seen and where he figured he'd take the two of them and for how much and Daddy said Uncle Jack swore another time with appreciable venom and Mr. J. T. London said just after him, "Willifords," and spat and swore with some venom himself.

He sold them a mule to ride as he had a policy against letting out his animals on account of their rarefied cultivation, he told it, and exclusive breeding. Actually he sold them eight mules all at once so as to give Uncle Jack his best eight-mule price which he explained he could not give for the one mule by itself since one mule by itself did not constitute a wholesale arrangement, but of course Mr. J. T. London figured Uncle Jack would have been good for eight mules anyhow and wondered didn't Uncle Jack figure the same thing and then pinched up a portion of Uncle Jack's neckskin between his fingers and squeezed it some. Aunt Della fetched the rifle and the shells and what tack they needed out from the wagon with the sides and the roof to it and her and Uncle Jack climbed up together onto the same animal and went off at what was not so extraordinary a velocity which did not improve and accelerate once they got out from the corral and away from the barn and on down the road some, and Daddy said Uncle Jack didn't have to get down and walk until halfway to town and Aunt Della didn't have to get down and walk until near about three quarters and they did not have to tie the mule up and leave him until the first building they arrived at and so continued just on foot with no mule in tow direct to the general drygoods with the Williford still sprawled up against the front of it his arms atop his belly and his feet crossed before him.

Daddy said Uncle Jack wanted to hear from the Williford what he'd heard from Aunt Della and so the Williford obliged him with what details he could recollect which would mostly be just the mule and just the indian and just the speculation as to where it was they'd ended up on account of the Williford was not a man with much eye for particulars though he did recollect the 15 cents to the penny and counted it from his left hand into his right hand once he had it all to count. Then he got unsprawled and upright as best he could and stretched himself and worked his joints and ever so eventually stepped down off the plank sidewalk into the road and crossed it to the far side with Uncle Jack and Aunt Della crossing it behind him and proceeded north to an alleyway which he turned into with Uncle Jack and Aunt Della turning into it behind him and he come out the other side and proceeded north some more prior to stopping dead in the road with Uncle Jack and Aunt Della stopping dead behind him. Then he pointed and indicated, Daddy said, though not in the usual fashion of Williford pointing and indicating but with some purpose and accuracy and considerable good effect as Uncle Jack and Aunt Della too both saw little Spud at the same time tied up to a rail not so very awful far down the road.

Daddy said he figured it was maybe seventy-five yards altogether which came out to near about a penny every five steps and Daddy said Uncle Jack, who had a head for ciphers himself, figured pretty much the same thing straightoff and so called the Williford a name directly and suggested how he did not know which was the worse, the bastard that had took the mule in the first place or the bastard that had seen him do it, but the Williford did not appear much affected by any of what he got told or any of what he got called and it was only when Uncle Jack drew back his arm to hit him that the Williford grew truly animated and made off like you would not expect from a man that could sprawl and lay about so. Consequently, then, it was just Uncle Jack and just Aunt Della that continued on up the road to where little Spud had got tied up out front of the lowslung building and Aunt Della suggested, as there was not anybody much roundabout, that they just loose little Spud and be gratified to get him back, and Daddy said Uncle Jack considered the proposition and it seemed to him sound and seemed to him logical but he loaded the rifle anyhow and gave it over to Aunt Della along with what cartridges she could fit in her hand and he told her just exactly how far he'd come from home and just exactly where he'd got lost on the way and how and just exactly who'd done and swindled him now that he was where he'd got to be and not just done and not just swindled but robbed on top of it and then Uncle Jack blew out a breath and told Aunt Della he'd be goddammed if he wasn't going to wale the shit out of somebody and he figured it might as well be an indian on account of he'd never waled the shit out of an indian before and he looked forward to the novelty of it.

So Aunt Della got the rifle and got what shells she could fit in her hand and Uncle Jack set himself to wale and beat and pummel an indian just in your general way that men set themselves to wale and beat and pummel most anybody which includes a rolling up of the sleeves and a throwing back of the shoulders and a firming and tightening up of what muscles can be firmed and tightened to much effect along with some demonstrative inhaling and some demonstrative exhaling too afterwhich Uncle Jack stomped on down the road to the lowslung building, stepped up onto the plank sidewalk, and bounded direct in through the open doorway which Daddy said put him pretty much into full darkness or what was as good as full darkness anyhow on account of Uncle Jack could not see but the little lines and dots left over from the sunlight which Daddy figured would have slowed and hindered most men but did not noticeably slow and hinder Uncle Jack who advanced direct into a table and stopped only once he could not get through it or around it either, stopped with the edge of it against his thighs and then drew off a breath and inquired, Daddy called it, "Which of you pilfering sons-of-bitches stole my mule?"

And Aunt Sister said, "Foolishness," just like she'd said it previously and said, "Blood thing," just like she'd said that too and this time it was Momma that tried "Passion" and it was Momma that tried "Temperament" but Aunt Sister told her, "Foolishness," again like maybe she had not quite heard it the first time and Aunt Sister added "Plain" and added "Simple" after it and did not get told anything contrary back as Momma hardly ever was contrary much except with Daddy every now and again. And Daddy said Uncle Jack still could not see but the lines and could not see but the dots after he said and inquired what he did say and inquire and so just stood with his thighs against the table edge and listened to the chairlegs on the wood floor and the bootheels too and then at last saw something other than dots and something other than lines which was just your shapes mostly, your indian shapes all standing and upright and spread roundabout Uncle Jack on three sides anyhow and Daddy said Uncle Jack did not but draw off a second breath and did not but inquire again just exactly what he had inquired before and then waited to get told what it was he desired to know which he did get told near about straightaway and by an indian direct across the tabletop from him, an indian Uncle Jack could almost see some of, or anyhow could almost see some of aside from the shape and the bulk of him which Daddy said was considerable, more considerable by far than most all the rest of the shapes and the bulks Uncle Jack could make out, and Uncle Jack asked the indian that had fessed up to taking the mule just exactly why in the hell he'd done what he did in case there was a legitimate reason for it as Uncle Jack had sized up the shape and had measured out the bulk and so had calculated and arrived at the likelihood of his doing some waling versus the likelihood of his getting some and since it did not seem to him he could stand at the time to die in Oklahoma he wondered if maybe there wasn't an excuse for all of it and so asked the indian was there and in return got called a particular item straightoff, an especially unsavory and indelicate particular item, Daddy said, which affected Uncle Jack in an immediate sort of way and he said, "Well," and he said, "Shit," after and then dove direct across the tabletop.

Now Daddy says your regular variety of fistfight does not ever come up to the kind of thing on the television where a man gets stood up with one hand and punched with another and then sort of sails backwards to bust up what furniture he can. Daddy says your regular variety of fistfight does not generally have much to do with fists and punching and beating and whatnot but is just your basic grappling mostly and wrenching around and rolling about and such along with some headbutting and teethgritting and grunting and groaning and spitting and considerable swearing and name calling, and Daddy said as Uncle Jack was the one that dove straightaway and the indian was the one that got dove at, Uncle Jack had the best of it there at the first since he wrapped his arms roundabout the indian's thighs and pitched over atop him where he was able to lay the crown of his head against the point of the indian's chin with some force and zeal and Uncle Jack grunted while the indian groaned and gnashed his teeth some and the two of them together pitched and rolled first to the one side and then to the other and Uncle Jack kept what he had hold of and butted what he could butt against while the indian tried to get loose and tried to get free and in the process swore Uncle Jack and called him one thing and another which Daddy says is traditionally left to the man on the bottom as he has the most to be profane about, and Daddy said Uncle Jack was fairly well established there with his weight laid like it was laid and his arms wrapped like they were wrapped and his head butting what it was butting, so did not anything in particular happen for a spell except for the swearing and except for the butting that produced it until that indian managed to swing his chin roundabout some and so avoid Uncle Jack's topnotch which put him in an excellent strategic position, Daddy called it, on account of how when Uncle Jack lunged to butt all that indian had to do was open his mouth and a piece of ear went direct into it and Daddy said he closed his teeth on it and bore down appreciably which moved and impressed Uncle Jack straightaway.

And Aunt Sister told Daddy she'd never heard of such and told Momma the same thing behind it and then dabbed at the underside of her nose with a raggedy little ball of powderblue Kleenex and said, "Savages," that way she says Catholics sometimes, but Daddy told her in your regular variety of fistfight earbiting and headbutting and such are not at all extraordinary as they are so effective in a consistent sort of way and Daddy said that indian did not but chomp down and hold on and of a sudden the butting left off entirely and though a little swearing set in in place of it, Daddy said it was not any manner of intolerable swearing, not nearly so harsh and objectionable as the butting anyhow and Daddy said Uncle Jack could not lunge forward and could not pull back, could not go anywhere really without surrendering a mouthful of himself to the indian who kind of ground the top of Uncle Jack's ear between his molars and grunted while Uncle Jack called him most every unseemly thing he could think of and grunted some himself, and Daddy said as the swearing and his

portion of the grunting did not seem to be aiding Uncle Jack
any he loosed his grip from around the indian's midsection
and commenced to poke his fingertips into what recesses of the
indian's face he could manage to poke them into thereby
distracting and annoying the indian sufficiently to get himself
thrown partway across the room along with the whole of his
unaffected ear and the vast majority of his bit one, and Daddy
said Uncle Jack, chewed on and afflicted as he was, did not
clamber up from the floor like he might have otherwise and so
got kicked one time in the ribcage and then got hit one time
across the bridge of the nose which Daddy said was not to be
confused with a regular punch in the nose on account of the
indian had been attempting to punch Uncle Jack up side of his
head but had ended up hitting Uncle Jack's nose instead with a
piece of his wrist though Daddy did not imagine the
discrepancy was much noticed by the indian at the time or
Uncle Jack either who could not see of a sudden and so leapt
upright and straightaway fell over a chair which spun round
with considerable velocity and a leg of it jabbed the indian
square in the inseam and took his breath temporarily, allowing
Uncle Jack to stand upright all over again and wipe his eyes
some and as he was not much of a puncher himself but more of
a butter and a grabber he charged full onto the indian and took
him on out the door and across the plank sidewalk and down
onto the road where he commenced to butt what he could butt
and grab what he could grab and swear when he could muster
the breath for it.

Now Aunt Della had been listening to all of it from out in the
road with her one hand full of cartridges and the fingers of her
other wrapped roundabout Uncle Jack's rifle which Daddy said
was not just your ordinary sort of weapon but was special and
particular though not precisely special and particular in the
way Uncle Jack thought it was when he bought it. Daddy said it
was Mr. Hubert Jukes of Ruffin that sold the thing to him once
he learned how Uncle Jack was taking up from Mr. Nunnely
what he took up from him, and

Daddy said as Mr. Hubert Jukes had a talent for making people want what they did not need, him and Uncle Jack struck in on a bargain straightoff on account of Uncle Jack generally wanted what he did not need in the natural way of things and so did not require hardly any encouraging or much finagling either. Mr. Jukes wanted to know had Uncle Jack ever laid eyes on a Sharps .50 caliber buffalo rifle and when he got told no he held up his own gun and said it was one which Uncle Jack did not have any reason to doubt as not anywhere on the bore or the stock or the trigger guard either was there an inscription to the contrary and Uncle Jack hefted the thing and looked it over and hefted it again and then told Mr. Hubert Jukes he was pleased to at last lay his eyes on a Sharps .50 caliber buffalo rifle as he had always heard tell of them, and Mr. Jukes told him that his was not just your regular Sharps . 50 caliber buffalo rifle but was actually the mule trader variety of buffalo rifle made especially by Mr. Sharp for mule traders and Mr. Jukes told how the barrel on the mule trader variety was a little shorter and Uncle Jack pondered the barrel and agreed that it was a little shorter though he did not know shorter than what exactly, and Mr. Jukes just let him hold the thing and heft it and aim it and look at it which Daddy said was all he needed to do on account of the way Uncle Jack could commence to want a thing on his own, and he did commence to want it, Daddy said, even saw himself with it out on the plains shooting one thing or another or just standing with the barrel of it canted up on his shoulder like he figured regular frontiersmen usually stood. So he wondered at Mr. Hubert Jukes could he get it somehow and Mr. Hubert Jukes dropped his mouth and stared back at him all astounded and put out and since Uncle Jack was too busy wanting the buffalo rifle to appreciate the subtleties of Mr. Jukes' expression he wondered at Mr. Jukes could it maybe be bought with regular money or if not money get traded for outright and Uncle Jack told how he had his daddy's over-and-under and figured that maybe they could work up a swap but Mr. Jukes only lowered his jaw all over again and announced to Uncle Jack just precisely what a rare item it was he held in his hands and Daddy said Mr. Jukes set in to tracing the origins of this particular Sharps .50 caliber buffalo rifle which seemed to have been owned by most every notable somebody throughout the country but for Thomas Jefferson and Daniel Boone who Mr. Jukes could not work into the lineage somehow. Naturally, though, Unde Jack did not want the gun but twice as much over as soon as he discovered what little chance he had of getting it so it was not just the money or the over-and-under but came to be the money and the over-and-under together which Mr. Jukes considered with his jaw near about shut and did not seem to take any open offense at and then it was not just the over-and-under and the first bit of money but the over-and-under and a second bit of money along with it and Mr. Jukes shut his mouth completely and pondered the whole deal at once and then lowered his jaw again and suggested the over-and-under and the second bit of money along with a birch hayfork he'd had his eye on for a spell and right then it was done.

So Uncle Jack got what he wanted, Daddy said, and gave up what he gave up and Mr. Jukes threw in what seemed to be a full carton of shells until Uncle Jack opened it and discovered it was mostly a full canon of casings and just somewhat a full carton of shells and he decided he would fire not more than two as a means of testing his Sharps .50 caliber buffalo rifle on account of how Uncle Jack followed most all his excesses with bouts of frugality, so him and Mr. Jukes hunted up a stomach tar bottle in the weeds by Uncle Jack's hogpen and they set the thing up on a fencepost and drew off from it a ways and Mr. Jukes showed Uncle Jack where the bullet went and how and told Uncle Jack just precisely where he should aim to hit the stomach tar bottle, which was not truly at the stomach tar bottle exactly, and Mr. Jukes told how it would bust up and disappear and go off everywhere into thousands and thousands of tiny little pieces and then he licked his thumb and put some spit on the barrel sight and backed away as

Uncle Jack brought the rifle butt up firm against his shoulder and aimed along the bore and breathed in and breathed out and breathed in and breathed out just somewhat and then squeezed off the shot like his daddy had taught him with the trigger right square in his first finger joint, but even after the explosion, and Daddy said with a .50 caliber rifle it is an explosion mostly and not hardly a report, there was some smoke to get beat away and Uncle Jack's shoulder to get worked and adjusted some and also the stomach tar bottle to shoot at all over again on account of it was still where it had been, looking a little smaller for having been shot wide of and maybe a little belligerent too. So Uncle Jack prized out the empty casing with his fingernail, which was the method of prizing out empty casings with Mr. Jukes's particular Sharps . 50 caliber buffalo rifle, and inserted the second bullet like he'd got told to and laid some spit to the barrel sight like he'd got shown to and aimed this time where he figured maybe he ought to and breathed in and out like he knew how and squeezed like his daddy had taught him and then beat the smoke and adjusted his shoulder and looked at the bottle again.

"Has a good feel to it," Uncle Jack said.

And Mr. Jukes told him, "Yes sir."

"Potent," Uncle Jack said.

And Mr. Jukes told him, "Yes sir."

"Don't sight quite square," Uncle Jack said.

And Mr. Jukes told him, "Maybe not."

"But I like it fine," Uncle Jack said and took up his cartridge box and slid shut the lid of it while Mr. Jukes explained to him just how that rifle could make a bottle bust up and disappear and go off everywhere into thousands and thousands of tiny little pieces, just how he'd seen it do exactly that and Uncle Jack told how he did not doubt it but still did not load up and still did not fire a third time as he had decided in his own mind he would not fire but twice though after Mr. Hubert Jukes climbed onto his wagonseat and set off towards Ruffin Uncle Jack did snatch the stomach tar bottle from the fencepost top and did break it on a rock into pieces enough to suit him which was not thousands and thousands of tiny little ones exactly.

And Daddy said it had not got shot since that he knew of, since in this case being between the stomach tar bottle and the indian which was a space of some weeks, and Daddy said it followed then that the Sharps .50 caliber buffalo rifle had not got shot ever by Aunt Della who stood at the edge of a backstreet in Hartshorne Oklahoma cradling the loaded gun in her one hand and holding the spare cartridges in her other and at first just listening to the grunting and the butting and the swearing and the tumbling and the grappling about and then seeing some of it for her own self as Uncle Jack and the indian came out the open door together and across the plank sidewalk and pitched on into the street with Uncle Jack on the top straightoff and the indian on the bottom and the dust rising in little plumes and wisps all roundabout them as they kicked and clawed and scratched it up. Aunt Della did not see as she could help things much there at the outset and so just watched what butting there was to see and listened to what swearing and heard what groaning along with the leftover indians that collected and lingered in the doorway and the stray regular white men who came out from shops and down through alleys and stopped wherever they found to suit them so as to watch the proceedings mostly with their hands stuck snug into their back pockets, and Daddy said for a considerable spell there was not much to watch but the butting and there was not much to hear but the swearing and the groaning until the indian, by what Aunt Sister called your usual red man's wiles and ways, managed to lock his teeth onto the most of Uncle Jack's cowlick which Daddy said was not one of your crown of the head cowlicks but was instead one of your front of the head cowlicks that stood up just where the part commenced and as Uncle Jack could not guard his ears and guard his cowlick and continue to butt with much drive and effect to speak of he left himself vulnerable there at the part and the indian closed his teeth on a sizeable hank of hair just like he'd closed his teeth on the earflesh previously.

Daddy said Uncle Jack was affected straightoff and could not drive forward and could not draw back and instantaneously discovered how relatively pleasant the earbite had been in comparison to the hairbite which troubled and pained him most acutely and produced what Daddy called a wondrous outpouring of profanation which was not the sort of thing Aunt Sister would have allowed from the indian or the Sadler Montgomery or such as that but seemed well-suited to Uncle Jack as far as she could tell and she said, "Yes yes," and admired the phrase. According to Daddy that indian kind of chucked Uncle Jack around with his teeth, or anyhow that's what Daddy said he'd heard though he had not ever suspected a cowlick could stand much chucking around previously, but Daddy said he'd heard Uncle Jack had got chucked around and he'd heard that was what he'd got chucked around by and soon enough the indian was not on the bottom anymore but was kind of partway on the top and so let loose of the cowlick, Daddy said, or anyhow let loose of what cowlick was left to let loose of and laid his knee and shinbone up along Uncle Jack's rib-cage which Daddy said was not the kind of thing to promote much breathing to speak of and Daddy said that indian reached back into his boot, and Daddy said it was a soft leathery boot with thongs and beads and such dangling all roundabout it, and drew out from the inside of it a bonehandled knife with a long silvery blade that glinted and glistened in the sunlight, and Aunt Sister dabbed at her nose and said, "Yes yes," mostly on account of the glinting and the glistening and the general drama of the episode and then she added a word or two against indians as a species and Momma sort of threw in with her but insisted, just like in everything, there were your good indians too and Aunt Sister told her, "Alright, where?" and Momma said it was just like your negroes, said there were the bad ones but there were the good ones too and Aunt Sister told her, "Uh huh," which was truly a manner of abbreviation so Momma named off Sharena Moncrief that cleaned for us on Thursdays and Aunt Lavinia Goins that cleaned for Mrs. Phillip J. King and Memaw Harper and her brother's girl that took in washing together but Aunt Sister said they all drank liquor and all ran with men but Momma told her Aunt Lavinia did not drink liquor but Aunt Sister told her Aunt Lavinia ran with men that drank liquor which Aunt Sister said was worse and Momma asked her, "Alright, how?" and Aunt Sister told her it just was and then dabbed at her nose and looked at Momma all firm and irrefutable, and Daddy wondered at the both of them could they maybe get back to indians, maybe Cherokee indians, maybe one particular Cherokee indian with his knifeblade all glinting and glistening and Momma humphed like she did sometimes and Aunt Sister humphed like she did sometimes too and Daddy had said near about five words still on the knifeblade and still on the bone handle when Momma told Aunt Sister, "George Washington Carver," and Aunt Sister admitted while she had not known that one what Carvers she did know could not hardly be recommended and Momma told her back this one was not from what Carvers she did know and Daddy told the both of them at once, "Sweet creeping Jesus," and of a sudden negroes did not seem so extraordinarily crucial and Momma and Aunt Sister joined up together and pitched a fit.

And Daddy said he raised it into the air, raised it high above his head holding it overhand with the knuckles up and set himself to plunge it, Daddy said, set himself to drive it on into the road with Uncle Jack just a thing to get through on the way and Daddy said Uncle Jack squirmed and wrenched about but could not work his ribcage free or any of the rest of himself either, could not even draw off breath to swear with, and so watched the knifeblade glint and glisten and jerked and moved what parts of himself he could jerk and

move and fairly much waited to get stuck and skewered and generally done in which Daddy said was along about when Aunt Della saw the glinting and saw the glistening her own self and straightaway she raised the Sharps .50 caliber buffalo rifle and did not aim it, did not even lay spit to the sight, but just pointed the thing and shot it and her shoulder headed north with the rifle butt and she figured she'd best go on with it and so sailed for a few feet all laid out in the air and landed full on her backside athwart a rut in the road from where she could not see anything much but the sky and the tops of the storefronts either side of her, from where she certainly could not see the indian let loose of the knife with his fingers so as to take hold of his bullethole with them, but from where she could hear all the swearing and all the stomping around well enough, the swearing being Uncle Jack's and the stomping around being his and the indian's together, and then it was not just the sky and the storefront tops but Uncle Jack too standing over her with just his neck bent and the bonehandled knife in his fingers and he looked down at Aunt Della and Aunt Della looked up at him and Uncle Jack licked his lips and said it was a mite high and left of center and as best as he could figure it was a good thing that indian had not been a stomach tar bottle, and Aunt Della listened to him and pondered what she heard but did not find it held any sense for her and she said to Uncle Jack, "Daddy, get me up from here."

Three

They figured it was the kind of thing that stuck and stayed with a man, or anyhow Daddy said that's how Granddaddy figured it and that's how Granddaddy persuaded him to figure it too on account of the oath mostly, which Granddaddy said was not an item you could give a man the one day and draw back from him the next. Granddaddy said it was a solemn thing, said it was a sacred thing, said it did not expire ever but stuck and stayed with a man and did not quit him, so Daddy got made to believe it too, got made to believe what Granddaddy had already convinced himself of and consequently did not go with Granddaddy just to watch him and just to soothe him like Grandmomma figured Granddaddy needed watching and needed soothing but went on account of he'd subscribed to it, on account of he'd put in and joined up and like Granddaddy had bound himself to the notion that just that one little thing would make it all square and make it all proper which Daddy said he did not imagine he could have made anybody else believe but for Granddaddy and but for his own self and but for Mr. Clay Weathers too who Daddy said had been idling about the house likely waiting for something to believe in and take to.

He lived back off the old Stacy road, a considerable ways back off it in a pocket of trees and with his neighbors to the south of him and his neighbors to the north of him too right slam up on the blacktop which made it seem near about rural where he was though there was not any of it truly rural anymore, Daddy said, not any of it cultivated like before or grazed on but just cleared and subdivided and built atop of with room for a driveway to one side or the other and some bushes at the frontstoop and maybe a dogwood midway down the yard but not spacious anyhow and not hardly picturesque, Daddy said, like Mr. Clay Weathers's little frame house back in his pocket of trees with the long straight drive up to it that was not anything but ruts with a hump between them. He had raised hounds, not to get a living but just for the pleasure and worry of it, which was how come they'd sworn him when they did as they'd needed hounds and he'd had a pair handy, the one of them a saddle-brown black-spotted male called Sergeant Bilko and the other of them a pitch-black brown-spotted male called Lester, the first having got named off the radio and the second having got named off the late Mrs. Clay Weathers's middle brother that looked at folks like the dog looked at folks whenever anybody talked direct at him. Weren't any more breeding bitches even then on account of how the pleasure had given way mostly to the worry and Sergeant Bilko had the bursitis in his forelegs but could get along well enough so they gave him the oath, Daddy said, though not just him by himself but the whole bunch they'd collected together to give the oath to, which Daddy said was not even the first bunch and maybe not even the second either.

Daddy said it was a regular fullblown manhunt which everybody figured had commenced with a runaway Odom while they were searching and probing around for him, but Daddy said once you backed off from the thing some you could see plain enough that it had not commenced with the Odom really but just had got confused and complicated by him which was hardly his fault on account of he was dead through most of it, actually was dead before the first deputy got sworn in and the first hound put his nose to the dirt. He'd got sent up to Caledonia for aggravated assault. Daddy said that would be Ricky Odom of Matrimony Creek who was not to be confused with his cousin Donald Bud Odom of Wentworth who was the one that ended up at the Central Prison in Raleigh on account of Mr. H. Upton Mc-Graw's tobacco barn that Donald Bud Odom burnt to the ground though he had not aimed to really. He was after a cat, Daddy said, not even Mr. H. Upton McGraw's cat but just a regular wild cat and it happened to run into Mr. H. Upton McGraw's tobacco barn and climbed up among the rafters and the poles where Donald Bud Odom could not get at it and so he went ahead and set fire to the whole place as a manner of driving the cat back outside which did not seem a squanderous thing to him on account of it was not his barn anyway and on account of the smoke and the flames too did in fact drive the cat out through the little squat doorway and Donald Bud Odom shot it with a load of number 8 in his 20 gauge, mostly because he did not like cats much, or anyhow that was what defense he offered and what defense he got convicted on by Judge Benjamin Mortenson, Daddy said, who took a kind of hard view of your criminal element and so called the barn occupied without bothering to say was it President Truman or a wild cat but just plain occupied which meant life usually or as good as it anyhow.

But Daddy said it was not that Odom and was instead the Matrimony Creek one who did not burn anything and did not kill anything and did not hardly hurt anybody but somewhat and so got time at Caledonia on aggravated assault which Daddy said was near about as natural for an Odom as an egg at breakfast, Odoms being given to aggravation and being given to assault. And as Daddy figured it that Odom would have likely served out his time, which he recollected was not considerable or burdensome in a relative sort of way, and then got cut loose and been done with it but for a bond that developed there behind the prison fence. Daddy said it was not your natural and regular sort of bond but was just your kind of bond that did develop behind prison fences sometimes and was in this case a one-sided unrequited bond that rose up between the Matrimony Creek Odom and a particularly larcenous Garrity with the bulk of the affection falling to the Garrity and the bulk of the unrequiting falling to the Odom on account of the Odom could not much stomach and tolerate getting called cute and comely by any creature that had reason to shave more than its legs and armpits.

Daddy said the Garrity was not at all your dainty sort and likely the Odom would rather have gotten children by a horned toad than have any little piece of his own self touch any little piece of the Garrity but the Garrity had this way of laying his own flesh against the Odom's flesh even if it was just armskin or fingerskin or some such innocent part as that and the Odom would go all tight and sweaty of a sudden and call the Garrity the first abusive thing that came into his head which was generally some manner of fucker as that was the Odom's usual species of abuse which he did come to regret on account of how the Garrity ordinarily agreed with him. So they got on better than the Odom liked and got on worse than the Garrity wanted on account of the Garrity had a kind of ache in his heart for the Matrimony Creek Odom and, unfortunately, a kind of ache elsewhere too which was truly the troublesome ache as far as the Odom was concerned as he did not wish his orifices afflicted and enlarged and generally reamed out especially by the item the Garrity hauled roundabout to do such with and consequently there was palpable friction, Daddy called it, and constant tension and anguish too especially on the part of the Odom who commenced to stay puckered up all over every minute and hour of every day which Daddy said can drain and wear on a man and did drain and wear on the Odom who got sent with the Garrity on work detail to the potato field outside the prison fence where one of the guards watched the whole bunch of them from a chair under a pecan tree while the other guard drove the tractor that plowed up the potatoes that the prisoners collected in five-gallon buckets and dumped into gunny sacks, and Daddy said the Matrimony Creek Odom was just puckered like usual and just tense and maybe a little extra wary on account of how he was having to squat and stoop and who was behind him to see it when the Garrity caught his eye and showed to him a particularly deformed and elongated potato which the Garrity put to use straightaway as an implement in an elaborate and extraordinarily vivid dumbshow and Daddy said it had an appreciable impact on the Odom rightoff and sort of naturally compounded all the puckering and all the tension but somehow affected the wariness otherwise on account of when the Odom reached the end of the row he proceeded on out of the field and into the woods beyond, just walking like he'd walked the rows, and likely he'd have gotten away clean but for the Garrity who commenced to scream and wail.

Daddy said the guard under the pecan tree had not seemed asleep until he woke up and he did not know which way to run or who to shoot at straightoff and so ran most everywhere and shot in most every direction and then set in to chasing the

Garrity who'd set in to chasing the Odom and caught up with him right at the edge of the woods which the Garrity pointed and indicated into prior to wailing and screaming and stomping about. The guard on the tractor struck out for the prison gate to fetch the guards that would fetch the dogs and the guard at the treeline fired his shotgun randomly into the woods which did not seem to please the Garrity much who reached out and took hold of the barrel and suggested to the guard he might do with the shotgun what he had indicated to the Odom he might do with the potato and as the Garrity was a particularly sizeable and gruesome individual the guard considered his suggestion with special care and attention and found he was sympathetic and agreeable. Meantime of course the Matrimony Creek Odom had woke up to just what it was he was getting away from and had woke up to just how things would go with him if he did not get away entirely and so he commenced to move through the trees with some velocity and headed downslope towards the Neuse riverbed where he figured he could put off the hounds and lose the guards and where Daddy said he did in fact put off the hounds and lose the guards but not quite like he had anticipated he would.

Daddy said the Odom could not but beat around in water and it wasn't the kind of beating around that some people manage to stay afloat with but was essentially your purely counterproductive beating around which sunk him sooner than he would have got sunk otherwise. It had not looked a deep river from the bank and had not looked a fast one and was not generally deep or fast either but had got swelled somewhat with rain and so flowed like it usually did not and sort of snatched the Matrimony Creek Odom off his feet before he was in it good and carried him on out to midstream where he set in with his brand of stroking and his brand of kicking and went under fairly much straightaway. Daddy said he got jammed up between two rocks where the dogs couldn't smell him and the guards couldn't see him and the air couldn't get at him either which left the Matrimony Creek Odom well hid but dead from it and Daddy said he stayed stuck where he was while the guards and the dogs too combed the woods all roundabout him and the state troopers blocked off the nearby roads and the just regular people loaded their guns and sighted down the barrels of them, and word of the Odom went on the radio, Daddy said, and went in the newspapers and got spread around mouth to mouth so naturally people commenced to see him all over the place and the guards and the dogs and the troopers and the just regular people too chased him up the riverbank and chased him down the riverbank and chased him out from the riverbank in every conceivable direction and did not but just miss him every time and Daddy said as night fell scores of widowwomen throughout the county called relatives and sheriffs and troopers and told how the Matrimony Creek Odom had just peered in at them through their sidewindows and their backwindows and had seen them in their full slips and their housecoats like maybe that was what he'd got out from prison for.

Daddy said for a week straight they had him cornered somewhere at least twice a day but could not seem to latch on to him and the warden at Caledonia insisted it was because he was wily and sly and ruthless too, especially ruthless, the warden said, most particularly savage and lawless and hardened which Daddy said got more bullets put in more guns and got more barrels sighted down and just generally pitched up the whole business some now that he was not just escaped but was mean and was smart on top of it, and the troopers and the guards and the regular people all banded up together to look for him and hunted where they'd hunted already and hunted where they'd neglected to hunt but did not find any trace of him and, after a while, could not even figure where to look anymore which Daddy said was about when the Mimses, who would in this case be Ray Mims and his wife Lydia Lucas Mims all the way over in Stacey where nobody had even thought to look, had what discussion they did have there in the Mims bedroom with Ray Mims home early from the cotton mill on account of the nausea and with Lydia Lucas Mims stretched out atop the bedcovers naked mostly but for her right knee that was wearing all of her panties and her left elbow that was wearing all of her brassiere and Daddy said Ray Mims looked from his naked wife to the open window over by the dresser that the curtain-ends had got sucked out of and then back at his naked wife again who heaved and gasped some and told him for a second time, "Odom," which Daddy said suggested sly and wily and ruthless and savage and lawless just like the warden had suggested them but suggested hardened somehow otherwise.

Ray Mims and Lydia Lucas Mims lived with a whole load of Mimses out from the Stacey limits on a parcel of Mims property, anyhow lived within sight of a whole load of Mimses though in their own little house off from the main one which itself was circled around by an assortment of little houses full of other Mimses and their wives and their husbands and their children which left the big house for Ray Mims's granddaddy and grandmomma and their idiot daughter Lois Marie Mims who was considerably past fifty and wore frocks and shiny black shoes and had her hair cut like a boy's. Ray Mims's little house was slam up next to his brother Roy Mims's little house which was slam up next to their Uncle Lloyd Mims's little house and the three of them shared a Ford truck that each of them drove to the cotton mill when his shift came on so as to give it over to whoever it was that was coming off which would be Lloyd in the afternoon and Ray at midnight and Roy in the morning. Lloyd had married a Cummings that left him early on and took up with a Sugg so he lived in his little house with just his tomcat and just his whiskey and just the general filth and dishevelment the two of them together can bring about. Roy, that had served two hitches in the marines, could not see clear to marry himself and so just took up with women in a loose and unsanctified sort of way and generally kept after the same woman for a couple of months prior to getting a whiff of somebody else somewhere otherwise and turning his attention to her for a while. Roy was two years older than Ray and the two of them favored at the eyes but most everywhere else did not much look like relations on account of Ray could not get any bulk on him and did not ever have much in the way of healthful color while Roy possessed the kind of physique women generally suck air over. Daddy said he was all broad and strapping and ripply roundabout his stomach and had on the round of his left shoulder socket a colorful tattoo of an eagle with arrows in its one claw and serpents in its other and with its head turned up some and sideways towards a hairless mole that it seemed set to peck at.

Daddy said Roy and Ray and Lloyd too all seemed to get on well enough though they did not have much occasion to do otherwise as Lloyd was at work when Ray and Roy were at home and when Ray and Roy were at home Roy was usually asleep and hardly ever woke up until after Ray had left with the truck that Lloyd drove home in so as to have it there for Roy to drive to the mill when he came on to relieve Ray who drove the truck home for Lloyd to have to come on for Roy in. So they did not but pass each other, Daddy said, and were not but rarely all home and all awake and upright at one time and consequently did not get much news of each other and did not get much news of anything else either but through Lydia Lucas Mims that had Ray to talk to in the morning and Lloyd to talk to in the afternoon and Roy to talk to in the evening and most of the rest of the time the idiot Lois Marie Mims to talk to who generally liked to discuss everything all at once when she was not otherwise engaged with the bending and the twisting and the knotting up of her fingers.

Now Daddy said the Granddaddy Mims and the Grandmomma Mims did not much approve of Lydia Lucas Mims, or anyhow the Grandmomma Mims did not much approve of her and persuaded the Granddaddy Mims it would be in his best interest to not much approve of her either though Lydia Lucas Mims was truly not the sort of creature a man could fail to approve of at least somewhat just as she was truly not the sort of creature a woman could help but despise and vilify straightoff. Daddy said she was a comely woman, more comely far off than tight and up close but comely anyhow with long slender legs and long slender arms and a flat stomach and a little rounded behind and long black hair as thick as hog bristles. And Daddy said she was skilled and artful with what she had and kept her fingernails and her toenails fairly completely painted and kept the blusher on her cheeks and the bloodred gloss on her lips and maintained her eyelids at a kind of a glistening purple that Daddy said was like two sunsets seen through the bottom of a milk of magnesia bottle, and Daddy said she kind of highlighted and accentuated the whole business with the nightgowns she went roundabout in which Daddy said were generally of the sheer and lacy variety and most usually were cut clear up to the fender wells, Daddy called them.

So naturally she had a way with men, even had a way with the men she was not supposed to have a way with like Granddaddy Mims who tried to disapprove of her and tried not to say but ill and unseemly things about her but still got all silly and shitfaced anyhow, Daddy said, whenever she told a thing to him and threw back her hair and pinched up his cheek like she tended to. Of course Lloyd liked her well enough but she did not see awful much of Lloyd on account of he generally commenced with his Henry McKenna sedative as soon as he could get the glass out to take it in which left mostly just Ray in the mornings and just Roy in the evenings and just the idiot Lois Marie Mims the rest of the time so Daddy said it was not surprising really that things developed like they did develop as Lydia Lucas Mims was the sort of woman she was and possessed the kind of attributes she did possess which would be the legs and the arms and the stomach and the little rounded behind mostly and as Ray Mim's brother Roy was the kind of man he was and possessed the kind of attributes he did possess which would be the broad and the strapping and the ripply, Daddy said, in addition to a general tendency to touch and hold with his ten fingers whatever it might be he was not supposed to touch and hold. So they commenced with just talk, just plain talk of an evening at the eating table in Ray and Lydia Mims's little house with Lydia Lucas Mims in a chair on the one side of the table and Roy Mims in a chair on the other and just two houses down Lloyd Mims asleep in his chair with his cat in his lap and cathair in his liquor glass and across the yard in the big house Grandmomma Mims setting the kitchen to rights with Granddaddy Mims at the table still, a Maalox in his mouth and his face in the newspaper, and lurking somewhere roundabout the idiot Lois Marie Mims in her frock and her shiny shoes and off at the cotton mill working his shift Ray Mims who did not ever get home unexpected as he did not have the truck to get home in.

There was occasion then, Daddy said, and opportunity, Daddy said, and certainly disposition, Daddy said, but did not anything flare up straightaway and they just sat across the tabletop from each other and just talked about some things and just implied and suggested other things and just wondered over and envisioned more things still that they could not hardly bring themselves to talk about or even imply and suggest either but did not anything truly flare up for a considerable while which Daddy said was not at all scruples and not at all principles and was not truly ethics but in trace amounts and so was not meant to indicate goodliness and reserve on the part of Lydia Lucas Mims or goodliness and reserve on the part of Roy Mims too but instead indicated mostly a thing or two about Ray Mims who Daddy said was naturally decent and kind and compassionate, in fact so naturally decent and kind and compassionate that could not Roy Mims, who was a lout, and could not Lydia Lucas Mims, who was a harlot, bring themselves to sin against him, at least not for a spell. So Daddy said they had to reason the thing out and had to work their way roundabout it and had to do the whole of it with just the implying and just the suggesting and not in any way directly or flatout as somehow that seemed to them potentially more offensive than what fornicating they might manage in the bed, and Daddy said it was purely fornicating they were attempting to manage and was purely fornicating they were ever implying and were ever suggesting but Ray Mims was Roy Mims's own brother and he liked him well enough and Ray Mims was Lydia Lucas Mims's own husband and she liked him well enough too which gummed up the whole business at least somewhat on account of how Roy Mims and Lydia Lucas Mims could not decide just how it was that Ray Mims had what he was about to get coming to him and he did need to have it coming to him at least slightly and somewhat for Lydia Lucas Mims and Roy Mims in combination to inflict it upon him in the first place which Daddy said was not scruples and was not principles and was not hardly ethics but maybe only barely.

So they figured and wondered and speculated and it was Roy Mims who at last drew up and concluded what it was that got drawn up and concluded and that just in the course of the regular conversation and the regular implying and suggesting so as not to seem to have got figured and wondered and speculated at and especially so as not to seem to have got agreed upon, but it did get agreed upon anyhow, Daddy said, got agreed upon by Lydia Lucas Mims who heard it and by Roy Mims who thought it up and proposed it and together they concluded that it would all be proper and would all be just and fitting on account of how Ray Mims was simply too goddam nice for his own good, Roy Mims called it, and Lydia Lucas Mims nodded her head yes and said right behind him, "Nice," with her mouth turned all inside out like maybe it was leprosy or syphilis or some other manner of throughgoing rot and disease. Roy Mims, though still just implying and still just suggesting, told how there was people that did not have sufficient bite to them, that could not be mean and could not be spiteful even when nothing but meanness and spite would do and he feared his brother Ray was of the type, feared he was altogether too kind and too decent and too vulnerable and needed to get hardened, needed to get toughened, needed to get generally instructed, Roy Mims called it, and Lydia Lucas Mims nodded her head yes and said right behind him, "Instructed," and then laid her tongue out where she laid it sometimes.

But still they did not fornicate straightoff as they had not arrived at the fornicating part of it with merely the justification for fornicating. Daddy says it is not that simple a business but is instead a bristly and complicated procedure with a variety of phases to it, a whole assortment of ceremonies and rituals and whatnot that climax and culminate with the actual fornicating, or anyhow Daddy says that is the general view of it though he himself is of a mind that the actual fornicating is not truly the climax and culmination but maybe just the appendix or the afterword as what gets put where and worked how is not but the tiniest part of the whole undertaking since there is the sober talking firstoff and then the silly talking and then the extended giggling and then the touching with the fingertips though not of your private and indecent places but just your knees and your forearms and your cheeks and hands and such followed by the innocent kissing and then the deep and meaningful kissing and then the fully clothed rolling around anywhere but in a bed and then the partly clothed rolling around in a bed just sometimes though usually not and then the fullblown nakedness which does not always mean fornication but sometimes instead brings about just your grunting and your aggravation for the man and your sobbing and your apprehension for the woman and then maybe the fornication if there is to be fornication at all and Daddy says it is generally not anything extravagant but is just ordinarily a minute and a half of curious agitation followed by what seems to be interminable indifference. As for himself, Daddy says he has had better fun fishing and Daddy does not much like to fish.

However, Daddy says, there are men with inclinations otherwise just as there are women with inclinations otherwise too and while Roy Mims was one of the first Lydia Lucas Mims was one of the second which Daddy said simply meant that Roy Mims was of a sort that would follow his upright instrument off the edge of the earth and Lydia Lucas Mims was the sort that would point him the way. So they got on, Daddy said, got on from the first and likely knew straightoff even before the suggesting and the implying just how it was they would climax and culminate and consequently it was not so much a thing that got decided over the tabletop but was just a thing that got articulated there when at last it did get articulated which was after the implying and the suggesting and the justifying too and likely would not have happened just precisely when it did happen but for the sleeveless t-shirt which Daddy said was one of your regular gauzy sleeveless t-shirts with ribs down it, though truly it was not the t-shirt itself that did anything much but more what came out from it in the way of your broad and your strapping and your ripply parts and your eagle too with the arrows and the serpents and the mole to peck at. And Daddy said Lydia Mims just looked at what she saw there across the tabletop and just ran her tongue in and out like she did sometimes and just tried to talk about your regular sorts of things and just tried to think about most anything but what she was thinking about and she fought it off and fought it off and fought it off but got up anyhow and walked on around the table so as to come up on Roy Mims from behind and she laid her palms on his shoulders and then ran her fingertips down off them to his elbows and he reached back behind himself and took up two handfuls of her little rounded behind and Daddy said that was about the end of all the implying and the suggesting, and things progressed at a somewhat accelerated rate, Roy Mims being his type and Lydia Lucas Mims being hers.

Naturally there was confusion rightoff on account of how Roy Mims figured he'd best get up out of his chair just as Lydia

Lucas Mims decided she'd best sit down in it with him and so they kind of passed each other there at first but presently came together in a standing clinch and fairly much condensed and combined most all the ceremonies and most all the rituals, and Daddy said if there was any doubt left about the fornicating it got cleared up and resolved by Lydia Lucas Mims who drew back for a breath and expressed her sentiments of the matter in just two words which Daddy said were not the sorts of words you usually hear from women, especially not the first one and especially not with the second, but Daddy admitted that together they made for just precisely the kind of expression to do what articulating needed to be done. Anyhow it was the sort of thing Roy Mims could comprehend well enough and he set out in his own way to fulfill what Daddy called Lydia Lucas Mims's directive, that is he laid his hands and fingers on the high parts of her and laid his hands and fingers on the low parts of her and then ran them back and forth in between thereby causing considerable friction and prompting Lydia Lucas Mims to several extended outbursts of noisesome mouth-breathing.

He wanted to carry her off to the bedroom with drama and flair, wanted to whisk her up in his arms where she would lay all limp and quivery and proceed with her down the back hallway and into the bedroom where he intended to lay her ever so gently atop the bedcovers, but when he went to whisk her she got kind of turned around sideways and her legskin and his armskin caught against each other that way skin will sometimes and made for some general uneasiness that had to get corrected partway down the hall where he set her down so she could get turned and get situated and then whisked her up a second time but still she could not manage an easeful position and so got let to the floor and walked on into the bedroom and laid her own self atop the bedcovers which failed to diminish the atmosphere much partly on account of Lydia Lucas Mims's persistent noisesome mouthbreathing and partly on account of how she squirmed and writhed and pitched about on the bed which pretty much put the awkward whisking entirely out from Roy Mims's mind and he commenced a lively and energetic laying on of hands that pitched up the mouthbreathing some and pitched up the tossing about to the point where Lydia Lucas Mims and Roy Mims got all tangled and twisted up together and could not hardly tell who belonged to what pieces they had their fingers on. Then came the general disrobing, Daddy said, which was initiated by Lydia Lucas Mims who pulled and tugged at the sleeveless undershirt though not in a direction that could possibly remove it but just in the best direction she could manage which was kind of out and kind of down too and which served to suggest and served to imply to Roy Mims Lydia Lucas Mims's wishes and desires and so he took the thing off himself and thereby revealed the most of his broad and strapping and ripply torso that Lydia Lucas Mims commenced to touch straightaway and commenced to rake over with her fingertips. Roy Mims helped himself to the sheer lacy part of the nightgown which he drew up over Lydia Lucas Mims's head and managed to get entirely off her once he loosed her hair from the ornamental buttons at the neck and then he set in straightaway on the brassiere but Daddy said a brassiere is simply not the kind of thing a man can ever operate with much success and Roy Mims could as well have flown a jet as got the thing unhooked like it was meant and designed to get unhooked, so Lydia Lucas Mims reached back behind herself and did with just two fingers what Roy Mims could not manage with all of his and she let the strap off her right arm and slid the whole garment down around her left elbow which exposed what parts Roy Mims had intended to get exposed and he looked and gazed at them that way people tend to look and gaze out off a high place all stuck on and transfixed by the view.

Daddy said Lydia Lucas Mims decided there was an item she'd like to see herself and so she set in to fishing around for it which prompted an outburst of noisesome mouthbreathing on the part of Roy Mims who had not but panted a little previously and he squirmed some and writhed and pitched about himself as Lydia Lucas Mims unclasped the clasp and unzippered the zipper and finally found with her fingers what she'd been hunting for and straightaway Roy Mims struck out after the corresponding item and discovered that he could manipulate the frilly panties well enough on his own and slid them down entirely off the left leg and off the right leg to the knee anyhow and got joined in on his own noisesome mouthbreathing by Lydia Lucas Mims and together they kicked up quite a fuss which Daddy said was likely how come they did not hear the carmotor and which was likely how come they did not hear the cardoor and which was likely how come they did not hear the screen one either until it had bounced off the jamb one time, and of a sudden they left off mouthbreathing, left off nosebreathing too, left off most every variety of undertaking except for listening hard and did not even do that but ever so briefly which was long enough anyhow for Roy Mims and Lydia Lucas Mims as well to figure out what noise it was and who had made it and Roy Mims snatched his sleeveless t-shirt up off the floor and held his pants up with his closed fist as he hurled himself through the open window by the dresser, punching out the screen on the way and landing atop it in the sideyard.

It was foods in combination, Daddy said, foods that had mixed and mingled well enough there at first but then had got touched off and had got aggravated in the stomach sack like foods will sometimes, and Daddy mentioned red pepper and mentioned 7-Up. As he heard it there was pimento cheese mainly and mayonnaise, which Daddy said can ever be threatening and troublesome, along with Wise potato chips out of the green bag and sweet milk drunk from the carton which altogether was not a disharmonious combination, Daddy said, and settled into Ray Mims's stomach without much fuss and hardly any gas to speak of except from the milk every now and again, and as Daddy figured it, and Daddy is one to contemplate this sort of thing at some length as he is a constant sufferer himself, Ray Mims would not have got himself afflicted and so would not have done what he ended up doing if he had only not added to what food he'd eaten what he added to it which Daddy seemed to recollect was a Mounds bar, meaning of course chocolate and meaning of course coconut, and Daddy said the pimento cheese and the mayonnaise and the potato chips and the milk he had ingested at home reacted straightaway with the candy bar he ingested at the mill and the whole batch of items churned and fulminated, Daddy called it, in Ray Mims's stomach sack and just generally cut up in a chemical sort of way which inflicted upon Ray Mims measurable discomfort and agitation not to mention your general perspiration on the brow and along the lipline, so Ray Mims took leave of his machinery, Daddy said, and retired to the men's room back behind the water cooler where he stood before the lavatory and looked at his wan self in the mirror on account of he knew something was going to get discharged but could not decide from which end exactly and so was afraid to commit to sitting and was afraid to commit to kneeling which left just your regular standing around that he did before the sink so as to see in the mirror what he saw, and he did considerable peering at himself but did not anything much happen in the way of an evacuation and so he touched his own stomach and felt the heat of it and touched his own forehead and felt the heat of that and dabbed off with his shirttail what sweat he could dab off with it but did not anything come up and did not anything surge down and there were several times the doorknob jiggled from the outside as there were actually a number of other men in the mill with bladders and colons and such of their own to see to. So Ray Mims figured he'd best do what evacuating he was going to do and then clear out but he still could not determine should he sit or should he kneel which Daddy said is always a problem of a sort evacuationally speaking since a man cannot know what part of himself to grunt and strain against until he decides what direction it is his bile is heading for and Ray Mims simply could not decide and so he came out pretty much like he'd gone in and went back to his machine feeling pretty much like he'd felt and he stood there for a time churning and fulminating and perspiring too and tasting in his mouth that taste people usually taste when they do churn and fulminate and perspire and he jumped up off his feet a time or two and landed hard and jiggled himself around some so as to test his general fortitude and decided at last he did not have much fortitude to speak of on account of the bile that would not go up and would not go down but would just churn and would just fulminate.

He got a ride with the foreman's cousin that was going towards Stacey anyhow and that dropped him off two feet from his own door there in the Mims compound, and Daddy said likely Ray Mims would have heard what there was to hear, which would be the noisesome mouthbreathing and the general pop and give of the bedsprings, but was just listening at his bad stomach instead like some men listen at their bad hearts and so did not ever hear anything really in the way of the moaning and in the way of the pitching about and actually did not truly hear the windowscreen get knocked out like it got knocked out but instead was just jarred and stirred by the noise of it without knowing what noise it was and he proceeded on down the hallway to the bedroom and stopped there at the foot of the bed where he set himself to speak of the churning and speak of the fulminating but when he lifted his head and dropped his chin would not any words come out on account of the brassiere roundabout the elbow and the panties roundabout the knee and the naked parts all in between which was not what he had expected and was not what he had anticipated and so he did not say nausea and did not say bile and did not say Mounds bar like he had planned to but just stood with his jaw all sagged down and got told, "Odom," by Lydia Lucas Mims who had read the Chronicle and who had listened to the radio and so had known what to say without hardly having to think to say it, and Ray Mims looked at his wife's naked parts and looked at her brassiere and at her panties prior to gazing off from her to the dresser and beyond that to the open window with the curtainends sucked out it, and when at last he did tell her something back what he told her back was, "Odom?" and Lydia Lucas Mims worked her arms and worked her legs too in a tortured and agonized sort of way and said to her husband, "Ravaged," and grew all pouty and puckered roundabout the mouth and all teary and forlorn roundabout the eyes.

Daddy said the nausea cleared up straightaway but the churning and the fulminating lingered and persisted though somewhat redirected and somewhat changed and altered and Ray Mims grew hot and grew wild and grew agitated and then grew profane on top of all of it which would be the part of the business Roy Mims got wind of from his little house next door where he was wondering just how he would keep from getting murdered since from what he could hear it seemed to him that murdered was what he was going to have to keep from getting, and murdered was likely what he would have gotten had Ray Mims bothered to suspect it was maybe not the Odom but maybe somebody otherwise which he did not bother to suspect on account of what regard he had for Lydia Lucas Mims that maybe she did not wholly rate as she was not decent and was not kind and was not hardly nice like Ray Mims was decent and kind and nice but was just ordinary, Daddy said, or maybe even less than ordinary as she had circulated widely before her and Ray Mims ever took up together and Daddy suspected she had turned over her odometer at least one time which did not seem to bother Ray Mims much who claimed her and had her for his own self not because nobody else would but surely after most everybody else already had and he knew near about all she'd done and knew near about everybody she'd done it with but absolved her and forgave her and went ahead and adored her anyhow as he was decent and was kind and was nice and did not have much meanness or spite to him which let him think just Odom when he got told Odom and let him think just Odom when he got told Ravaged and let him think just Odom all throughout after until he found but otherwise which he would not believe even then until he could not help but do it.

So he fetched out from the coatcloset his shotgun and pumped it one time so as to send a shell into the chamber and covered Lydia Lucas Mims over with the bedsheet while he excused himself to her and charged on out the door and around the corner of the house down towards his brother's place and Roy Mims watched him through a side window and wondered what chances there were that he would not have some part of himself separated from the rest of himself and distributed haphazardly roundabout the room which, once he thought about it, seemed altogether too likely and probable to suit him and so he lifted the grate off from the main floorduct in the hall and was commencing to climb down into the crawlspace with the furnace when Ray Mims, that had charged out from his own house and down through his sideyard, charged on into his brother's house and came up on Roy Mims once he'd got mostly under the floorboards and was attempting to pull the grate into place behind him and Ray Mims stopped short there in the hallway with the shotgun laid athwart himself at an angle and did not say anything straightoff and did not do anything straightoff either thereby providing Roy Mims with the opportunity to recalculate and refigure and rewonder at his chances of not getting somehow separated and of not getting somehow distributed and he found altogether more likelihood and altogether more probability and so decided to speak out in his own defense, decided to call upon brotherly love and decided to call upon basic human decency and decided to call upon whatever else might pop into his head when he needed a thing to call upon and he wet his lips with what spit he could muster to wet them with and drew what air he could manage to draw and brought himself somewhat out of the ducthole and said to his brother, "Hi," and Daddy said it had a kind of earnestness to it that anymore you don't find much in your basic salutations.

Ray Mims, by way of adjusting and easing himself, swung round the shotgun and sort of pointed it at Roy Mims on the way to laying the barrel across his shoulder and Daddy said Roy Mims vanished entirely into the ducthole and commenced to talk and jabber with appreciable velocity but between the furnace and the reaches of the crawlspace the words did not but bounce around beneath the floorboards mostly and so would not have been truly comprehensible to Ray Mims even if he had been attempting to truly comprehend them which apparently he was not judging from how he had set in to talking himself along about when Roy Mims did and as Roy Mims's kind of talk was your earnest and sincere and apologetic sort of talk, which Daddy said does not generally call for much volume, he got drowned out almost straightaway by Ray Mims who was engaging in your more irate and incensed sort of talk that needs a little pitch to it. So Ray Mims did not hear Roy Mims at all and Roy Mims did not hear Ray Mims rightoff but did commence to pay some attention to him along about "purely dead son-of-a-bitch" which arrived at the furnace whole and intact and as Roy Mims figured quite naturally he was the son-of-a-bitch that was about to get purely dead he set himself to fill up his ears with his pointing fingers on account of how he had not ever cared much for shotgun blasts even outside in the open and surely did not think he could tolerate one in a ducthole, but before he could lay his fingers where he intended to lay them he heard himself get told, "Odom," and heard himself get told a vile thing after it and he raised a little piece of his head up out of the ducthole and said to Ray Mims, "Odom?" and said to Ray Mims the vile thing back, and Ray Mims told him, "Ravaged," and told him what and and told him just by whom exactly, and Roy Mims said back, "Odom," again like it had properties to it, strange and altogether mystical properties and he came out of the ducthole up to his collarbone.

"That loose crik Odom," Ray Mims said and he explained somewhat about the brassiere and somewhat about the panties though not so much as to be indecent and then proceeded to the window and the punched-out windowscreen.

And Roy Mims looked up out of the ducthole not at Ray Mims directly but mostly just into the vacant air and he said, "Ravaged," like maybe it had properties too and Ray Mims set about describing ravaged to him though in a delicate sort of way and he again mentioned what and again mentioned by whom and then said the vile thing once more prior to covering the both of his eyes with his free hand and laying his head back some, and Daddy said Roy Mims came out of the ducthole to the waist and beat his fist one time on the floorboards. "Let's get that bastard," he said and then he added the vile thing himself and climbed out of the hole entirely.

They roused up Lloyd firstoff who was quite completely sedated and so required some considerable rousing up which included not just your shouting and your shaking about but a partial waterbath on top of it and eventually Lloyd did in fact come around but for the longest time he did not seem to know but the word "what?" that came out from his mouth whenever he managed to open it and Ray Mims and Roy Mims together told him about the loose Matrimony Creek Odom and told him what had got done and to whom and Lloyd Mims told them back, "What?" and looked all roundabout himself with his eyes as wide open as they could get and he looked at the walls and at the ceiling and at the floor too and particularly at Ray Mims with his shotgun and at Roy Mims with his .30/06 over his folded arm and a pistol in his pants and he opened his mouth and asked the both of them, "What?" pretty much like he'd asked them it all along and they yanked him up out from his soft chair and turned him loose to cast and amble across the room and he had not taken three full strides when he stepped direct on the cat that squirted out from under his foot like a soapcake.

Then it was the three of them all bristling with guns and all bulging with cartridges that crossed the yard to the big house and came up on Granddaddy Mims still at the table in the kitchen with the white Maalox residue in the corners of his mouth and his nose near about touching the Chronicle at the crease of it and they told him what had got done and by whom and he looked at Grandmomma Mims over by the sink who looked back at him there at the table and did not anybody speak for a time except Lois Marie Mims off in the dining room who chanted to herself in her raspy idiot voice, and finally when words did get said again it was just one of them and it was just Granddaddy Mims that said it. "Odom?" And he folded the paper, laid it on the tabletop, and crossed his arms over himself and did not anybody speak again for a time except Lois Marie Mims off in the dining room who had not ever stopped. Then Roy Mims repeated all of it so as to save Ray Mims the pain of having to, repeated all of it with appreciable vigor and zeal and Granddaddy Mims pondered what it was he had heard once he had heard it and looked across the kitchen at Grandmomma Mims who stood with her posterior to the sink and her face all turned down in disapproval but Granddaddy Mims told her anyhow, "Call the law," and he grunted hard one time and got up on his feet so as to fetch his own rifle and so as to beat the bushes roundabout.

Daddy said they did not turn up anything straightoff because straightoff was not enough of them to turn up anything much as it was only the Mimses and as it was only Sheriff Browner too who interviewed Lydia Lucas Mims and got told where the Odom had come in and how and got showed where the Odom had gone out and got suggested and implied to him what the Odom had managed in the meantime which Lydia Lucas Mims could not bring herself to speak of but in a tiny whispery voice that tended to give out in a regular sort of way and so the sheriff got the thing in little snatches and pieces and laid it all together for himself but still did not anybody get deputized straightoff so it was only the Mimses, who did not find anything anyway, and only the sheriff himself and only his regular deputy who was at that time a Pender along with Mr. Demitt and Mr. Fontain that mostly just clogged intersections at funerals. And Daddy said Sheriff Browner and his regular deputy Mr. Pender too dropped by Matrimony Creek and interviewed an assortment of your unjailed Odoms but did not find out anything much they were looking to find out and did not find out anything much they were not looking to find out either but in fact almost came away knowing less than they'd gone in with as the Matrimony Creek Odoms did not tell them anything much and certainly did not tell them anything true and verifiable out of what little they did tell them so the sheriff and his deputy Mr. Pender went knowing just somewhat and came back knowing less and that wrong. Consequently, then, they did not have much idea where the loose Odom might be as he could have been just about anywhere so the sheriff did not consider it feasible to actively look for him everywhere they would have to, which would be in fact everywhere really and no special where in particular, and he explained his predicament to the Mimses commencing with Granddaddy Mims who took it well enough and Lloyd Mims who took it even better and then Roy Mims who was agreeable in an enthusiastic son of way afterwhich the sheriff explained to Ray and Lydia Lucas Mims together how he could not look everywhere and would not even try to, which Lydia Lucas Mims did not hardly twitch at but Ray Mims got hot of a sudden and irate and indignant and reminded the sheriff what had got done and to whom and then suggested how he himself would find the Odom and suggested what he himself would do to him.

But somehow, Daddy said, Ray Mims did not find the Odom and so could not do to him what he had suggested he would and Daddy figured likely would not have anybody else bothered to look for him either, especially not the great mass and throng of people that did eventually look for him when he did in fact get looked for if the Odom himself had not struck again and so caused things to get stirred and pitched up like they did get stirred and did get pitched and Daddy said it was an Underwood this time which was how come precisely, as there are your Mimses in this world and then there are your Underwoods too. They were Presbyterians primarily, practicing God-fearing Presbyterians and business people otherwise and the Democrats had elected one of their relations lieutenant governor in 1892 which could not any of them seem to forget even for the least little moment. Daddy said they had all married well, Daddy said it was a habit with Underwoods to marry well like it was a habit with some people to bathe and eat, and it seemed to Daddy that the Underwood men had got the best of the bargain as the Underwood men tended to be prettier than the Underwood women primarily on account of the Underwood nose which Daddy insisted was noble on a man but just conspicuous on a woman, and Daddy said did not but all the Underwoods seem happy in marriage in that way people of money and prominence tend to seem happy in marriage which is not ever anything open and giddy but just your basic blank and civil harmony that people like Underwoods call bliss. And as best as Daddy recollected, it was Mr. Robert Rosemont Underwood and his wife, Mrs. Sophia Jane Womack Underwood, that were the most noticeably blank and civil and so likely the most utterly blissful of any of the remaining bulk of Underwoods and there was a considerable bulk of them.

They lived on the golf course back behind the seventh green though not quite far enough back behind the seventh green judging from the golf balls that hit on the patio and bounced off the iron furniture and off the siding and off the paneled door and through the windows every now and again which Daddy said was not on account of bad golf really but mostly on account of poor club selection which in turn was due almost exclusively to how the limbs hung roundabout the green and how the shade got thrown which together suggested and implied a kind of depth and distance that the hole did not truly have much of as it was only no yards from the back of the tee to the middle of the green and that not entirely accurate but likely overshot too. So would not anybody ever hit a wedge, Daddy said, and would not hardly anybody ever hit a 9 iron except those people that should have hit a wedge which left not but everybody else to hit something otherwise that the most of them surely would not have hit if they'd known where it would go and what it would do when it got there. Daddy said he had even played the thing himself one time back when him and Momma thought they might like golf as an alternative to sitting on the glider, and as best as Daddy could recall Momma hit a driver on account of it was from a tee after all and Momma figured that was all you could hit from a tee and Daddy said she would have probably sent her ball on through the Underwoods' living room if she had hit it flush and square but Momma did not have the kind of swing that ever produced any manner of flush and square contact and so instead she cleared the roadside to the left in the direction of the clubhouse and rolled her shot up on the practice green. Daddy seemed to remember he hit a 3 iron on account of he had thrown up some grass and had watched it blow back behind him which somehow told Daddy 3 iron and he poised himself over the ball, which Momma said was the best part of Daddy's swing, and drew back his club altogether sedately prior to making a kind of frantic and exasperated lunge forward with his hips first and then the club after like maybe he was trying to kill a pit viper, and Daddy said it was perhaps the most majestic shot he ever struck and sailed high up into the air in the precise direction of the flagstick and Daddy recalled how he had even followed through on the thing and then let the clubshaft slip down through his fingers like a real golfer does and he watched it climb and watched it sail and waited for it to drop onto the green and maybe even spin backwards some but it did not seem disposed to drop on the green and he waited for it to drop into the sandtrap just behind the green but it did not seem disposed to drop there either so he waited for it to hit on the patio and rattle around amongst the iron furniture but it did not seem disposed to do that and appeared set instead to bust out the most of the upstairs bay window which Daddy said was when he closed his eyes and which Daddy figured was when it sailed on over the roof of the house and out of sight.

So, with his own experience to gauge by, Daddy figured it must have been about a 7 iron or maybe a firm 8 as it cleared the patio wall on the fly and landed direct in a planterbox full of petunias which Mrs. Sophia Jane Womack Underwood was not sitting dangerously close to but was sitting somewhat close to anyhow in her gauzy robe and with an open Chronicle on her lap. Daddy said it was a Morgan from Lawsonville that hit it and he ran with his club in his hand direct from the tee, on past the green, and up onto the Underwood patio to see after what harm and what damage he'd done and to apologize and make amends for it and he did not realize Mrs. Underwood was in her gauzy bathrobe until he got right up on her which gave him another thing to be sorry about aside from the golf ball and the general scare of it so he talked at Mrs. Underwood and apologized at her without seeming to look at her too as she did not appear to be dressed for looking at especially by a man she was not acquainted with who had put her in somehow measurable danger with a golf club and a Titleist in combination. But she took it all well enough, Daddy said, even though she was not a woman known for taking things well but then the Morgan from Lawsonville was fairly young and sturdy and cut an altogether handsome figure and Daddy said they spoke at first just of the golfball and just of the petunias too and then of the golf-hole itself as a prickly item and then of the sport of golf in general and then of golfers themselves in a vague and circumstantial sort of way that led eventually just to people in the ordinary sense and just to plain talk after the ordinary fashion and Daddy said naturally as they were speaking to one another anyhow they went ahead and looked at one another too at first just the way people usually look at one another when they speak but after a spell they commenced to look at each other more that way men and women do look at each other sometimes, most especially those men and women that shouldn't, and Daddy said all it needed was music, violins in particular, so as to set off the whole business which might have seemed regular enough from down on the green or back at the tee but actually was not hardly anything blank and was not hardly anything civil about it.

Mr. Robert Underwood traveled roundabout the state on behalf of the shirt factory below Wentworth that most all the Underwoods had an interest in and share of, and while he did not actually sell the shirts himself—he carried a man with him to do that—he paid attention as to how they were laid out and displayed and undertook to cultivate, Daddy called it, your store managers and such who were not hardly ever much match for an Underwood of the 1892 lieutenant governor Underwoods. And as best as Daddy recollected it was along about a Thursday evening two or three days after what had happened to Lydia Lucas Mims had happened to her, or anyhow two or three days after she had done what she did which she still was calling ravaged and still was calling brutalized as well when she could think to, that Mr. Robert Rosemont Underwood who was supposed to be displaying and laying out and cultivating in Statesville stepped in through his sidedoor and shut it hard behind him, hard enough anyhow to rouse up Mrs. Sophia Jane Womack Underwood and to rouse up the Lawsonville Morgan too who had not been sleeping exactly, Daddy said, but had been occupied and distracted doing what it was it had become pretty much a habit with them to do in the course of the few weeks after the first time they did it, and Daddy said the Lawsonville Morgan did not know straightoff should he scamper roundabout the room collecting his clothes and then leap with them to his death out the window or maybe just crawl under the covers down to the foot of the bed and make like a lumpy place and as he could not decide directly which would be better or if anything otherwise would suit he commenced to do most everything he thought of as he thought of it which meant scampering and meant crawling and meant just your agitated leaping about all of which combined together did not make for truly anything much in the way of escape and in the way of evasion so Mrs. Sophia Jane Womack Underwood collected up the Lawsonville Morgan's socks and shoes and trousers and shirt and undershorts along with the Lawsonville Morgan himself and shut them all up in the clothesdoset afterwhich she overturned the chair by the dresser and dumped out her jewelbox on the carpet and threw open the window by the bed and then laid and sprawled herself across the mattress in an ungainly sort of way and as she was a woman that read the Chronicle and as she was a woman that heard the radio she did not hesitate when at last Mr. Robert Rosemont Underwood stepped into the bedroom to tell him flatout, "Odom," and then groaned somewhat so as to suggest ravaged and so as to suggest brutalized.

And it was a full-fledged manhunt, Daddy said, full-fledged straightaway on account of how Mr. Robert Rosemont Underwood would not hardly consider any partly fledged sort of undertaking and Daddy said of a sudden there were deputies everywhere and guns and bullets and hard talk as a single Underwood had considerably more to bring to bear than a whole slew of Mimses could possibly muster, and there was a nurse too, Daddy said, a nurse for Mrs. Sophia Jane Womack Underwood who had after all got traumatized in the course of getting ravaged and brutalized and so did suffer and did need nursing but did not hardly suffer so much as the Lawsonville Morgan who was fifteen hours naked in the coatcloset that he could not but squat in. However he did make off eventually and made off clean, Daddy said, so there was not but the Odom to look for and not but most every male in the county to look for him, and Daddy said Sheriff Browner organized the whole thing with the aid of various Underwoods who had notions of where the Odom might be as they had closely considered where they would be if they were the Odom, so deputy squads and deputy platoons and just your regular unordained mobs as well commenced to poke around wherever it seemed likely the

Odom might be which was most places truly and everywhere else too, and at the request of the sheriff who was acting upon the request of the prime Underwood the warden at Caledonia mailed to city hall an article of the Odom's clothing which turned out to be a single white sock with two green stripes at the top of it, so then there were not just the men and the guns and the bullets and the hard talk but there were the hounds too including Sergeant Bilko and including Lester and Daddy said as Mr. Clay Weathers told it he was three full days in every woods and thicket and scraggly-assed stand of trees roundabout and did not scare up but chiggers and ticks and one altogether unfortunate copperhead that got shot to pieces by twenty men at once.

But they kept looking nonetheless, Daddy said and got joined in the hunt by a handful of state troopers that parked their silver Chevrolets on the roadsides and stood canted against the fenders of them with their arms crossed over themselves so as to be handy and apparent and support the effort in almost a purely spiritual sort of way, and Daddy said the enthusiasm commenced to flag after a general fashion when did not anybody find the Odom or even any evidence of him, commenced to flag that is for everybody but the Underwoods and everybody but the Mimses who maintained a zeal for the hunt, especially Robert Rosemont Underwood and especially Ray Mims as they had the most to be zealous about, but could not sheer manpower and dogpower and zeal too cause the Odom to get found and discovered though he did in fact get found and did in fact get discovered but Daddy said it was not manpower or dogpower or zeal either that did it but just a number 10 hook on 60-pound testline. Daddy said it was a colored Scott that was doing the casting and doing the reeling and he threw out his line upstream and let the current carry it down amongst the rocks where he figured some fish might be lurking and swimming about and some fish were, Daddy said, as the colored Scott had brought in two catfish and a river eel before he ever snagged the Odom but had not the catfish and certainly had not the eel pulled like the Odom pulled and resisted like the Odom resisted and naturally straightaway the colored Scott figured him for a carp and if not a carp then some manner of gar maybe though he was not rigged for gar and did not hardly catch them when he was and there at first when the Odom just pulled and just resisted and did not move whatsoever he figured maybe a treelimb too but then he did in fact budge him some and move him some and worked the Odom out into the flow where the current pushed him upwards and he broke surface which likely would have suggested and would have indicated to the Scott that the Odom was what he turned out to be but just for how he broke surface exactly and wearing what which would be back foremost and which would be a gray prison skivvy. So naturally there at the first sight of the Odom the colored Scott did not think human and did not think corpse but thought instead porpoise and thought instead shark and said just precisely what he might have said if he had thought human and had thought corpse which was "Sweet Jesus!" two times right atop each other and the colored Scott's brother downstream a ways grew curious and came up the bank and the colored Scott's boy upstream a ways grew curious too and came down the bank and the three of them together watched the Matrimony Creek Odom float and bob on the water and the colored Scott, with his foot set against a rock and his back foot set against an exposed treeroot, said, "Whale maybe," and got told back by his brother, "Maybe," and the two of them together looked at the colored Scott's boy that went to community college and the colored Scott's boy pondered the thing himself and then told his daddy and told his uncle too, "Sea manatee," which did not either one of them seem much impressed by and taken with.

The three of them together landed the Odom when at last he did get landed with the colored Scott on the pole and his brother and his boy on the line and still they did not think human and did not think corpse for a considerable while but thought instead fritters and thought instead fishsteaks right up until they had him in and right up until they rolled him over and so saw for certain that it was not a shark or a porpoise or a sea manatee either but just a dead swole-up white man which could not the colored Scott or his brother or his boy get much enthused about. And Daddy said the word got back directly, got back to Sheriff Browner who did not let it out like some folks would have on account of he comprehended and on account of he understood just what a dead Odom still in plain sight of Caledonia meant to a Mims and meant to an Underwood and so he kept it to himself, or anyhow kept it to himself but for his deputy the Pender that was to tell just the troopers so as to get shed of them but told the Fontain too and told the Demitt and then it was fairly much out altogether, and Mr. Clay Weathers said it got to them in a cow pasture which was not just him and not just his dogs and not just regular people too but all four Mimses as well, and Mr. Clay Weathers said while it did not get to them all at once it did spread and did circulate to everybody else first and then to the Mimses themselves at last, or anyhow got told to the Granddaddy Mims that told it to Lloyd Mims and told it to Roy Mims and finally told it to Ray Mims too who said direct back to his granddaddy, "No," and just behind it said No again to everybody else.

As best as Daddy recollected did not anybody know what the Underwood did and what the Underwood said, anyhow not anybody but Sheriff Browner that called him in to tell him and could not the mayor's secretary say but how he came out just like he went in which was all pure Underwood with the blazer buttoned shut and the tie-knot straight and the silk handkerchief out from the breastpocket corner foremost and she said he told her, "Good afternoon," going out just like he'd told her, "Good afternoon," coming in, and as far as Daddy knew did not the Underwood ever say anything and did not the Underwood ever do anything and did not the Underwood ever seem perturbed or distressed at all by what talk went around on the topic of what he should have said and on the topic of what he should have done, but then Daddy insisted that saying nothing and doing nothing and ignoring everything is what civilized means sometimes aside from bland and aside from harmonious, so they went on after like they'd gone on before and did not people even tell each other Whore and did not people even tell each other Slut on account of who they were and on account of what they had and on account of how they did not either one let on that the Whore and the Slut too had ever suited or even could conceivably suit, so it all got put off otherwise, Daddy said, got put off on the Mimses as they were just Mimses after all and were not given to saying nothing and were not given to doing nothing and did not hardly have much of anything that did not most everybody else have more of, so Lydia Lucas Mims got the bulk of the hard talk, got the Whore and got the Slut too which did not either one run contrary to the lacy nightgowns and the painted nails and the flat stomach and the little round behind and the thick black hair and the blush and the gloss and the eyeshade and people said she got beat for it, said she got thrashed and slapped roundabout, but she did not ever get beat really or thrashed or even slapped either as Daddy said Ray Mims was not the sort for pounding a woman, was not hardly the sort for pounding a man, and did not truly want to get even and did not truly want to get vented but mostly just wanted to get apologized at and could not have that even on account of Lydia Lucas Mims was not the sort to be sorry for anything she had not done purely by accident and somehow could not any of this be made out as accidental.

Of course as she would not tell who and would not tell how often, Ray Mims figured everybody straightoff and figured all the time which did not hardly contradict the consensus roundabout and Daddy imagined he would not have ever found out who and would not have ever found out how little really that he did not ever believe anyhow if he had not done what he did in his granddaddy's house across his grand-daddy's linoleum, which was stomp mostly and wave his arms somewhat, and if he had not said what he said which was

almost exclusively "Odom" in a riled and peevish sort of way
and from off in the dining room with her legs and her shiny
shoes drawn up beneath her frock the idiot Lois Marie Mims
chanted what she'd chanted previously and pulled at and
twisted her fingers and Ray Mims stomped back in the
direction he'd come from and said "Odom" again like he'd said
it before and the idiot Lois Marie Mims chanted what she'd
chanted and pulled at and twisted her fingers like she generally
did and actually got heard this time though did not get
understood straightoff and Ray Mims stopped still on the
linoleum just at the dining room doorway and said out of the
kitchen and into the dining room "Odom" again and got
chanted at directly which he actually made out but could not
truly believe it was what it was and so he looked at his
granddaddy there at the table and looked at his grandmomma
there at the sink and stepped on into the dining room proper
with him behind him and her behind him too and he squatted
on his heels just before the idiot Lois Marie Mims who looked
up at him with her eyes all empty like usual and her lips all
twitchy and her fingers all twisted and pulled at and Ray Mims
dropped his chin some and said to her, "Odom," and
straightoff she told him back, "roymims roymims roy-mims,"
like she'd been saying it all along.

So Granddaddy figured it was a thing that stuck and stayed on
account of it was sworn and sworn things did not ever but stick
and did not ever but stay and Daddy said he looked for a gap in
it but truly could not find one and so threw in and held with
Granddaddy who explained to Mr. Clay Weathers about the
oath and about the general potency of it which Mr. Clay
Weathers did not have any quarrel with either as he was not
particularly bound up with engagements and such and so
guessed he could stand to hunt down a nigger carthief, and

Daddy said as they did not know where to go precisely they
decided they would just go everywhere, or anyhow
Granddaddy decided they would just go everywhere on

account of as Granddaddy saw it his job was to do the deciding and the directing and Daddy's job was to do the driving and Mr. Clay Weathers's job was just to sit in the backseat and be sworn until he got called upon for purposes otherwise. So they rode around, Daddy said, and stopped to talk most every time they saw somebody to stop and talk at which at first was white folks almost exclusively and Granddaddy would tell about the Bel Air and would tell about the lye scars and would tell about the green shirt and the brown pants and the black sneakers with the laces out and the tongues flapping and could not anybody but tell him back just who it was and could not anybody but tell him back just where to find him and sometimes they did come across just who they were set on and sometimes he was in fact lye-scarred and green-shirted and brown-pantsed and black-sneakered but somehow he was not ever the nigger they wanted and most usually had several dozen relations on hand to swear just what nigger he was and just what nigger he wasn't.

Consequently, then, they did not find but everybody and not any of them who they were after so far as Granddaddy and Daddy and Mr. Clay Weathers too could tell, and Daddy said they drove near about clean to Danville before they turned around and even then did not drive straight back but headed off in a westerly sort of way and then an easterly sort of way and then a westerly sort of way again and Granddaddy and Mr. Clay Weathers looked for Bel Airs and saw some too but not ever the right Bel Air and saw some Impalas that they thought were Bel Airs and Mr. Clay Weathers mistook a Pontiac but just the one time on account of Granddaddy let him know straight-out what little use he had for a man that could not tell a Chevrolet from most anything otherwise, so then it was just Granddaddy that looked for Bel Airs and just Mr. Clay Weathers that told him Yes sir after he'd found one but were not hardly any of them two-tone like Aunt Sister's was two-tone and were not any of them at all your dark turquoise and your light aquamarine like Aunt Sister's was dark turquoise and was light aquamarine too, and Daddy said they zigged and they zagged and Granddaddy spied what Bel Airs there were to get spied and Mr. Clay Weathers confirmed them and directly they rolled on into Neely proper still having seen but just the type and not yet the item itself, and they tried the alleyways and tried the oiled back-roads and Daddy said he'd gone most everywhere he cared to go when Granddaddy told him, "Sumter's," like Daddy was expecting to get told Sumter's and Daddy told Granddaddy back, "Alright, chief," like he still says alright mostly.

Sumter's was what we called all of it, is what we call all of it still, even them too that live there and know it is something otherwise as Sumter's is just the block store in the middle of it that is not even Sumter's anymore but is Colemont's now and has not been Sumter's since back when it was white all over and not black anywhere at all though hardly ever even average white, Daddy said, but lowly white always and then black somewhat and then black altogether, and by that time it was already truly not Sumter's as Mr. Sumter that had got his living from loafbread and canned meat and milk and cigarettes and Pepsi-Colas had succumbed already to the angina before it was even black mostly and the place got emptied and the windows got boarded up and the door got bolted fast but it stayed Sumter's nonetheless as that was what the tin sign out front still said it was, and then there was the Colemont after who was a black Colemont that bought the building and the little slip of property it sat on and he unboarded it and unlocked it and cleaned it and painted it and called it Colemont's where he sold loafbread and canned meat and milk and cigarettes and Pepsi-Colas as well as those parts of the chicken and those parts of the pig that do not but colored people eat. But it stayed Sumter's anyhow, Daddy said, stayed Sumter's not just with the white people that had reason for it but with the colored people too as there is ever a general reluctance roundabout, Daddy explained it, to let loose of most any item whether or not it has passed completely and quite irrevocably from the face of the earth which Daddy says is why Aunt Sister can stand out front of the homeplace that do not even Younts live in anymore and point across the yard to where the new road goes and tell about the apple tree that would be in the westerly lane if it still was at all, tell how she would climb it as a little girl and sit high up in the top of it and then she just stares and gapes where the road goes like she is seeing limbs and blossoms and leaves and maybe fruit too when there is nothing but wavy air rising off the asphalt.

So it was still Sumter's even actually after it wasn't anymore, and it was all Sumter's, blocks away it was Sumter's even though there were other stores with other names on them aside from the Colemont's that had been the Sumter's firstoff and there was not but one way to get into it and was not but one way to get out of it either which was down B Street that could not anybody explain the how come of as there was not an A Street and was not a C Street either, was not any alphabetical streets other than the B one and did not anybody know was it meant to be alphabetical anyhow or was it meant to stand for a thing though Bill Ed Myrick jr. said his daddy told him it stood for bastards on account of how most everybody that lived on it was one. It started up on Dundee Avenue off the boulevard and dropped steeply down to the creekbottom and then climbed just as steeply after and did not level off until Colemont's grocery, beyond which it proceeded flat for about a quarter mile and then just quit at the trainyard with only a steel barricade and a honeysuckle thicket between the pavement and the tracks. Of course there were sideroads every halfblock along the way and roads off them and roads off them too but did not any of them go anywhere much and did not any of them lead out to anywhere except in so much as they all went back to B Street that went up to Dundee Avenue off the boulevard.

I have not ever been down into Sumter's but a few times and then mostly with Daddy in Momma's Buick so as to drop off

Shareena Moncrief that would iron for Momma alternate Thursdays and she did not live awful far up from the creek, not even so far as Colemont's, and in a neat little house with paint on it and shutters that even white people could have lived in but maybe for the gardenias in the yard and the statuary where the sidewalk met the curb, and she would not ever get but partway out the backseat when her dog that was half German shepherd and half something squat and low and otherwise ill-bred would charge out from under the house and writhe all about her feet rolling and snapping and wailing too like any dog anywhere. And I do not recall that I saw the other one the first time or even the second time either, maybe on account of the dog and maybe on account of he just did not move much and did not say anything hardly but the third time I saw him plain enough, him that Shareena Moncrief called her boarder and him that Daddy and that Momma called her boarder too though saying it not like Shareena Moncrief did but more like it was not even English really, and he stood up out from his iron chair on the porch and said "Hello" I suppose but with such a low deep voice that did not but the vibration of it get to us and I asked Shareena Moncrief out the carwindow, "Who is that?" and Daddy pinched me on the knee with all five of his fingers and told her "Good evening" like he always did and got told back "Night" like always too.

And then there was the time without Daddy and without Shareena Moncrief and without even the Buick to be closed up and safe in which was the time we walked in and which was the time we walked back out again because Jack Vestal said we wouldn't, said he wouldn't either not even for fifty dollars and a chance to see and touch Angela Kirstan Little's naked parts which he surely would have got the chance to do if only he'd been old enough to do it as most everybody else old enough to do it got the chance, but me and Marcus Bowles together told him we didn't need fifty dollars and didn't need our fingers on anybody's naked parts but would walk in and would walk out for nothing, would walk clean to the trainyard and would turn around and come clean back and Jack Vestal said we wouldn't either so then we had to and Marcus Bowles set down his books at the B Street and Dundee Avenue signpost and I set mine down on top of them and Jack Vestal told us a thing he'd heard colored people do to white boys and Marcus Bowles told him back he was a dumb fuck and a pissant and said there wasn't anything different about colored people but that they weren't white but did not any of us believe that, not even Marcus Bowles that said it.

So Jack Vestal told us, "Go on then," and flung his arm towards the creekbottom and we told him back, "Alright," but did not go on exactly, not straightaway anyhow, and made out to fix ourselves and made out to prepare for what it was we were setting to do and Jack Vestal said we should each carry honeysuckle back or not any of it would count for anything and Marcus Bowles told him he wasn't hauling any shrubbery out for anybody and asked Jack Vestal if he wanted honeysuckle why didn't he go fetch it his own self and Jack Vestal said he weren't crazed like some people and then sat down on the Dundee Avenue curb and spat between his legs and made out not to watch us when we finally went like we knew we had to and Marcus Bowles told me out from the side of his mouth not to but walk like I usually walked and not to but seem like I usually seemed and he picked up a rock from out of the road and threw it towards the creek and I picked up a rock and threw it somewhere too.

There was not much to the thing there at first as there weren't but vacant properties the Dundee Avenue side of the creek and not but vacant properties the other side for a ways either but then beyond there was houses just purely, houses piled one on another both sides up the slope and on over the crest out of sight and some of them neat houses like Shareena Moncrief's with lively paint and ornamental items in the yard but most of them not, not neat, not painted, not in any way ornamental but just plain wood on top of plain dirt and with the sashes flung up and the doors standing open and not a screen-wire anywhere in sight. But it was not the general shabbiness that put us off and caused us to taste in our mouths what we tasted and caused us to figure and anticipate what we figured and what we anticipated; we were through the cotton mill village every day and it was beyond shabbiness even and beyond filth too and clean to squalor but they were all white people like we were white people, maybe dirtier and sorrier and meaner too but white and that counted for something as we could always make out why they would do what they did since they were not but us beat back and near about defeated and we were not but them some small quarter down deep, but it was different with the colored people whose daddies and granddaddies and great-granddaddies had come from a place we did not know and had endured a thing we could not comprehend and so we could not but guess at them and could not but puzzle over them and could not but be mystified and confounded in the face of how they would act towards us like they acted and do to each other what they did and consequently there is not any observation a white man ever makes that he is more sure of than the one he makes about a negro that is not ever with particular phrases or particular words or particular noises either but is instead with the entire head that gets worked first one way and then the other.

Marcus Bowles was quite utterly convinced that we were going to perish and I was becoming persuaded and we decided he should make up some sort of escape plan as he had an uncle that had been a marine in Korea and Marcus Bowles said did not just anybody get to be a marine but only your individuals specially bred for it, like Bowleses, he told me, and so we both voted and he won and thought on the thing for a spell prior to announcing that we should split up whenever that pack of negroes with knives and sticks that we were certain was going to chase us did in fact commence to and he said as best as he could figure it I should head east, and he pointed north across the road, while he would run west, and he pointed south to the other side, and then the both of us would circle down south, and he pointed east towards the creekbed, and wade on out into a wide spot so as to discourage the negroes who Marcus Bowles reasoned probably would not be up to getting wet just for two white boys as they are not hardly ever up for getting wet anyhow, and Marcus Bowles said when the coast was clear he would whistle like a bullfinch, and he puckered his lips and let out a kind of a noise through them, and we would rendezvous, he called it, at the Dundee Avenue B Street signpost where he figured the two of us together could pummel Jack Vestal as it was mostly his fault anyway. And somehow the plan spunked us up appreciably and we felt braver and surer and more resolved and there was even brief talk of actually carrying back honeysuckle but shortly, as we came up out of the creekbottom, we gained that part of the hill where the houses set in and saw our first actual negroes in the chairs on the porches and saw their dogs too that came out from under the front-stairs and around the corners from the sideyards and down off the porchplanks themselves to bark at us like our dogs come out to bark at them.

Straightoff it was just old negroes with not anything to do otherwise but sit and look and fan at themselves and did not any of them tell us even Hello like Shareena Moncrief's boarder had told Hello to me and to Daddy and did not many of them bother to look at us much past glancing not even Uncle Hobart that passed the schoolyard daily and hardly managed three or four steps at the time without saying, "Well, hey there," to most anybody that eyed him through the fence. He just sat like the rest of them sat and just fanned like the rest of them fanned and just considered and perused everything there was to consider and peruse but me and but Marcus Bowles that had both figured we bore some viewing and bore some scrutiny but did not get hardly any of either, and then there was the little negroes too, little shirtless and shoeless negroes playing in the yards and playing at the curbing though not generally with any sort of item that had meant to be played with but just kitchen ladles and glass bottles and sticks and car motor parts and such and while they did not talk at us either they looked at us plain enough, stood up and just gaped at us outright and Marcus Bowles pointed at one little lightskinned boy whose head was all covered over with pieces of string and lint and general trash and he said to me mostly it looked like somebody had took him up by the ankles and dusted the floor with him and then Marcus Bowles laughed that laugh of his that is always too loud anywhere but was near about deafening in the middle of niggertown and a woman back in the house we were just then in front of hollered, "Come on," and all the children together went which left just me and just Marcus Bowles and just the dogs to bark and yap at us and I told Marcus Bowles that if somehow I died and he didn't, if somehow I got beat and cut to pieces and he made off clean, then I would come back for him all bloody in the night and scare and terrify him so bad he'd piss himself and so leave nothing behind but a wetspot on the bedsheet and Marcus Bowles did not laugh this time likely on account of how my eyes had got so big and my face had gone so white that maybe I looked like I meant it. I know I surely felt like I meant it, especially the beat and cut to pieces part and Marcus Bowles told me "Remember" in a low breathy voice and then he pointed his finger at me and said "East" and pointed his finger at himself and said "West" but I do not recall being much soothed on account of it.

Of course did not but both of us want to turn and run which naturally would have drawn the dogs but we figured we could manage dogs well enough as we understood and comprehended dogs at least somewhat but then there was Jack Vestal too and there was what he would say and there was who he would tell and there was how he would tell it, so we kept on like we'd set out and walked not much towards the one curb and not much towards the other either but fairly completely in the pure middle of the road and crested the hill together near about in lockstep and Lord I do recall how there was not anything but negroes, negroes not on porches in chairs with

paperfans but negroes loose everywhere with the great bulk of
them out front of Colemont's just standing and just hooting
and talking and apparently just waiting for something to get
distracted and diverted by like maybe two white boys with not
any good sense much, and we figured everything would just
leave off at once, all the hooting and all the talking and all the
general ruckus negroes can make, and we would get looked at
for a spell and then would get beat and would get cut up likely
by the big ones primarily that had those arms and had those
shoulders that seemed just special made for tearing folks apart
at the joints, but everything did not leave off, did not hardly
anything leave off actually, and Marcus Bowles set in with his
breathy voice to tell me what I thought would be East and what
I thought would be West all over again but was plain
"Godalmighty" instead which soothed me even less somehow.
And then we both together saw the poolhall that we both
together had forgotten was even there in the first place and we
both together drew air and both together let it out again and
both together fully prepared to perish on account of how we
both together had recalled all at once and of a sudden how one
man had already got killed in the poolhall, near about a white
man, or anyhow the ambulance driver that was a Battle had
taken him for a white man and had let out that that was what
he was and he was stabbed and killed by a colored woman that
did not get hunted down for several days on account of Sheriff
Browner and Deputy Burton could not discover who she was
truly as she went by Betty sometimes and went by Laona
sometimes and went by K. T. the rest of the time and naturally
had not ever troubled herself with a last name for any of them
as she had so many first ones to keep up with, but they found
her eventually anyhow which was along about when it got out
that the stabbed and killed man was not white after all but just
high yellow which cooled off the Baptists considerably and Mr.
H. Monroe Aycock wrote up the whole thing in the Chronicle
and told just what had happened and just why so that could
not anybody understand it, anyhow not anybody but Daddy
who said it was surely just the failure of the one to pay the

other and the failure of the other to stand for it, but did not the why of it and did not truly the who of it come to mind at the sight of the poolhall and we just thought stabbed mostly and just thought killed behind it and I set myself to tell Marcus Bowles Godalmighty but he was already telling it to me again.

That was surely where the worst ones were, partly outside in the dooryard and partly inside roundabout the tables and along the walls, and Marcus Bowles suggested to me out the side of his mouth that I should not look at any of them which was likely as fine and as true a gem of advice as has ever been given but of course like most fine and true gems of advice it was not anything I could manage and so I did look and Marcus Bowles looked too once he saw I was looking and we saw the ones outside and saw the ones inside and there together grew so entirely certain that they would all fall in on us and kill us that maybe we were a little disappointed when they didn't, didn't not just not fall in on us and not just not kill us but didn't even see us back as far as we could tell. I mean they looked, or anyhow turned their faces on us, but did not seem much impressed or affected, did not truly seem impressed or affected at all like maybe we weren't white or actually like maybe we just weren't, like maybe they picked up their heads and like maybe they looked but did not see but the pavement and the curbing beyond it and the housefront beyond that and certainly not two white boys, not two boys at all, not anything but the empty road and the empty gutter and the empy air all roundabout and it did not seem to me any fine sensation to get looked at and not to get seen not even by the men that I figured would beat me and would cut me to pieces as it takes at least something for spite and for venom, not awful much but something anyhow, and they would not even give us that but just saw the empty road and just saw the empty gutter and maybe as well the blank housefront beyond them and surely not Marcus Bowles and surely not me either.

So I did not ever run east and Marcus Bowles did not ever run west and we did not ever meet up and rendezvous in the creekbed but just proceeded direct to the barricade where we snatched a sprig of honeysuckle apiece out from the thicket and turned round to go back where we'd come from and again we just walked and did not but get barked at by the dogs and did not but get looked at by the little colored children and did not but get ignored every way otherwise and I do not recollect we ever ran any except down the hill to the creekbottom because it was easier to let loose and run than to hold back and walk and then we stopped and got our breath so as not to seem tired for Jack Vestal and so as not to seem worked up and agitated and we walked together up the hill to Dundee Avenue with our honeysuckle behind our ears and we did not see that Jack Vestal had gone home until we got near about to the signpost and we did not see that he had done what he did with our books until we had reviled and had cursed him some and so we reviled and cursed him some more and Marcus Bowles, on account of his long arms, was the one that laid flush on his stomach and I was the one that held his legs while he hung partway down in the sewer and fetched back everything he could reach which was everything Jack Vestal had put in the sewer in the first place but for my ballpoint pen that wrote in two colors and we decided we would go straight to Jack Vestal's house and we would drag Jack Vestal into his front yard and Marcus Bowles would sit on him while I gave him indian burns but our enthusiasm piddled out almost straightaway as it was just a pen after all and just Jack Vestal too.

But Daddy said it was different then, not different down deep but different seeming anyhow as not much had got said then that would get said and not much had got done then that would get done and so it was just us and just them not opposed like would come but not ever united either and so just apart with them doing for us what it was they did and us doing for them what it was we did back and all of it decent and all of it

civil and gracious and kind but not any of it different truly
except for the decent and the civil and the gracious and the
kind that at last fell away when things did in fact get said and
did in fact get done, but Daddy said just the seeming was
enough somehow, at least was enough for us that did not want
to ponder just who they were and just what they'd come for
and so took what goodwill we could get even if it was not
goodwill really and gave back what goodwill we could give back
even if that was not goodwill really either, but Daddy said it
was all enough somehow which was why they could go to
Sumter's, three white men together in a Buick towards
eveningtime and one of them not just regular and not just
ordinary but purely enraged and hunting down what he would
not call but a nigger even there circled roundabout by what he
would not call but niggertown, and Daddy said Mr. Clay
Weathers slunked and slid down in the backseat near about so
far as to be sitting on his shoulderblades and Granddaddy laid
his elbow out the sidewindow and looked at the people on the
porches and the people in the yards and the people lingering at
the street and every now and again he would observe a thing,
Daddy said, most usually a niggery thing that was meant for
just Daddy and for just Mr. Clay Weathers but went
everywhere nonetheless on account of how Granddaddy said it
and on account of what direction he said it in.

Daddy said there was a regular colored throng out front of
Cole-mont's which was not anything much like your white
throngs that collect at fires and wrecks and such as a colored
throng does not generally pay much attention to anything but
itself, and Daddy said there was considerable boiling and
moving about though he could not tell on account of what
exactly and considerable laughing from the men and
considerable shrieking from the women, what Daddy called
your earpiercing windowbusting variety of shrieking that
colored women just seem to have a natural inclination for, and
Daddy said did not any of it leave off with the arrival of the
Buick that he brought direct up to the curbing so Granddaddy

could lay out the sidewindow and say whatever it was he might feel inclined to say which Daddy said he was a little anxious to hear himself and which Mr. Clay Weathers seemed just as anxious to keep from hearing judging from how he slunked and slid on top of what slunking and sliding he'd done previously and so fairly much ended up sitting on the back of his head. But straightoff, Daddy said, Granddaddy did not let out anything offensive, did not let out anything at all, but just studied the throng in all of its appreciable diversity, Daddy called it, and got fairly soundly ignored by most everybody but for one particular Broadnax who had some ponderous girth and bulk to her and Daddy said she looked all baldfaced direct at Granddaddy and said to him, "What you looking at?" loud enough for it to get heard but not so loud so as to seem to have got asked outright, and Daddy said Granddaddy just looked at her back and looked roundabout at everybody else he could see plain and still did not get but ignored even after he'd hollered "Robert" one time, even after he'd hollered "Robert Gotner" just behind it, and then he grew truly agitated, Daddy said, and so hollered out the window louder than he'd hollered Robert the first time and Robert Gotner the second time too, "One a you boys come over here," and Daddy said Mr. Clay Weathers disappeared altogether onto the floorboard but Granddaddy just hung out the window like he'd been hanging out it and waited to get approached like he did get approached by a man Daddy could not see but the midsection of and so could not tell had he come on account of the summons or maybe just to hoist up the Buick and turn it topunder.

Granddaddy told him just plain "Robert Gotner" again and Daddy said got told a thing back that could not Daddy understand on account of where he was, he figured, clean across the Buick but could not

Granddaddy seem to get ahold of it either and so he said "Robert Gotner" a second time with appreciable emphasis throughout it and got told another thing, or maybe the same

thing all over, Daddy could not tell this time either and
Granddaddy did not seem much enlightened himself and so
said just "Robert Gotner" yet again like maybe it was his axe
and that colored man the tree he was bound to fell with it and
before Granddaddy could get told another low and
indecipherable thing, which might have been the same thing
all along, he fired off two more Robert Gotners headlong so as
to attempt with sheer volume and magnitude what he could
not seem to succeed at otherwise and Daddy said of a sudden
the colored man's midsection became the colored man's
backside and he receded fairly much like he had approached
without bothering to indicate was he going to fetch who it was
Granddaddy wanted him to fetch or was he just plain going
and Granddaddy kept himself partway out the window like
he'd been and watched the throng open up for that colored
man and then close up behind him and Daddy said, "Chief,"
and Granddaddy told him, "Hold on," and stayed just like he
was and Daddy said, "Chief," again and Granddaddy just laid
out where he'd been laying like he'd been doing it and did not
tell anything back to Daddy that said, "Chief," a third time and
then added to it, "Let's leave this place," and while
Granddaddy did not but stay where he was and did not but
look where he'd been looking Daddy felt himself get kicked or
kneed or elbowed or some such in the kidneys and heard
himself get told, "Yes sir Yes sir," by Mr. Clay Weathers that
raised up just long enough to say it and then went back to
where he'd been.

But the Gotner did come out, Daddy said, and out of all the
Gotners it could be, as there were considerable Gotners most
everywhere, it was in fact the right Gotner, was even the right
Robert Gotner out of the half dozen Robert Gotners it could
have been which would be the Robert Gotner that helped
Granddaddy with the shrubbery and helped Granddaddy with
the yard and even took lunch most times with Grandmomma
and Granddaddy too right there at the breakfast room table,
but Daddy said he did not look much like that Robert Gotner

straightoff, anyhow did not look much like that Robert Gotner when the throng parted and let him out of it on account of how he held himself there at the first with his shoulders bowed back and his chin raised and canted to one side and with his arms swinging loose and free and his feet stepping not like they usually stepped but kind of higher and kind of firmer too and Daddy said he was all set to wonder at Granddaddy just what in the world had Robert Gotner come to be possessed by when of a sudden he commenced to change and commenced to transform and alter, or anyhow commenced to shrink up and dwindle and draw in his various parts so that by the time he arrived at the side-window he was not all bowed and canted and lively most everywhere but was just Robert Gotner like usual and Granddaddy said to him, "Robert," and Robert Gotner crouched at the doorpanel and said back, "Yes sir, Mr. Buck."

And Daddy said Granddaddy told about the Bel Air and where it had got gone and who by and he dwelled some on the nigger that took it which he even called the nigger that took it direct at Robert Gotner which got Daddy a little kidney kicking and elbowing and kneeing but did not seem to affect Robert Gotner himself in a measurable sort of way and he told Granddaddy, "Yes sir, Mr. Buck," most every time there was an occasion for it and some times otherwise as well, and Granddaddy repeated the lye scars part and the green shirt part and the brown pants part and the black laceless sneakers part too so as to have it all sink in and have it all stay and then Granddaddy said a few sharp words against colored people in general but apologized for it straightaway and explained to Robert Gotner how he was simply down on niggers just then and wanted to know did Robert Gotner see how come and got told back, "Yes sir, Mr. Buck," that way Robert Gotner always said Yes sir and always said Mr. Buck even when he should have said some other thing some other how. And then he got dismissed, Daddy said, or anyhow got waved at by the back of Grand-daddy's hand and got told, "Go on," and said back just "Yes sir, Mr. Buck" and stood up and kind of plain slunked away, Daddy said, kind of plain slunked on back to the throng where, just before he stepped into it and vanished entirely from sight, he got all bowed and inflated and lively and canted too and Granddaddy watched him get gone from there at the sidewindow and said, "Niggers," and blew a breath and Daddy said he blew a breath himself which seemed Yes sir enough at the time and Mr. Clay Weathers raised up off the floorboard far enough to see over the frontseatback and asked Granddaddy in a sort of an anxious and scratchy whispher, "Whereabouts?"

ii

Aunt Sister told him he left it out, insisted he left it out, and said she would not stand for it to get left out as it was a crucial thing, but Daddy told her back he hadn't left it out at all on account of it hadn't ever been and so wasn't in the first place, but Aunt Sister insisted all over again and when Aunt Sister set in to insisting she did not hardly ever retreat from it which Daddy knew and which Momma knew and which even I knew too and then she dabbed at her nose with her little ball of frayed and partly decomposed powerblue Kleenex and she commenced to say a word about how she liked a thing to be true and liked a thing to be honest and above all liked a thing to be wholly accurate that Aunt Sister said akerate and did not get corrected on since Momma and Daddy and even me too knew her mouth could not mold it and could not give it out as anything but akerate anyhow. But Daddy stayed with his side of it and said it hadn't ever been and said it wasn't, and Aunt Sister wondered back how would he know anyhow since weren't any of them his people in the first place but through the vows that Aunt Sister said was not any bond much to speak of, not so potent as to make a Benfield a Yount or a Yount a Benfield or a Hoover a Roosevelt, she said, and Daddy told her he had eyes and he had ears and he knew what he'd seen and he knew what he'd heard and Aunt Sister told him back she had all the parts he had and could do with hers everything he could do with his and she said she was privy anyway, privy when he wasn't and couldn't have been, privy when there wasn't even a him to be privy, and she said she'd seen everything he'd seen and more and she said she'd heard everything he'd heard and more of that too, and Daddy told her, "Alright," though not the way he says it most times to Momma and to everybody else too but instead the way he does not hardly ever say it anywhere to anybody but Aunt Sister which is the way that serves as preface and the way that serves as preamble to what he is setting himself to tell when he says it, and Momma, that had not uttered anything much and had not but twitched some in her chair, heard what Alright it was exactly and so told Daddy straightaway, "Louis," all soft and flexible like she will every now and again and then she told Aunt Sister, "Sister," pretty much the same way and said to the both of them, "Now really," all quick and light and Aunt Sister laid her Kleenex to her noseholes and ignored Momma and while Daddy did not move or shift in any appreciable sort of way he managed to make it clear enough that he was ignoring Momma too, and Aunt Sister said to him, "You are muleheaded, Louis Benfield," and Daddy told her back, "No ma'm, just akerate."

Now Aunt Sister is a woman to grow offended like dead flesh is a thing to grow mortified which is to say it does not take but one hard item, one moderately fiery exchange to wound and pierce her and once she is wounded and once she is pierced she does not hardly ever recover but most usually perishes absolutely, and Daddy's akerate had hit her fairly much full on as she was particularly sensitive about what noises her mouth came out with when she was attempting to manufacture sounds otherwise and so she watched herself unclump her Kleenex with all eight of her fingers and both her thumbs and then watched herself clump it again and she said, "Well," all breathy and forlorn down her dressfront and Momma kind of hissed at Daddy and kind of made like to kick him and jerked her head at Aunt Sister and hissed and jerked her head at Aunt

Sister again and Daddy saw just what he'd best do which was what he generally saw only after he'd done whatever he usually did and he said to Aunt Sister, "Now Sister," in a tone that was for him pure sweetness but just plain and regular in anybody otherwise, "just what is it you want and where is it you want it to go?"

And Aunt Sister did not tell him anything back for a spell but just gaped across at the far wall like maybe it had a window to see out of which it didn't and when she did in fact fix herself to talk she did not say anything but "No" straightoff and that not one of your firm and negative noes but just a kind of nothankyou no give out all sad and breathy and direct down the dressfront like the Well before it.

And Daddy said to her again, "Now Sister," which approached near about soft and gentle even for regular people. "It just didn't strike me as suitable," he told her.

"We're capable," Aunt Sister told him back all lively of a sudden. "We're even given to it," she insisted. "Aren't we given to it, Inez?" And Momma kind of wagged her head roundabout in a way that did not mean but yes and no and everything else too.

"But not like some people," Daddy said. "You'll admit not like some people."

"Not like Messicks maybe," Aunt Sister said, "all sloppy and weepy most always, but like regular people anyhow."

And Daddy told her, "Alright, alright the women," and he waved his hand like he was surrendering most every surrenderable item.

"Of course the women," Aunt Sister said, "but most all the men too."

"Which?" Daddy wanted to know and was not much pure sweetness detectable any longer. "Certainly not your daddy."

And Aunt Sister drew herself all stiff and upright or anyhow as stiff and upright as she could get without actually standing and she said, "My daddy could be the gentlest man on the face of God's earth when the mood came over him."

"Your daddy? The chief's daddy? The same daddy?"

"Yes sir, him," Aunt Sister said and pulled at and kneaded her Kleenex with her fingertips.

And Daddy said back, "Now this is the man that shot Mrs. Robertson's cat off her own fence in her own yard?"

"He had call to," Aunt Sister told him.

"Something about catshit I recollect," Daddy said and Momma looked direct through him that way she does sometimes.

"Well hadn't you ever done any regrettable thing your own self, Louis Benfield?" Aunt Sister wanted to know and Daddy thought on it for a time and told her he guessed he had but then didn't anybody ever figure him for the gentlest man on the face of God's earth and Aunt Sister shot back how it was a tomcat anyhow and left more of what cats most usually leave and right there at the doorstep near about where it could get smelled and tracked in and she said anyway Daddy did not know Robertsons like she knew Robertsons and did not know hardly how it was like she knew how it was and Daddy said, "Maybe not," like he said Alright usually and shifted things over some to Aunt Sister's first cousin Jarrod Yount that had fairly thoroughly stomped a Methodist tenor on account of "Jesus Christ Is Risen Today" that the Methodist tenor sang the alleluias to in an objectionable sort of way, objectionable anyhow to a Yount, Daddy said, and so the tenor got called out and the matter got discussed and the discussion got punctuated and Daddy said all of it on Easter Sunday right there in the graveled sanctuary lot, but Aunt Sister and Momma together threw in against him and told him and me too how Jarrod had a special problem that the both of them said Daddy knew already and told him and me too how Jarrod had not got medicated for it, not until after that Easter anyhow, which the both of them said Daddy knew already too, and Momma told us it was a special problem, Momma told us it was chemical, and then she looked at Aunt Sister so as to allow her to say yes, special, and to say yes, chemical, but while Aunt Sister did not say special and did not say chemical either she did say yes and then she said, "Passion," like it was a thing she'd up and found once she'd forgotten she was even looking for it.

"Lunacy more like it," Daddy told her.

And Aunt Sister said back, "No sir," and said back, "Passion. Wrongheaded maybe but still it."

And Daddy told her, "Alright," not that way that means no and not that way that means less than no really but more that way that means so fucking what which only comes out as Alright for Momma and for Aunt Sister but exits otherwise most every place elsewhere.

"Misdirected," Aunt Sister said. "Wild and unmedicated," Aunt Sister said, "but there anyhow and not just Jarrod that hit the tenor and not just Daddy that killed the cat but the whole line up and the whole line down too and not hardly always wild and not hardly always misdirected but right sometimes and good and kind and gentle and sweet and just, well just passion like people most always mean it when it gets said."

"Who in, exactly?" Daddy wanted to know.

217

"The bunch of us," Aunt Sister told him.

"Who in, exactly?" Daddy insisted.

And Aunt Sister told him, "Well, William Elsworth Yount for one." "The chief?" Daddy asked her back.

And Aunt Sister told him, "Yes sir, himself."

"William Elsworth Buck Yount?" Daddy wanted to know.

"Him, Louis," Aunt Sister said.

"Alright then tell it," Daddy told her, "and just exactly like it was with not anything touched or altered or swung roundabout to suit you." "I can tell a thing square," Aunt Sister said all drawn up and stiff

of a sudden. "You might mosttimes drive the car, Louis Benfield, but you don't own the highway."

"Tell it then," Daddy said. "Tell it."

"Alright," Aunt Sister said back and then closed all but the pointing finger of her right hand roundabout her powderblue Kleenex and shook the whole item as near to Daddy's face as she could manage to shake it, "I will," she said, "I purely will."

Aunt Sister did not recollect it was the winter of 19 and 57, she called it, did not recollect straightoff just what winter it was exactly but knew well enough it was not in fact the winter of 19 and 57 because 19 and 57 was the year of the big snow and Aunt Sister did not suppose she would misplace a thing that happened sometime in the year of the big snow, especially not in the winter of the big snow, especially not in a snow itself which likely might have been the big snow if she had not recollected that it wasn't, and she asked Momma and she asked Daddy too didn't they remember the big snow January ninth, she said, 19 and 57 and they both told her they did and Aunt Sister looked off at the ceiling somewhat and said at it, "Full eight inches, eight and a half places," and Daddy told her, "six and three quarters tops," and Aunt Sister did not leave off looking at the ceiling but just said back at it, "Six and three quarters in town, eight, eight and a half places otherwise. Seems almost nine at the homeplace. Yes, I do recollect near about it. Ten up against the shed," and then once she'd just looked some and had not talked for a spell she said, "No, not that one, not 19 and 57, but previous to it sometime, sometime previous to it."

And she thought 19 and 55 for a spell, December of 19 and 55 which she recollected as extraordinarily mild for December but with maybe some snow and with maybe some sleet and with some freezing rain especially and she pondered 19 and 55 and pondered the mild December and the weather of it and Momma seemed to recall how they had buried Mr. Jennings W. Hayes in December of 19 and 55 and so Aunt Sister pondered Mr. Jennings W. Hayes along with the sleet and the snow and the freezing rain and she looked off to where the ceiling joined up with the far wall and thought for a time with her face all creased and puckered and then it came to her of a sudden and she said, "They dropped him," which spurred Momma to recollect it too and she said, "They did drop him, didn't they," and Aunt Sister told her, "They surely did, and he slid too," and Momma said, "Why he did slide," and Momma said, "Didn't he."

She did not recall it was snow, or anyhow did not recall it was snow much but just sleet mostly and maybe rain somewhat but not anything you could see anyway, not anything you could see there on the sidewalk unless of course the light hit it so as to make it sparkle and make it shine, but Aunt Sister said it was all wintry gray and dark and asked Momma didn't she recall it was just that precisely and Momma shook her head yes. So they did not know it was slick like it was slick, did not truly have call to suspect it, and Aunt Sister said everybody stood up like people always do and she recollected it was just four of them to carry him, two of them brothers and one of them a cousin and one of them just with the funeral home and Mr. Jennings W. Hayes, that had not been all airy and light upright, was surely not hardly more of either laid out and dead and in the commander's maroon Gloriosa which was near about the pinnacle of the casket line and so had your extra padding and your goosedown pillow and your solid handles and your heavy-grade sheathing all round, and Aunt Sister said the commander, which would be Commander Jack, struck out there at the first all emptyhanded to lead the procession and was followed by the four bearers that tried to look proper and mournful but kind of weaved and kind of listed like maybe they were hauling stone to the pyramids and behind them came the widow herself and her daughters and her nephew Laurence Tilley that was like her own boy, and Aunt Sister said the commander stepped on out the chapel doorway and onto the sidewalk and did not seem much troubled by what was underfoot, not at first anyhow, and he got followed fairly much straightaway by the casket and the bearers either side of it after they had paused and had fixed and adjusted themselves on the chapel steps, and as best as Aunt Sister recollected it was Mr. Jennings W. Hayes's least brother, Mr. Charles Kenly Hayes, that went down first on account of it was Mr. Charles Kenly Hayes that had on the crepe-soled shoes and they just kind of both of them went north at once and Mr. Charles Kenly Hayes, in an attempt to right himself, kept hold of the casket handle with the hand he'd had hold of it with all along and took hold of the casket handle with his freeswinging hand too and kind of laid all his weight to the thing and as lightness and airiness are simply not traits Hayeses

ever tend to possess, the weight of the dead Hayes and the weight of the live Hayes too mingled and combined together

and made a considerable impression on the remaining three
bearers that simultaneously crumpled at the knees and let
loose of the casket so as maybe not to get crushed and mangled
by it which not any of them did get, not even Mr. Charles Kenly
Hayes that had caused it all and still had hold of the thing
when nobody else did, or anyhow did not any of them get truly
crushed or truly mangled though the commander himself got
something in the way of assaulted and blindsided likely, Aunt
Sister said, on account of he did not figure he was hearing what
he was hearing just exactly when he heard it but had to ponder
the ruckus momentarily and so did not draw his chin back
round to his shoulder until fairly well after he'd heard what he
heard and naturally by then Mr. Jennings W. Hayes was
already commencing to travel some on his own, not altogether
quickly straightoff but quickly soon enough since the sidewalk
was not just glazed over and slick but was slopey too and since
Mr. Jennings W. Hayes was not just dead and not just laid out
but was not light and was not airy as well, so Aunt Sister said it
was just plain physics and asked Daddy wasn't it just plain
physics ancTDaddy said he guessed it must have been physics
mostly if it was anything much and Aunt Sister said it was
something alright, said she'd seen it herself and so knew it was
something alright, or actually had not seen truly the bulk of it
firsthand but had seen how the commander's eyes opened up
and how the commander's face stretched out when he himself
saw the bulk of it and altogether entirely too firsthand, saw the
bulk of it sliding at him down the sidewalk which would be the
Gloriosa closed roundabout Mr. Jennings W. Hayes and the
both of them moving like they were moving on account of laws,
Aunt Sister said, and on account of properties, and Aunt Sister
said one moment she was looking at the commander from the
shoulders up and the next moment he just was not there
anymore to look at which she did not know the why of
straightaway but came to understand and appreciate shortly
when Mr. Jennings W. Hayes's Gloriosa slid into view there on
the sidewalk with Commander Jack atop it frontside
downwards and backside foremost.

Naturally they accelerated, Aunt Sister said, on account of the slope and the ice and the bulk and the weight and your properties and laws in general and together they commenced to move at a speed quite appreciable for a casket with a funeral home director atop it and Aunt Sister said the commander's jacketflap got caught in the wind and the general turbulence and flopped up on the commander's back thereby hindering him from seeing just where it was he was going which likely he suspected anyway and so did not truly want to see since he was not going much of anywhere he would have chosen to go atop a casket frontside downwards and backside foremost and certainly not at the speed he would have chosen to go there since it wasn't but steps down to the curbing and wasn't but the broadside of hearse number i after that. Aunt Sister was convinced he would have been killed or just maybe broken to pieces and was equally convinced that Mr. Jennings W. Hayes, had he not been dead already, would have got purely done in, so Daddy said it was a good thing he was dead already since it is widely considered bad form for a man to die at his own funeral and Aunt Sister drew up some and said she was simply making a point as to the speed and as to the acceleration and if she did in fact need advice on form she would just as soon consult a housecat all of which Daddy said "Alright" at without particular venom or bite.

So they both would have got killed, the one that was alive would have got killed and the one that was dead would have got killed too if he'd been alive to get it, and as far as Aunt Sister could tell still from the chapel and still just looking out it and still with only the commander's eyes and the commander's face to judge by, the commander himself appeared to have fairly thoroughly figured out that killed was what he would in fact get if he stayed where he was to get it so he set himself to bail off the Gloriosa, set himself to roll to the one side of it or to the other, anywhere really just to get clear, but he could not quite bring himself to do any actual bailing on account of the actual landing that would have to follow it and the commander could not seem to see the advantage in jumping to his destruction as opposed to just riding to it, so when he did in fact leave the Gloriosa it was not because he actually leapt from it but more on account of he got snatched pure off the top of it by the iron rail that he managed to get hold of with a backhanded swipe there at the head of the stairs and consequently the commander stopped in a considerable hurry, which Daddy says is generally the trouble with going fast in the first place. Of course the Gloriosa stopped in a considerable hurry shortly thereafter and Aunt Sister said from the chapel doorway she saw the backend of it pitch up some as the frontend of it set off down the stairway and then she did not see any of it anymore but almost straightaway heard the crash and almost straightaway saw the entire hearse shiver one time.

And it was over, Aunt Sister said, not a half minute after it had started up and it had a kind of aftermath to it that most things that do not last but a half minute generally don't have, left a kind of a trail of what Aunt Sister called woe and mayhem with four sprawled pallbearers at the top of it and one sprawled funeral director at the middle of it and one caved in quarterpanel at the end of it with the Gloriosa itself that had brought about and caused it all in conjunction with the ice and in conjunction with the crepe soles laying sideup a ways down the curbing where it had slid to after the collision. And Aunt Sister said was not anything to hear but queer silence rightoff like usual after a calamity, and then not anything after that but the widow Mrs. Jennings W. Hayes shrieking, "J. W., J. W.," which was just as queer itself on account of with all the fallen live ones that could have got killed the uproar straightoff was for the one that had been dead to begin with.

Now Aunt Sister said it had seemed to her rightoff that somehow this was not the sort of thing that could much benefit the commander as it did not appear to have any good to it truly what with the brothers of the deceased sprawled out on their backsides atop an icy sidewalk, atop the commander's own icy sidewalk, and the commander himself sprawled a little too and with his worsted wool navy trousers tore at both knees, and with the commander's number i hearse all collided with and caved in at the quarterpanel and with the late Mr. Jennings W. Hayes tipped sideupwards near about in the road where he affected traffic like he had not ever before. Aunt Sister said it simply did not strike her as a proper testimonial to just what the commander was up to in a business sort of way on account of was not any of it suitably grim and sober but just mucked up mostly instead and the widow herself did not help things much with her shrieking as it was not the kind of scene that shrieking could much help, was not the kind of scene that anything could much help as far as the commander could tell from there at the iron handrail unless of course Mrs. Commander Jack Tuttle laid her pointy knee in his ribcage like usual and so woke him up under his own bedcovers but did not that seem likely. So the commander kind of set himself upright and looked first down the stairway to what he called in his own mind the impact area that was all dented in and creased and scarred just behind the right rear tire and then he turned his head somewhat so as to ponder Mr. Jennings W. Hayes's Gloriosa that he called in his own mind the projectile afterwhich he brought himself round to the chapel doorway all choked with grievers that he called in his own mind the witnesses and finally he looked full on the pallbearers, three of them Hayeses and one of them a Dunn, that he called in his own mind the plaintiffs.

Like is the way with most calamities, could not anybody seem to do anything at first but just stand and just look except of course for the widow Mrs. Jennings W. Hayes who just stood and just looked but just shrieked too, and then of a sudden everybody stopped doing nothing and set in to doing everything and not so much together as just simultaneously and consequently it was not the sort of doing something that accomplished much but just the sort of doing something that was not doing plain nothing anymore and so people just slipped and just slid mostly and just knocked back over what pallbearers they had managed to pick up and kind of skidded all roundabout the chapel-yard making suggestions and giving orders and rendering up your general variety of observation every now and again. So did not anything truly get done straightaway except that the people that had commenced upright ended up overturned and the people that had commenced overturned finally ended up upright and so helped up the people that had started out upright in the first place and the commander chose out six of the sure-footedest ones he could find and sent them to fetch Mr. Jennings W. Hayes who Mrs. Jennings W. Hayes had not ever stopped shrieking at once she had started. Of course the commander figured Mr. Jennings W. Hayes would need some work as did most everybody else that guessed they would need some work themselves if they had hit a hearse like Mr. Jennings W. Hayes had hit a hearse, and so the six sure-footed ones hauled the Gloriosa back up the steps and on in through the chapel to a private viewing room where the commander himself inspected the exterior of the casket and found it to be in remarkable condition considering where it had been and what it had done and the commander himself backed out the screws from the lid and lifted the thing up and saw what he considered to be something else altogether remarkable which was just Mr. Jennings W.

Hayes laid out like he'd been laid out and not hardly mussed and not hardly upset except for his eyeglasses that had rode up some on his forehead, and the commander set to rights what little needed setting to rights and then ushered in the widow Mrs. Hayes and her daughters and her nephew too who had not expected to be looking at Mr. Jennings W. Hayes again, at least not so soon anyhow.

So it was not hardly so bad as it could have been, Aunt Sister said, not hardly so bad on the widow and the widow's relations except for Mr. Charles Kenly Hayes that had got told earlier in the day by Mrs. Charles Kenly Hayes not to wear his crepe-soled shoes though not because of a premonition on her part but just on account of the suit was gray and the shoes were a kind of a brownish tan and she did not care for the combination much and so suggested the black ones instead but Mr. Charles Kenly Hayes explained to her how the black ones pinched him and explained to her where and she told him he should just suit his own self then though in a way that meant something altogether otherwise. So naturally when Mr. Charles Kenly Hayes got picked up and then knocked over and picked up again and set in to explaining how his soles had not gripped and how his feet had made off like they did, Mrs. Charles Kenly Hayes told him would not any of it have happened if he had worn the black shoes like she had suggested he should, and once the brother and the cousin had got picked up and knocked over and picked up again they themselves set in to wondering at Charles Kenly Hayes just why he had not worn the black shoes like had got told and suggested to him and Charles Kenly Hayes explained to them about the pinching and explained to them where but somehow cramped feet did not hardly measure up with a dropped casket and a wrecked hearse and a brother and a cousin with sore backsides, so most everybody with reason to blame somebody for all of it went ahead and blamed Mr. Charles Kenly Hayes and did not anybody think to lay off even a piece of it on the commander that did not get plaintiffs and did not get witnesses but just got a notion instead, a notion about the Gloriosa that had not got dented and had not got scarred and had not dumped Mr. Jennings W. Hayes out in the gutter or even let him get much rearranged but for his eyeglasses.

Aunt Sister said the insurance adjuster Mr. Sikes from the mutual guessed a Ford coupe straightoff and guessed a Rambler after when he got told it was not a coupe but he still insisted it seemed to him more of a coupe dent than any manner of vehicular dent otherwise and it was the commander himself that said to Mr. Sikes, "Gloriosa," when at last Gloriosa got said to him and Mr. Sikes wanted to know was it foreign and rare on account of he had not ever ridden in one his own self, but the commander told him it was a domestic model and led Mr. Sikes on into the Heavenly Rest where he showed him a Gloriosa and Mr. Sikes stood off from it a ways and studied the thing with his chin in his hand and then observed to the commander how it looked to him awful much like a casket. And that was truly how it all commenced with the commander or actually how it all jelled for him on account of he had got the inkling and had got the inclination previous but was not convinced he would do what he did until Mr. Sikes told him coupe and told him Rambler and told him casket too which was when the commander decided and he wrote up the copy his own self and clipped out the picture from a catalog and personally carried the whole business down to the offices of the Chronicle where Mr. H. Monroe Aycock that wrote the exposes and wrote the human interest and wrote the politics too also handled most all the advertising and so consulted with Commander Jack and advised him and together they decided where to put what and how to say which thing so as to make it all dynamic and scintillating, Mr. H. Monroe Aycock called it, but still appropriately earnest and grim too somehow and they settled at last on a full page in the Saturday edition with the picture of the Gloriosa square in the middle and writing all roundabout the borders, writing mostly about the Jennings W. Hayes episode that did not get called the Jennings W. Hayes episode exactly but just "a recent mishap" instead since everybody knew anyway what had happened and who to and the commander did not mention the ice or the crepe soles either but just made vague reference to "various unfortunate circumstances" that had contributed to the "recent mishap" which left the Gloriosa itself as the only solid and firm item in the whole affair since most everything else was sort of sketchy and sort of roundabout.

As Aunt Sister recollected it the commander did say coupe and did say Rambler and then discussed at some length what alloys were on the outside of the thing and what pads and fabrics on the inside and without saying as much directly he made certain to communicate how a Gloriosa was not the sort of item that would dump out anybody's dead relations no matter what variety of general cataclysm it had to endure be it hearse ramming or a more lively and potent something otherwise, and then he left the rest of the talking and the rest of the communicating to the photograph itself which had been taken not endwise or sidewise either but kind of slantwise mostly down the length of the casket with light coming off the handles and coming off the casketlid so as maybe to suggest a presence holy and divine, and Aunt Sister said it looked all sleek and invincible, looked all sleek and invincible just like a—she could not think straightoff what it looked all sleek and invincible just like and so drew a breath and fingered her powderblue Kleenex and then it came to her of a sudden and she said, "Throat lozenge."

"Sleek and invincible like a throat lozenge?" Daddy asked her.

And Aunt Sister told him, "Just precisely."

"I don't see it," Daddy said.

And Momma told him, "Just precisely," too which meant it was all up for Daddy no matter if a throat lozenge was not particularly sleek or particularly invincible either and Aunt Sister told him, "You know what I mean, Louis Benfield," and Momma, like she will sometimes, told Aunt Sister on Daddy's behalf, "He does," and Daddy fished out a Tareyton from his shirtpocket and fished out a matchpack from alongside the chaircushion and said, "Holy," and said, "Divine," and said, "Sleek," and said, "Invincible," and said, "Throat lozenge," and then bumped the match on the striker and lit the Tareyton and told Aunt Sister through the first smoke of it, "Go on."

She said it did the thing it was meant to do and that was the point anyhow, she said it kind of opened people's eyes to the fact that there were your caskets and then there were your caskets when mostly people had just looked for color on the outside and color on the inside without paying much mind to . . .

"Sleekness," Daddy said, "and invincibility."

And Aunt Sister told him back, "Cataclysms," without paying hardly any mind to cataclysms but just color on the outside and just color on the inside too which the commander changed and altered appreciably with his advertisement and folks started to figure that on the day of judgment maybe they would like to have just their eyeglasses to straighten and nothing otherwise.

So there was a run, Aunt Sister said, a pure run on Gloriosas and for a stretch there did not anybody that got buried get buried but in one, and Aunt Sister said an extraordinary lot of people did in fact get buried, and then she stopped talking one more time and pulled at her Kleenex and watched herself do it and she did not say anything more until she said, "Green December," to herself almost exclusively and then "Green December" to Momma and to Daddy and to me too and Momma said, "Fat graveyard," back at her and Aunt Sister told her, "Yes, ma'm," and so said it was not that one either she guessed on account of not just the December was green but as she recollected it the January and the February and all throughout the March was green too so it could not have been that one with just some ice and just some sleet and just some freezing rain that not any of which was snow at all, and Aunt Sister said to herself "19 and 57" and said to herself, "19 and 55" and then mulled and pondered noticeably and finally said, "Sometime, sometime with a snow and near about March, I do recollect, maybe full into March proper, but sometime with a snow."

So she said she could not tell just when but knew it was her and my granddaddy and my grandmomma and great-grandmomma Yount that was Aunt Sister's momma and Granddaddy's momma too and that was very old even then and slight and brittle and wore her white hair all swept back in a knot and the five print dresses made from the same bolt of material which were the five print dresses she was not hardly ever out of, and Aunt Sister said there was not but her left from all her sisters and her brothers and Great-granddaddy too, her husband, and as she was so very old then and slight and brittle she had moved in with Grandmomma and with Granddaddy and stayed in the extra room across from the plank door at a diagonal where she had her bed with the board under the mattress of it and her chair with the cushions and the pillows and her laminated highboy with the pictures all across the top of it, pictures of babies and children mostly that had since got big and grown and were actual adult nieces and nephews and cousins and such everywhere but on Great-grandmomma's highboy where they were just babies and just children too but for Uncle Jack and but for Aunt Della that were all grown in front of their wagon and in front of their mule. She had not ever been one to talk, Aunt Sister said, had not ever been one to just chatter like women will sometimes and did not read the paper or listen to the radio but liked to sit primarily and enjoyed a pinch of Tuberose of a late afternoon or an evening and mostly she sat in her chair with the cushions and the pillows but sometimes she sat with Grandmomma in the room with the carriagehouse doors and Grandmomma did the bulk of what talking got done and hardly ever gave way but for a yes and but for a no sometimes which was the way of it too at the suppertable where Grandmomma did not just the most of the talking but the most of the eating as well while Granddaddy, that did not have much passion for food, sat and piddled with his fork and while Great-grandmomma, that he had gotten all of it from, sat and piddled some herself.

But they got on well enough, Aunt Sister said, and were not ever sharp and hard with each other except in the usual course of things and Aunt Sister told how she would sometimes herself sit with Grandmomma and Great-grandmomma in the room with the carriagehouse doors and her and Grandmomma mostly would recollect people they did not know they had forgotten completely about until they recollected them and usually it was Aunt Sister that wondered what had went with whoever it was they were recollecting and usually it was Grandmomma that told her she did not have any notion and then usually it was Great-grandmomma that would mention a person and sometimes it would be the very person they were actually speaking of or at least some manner of relation but mostly it was just somebody else entirely that had come into Great-grandmomma's head and so had come out of Great-grandmomma's mouth and she would tell what she had to tell and then usually tell the very same thing a second time just behind it and then she would spit into her tomato can and dab at her lips with the lacy linen handkerchief she usually dabbed at lips with which Aunt Sister told us was not hardly what lacy linen handkerchiefs were intended for.

And then there was the time it snowed, Aunt Sister said, which was what she'd set out on anyway which would be the time that was not 19 and 57 and not 19 and 55 but some winter otherwise, Aunt Sister said, some late winter otherwise, near about March when it was not supposed to snow anymore which it had not done even once all winter anyhow, when it was not supposed to frost even, but did snow and did frost and did freeze up everywhere without anybody anticipating it would, of course not your regular people that got stunned and overcome with every out of the way thing anyhow, but not your weather-oriented people either who could generally call for and prediet a thing along about when it was set to commence.

But Aunt Sister said this one just came up, came up almost like a rainshower, and set in near about fullblown and entirely unforecasted and unprognosticated which made it worse somehow for some people and made it better somehow for others, and Aunt Sister said it commenced just around midday with scant flakes that did not look but like chimney ash and then it picked up directly and got thick and wild and slantwise from most everywhere and caught up against treetrunks and windowpanes and fencing and anything else it could get caught up against and what had landed already got picked back up and blown all roundabout with what had not landed yet. And Aunt Sister said everybody went out in it, not just the children and not just those adults that did not but seem children twelve months of the year, but everybody that could get up and get out and not to do anything special but just to stand primarily and just to catch snowflakes on their hands and on their jacketsleeves and just to spy and marvel at all the rest of the ones they could not catch. And there was no traffic of a sudden, Aunt Sister said, not motors anywhere and not tires and just not noise much but for the whistle at the cotton mill and the midday freight to Greensboro and but for the laughing too, she said, the wondrous sort of laughing that people will laugh sometimes, even people that do not seem much capable of merriment.

And it did not let up, Aunt Sister said, did not let up for hours but fell and blew all thick and wild into the dusk when it commenced to slacken ever so slightly but still did not even begin to leave off until well past dark and by then it was all blown and piled and swirled up most everywhere and smooth mostly but for the places the footprints had been and blue too from the mercury lights along the street which with the swirls and the drifts and the elegant contours made it all seem like somewhere else really and not hardly where it was which generally had no swirls and no drifts and nothing elegant about it, and Aunt Sister said she took supper with Grandmomma and Granddaddy and Great-grandmomma too as she could not but have walked to get home and did not want to do that and Grandmomma made a stew with beef and onions and whole potatoes that did not even need a bowl to be had out of and then she sent Granddaddy into the backyard with a pot and a ladle after snow and Grandmomma mixed up the milk and the sugar and the vanilla in a mayonnaise jar and Aunt

Sister told how much she put of which and Great-grandmomma told how much she put of which but only after Grandmomma had already put what she put of which and had shook it and mixed it all up in the jar and Granddaddy brought back the pot near about full but had got a piece of a stick and some fruit tree leaves and little flecks of what looked to be actual dirt in with the snow that Great-grandmomma said she would not eat any of if it had sticks and leaves and dirt in it and Grandmomma and Aunt Sister together asked Granddaddy if out of all the snow that fell couldn't he find one stickless leafless dirt-less spot of it and Granddaddy got ill somewhat on account of it was just him alone and a whole gang of them together and he said he wasn't a bat anyhow and couldn't hardly ever see without some light to see by so Grandmomma opened the drawer in the kitchen where they kept everything that they could not find anywhere else to keep and she fetched out both the flashlights but the one with the bulb did not have any batteries and the one with the batteries did not have any bulb so she took the batteries out of the bulbless one and put them in the other and turned it on and it did in fact come on kind of but only in a dim and yellow sort of way and Granddaddy took it anyhow and beat it on his hand one time and it got unaccountably brighter so he beat it on his hand again and it shut off completely and would not come back on at all no matter how he slapped it and shook it and swore it too so he went out with just his pot and just his ladle and just his tainted snow that would not anybody eat and from the doorway Grandmomma directed him to a place where she said she would dig if she was him and he dug there and did not this time bring back sticks or leaves or dirtflecks either but just plain snow that Grandmomma emptied her mayonnaise jar into and then stirred after and doled out at last and did not anybody say anything straightaway but just ate and then Aunt Sister said it made her teeth hurt and Granddaddy, that did not have but plates, said it did not affect his much and Grandmomma smacked at some in her mouth and wondered was it maybe too sweet but did not anybody think so and Great-grandmomma said it tasted different to her and Grandmomma asked her different how and Great-grandmomma told her different from what it used to taste like when she was a little girl. She said it did not taste so pure anymore, did not taste so clean, and Granddaddy told her he'd gone to the place Grandmomma had told him to go to and Aunt Sister told Granddaddy she had not meant clean like sticks and leaves and dirtflecks and then she asked Great-grandmomma hadn't she not meant sticks and leaves and dirtflecks but maybe something otherwise, something atmospheric, Aunt Sister called it, and Great-grandmomma spooned a heap of snowcream into her mouth and held it there for a time and then swallowed it in a rush and told Aunt Sister, "This makes my teeth hurt," and Aunt Sister told her back, "Momma, your teeth are on the nightstand."

"Well," Great-grandmomma said, "it makes something hurt anyhow."

Aunt Sister said she was going to sleep on the sofa as there were not any beds vacant but Grandmomma would not let Granddaddy let Aunt Sister sleep on the sofa and made Granddaddy, who did not care if Aunt Sister slept on the sofa anyway, sleep on the sofa himself with just a blanket and a sheet and a little square throwpillow and Granddaddy could not even stretch full out but had to sleep with his knees up and so awoke with his knees up and straightaway broke his customary morning wind which had a kind of uncharacteristic resonance to it on account of he was not stretched out like usual and so could not stifle and cloak the thing with much effect and it rousted Aunt Sister directly and she wrapped up in Grandmomma's robe and hurried to the front door so as to look out the little window of it and see who had pressed the buzzer.

She recollected it was a gray day though not a bleak and oppressive gray day as there was white snow on the ground and in the treelimbs and as the sky was not low gray and threatening gray but just high light gray, and Grandmomma made coffee and fried bacon and scrambled eggs and cooked oatmeal too and Granddaddy read to Great-grandmomma out of the newspaper how Mrs. Bradshaw's cousin in Mayodan had died in the night though Granddaddy was not sure which night exactly but then Great-grandmomma was not sure which Bradshaw exactly either and thought for a time it was maybe Camille Bradshaw but Grandmomma reminded her how Camille Bradshaw had died in July so Great-grandmomma figured maybe it was some other Bradshaw instead and she asked Grandmomma had Camille Bradshaw died in that wreck out the Richardson road but Grandmomma reminded her how the wreck out the Richardson road had not happened until October and it wasn't Bradshaws anyhow but Littlejohns and Greers and did not anybody get killed except for Mrs. Littlejohn's lapdog that got squashed against the glovebox door but Granddaddy said he thought it was the Greers's dog that got squashed against the glovebox door and Grandmomma reminded him how the Mrs. and the Mr. Greer both were so slight and spindly that the two of them together could throw themselves on a fieldmouse and not do him any harm while Mrs. Littlejohn alone could sit down hard and snap a collie in two and Great-grandmomma observed how a collie did not seem to her a suitable lapdog and Aunt Sister explained to her that it had not been a collie that had got squashed against the glovebox door. The collie had been merely what Aunt Sister called an illustration, and Great-grandmomma said, "Oh," that way she said Oh when she did not know just what to say exactly.

Granddaddy figured he would shovel some, maybe clear the walk and the frontsteps and the driveway runners and as he did not have any proper snowclothes he just put on two of most everything but briefs on account of he did not wish to get altogether constricted and confined and in place of regular snowboots he wore his Red Wing bro-gans all slick and shiny with mink oil and Grandmomma told him they would not keep out the snow but Granddaddy told her back he could wear them in the bathtub and not get his feet wet and Grandmomma wondered couldn't she wrap and swaddle them up in plastic so as to make them purely watertight but Granddaddy said he would not be seen in the out of doors with his feet wrapped and swaddled and Grandmomma said he could suit himself then and catch pneumonia and Aunt Sister, that had not said anything, called Granddaddy pigheaded like usual and Granddaddy went up the back hall to the basement steps walking hard and shut the door firm behind him. Of course he didn't own a true and verifiable snowshovel but just a longhandled pointyended shovel and a shorthandled squareended spade and while the shorthandled squareended spade served well enough to plant bushes with, it did not do much on snow but cause back trouble which left the longhandled pointyended shovel that tended to chip and scar the concrete but did not generally afflict the shoveler much. And Aunt Sister said by the time Granddaddy got outside they were already running the road out front of the house on sleds and pieces of boxes and just their shoebottoms and pantseats too which would be all four of the Gardner boys and their sister Mary Alice that was twins with one of them and both the Mayberrys and Mr. Suggs's nephew from Wentworth that had got stranded and Mrs. Suggs herself that Aunt Sister said did not ever act like a grown person, and she said her and Grandmomma and Great-grandmomma too looked out the front window at Granddaddy chipping away at the icy steps and off behind him at the sleds that would go by one two three and sometimes four at the time and with considerable speed too as they were already halfway down at Granddaddy's and ran clean to the rise that slowed them enough to let them butt into the curb and not get hurt by it, and Aunt Sister said Granddaddy did just shovel and did just chip and pick at the ice and her and Grandmomma and Great-grand-momma too did just watch him for a spell up until the middle Gardner boy that Aunt Sister said got an urge in his bladder left his sled there where Granddaddy's walk met the roadway and went off home for relief and did not Grandmomma or Aunt Sister or Great-grandmomma either see Granddaddy look at it like he looked at it and then look away like he looked away and so they did not hardly expea and anticipate that he would drop the shovel like he did drop it and go where he went and take up what he took up and run with it all spry and nimble like he ran with it and then throw it down and throw himself down on it with unflinching grace and flair so he was near about already gone before they could see where he went and on what, and Aunt Sister said the three of them together stepped out onto the front porch in just their housedresses and just their sweaters and just their regular shoes and Grandmomma called after Granddaddy, "William Elsworth," all serious and earnest and did not get back but a yip from somewhere along the road so they all three together helped each other down the steps with Grandmomma, that had the bulk and weight to her, going first so if she slipped and fell she would not crush the other two, and they all three together helped each other along the walkway to the curbing where they all three together looked down the road and saw Mayberrys and Gardners and Suggs and two colored Robinsons along with Granddaddy himself flatout on his stomach with his feet upwards and yipping and hooting and overtaking the whole bunch of them.

Aunt Sister said he did not run into the curb himself but instead executed an elaborate turning maneuver that slowed him and then stopped him entirely and the Mayberrys and the

Suggs and the Gardners and the Robinsons too tried it themselves but ran into the curb anyhow. And then the whole bunch of them walked up together, Aunt Sister said, walked up together strung clean out across the road some pulling their sleds behind them, some carrying them caught up under their arms like Granddaddy and when he got back up to the house with the Mayberrys and the Suggs and the Gardners and the Robinsons, Grandmomma said at him, "William Elsworth," but not with bite truly and more with pure wonder though she seemed to want to get on him some on account of he could have broke his neck, she told him, on account of he could have injured an organ, she told' him, and Aunt Sister said Grandmomma was working up some heat and working up some snap too when she heard not the carmotor but just the tires or actually not the tires but the snow crunching underneath them like snow will and so left off talking of a sudden and looked at the vehicle like everybody else had already which was not at all like it was a plain car with a plain driver at the wheel of it but more like it was altogether exotic and farfetched, and it was at least a little farfetched anyhow, Aunt Sister said, on account of it was Mrs. Nettles in her Pontiac who did not hardly go anywhere in clear weather and could not hardly drive then and so was purely up against it on ice and snow, especially in a car with the considerable tonnage of a Pontiac and nothing to manage it but disc brakes which Aunt Sister said Mrs. Nettles applied full on a quarterway down the hill but not with any effect much except to lock the tires that slid and skidded with appreciably more velocity than they had managed on the roll, and Aunt Sister said she stayed headlong and stayed grillfirst for a ways and passed the bunch of them there at the curbing fairly straight in the road and Aunt Sister said she was all hunkered down like usual with her hands up high on the steering wheel and her nose underneath the arc of it and so did not look but to be driving like she ordinarily did drive except of course that the wheels were not turning like they ordinarily did turn, and Aunt Sister said she picked up noticeable momentum where the road dropped off

some below Granddaddy's house and she commenced to skate
and slide not so much headlong and grillfirst and straight in
the road anymore but somewhat at the diagonal and still
hunkered like usual and with her hands where they had been
and her nose where it was and then she was not diagonal
anymore but was purely sideways and proceeded like that for a
spell still hunkered and still latched to the wheel and still
peering out the windshield that was not even frontwards and
then was not even sidewards either once the Pontiac
commenced to trade ends which it did entirely on its own as
Mrs. Nettles just held the wheel and did not attempt to do any
actual steering with it, so the car slid backwards like it had slid
frontwards and sideways previous and Mrs. Nettles held the
wheel and looked out where she'd been just precisely like she'd
looked out where she was going and did not but look and but
slide and but hold the wheel for a time until it seemed that she
would travel clear to Lawsonville without putting the first
tenth of a mile on her odometer or wearing her tires but in one
little patch apiece, so it was just when it appeared that she was
incapable of anything but gripping and peering and sliding
that Mrs. Nettles of a sudden left off braking with her braking
foot and laid on accelerating with her accelerating foot which
for Mrs. Nettles were not the same feet and so allowed her to
brake and accelerate simultaneously whenever she chose to
which Mr. Nettles generally complained about and got
nauseous on account of whenever he was along for the ride.
But Aunt Sister said it was just pure acceleration this time, was
just pure acceleration as far as she could tell from the way the
engine roared and groaned and from the way the snow spewed
and from the way the rear tires wheezed as they spun overtop
it prior to actually taking hold at least somewhat, enough
anyhow to halt the backsliding and initiate some verifiable
forward progress though not any considerable verifiable
forward progress straightaway but some anyhow and then
more after and then more after that until Mrs. Nettles was
actually climbing the hill frontwards that she had just finished
sliding down frontwards a little and sideways some and

backwards too and still hunkered like usual and with her hands where they had been and her nose where it was and Aunt Sister said she passed the whole bunch of them there going up the hill just like she'd passed the whole bunch of them going down it and the Gardners and the May-berrys and the Suggs and the two colored Robinsons and Grandmomma and Granddaddy and even Great-grandmomma too all watched her gain level ground and then hooted and cheered and just generally vented themselves with an ovation. And Aunt Sister said it was not the children, not the white ones or the colored ones or even the adult Suggs that acted like either and both who said, "Come on, now," when it got said but was instead Granddaddy himself that put down the Gardner's sled in the road and then said, "Come on, now," a second time and waved at Grandmomma again like he had waved at her straightoff and Grandmomma said back, "William Elsworth!" though not hard and not stern and Granddaddy told her, "Come on," again and got told "William Elsworth!" all over but she was already on her way to him by then and Granddaddy took hold of her fingers with one hand and took hold of her elbow with the other and said, "Come on," yet once more but not to Grandmomma this time who had already come on and instead to Aunt Sister mostly who was all set to tell him "no sir" on account of her neck that she could break and on account of her organs that she could injure when Great-grandmomma that he was not even talking at in the first place opened her mouth and told Granddaddy, "Alright," and then was off the walk and over the curb and was sitting upright on the frontend of the sled before Granddaddy could even let loose of Grandmomma's elbow and fingers long enough to take hold of Great-grandmomma's that did not hardly need taking hold of, and Great-grandmomma laid her feet on the steerer and turned partway around and said to Granddaddy and to Grandmomma too, "Well, come on."

Aunt Sister said Grandmomma got on behind Great-grandmomma and not with much ease or grace either as

Grandmomma was not built to sit down on a thing as low to the ground as a sled with much ease or much grace and she held on to Great-grandmomma's midsection and Great-grandmomma held on to the edges of the sled deck and Granddaddy stood upright behind the thing with his hands on Grandmomma's shoulders and his whole self all set to give a little shove and put the thing in motion, and Great-grandmomma, that was a little anxious to get started, said to him from the side of her mouth, "Push," and Grandmomma, that was a little anxious herself, said to him out from the side of her mouth, "Don't, don't," and Granddaddy, that had had the notion in the first place, went ahead and shoved some and then set about to find a spot for himself on the Gardner's sled that was appreciably burdened and crowded already.

As best as Aunt Sister could recollect he did not ever truly get situated in a proper sort of way which was the most of the trouble and so primarily brought about what got brought about. He did in fact get on the thing, kind of squatted there at the very back of it, and did in fact attempt to sit but could not find a suitable place for his feet and a suitable place for his backside and so just kind of sat down anyhow without truly anything to sit down on, anyway without truly a piece of the Gardner's sled to sit down on but with considerable snow to receive him and it did receive him and he kind of skidded along overtop it for a spell haunches downward while he tried to grab and tried to snatch at whatever he could grab and snatch at which turned out to be Grandmomma mostly who was pretty firmly situated herself but not nearly so firmly situated that Granddaddy could not remove and dislodge her like he did remove and did dislodge her and Grandmomma rolled over backwards and departed entirely from the sled herself but did not land on and skid across the snow like Granddaddy had landed on and skidded across the snow and instead just landed on Granddaddy who did her skidding for her and the two of them together slid down the hill a considerable ways before Granddaddy could dig his heels in sufficiently to stop them and then they just sat there for a time on their numb parts, Granddaddy's chilled from the snow and Grandmomma's from the icy wind up her dress, and collected up their faculties enough to wonder was Great-grand-momma wrecked and dead or just broken all to pieces on the roadside and it was Grandmomma that spied her first as it was Grandmomma that had the eyes for it and she pointed out to Granddaddy the sled down the hill a ways still gliding and skating along the packed snow and still with Great-Grandmomma atop it, and Aunt Sister said Granddaddy called, "Momma!" there from his backside and then stood up and cupped his hands around his mouth and called, "Momma!" again and Aunt Sister said she called, "Momma!" herself a time or two along with him but did not any of it seem to affect Great-grandmomma much who sat all stiff and upright with her feet on the steerer and Aunt Sister said she was already so old then, already so ancient near about and so shriveled and wiry and gnarled that even the Mayberrys and the Robinsons and the Gardners and the Suggs, that were all plain children but for the solitary adult that only acted like one, took notice of her in the way that children do not ordinarily notice a thing which is to say with considerable attention, Aunt Sister told it, and with considerable silence too, and so they all watched her as she gathered speed down towards the hillbottom and Aunt Sister said did not anybody know could she swing around like

Granddaddy had swung around and stop herself or could she run up on the curbing like the children ran up on the curbing and end the thing that way and so could not everybody but watch and could not everybody but wonder and Aunt Sister said she hit the hillbottom just sailing and with the hair worked loose from her bun standing straight out behind her and she started up the slight incline where Granddaddy had executed what maneuver he'd executed but she did not turn and did not whip sideways like Granddaddy had and proceeded on up to the brief level ground to where the children ran up on the curbing like they ran up on it but she did not swerve there either. "Couldn't," Aunt Sister said.

And Daddy that had not but watched and had not but listened and had not but smoked for the longest time said, "Or wouldn't," back at her.

And Aunt Sister considered the thing and said, "Wouldn't," too all sure and firm, and she said wouldn't swing round and wouldn't swerve, just wouldn't stop and quit the road and quit the sled and quit the ride mostly with the speed and the sharp cold air and the sound of the runners on the packed snow that is almost like silence but better maybe, better likely, and so she didn't, Aunt Sister said, wouldn't, and cleared the level ground and started back down again the other side of the rise and so just disappeared, Aunt Sister said, with the sled going first and then the bulk of herself after and the silvery back of her head last so was not anything left for Granddaddy and Grandmomma and Aunt Sister and the Mayberrys and the Robinsons and the Gardners and the Suggs to look at but where she'd been last which was not hardly where she was any longer, and Granddaddy that was standing up behind Grandmomma that was still sitting down opened his mouth and said, "I'll be damned," which generally would have gotten him an agitated "William Elsworth!" in return but did not get him one this time on account of Grandmomma opened her mouth and said, "I'll be damned," for herself and Aunt Sister admitted she even thought it somewhat as she stood there on the walkway and looked off at the place where Great-grandmomma had just dropped on out of sight, and then Granddaddy commenced to laugh, she said, just took hold of himself at the stomach and commenced to laugh full out and set off Grandmomma that had some considerable bulk to laugh with and so laughed with all of it from right there in the street that she could not get up off of by herself and that not even Granddaddy could lift her from at first somewhat on account of the general hysteria that caused his breath to go like it went and somewhat on account of the snow too that caused his feet to go like they went, so it was just Grandmomma sprawled out in the street with Granddaddy upright behind her and then Grandmomma and Granddaddy both sprawled out in the street and then just Grandmomma again partly sprawled but partly hoisted too by Granddaddy that had dug him a place to stand and so got her up halfway and then drew a breath and got her up entirely, and Aunt Sister said when she was actually standing on her very own two feet they both hooted and Granddaddy laid his arm roundabout Grandmomma's shoulders and laid his lips, Aunt Sister said, just here, and she put her own finger to her own cheek and told Momma and told Daddy too, "Here just precisely, and tender," she said, "and warm," she said, "and not hardly hard and not hardly rough," she said to Daddy mostly, and she said it was near about the same what with the sprawling and what with the picking up and asked Momma wasn't it and Momma said it purely seemed so and she asked Daddy too wasn't it the same near about and even Daddy said it seemed so as well, and Aunt Sister said, "Passion," and Daddy told her, "Alright," but not that way that meant alright exactly, and Aunt Sister said to Daddy, "Good and kind and gentle and sweet," and Daddy said, "Alright," behind it, and Aunt Sister said, "Given to it," and dabbed at herself and said, "all of us," and Daddy told her, "Alright," and Aunt Sister said it was a crucial thing, said it was a crucial thing especial, and Daddy told her, "Crucial," back and nodded one time and drew on his Tareyton, and Aunt Sister said Alright herself and unclumped her Kleenex and then clumped it back after, and Aunt Sister said Grandmomma did not slip down but one time on her way to the curb and Granddaddy that snatched and grabbed at her did not but slip down the same one time himself, and then they all stood on the walkway, Aunt Sister said, which was him and which was her and which was Grandmomma too, and they looked on down the hill and up the rise to where Great-grandmomma had been before she disappeared entirely, and Granddaddy said, "Well," and looked sideways at Grandmomma who said, "Well," back at him and then the two of them together pondered Aunt Sister so as to get a Well from her which they did get, and Aunt Sister said they all three looked back where they'd been looking and said they all three breathed out their mouths that way that is telling and significant and were in fact so caught up with looking and so caught up with breathing that did not any of them rightoff see that the Gardner who had left his sled where he left it so as to go off and do what he needed to do had actually come back and was pondering them from there at the curbing like they were pondering things otherwise and Aunt Sister said likely he could have stood and could have pondered and not have got noticed at all if he had not dropped his chin and said, "Mr. Buck," that way he did drop his chin and that way he did say Mr. Buck, and Aunt Sister told how Grandmomma looked at him quick and sideways with her hand laid across her chest and said, "Oh," kind of on the inhale, and Aunt Sister told how she looked at him a little slantwise her own self and said a thing too, and then she told how Granddaddy, that did not hardly ever do anything fast anyway, turned full around to study the Gardner on his own and laid his open hand atop the Gardner's green toboggan and said to him all slow and sweet, "Hello son."

Four

So Daddy said he still just looked at her for a while, him standing like he was standing just bent there at the neck and her sprawled and laid out across the wagonrut like she was sprawled and like she was laid out, and Daddy said he did not pick her up directly even after he got told what he got told and instead he moved and turned roundabout the bonehandled knife before his face and watched how the sunlight glinted and glistened off the silvery blade of it and he remarked, Daddy called it, as much to himself as to Aunt Della or anybody otherwise, "I like to got run clean through with this thing," and from there across the wagonrut in the dirt street Aunt Della told him, "Might still," and Uncle Jack of a sudden left off moving and turning roundabout the bonehandled knife and pondered Aunt Della still with just his neck bent and Aunt Della said to him, "Get me up from here," not all hot and fiery but with emphasis, Daddy called it, and considerable diction. So he stuck the knife in his own boot like he'd seen it in the boot of the indian and he stooped over and took up Aunt Della at the armjoints and snatched her direct to her feet where she shook herself free of what dirt and dust she could shake herself free of, and Daddy said Uncle Jack laid his arm full around Aunt Della's shoulders and Daddy said Uncle Jack squatted and leaned like he had to so as to put his lips where he put them and do with them what he did, and Daddy laid his own finger across his own cheek and said to Aunt Sister primarily, "Here," and straightaway Aunt Sister told him back, "Just precisely."

Uncle Jack gathered up the dropped cartridges and picked up the dropped rifle and Aunt Della herself fetched little Spud away from the roadhouse but did not either one of them or both of them too get up on him straightaway as Uncle Jack figured he might had been traumatized somewhat, might had been mistreated and abused and might just suffer effects from it all which Aunt Della took in that way she generally took in things with her head cocked a little and her mouth open some and she went along with it for a time at least so far as down the road and up the alleyway and out from it where she stopped herself and stopped little Spud and stopped Uncle Jack too and she told him how she'd been thinking on the thing and how it seemed to her that likely little Spud had got rid some and then had just got put upon to stand around after, while for her own self she'd walked the roads appreciably, had got robbed by an indian, had got aggravated by a Williford, and had fired a rifle that was near about as evil to shoot as it was to get shot by, and she asked Uncle Jack wasn't that traumatized and wasn't that mistreated and abused, and Uncle Jack that had a way of chewing on most every little dilemma put before him chewed on this one some and considered the walking and considered the indian and considered the Williford and the rifle too and then told Aunt Della how he supposed it was maybe traumatized and supposed it was maybe mistreated and abused and Aunt Della said she figured so and Uncle Jack said he guessed he figured so too and then he set in to walking again as he was satisfied in his own mind that he had settled and resolved the thing at least in a philosophical sort of way but Aunt Della did not set in to walking again straightoff and so did not set in to drawing the mule behind her on account of she had not truly just brought up the circumstances so Uncle Jack could be mindful of them but had intentions and had designs as she did not hardly ever say a thing so as to be hypothetical or theoretical or philosophical either, and before Uncle Jack got so far up the road that he could not any longer hear her plain and true she said to him, "Jack, I'll be perched on this creature directly," and Uncle Jack, with his one hand full of cartridges and his other hand full of rifle stock, turned roundabout so as to ponder and consider Aunt Della and so as to ponder and consider little Spud too and he chewed on the both of them for a time and when he did not appear about to do anything but ponder and consider and chew and mull and whatnot, Aunt Della went ahead and got perched like she'd said she would and then rode up alongside Uncle Jack as he finished off his various processes and he raised his head and beheld Aunt Della there atop little Spud and told her, "Alright."

So Uncle Jack walked and Aunt Della that had got traumatized and mistreated and abused rode on little Spud that had likely just got rid some and just got put upon to stand around after, and from up against his storefront the Williford, with his arms crossed over his bellytop, spat one time and hollered down to Aunt Della, "Nice piece of shooting, lady," and together Aunt Della and Uncle Jack too opened their mouths and reviled the Williford straightaway not with the same expression exactly but with purely the same spirit and enthusiasm and the Williford spat again and wiped himself with his knuckles and did not seem much affected. Daddy said naturally most everybody that was not out already came out to see the man that had got beat and gnawed on and yanked roundabout by the cowlick and near about skewered and run through along with the woman that had stopped things just shy of it and while it was not so extraordinary for a man to get beat and gnawed on and yanked roundabout and near about skewered and run through or even actually skewered and run through or even actually skewered and legitimately run through, it was a little out of the way for a woman to stop and prevent it, most especially a slight and dainty wiry woman with bangs and a buffalo rifle, so while they all looked at Uncle Jack and Aunt Della together they saw Aunt Della mostly since they got their regular fill of beat-up men but did not hardly ever lay eyes on a lethal woman and Daddy said she probably even looked a little dangerous with that bonnet cocked up the way she kept it cocked up and those bangs coming out from it and that sharp hooked nose and that pointy chin and that trace of snuff dribble out the corner of her mouth and with that mule underneath her that was not a J. T. London Oklahoma hybrid mule but was a full-sized regular mule that had not but got rid some and had not but stood around mostly and so was fresh and potent and maybe eager in as much as eager and mule can even get let out together. So they looked at her, Daddy said, and looked at him too but looked at her mostly and said things to each other there along the plank walk and along the roadedge that could not but they hear while Uncle Jack just walked a little scuffed and scraped and battered and sore in the ribcage where the knee had got put and Aunt Della just rode behind him and, as she did not have her can to spit in, spat in the actual street which the bystanders seemed to fully appreciate on account of how it fit and suited.

Uncle Jack figured that maybe this Oklahoma hybrid that he had tied up and left would be somewhat refreshed and somewhat rejuvenated by the time him and Aunt Della got back to it since it had gone relatively untaxed for a spell and so might have had occasion to retrieve what spunk and what vigor

it had commenced with which Uncle Jack guessed was maybe
some spunk and some vigor anyhow though likely not near so
much of the one or the other either as J. T. London had
suggested and had implied and had maybe even fairly much
insisted outright but when they came up on the creature where
they had left it all tethered up and played out it did not appear
to have recovered much and the sight of it there kind of drawn
up and stooped and scraggly against the shopfront did not
hardly render up spunk and did not hardly render up vigor, did
not but barely render up mule, and Uncle Jack did not even try
to ride it once he had untethered the thing and then had held
to it by the reins and circled roundabout it studying the various
contours, which would be the rises here and there and the dips
most everyplace otherwise, and instead he just set in to tugging
at it and set in to leading it and did not stop but to turn
roundabout and tell Aunt Della, "Actual. Inbred. Cultivated.
Horseshit."

Daddy said he ran them out eight deep behind the wagon with
the sides and the roof to it and let Aunt Della drive on little
Spud before them while he just sat there on the wagonseat
recovering, recovering not truly from the beating and the
gnawing and the yanking roundabout but recovering almost
exclusively from the treatment he'd got for it at the hands of
Mr. J. T. London who said he had seen them coming a ways off
and who said he had noticed straightaway how Uncle Jack was
all scraped and scuffed and so had went ahead and fetched his
salve that he'd made up special and kept roundabout the house
for such as scrapes and scuffs and even your bit places too and
consequently he already had the canful of it there in his one
hand by the time Aunt Della and Uncle Jack got back to the
corral fence and he had hunted up a stick to smear it with
before Aunt Della or Uncle Jack either could answer to J. T.
London's satisfaction just what exactly had happened and who
to, that is who to aside from Uncle Jack that appeared to Mr. J.
T. London to have received at least a part of what had
happened if not purely the bulk of it, and Aunt Della and Uncle

Jack together, that had likely been inclined to speak more of mules than indians, set in anyhow to telling Mr. J. T. London about the tussle and about the rolling around in the street and about the bonehandled knife and about the buffalo rifle too but Uncle Jack left the whole of the talking up to Aunt Della once Mr.

J. T. London commenced to spreading his special salve with his special spreading stick on account of Uncle Jack found himself preoccupied with some agony of a sudden.

Daddy said it was something like stomach tar though not formulated specially for stomachs like stomach tar but just kind of a general purpose pitch which Daddy said he could not begin to guess the origin of as there was not hardly a bush roundabout big enough to get plain sap from and truly not anything that would bear and produce pitch in a natural sort of way but Mr. J. T. London had a canful of it anyhow and had a stick to stir and spread it with and called it salve and called it balm and called it ointment too, called it everything but tar and everything but pitch and particularly everything but turpentine witch Daddy said it was purely weepy with, and Mr. J. T. London told Uncle Jack how it would soothe him and how it would promote healing and how it would discourage infection and then commenced to dab it and commenced to spread it first on the bit earlobe and then on the face scratches and then on the beat knuckles and scraped forearms and finally on the little raw place where the cowlick had been but wasn't hardly any longer and while Uncle Jack could not tell straightoff about the healing and could not tell straight-off about the discouraging he had an opinion directly as to the soothing on account of there was not any, in fact was not just not any soothing but was instead some appreciable aggravating and stinging and burning and Daddy said Uncle Jack set in to hopping and jumping and just generally dancing around in a wild and flagrant sort of way that was not much of an amusement to him but struck Aunt Della and Mr. J. T.

London too as a merry sort of thing and they eyed each other and showed each other their teeth and Uncle Jack hollered, "Christalmighty," one time and sort of pirouetted in midair and tried to blow on the top of his own head which people just were not made to be capable of.

So he got put off and distracted from talk of spunk and vigor and hybrids as intense pain and anguish will oftentimes tend to put off and distract a man and so Aunt Della helped Uncle Jack up onto the wagonseat while Mr. J. T. London himself tethered the eight bought mules to a hookeye on the back frame and then circled round to the front and got little Spud all buckled and situated and he bid Aunt Della a warm and cordial goodbye and bid Uncle Jack a warm and cordial goodbye too but did not get anything much in return except for the noise Aunt Della made in her cheek that was for the mule primarily and except for the whistly breezy sound Uncle Jack made with his lips that was mostly for what tarred places he could put wind on. And Daddy said they headed back pretty much the way they'd come only not direct through Hartshorne this time but roundabout it as wide as they could manage which was not altogether too wide as there was not but the one road through it and trails close in and no call for a bypass whatsoever so they kind of skirted parts of it and kind of went through parts of it too but did not get gaped at like they had been gaped at, did not hardly get remarked but for Uncle Jack this time that was chiefly looked at whenever anybody did look as he had just enough pitch on him to make folks wonder what coal bin he'd toured the bottom of.

Daddy said Mr. J. T. London, though he bred and cultivated the spunk and bred and cultivated the vigor without much measurable success to speak of, did breed and cultivate a high degree of general mulishness that seemed sometimes like spunk and seemed sometimes like vigor but was just your basic contrary energy that mules tend to have a talent for working up, apparently even your hybrid Oklahoma mules, and Uncle

Jack's eight of them towed like slab lumber or worse most times and decided they wanted to go near about everywhere the wagon wasn't and so struck out all eight together every now and again or half one way and half another and though they could not ever get just where it was they wanted to go they wrenched the wagon all roundabout well enough and jerked little Spud one direction and jerked him another and appreciably aggravated Aunt Della and quite apparently irritated Uncle Jack that was already measurably irritated from sources otherwise and did not need eight mules to contribute to it. Understandably, then, they did not make hardly the progress with the eight J. T. London hybrids that they would have made without them, that they would have made with even two dozen regular mules, and they did not get even out of Oklahoma entirely before they had to stop for the evening at the eastern border of a cattle ranch and the owner, that was riding his fences, come up on them along about when they were sitting down to their beans and their saltpork and so took a portion for himself along with a tin of coffee and he wandered roundabout the wagon with the sides and the roof to it and studied the animals tied to the hookeye at the backend prior to asking Uncle Jack, "What's these?"

"Mules," Uncle Jack told him.

And that fellow drew off some coffee and pondered those animals straighton and then squatted and looked underneath them like most people do Chevrolets anymore and at length stood upright again and said to Uncle Jack, "Mules," and directly got told back, "Yes sir."

So he circled round to the front of the wagon where little Spud had got unhitched and unharnessed and tied up separate and he studied and pondered him for a spell and squatted and stood upright again and eventually asked Uncle Jack, "What's this here?"

"Mule," Uncle Jack told him and got studied and pondered some himself on account of it and then that fellow drew on his coffee again and spooned up a mouthful of beans and looked from the eight hybrids to the regular mule and from the regular mule back to the eight hybrids so as to maybe suggest and imply his opinion in the matter and then he kind of glanced at Uncle Jack though not with any attention much there straightoff but directly he focused in somewhat and then squinted one time and focused in some more and then just plain peered and gaped for a while before he bothered to open his mouth and before he bothered to say, "What's that on you?" and he sort of threw out his arm and pointed in the direction of Uncle Jack's general self.

"Salve," Uncle Jack told him though Uncle Jack was not at all convinced it was salve since it did not have any soothing and balmlike qualities and Uncle Jack was of a mind that those were qualities a fine salve was supposed to possess but then he was not about to say Pine tar on account of he did not much care to admit to himself or a stranger either that he had let a man smear pitch on him with a stick and so he said Salve as much to ease his own mind as anybody else's and he thought soothing and he thought balmlike though evidence to the contrary still impressed itself upon him every time he twitched and every time he moved.

And Daddy said that fellow stepped on around the wagon and towards Uncle Jack and stopped there just before him and then put the bean tin in the hand that held the coffee tin already and reached out with his free fingers and laid one ever so briefly where Uncle Jack's cowlick had been and then brought it back towards himself and studied it and rubbed what was on it with his thumb and sniffed it and rubbed it some more and said to Uncle Jack, when at last he did say anything at all, "This here's pine tar."

"Salve," Uncle Jack told him.

"For boatbottoms," that fellow said back.

"Soothing," Uncle Jack told him. "Balmlike."

And that fellow stooped some and looked all roundabout Uncle Jack's person searching out the little pine tar smears and patches and when he was satisfied that he'd found all the ones that were out in the open to get found he brought himself upright again, picked up out from the beanplate a piece of saltpork with the finger and the thumb that still had a little bit of tar on them, and dropped it into his open mouth where he chewed it and ground it what seemed excessively and then swallowed one time and told Uncle Jack, "Bobcat," not at all speculative and wondrous but just plain and flat out.

"No sir," Uncle Jack said back and he took in a breath and set in to explain with, "You see my mule there," but he did not get to finish the thing out straightaway on account of the fellow with the beans and the coffee and the saltpork turned round and looked not at little Spud but at the string of spunky vigorous hybrids tethered to the hookeye and then turned back around and looked not really full at Uncle Jack's whole person but primarily at those parts of him that had got beat and gnawed and scraped and scuffed and tarred over and then he squatted of a sudden so as to bring his own face full level with Uncle Jack's and he said to him, "Well, shit in my boots," and Daddy said it was wondrous this time and maybe a little wild and speculative too, and Aunt Sister said it might just be wondrous and might just be wild and might just be speculative too but was purely uncalled for and Daddy told her it was only an expression like Christalmighty or some such and Aunt Sister said it was not hardly like Christalmighty and was not hadly only an expression but was profane and offensive and Aunt Sister said worse still, and then kind of picked at her Kleenex that way she did pick at it when Daddy worked her up like he worked her up, she said worse still it was heathenish and then she said it again, "Heathenish," and she told Momma and Daddy both how it seemed to her that heathens would say most anything, most anything at all, and Daddy shot back with, "Just precisely," and said how this heathen in particular, which was an

Oklahoma heathen, just opened his mouth and come out with what he come out with on account of that was the sort of most anything that heathens generally did open their mouths and come out with in Oklahoma and he wondered couldn't Aunt Sister see the sense of it and she said it was not but profane and said it was not but offensive and said it was not hardly sensible, said there is no sense to profanity and offense, is no sense to heathens in a general sort of way and then she cited a scripture verse that seemed sort of like a psalm there at the outset but went astray partway through and ended up all murky and inconclusive like maybe she had manufactured what portion she could not quite recall which was a habit with Aunt Sister who was as good a sheep as has ever been but could not ever be the shepherd with much effect, and she finished off the whole business with, "Heathens," all sharp and low and final like punctuation and then paid some inordinate attention to her powderblue Kleenex that was rapidly turning back into the little tiny pieces of whatever it had been made out of.

So Daddy said that Oklahoma heathen that had come out with what he come out with stayed squatted there where he'd squatted to and kept his face where he'd put it and opened his mouth a second time so as to say a thing direct after the heathenish thing he'd just finished saying and presently he come out with, "Mule?" which Daddy said was near about as speculative and wondrous as anything he'd come out with yet.

And Uncle Jack set back in with, "You see my mule there," just like he'd set in with it at the outset to get the whole business underway but again he wasn't hardly allowed to carry on like he'd intended to carry on as the Oklahoma heathen rancher heard mule again where he'd anticipated and expected and even had predicted bobcat and he said to Uncle Jack right there in the middle of what Uncle Jack was saying to him, "Well I'll be goddammed and bound up in hell," and Momma and Aunt Sister together set up a hue and cry and straightaway commenced to see the advantages of the shit in the boots over the goddammed and bound up in hell but Daddy seemed a little reluctant to go back to it on account of that was not truly the truth of the thing but Momma and Aunt Sister too insisted it was what they preferred far and away so Daddy said he guessed he would use it again if it would suit them to do so and they agreed enthusiastically that it would suit them fine and so Daddy told them, "Alright then," and told them just after, "Well, shit in my boots," and then looked full on the two of them with his lips laid out a little like maybe it was not the kind of thing he would say unless he got asked to.

"A mule?" that fellow said. "Gnawed and beat and scratched and just generally eat up all over by a mule?"

"What mule?" Uncle Jack asked him.

"Your mule there," the Oklahoma heathen told Uncle Jack and stood up and turned partway around and flung his free arm off in the direction of the wagon and the nine mules altogether.

"Weren't him that did this," Uncle Jack said and raised up his arms and inclined his head so as to make his tarred wounds more apparent. "Weren't him but what got took and stole there at the outset."

"Took and stole?" the Oklahoma heathen said. "Who by?"

And Uncle Jack told him, "Injun. Thieving injun bastard."

"My granddaddy's an injun," the Oklahoma heathen said and stiffened noticeably.

"Weren't him," Uncle Jack said back. "This boy ain't going to make it to granddaddy."

"Dead?" the Oklahoma heathen asked him.

"No sir," Uncle Jack told him. "Not last I saw but shot good enough to maybe get dead."

"What with?" the Oklahoma heathen wanted to know.

"Sharps," Uncle Jack said. ".50 caliber."

"Lord, get dead I guess," the Oklahoma heathen said back. "Where'd you hit him?"

"I didn't hit him anywhere," Uncle Jack said. "Weren't me that shot him."

"Who then?" the Oklahoma heathen wanted to know.

And Daddy said Uncle Jack showed all his teeth of a sudden and could not hardly seem to make his mouth shut enough so as to let him say who exactly and consequently he pointed straightoff and could not manage to come out with what he was trying to come out with until the Oklahoma heathen had already seen for himself what Uncle Jack had only been able to point at so far, and the Oklahoma heathen said, "Sweet Jesus," and Uncle Jack told him, "Her," and Aunt Della stirred the beanpot and poked the fire and looked kind of wiry and ordinary and, as far as the Oklahoma heathen could tell, wholly incapable.

"No sir," he said. "No sir, I can't see it."

"Her," Uncle Jack told him and he said, "Della, who shot that injun?"

And Daddy said Aunt Della, without ever not stirring her beanpot and without ever not poking the lire beneath it, told him back, "Me." So Uncle Jack said, "Her," again and the Oklahoma heathen said, "Her," his own self and then asked Uncle Jack, "Sharps?" and asked Uncle Jack, ".50 caliber?" and Uncle Jack fetched the thing out from the wagon with the sides and the roof to it and gave it over to the Oklahoma heathen who hefted it like he could not hardly and aimed it prior to hefting it like he could not hardly again and then he said to Aunt Della, "Got some bite don't it?"

And Aunt Della worked her shoulder that was mostly her fire-poking shoulder just then and told him back, "Bite sure enough."

And the Oklahoma heathen raised up the rifle another time and aimed it another time and lowered it another time too and then said to Uncle Jack, "Whereabouts?" and Uncle Jack that had a cartridge between his thumb and forefinger laid it point foremost against his own shoulder and the Oklahoma heathen asked him, "Clean through?" and Uncle Jack told him, "Yes sir," back and the Oklahoma heathen said, "Lordy," and Uncle Jack liked it well enough to say it himself.

Then did not anybody tell anybody else anything, Daddy said, at least not for a spell and Uncle Jack studied the bullet between his fingers and the Oklahoma heathen ate on his beans and drank on his coffee and pondered the air before him and Aunt Della stirred like she'd been stirring and poked like she'd been poking and the mules stamped and snorted like mules will sometimes though not with particular spunk or vigor either and Daddy said Uncle Jack said, "Well," one time so as to fill up the empty air and was about to say it again when a thought came to the Oklahoma heathen of a sudden and straightaway he asked Uncle Jack, "Where in the world were you?"

"In on it," Uncle Jack told him. "Tussling and tangling and near about run through."

"Stuck?" the Oklahoma heathen wanted to know.

"Stuck sure enough," Uncle Jack told him and he drew out from his boot the bonehandled knife and turned it in the air so the blade glinted and glistened even there in the failing light.

"Jesus, stuck I guess," the Oklahoma heathen said and whistled through his teeth. "So you was about to catch it?"

"Yes sir, just on this side of it."

"You was about to get purely done in," the Oklahoma heathen said. "Yes sir," Uncle Jack told him. "He had it out from his own boot and had it raised overhead and damned if I didn't figure it was all up with me. Damned if I wasn't cocksure of it."

"And then her?" the Oklahoma heathen said and jerked his head some.

"Her," Uncle Jack told him back. "Raised that thing and aimed it and squeezed off that shot and hit him direct in his stabbing shoulder and lord you could just hear the bones go."

And the Oklahoma heathen said, "Umph," in the back of his mouth and then snorted out through his nose and snorted in through his nose and said, "Umph," again prior to turning partway roundabout towards the fire and the beanpot and Aunt Della too that had done what she did and he pondered her there full on and then said for Uncle Jack mostly but for Aunt Della somewhat as well, "Fine woman." And straightaway Uncle Jack told him back, "Orblike," and nodded his head with more spunk and vigor than all eight of the hybrid mules together seemed capable of, and the Oklahoma heathen observed the nodding and considered the Orblike with his own head still but pitched and canted somewhat and when it was at last time for him to comment and reply he did not say but "Alright" that way that does not mean anything whatsover, not even alright.

Presently they did get clear of Oklahoma, Daddy said, though the mules did not seem enthusiastic at the prospect of going anywhere much truly and they traveled back through Poteau and across the border into Arkansas and as far as Fort Smith where they put up for two days so as to rest little Spud that had towed not just the wagon with the sides and the roof to it and Uncle Jack and Aunt Della and all their paraphernalia and whatnot but the eight Oklahoma hybrids on top of it that conserved their vast stores of inbred and cultivated energy and just let themselves get fairly much dragged along, and Daddy said Uncle Jack was all over Fort Smith with talk of indians and bone-handled knives and buffalo rifles, most especially out front of the mercantile where men tended to collect and linger, and he laid out the scene and expanded upon the circumstances and described the tussling and the tangling in the road, described his own perspective of it anyhow which tended to emphasize the biting both of the earlobe and of the cowlick and even sometimes of places otherwise that had not actually got bit but that seemed to him could have stood to, and then there was the shooting to speak of, first as he recollected it and then as Aunt Della must have seen it which neither one was precisely how it happened really on account of the knifeblade almost exclusively which had commenced raised up but Uncle Jack did not feel there was sufficient drama in a raised up knifeblade and so set about lowering it a little at the time until soon enough the pointy end of it was against his own chestflesh, had even sliced into it somewhat, and this was where Uncle Jack pulled open his shirt and showed off the scratch that could not anybody look at and say was not from a knife though it was from a fork truly, a fork that Uncle Jack had been a little wild and careless with, but had made a mark that could not anybody look at and say the pointy end of a bonehandled knife had not made, so it passed well enough and Uncle Jack told how it was to get near about laid open, told what it was he'd thought and what prayerful things it was he'd said, and then told how he'd heard the shot, how he'd heard the shot and seen the hole come there in the same instant, and he said, "Lord, you could just hear the bones go," which tended to have a kind of squirmy effect on folks, and he told how the knife had got dropped and the indian had got knocked backwards, and described just precisely and even accurately too how he took up the one and set out after the other but did not overtake him as he himself was beat and scraped and scratched and gnawed on and near about laid open while that indian was not hardly anything but shot and was an indian anyhow which meant feet and legs and purely astonishing velocity. And then there was the rifle to get took up and the spare cartridges and the shooter too that Uncle Jack jerked his head at whenever Aunt Della was somewhere roundabout to get a head jerked at her and sometimes he said just "Her" and sometimes he said "Orblike" too.

Daddy said the entire narrative grew a little puffed up and inflated on its way through Arkansas and the indian commenced to get extraordinarily large, commenced to get wild and inhuman along about Russellville and by Heber Springs the tangling and tussling in the street had accumulated and assumed a kind of savagery that most dogfights don't ever pitch up to, so the whole business was growing and swelling in a regular sort of way and by the time Uncle Jack and Aunt Della finally made Osceola to the east they brought with them not just a wagon with sides and a roof to it and not just a regular mule between the forks at the front of it and eight hybrid mules on the hook-eye at the back but brought with them as well a tale of truly epic proportions that Uncle Jack straightaway commenced to cast around for a place to spin and he found a livery partly down an alleyway that had a crowd roundabout the door of it, one of your slouching wall-laying crowds that looked, to Uncle Jack, purely ripe for what he had to tell them and so he proceeded down the alleyway to the livery door and commenced to slouch and lay up against the wall himself and presently, like usual, some one fellow that was more observant maybe than the rest or just closer anyhow and with eyes and a mouth too looked full on Uncle Jack and at length said to him, "What in the hell is that on you?"

"Salve," Uncle Jack told him back and got told himself, "Salve?" which was like usual too and he said, "Yes sir, for cuts and scrapes and wounds otherwise," and he drew a breath and waited like he tended to anymore on account of he knew now it would come, on account of he knew now there was just some things people could not stand not to know, and it did come and not even from the man that had said the first thing anyhow but from somebody else entirely that had got drawn in already and just happened to be the only one to get it out straightoff and not hardly the only one that wanted to but Uncle Jack did not even act like he'd heard it and just laid against the wall like he'd been laying against it and just kind of breathed in and just kind of breathed out and just waited for it to get said again on account of it always did and would get said firmer this time and louder and with appreciable irritation, Uncle Jack knew that already and so did not jump and did not twitch when he got asked it again, got asked it again not from the man that had asked it initially, who himself was not even the one that had started the whole thing in the first place, but from somebody else still, somebody the other side of Uncle Jack that barked direct in his ear but nonetheless did not make him jump and did not make him twitch, did not even prompt him to answer fast and direct and so thought that maybe he did not get heard clear and did not get understood and consequently the man that had said it the second time said it a third time too and even a fourth time along with it. "What from?" he wanted to know. "The cuts, the scrapes, the wounds otherwise. What from?" And Daddy said Uncle Jack wet his lips all roundabout and drew back his shoulders and puffed out his chest and inhaled deep and exhaled hard and told not just that third man that had spoke to him or the second one or the first that had commenced it all but told the whole crowd of them there together, "Well," which Daddy said was not just your ordinary well like most people say it most times but was Uncle Jack's own special epic sort of Well that Daddy said was all heavy and telling like that first long note violins play sometimes at the outset of a symphony.

He did not start in on the mule directly, anyhow did not start in on the mule directly in conjunction with the indian like he had started out the first few times he'd endeavored to tell it but started instead with just the mule as a kind of general item and then progressed to a brief history of little Spud emphasizing the sort and type and establishing thereby little Spud's particular brand of mulishness in such a way so as to draw and render him up as the type of creature a man could get bonded and attached to like Uncle Jack insisted he'd got bonded and got attached. And then he proceeded on to the indian that he dissected and discussed and just generally made plain like the mule previous afterwhich he kind of skipped roundabout and alternated between your various topics, which would be not just your mules and not just your indians but your thieving impulses as well and your scuffling and tussling techniques and your bonehandled knives and your buffalo rifles and what manner of harm could come from the one that maybe could not come from the other. Then Uncle Jack drew a breath, Daddy said, and took noticeable pause there at the livery doorway, pause so noticeable in fact and so complete that could not everybody roundabout him call up the courtesy to abide the silence with much grace to speak of and not the man that had talked at him first but the man that had talked at him second said, "Well?" and then got joined and contributed to by the man that had talked at him first and the man that had talked at him third too who said, "Well?" themselves like the second man had said Well before them, none of which were Wells of your symphonic sort but were instead more your pointy stick variety but still Unde Jack did not but persist in his pausing and laid himself back against the doorjamb in a casual and altogether unhurried sort of way that so irked and inflamed the crowd collected roundabout him that he got Welled at all over again and this time not even by the men that had Welled at him initially but by most everybody otherwise and Daddy said still Uncle Jack did not but lick his lips and did not but cross his arms over himself and did not but continue laying up against the jamb like he'd been laying up against it and naturally did not bother to speak until it commenced to look like maybe he would not get listened to anyway but just ripped apart at the bone sockets instead and even when he did open his mouth he did not say but two things there at first and let them hang in the air a time before he opened his mouth again and said the same two things all over. "Harts-horne," he told them, "Oklahoma."

Daddy said it was an art, said it was a gift, and said Uncle Jack had been purely blessed with it and so knew not just when to talk and what to say when he did but knew too just how not to say anything and when not to say it and had figured out between the talking and the not talking just when it was that some scant and partial talking might have an effect that could not much else have, your scant and your partial talking including of course your mouth and your nose noises that Uncle Jack used like words mostly and even used better than words sometimes, and so he said, "Hartshorne Oklahoma," and then said it again just after and then sucked spit through his tooth-gaps and so naturally made that noise that spit through a toothgap will make. Then he set in with the London, Daddy said, set in in a vague and discreet sort of way and did not get altogether particular about him but just said a thing or two and then went on to the mules that he did not get altogether particular about either as he was not himself looking to get irked and inflamed. Daddy said it was snuff after, was snuff for a while much in the way it had been mules and indians previously, was snuff up in the ether, Daddy said, snuff up on a plane other than the one the spit landed atop of, and then it was Sweet La La especial and the drygoods that stocked it and the Williford out front with his backside against the wall. Daddy said Uncle Jack painted the whole thing just like a picture with little flourishes in one place and another and gaudy colors here and there and he rendered up Aunt Della near about as true as he could render her up but without much particular emphasis on the hooked nose and the pointy joints and the general wiriness that he bunched altogether and let go as lilt thereby distinguishing and differentiating her from the Williford who did not get much lilt to speak of but just stomach mostly and some considerable saliva as well and thereby distinguishing and differentiating her from the indian too that did not get hardly anything but red skin and meanness at the outset and then just plain shot later, and Daddy said once Uncle Jack had established the principal items and forces of the thing, which was of course the mule and the meanness and the lilt and the saliva mostly, and had established the principal implements as well, which was the knife and the gun and the teeth and the knuckles and the knee that was to get put where it got put, he went on somewhat with the story of the thing though not purely full ahead on account of Daddy said Uncle Jack had a sense of pace and had a sense of timing and had a sense of rhythm too or anyhow had enough of a sense of pace and timing and rhythm so as to hinder and gum up whatever it was he might be inflicting his pace and timing and rhythm on which was in this case the actual theft of the mule which truly was not a lengthy and extended undertaking except in the telling of it as Uncle Jack felt obliged not just to give out what was happening to the mule at the hands of the indian but expended as well some appreciable breath on what was happening to Aunt Della and what was happening to the Williford and even speculated as to what was happening to his own self at the very same instant that what was happening to the mule was happening to him since Uncle Jack insisted does not everything stop happening to everybody everywhere when one particular thing starts happening to somebody somewhere else, or anyhow does not everything stop happening to everybody everywhere unless they are in earshot of somebody who's telling what's happening to everybody and everywhere it's happening to them since to hear talk of everything is to hear talk of nothing truly and the crowd collected roundabout the livery stable doorway commenced to get noticeably twitchy and agitated on account of they were not quite capable of comprehending as a group the nuances of the oral narrative as best as Uncle Jack could tell and being consummate and being accomplished, which was what Uncle Jack figured he was in the line of oral narrative and such, he adjusted and he compensated and allowed the indian, that had not even laid his fingers on the reins yet, to make off on the mule up the road and down the alleyway and the man that had talked at Unde Jack second and had seemed especially twitchy and had seemed especially agitated of a sudden grew offended as well and wondered how it was an indian could ride off on a tied-up mule and Uncle Jack told him back he'd untied the thing before he ever got on and the man that had talked at Uncle Jack second said he did not recollect any untying and the man that had talked at Uncle Jack first along with the one that had talked at him third and a few that had not talked at him at all previously said they did not recollect any untying either and so Uncle Jack touched himself where his cowlick had been that way he usually did even before it got bit off and he said he guessed he'd best start over so as to get everything square and proper but suddenly and straightaway a ride on a tied-up mule did not seem so farfetched and fantastic to the crowd at the livery stable doorway and several of them recollected together how they had struck out on tied-up horses a time or two themselves and they wondered why didn't Uncle Jack just go ahead with the thing and not even bother with the reins at all, wondered why they had set him off course in the first place, wondered what in the world had come over the bunch of them.

So Uncle Jack followed the indian down the alleyway and up the backstreet not so awful far to the roadhouse which he described with considerable attention from the outside and described with considerable attention from the inside too before he left off with the indian entirely for a spell and returned to Aunt Della in the drygoods and the Williford up against the front of it with his stomach and with his saliva and little otherwise to recommend him and Uncle Jack managed to work up considerable feeling against the Williford even before he'd ever opened his mouth other than to spit out of it, so when Aunt Della brought her lilty self out onto the plank sidewalk at last and saw just precisely what was gone from where and then got told what she got told by the Williford and how she got told it there was a pause in the progress of things while various factions of the crowd vented themselves against the sort of uncivilized creatures that the majority of them insisted Oklahoma was known for.

Naturally there was considerable traveling to make an accounting of and as getting from one place to another place and then back to the first place again is not generally all that lively and intriguing to actually undertake it is not hardly ever much to hear about either so Uncle Jack told somewhat of the walking but did not wear the thing out truly and then he changed over to the mulebite for a spell so as to break the monotony some and he made mention of the purply teeth-marks and made mention of the bloomers and where they got raised to and how fast and the entire episode produced some palpable levity among the men roundabout who were the sort to get all worked up and touched off by bloomers and by mulebites too so they were fairly much set to go back to Hartshorne when Uncle Jack got set himself to take them there and he did take them there but not hardly how him and Aunt Della had got there themselves which was both on the mule at the outset and then one on the mule and then none on the mule and then not even with the mule in tow but since Uncle Jack did not see as it would pay him to be accurate and truthful about what he'd bought eight of and hoped to sell off anyway he did not dwell much on the circumstances and various tribulations of the return trip but just mostly on the simple fact of it and he brought himself and Aunt Della and even the hybrid and cultivated mule too direct up to the drygoods which would have been fine if he'd done it all plain and slow but Uncle Jack figured that as long as he was taking the mule somewhere the mule had not truly got to be he might as well get him there somehow the mule could not truly travel which was at a kind of a fullblown romping gallop with Aunt Della clinging to his mane and Uncle Jack clinging to Aunt Della and he told how the animal ran full tilt clean up to the storefront and then to stop himself bunched up all four of his hooves together and plunged them into the loose dirt at the road-edge like spearpoints and then threw his head and snorted, and Uncle Jack fell silent for a time and let the image impress itself on the crowd roundabout him and it did impress itself but not just exactly how Uncle Jack had figured it would as he took it for a kind of harmless bending of the truth while the bunch of them there took it for plain horse-shit mostly, took it for plain horseshit straightaway, and so did not hardly need near the time to comprehend and appreciate the thing that Uncle Jack allowed them and the one that had talked at Uncle Jack third told him, "Go on," even before Uncle Jack could get his own head clear of the flowing mane and the hoofbeats and such that he was beginning to believe a little himself and the second one told him, "Go on," too and the third one threw in with a "Yes sir" after that meant purely Go on itself.

So Uncle Jack left off with the mule and went direct to the jackass

and told where he was and just how he laid up against what he laid up against and told what he said and where he spat and how he scratched and what parts he did it to and it all direct in front of a lady. "Lilty," Uncle Jack said. "Orblike." And Daddy said the crowd got all frothy and worked up together and said a few hard things against the Williford and said a few hard things against the sort of state that would breed his type and then a man back on the fringes of the crowd that had not spoke out previously expressed his preference for the grand state of Arkansas with a kind of fervor and enthusiasm that stirred everybody otherwise and he swore he'd be goddammed if he'd ever set foot in Oklahoma again and most everybody else swore they'd be goddammed if they ever would either though the bulk of them had yet to be out of Arkansas anyhow, and Daddy said Uncle Jack expressed his true and profound appreciation for their support and then he wondered, like maybe it was just plain purposeless wondering, what a man from Arkansas might charge a man from somewhere else for the trouble of walking across a street and down an alleyway and partly up a backroad so as to point out the solitary mule that had got stole from the man from somewhere else that could not get home without it and the man that had first preferred hell to Oklahoma spoke out again and insisted there was nary an individual in the entire state of Arkansas that would take money for such as that and he asked out loud in a general sort of way if that wasn't the truth of the thing and got told it surely was just precisely by most everybody at once and Uncle Jack laid his mouth and his chin and a piece of his nose in his open hand and shook his head one time and then said all slow and deliberate, "Fifteen cents," and shook his head another time and Daddy said the whole group together grew grumbly and ill and then near about outraged after and Daddy figured that if Oklahoma had been a frame house they'd have all set fire to it.

So he got led, Uncle Jack said, across the road and down the alleyway and partly up the backstreet to the roadhouse or actually not so far as the roadhouse proper but just to within sight of it truly where it could get pointed at and indicated with just a finger, Uncle Jack said, just a solitary raised finger, and then Uncle Jack laid his mouth and his chin and the piece of his nose where he'd laid them previously and he said again what he'd said before and so rejuvenated what ill will had seeped off from the crowd roundabout him and they were near about as ready for him to wail at the Williford as any savage otherwise when Uncle Jack told how he left Aunt Della in the street with the rifle and then broke off some from the progress of things to explain the gun and to explain the bullets and to explain what the two of them in combination could wreak upon a stomach tar bottle which was still a fairly completely theoretical sort of thing for Uncle Jack who guessed at it well enough anyhow and told it like he'd seen it plenty often. So then, Uncle Jack said, there was nothing left to do but fetch out the indian and impress upon him the foolhardiness of his escapade, Uncle Jack called it, and he said he patted his mule on the flank there in front of the roadhouse and looked him over for whelps and knots and such but did not find any and Uncle Jack guessed there was men that would have just untied the animal and took him off from there, guessed there was men that could do such and live with it, guessed it was maybe the smart thing, the sober thing, but he didn't figure it was the square thing and Uncle Jack announced there at the livery door how he was a man that stood and lived and breathed for the square thing and from the manner of noise that swelled up in reply it seemed for a time there that did not but everybody else stand and live and breathe for the square thing too. And Daddy said Uncle Jack told how he stepped in through the open roadhouse doorway and squinted in the halflight and could not see but shapes and could not see but forms and could not smell but indians all drawn up and circled roundabout him and then he said what he'd said and repeated it after on account of some few men in the back had not heard precisely what he said he'd said and wanted to know it just like it had come out when it first did come out and he told how he stood with his legs against the table edge and told how he waited and then told what he got told back and told from where, or anyhow indicated from where, Daddy said, indicated from where with his whole arm that he flung out before him and then looked down the length of like people will when they fling out their arms to indicate with, and Daddy said it was just for the drama of the thing mostly and not so as to really point and not so as to really indicate but once Uncle Jack had looked down his arm like he could not help but do he discovered it was really pointing and was really indicating and actually at some particular somebody off a ways up the sidestreet, some particular somebody that had crossed midway over it and had just happened to stop and had just happened to turn and had just happened to get pointed at and indicated by Uncle Jack that straightoff could not believe and could not comprehend it was who it was but soon enough commenced to believe it and soon enough commenced to comprehend it and said at last when at last he could bring himself to talk again, "Well, shit-fire."

Now Daddy says there are strange and wondrous forces at work in the universe, forces that purely defy sense, forces that purely defy rules and principles and just are strange and just are wondrous and just are not at all ordinary anyhow ordinary can be bent and construed. Momma holds with him somewhat but of course Momma calls it God and Aunt Sister won't say she holds with him outright but holds with him nonetheless and calls it Jesus which Momma says means God which Daddy says means forces strange and wondrous. When he calls it anything special and particular, or anyhow when he calls it anything special and particular aside from strange and wondrous forces, he calls it bizarre cosmic magnetism but Momma tends not to condone such talk under her roof as it seems to her somehow heathen or, maybe worse, pagan likely, so Daddy sticks to forces and Momma sticks to God and Aunt Sister sticks to Jesus but is not all of it but the same one thing that is in fact strange and is in fact wondrous and is in fact magnetic at least somewhat too judging from how Daddy tells what he tells about Mr. Russell Newberry and Mr. Russell Newberry's set of keys on a ring and the ocean they dropped into with its shifting tides and currents which Daddy says are metaphorical and allegorical and suggestive too of things other than tides and things other than currents and not but Aunt Sister usually objects on account of metaphorical generally sounds a little devilish to her somehow.

They were down at Kitty Hawk, Daddy said, Mr. Russell Newberry and Mrs. Russell Newberry like usual staying at the cottage they stayed at for two weeks every August and Daddy said they had been there eight days already and just as was ordinary for him Mr. Russell Newberry, that had passable good sense everywhere but on the beach, was already plenty raw and pink across the shoulders and raw and pink behind the knees and raw and pink atop the feet too which would have been the worst place he was raw and pink if not for his ears that he was raw and pink atop of as well and Mrs. Russell Newberry that did not go out much on the sand herself except at eveningtime and so had not got raw anywhere much and not hardly pink either tried to get Mr. Russell Newberry to stay off the sand but at eveningtime too, tried to get him to see the advantage and good sense of it, but Daddy said Mr. Russell Newberry was at the beach after all and Mr. Russell Newberry is just not himself in the presence of the ocean. So Mr. Russell Newberry hunted shells even in the heat of the day and would walk north until he was just a little speck in the distance and then would turn around and walk back south until he was just a little speck the other way and though he did take with him the hat Mrs. Russell Newberry insisted he take with him he did not ever put it on his actual head but instead filled it with whatever he picked up which was crab parts mostly and conch pieces and little busted bits of mysterious items otherwise.

He did go in the water, Daddy said, went in at least two times a day first so as to wake himself in the morning and then so as to soothe his raw pinkness in the afternoon and Daddy said the water off Kitty Hawk was generally just right to wake a man and was generally just right to soothe him too if getting numbed all over was the same as getting soothed which Daddy figured it was considering the rawness and considering the pinkness too, but then it was not a matter of just walking out and ducking down and raising up wet on account of the customary local turbulence which was rapid middling-sized waves on the topside and a near about purely vacuous undertow on the bottom-side so sea bathing at Kitty Hawk was primarily a kind of earnest confrontation and Daddy said just to stand an hour waistdeep in the ocean was like a week at the Y.M.C.A., and he figured it was the cold and figured it was the turbulence and figured it was maybe just the prospect of getting his upper half wrenched loose from his bottom half that distracted Mr. Russell Newberry on the afternoon that he did in fact get distracted, which Daddy said was a Tuesday, a bright sunny Tuesday afternoon that was having some bearing on the rawness and some bearing on the pinkness, so it was likely his own general discomfort and the prospect of rough icy water that prevented Mr. Russell Newberry from recollecting what he usually recollected and doing what he usually did which was to take out from his back pocket his wallet and take out from his side pocket his keyring and lay the both of them in with his shells and crab pieces and mysterious items otherwise.

Daddy said he was near about up to the armpits before he commenced to wonder with any sort of truly concentrated attention if what was supposed to be in his hat with his shells and such was actually in his hat at all as he could not remember putting the wallet in and putting the keys in on top of it like he generally did put the wallet and the keys in and so he felt his backside and discovered in his hip pocket what he'd hoped he would not discover there and he felt along his leg after and discovered in his side pocket what he'd hoped he would not discover there either, and Daddy said like people will when it comes to them how they have done a stupid thing Mr. Russell Newberry compounded his troubles with a second stupid thing which he figured, in his distracted state, might somehow improve and correct the first stupid thing and so he took his wallet out from his one pocket and took his keys out

273

from his other pocket and raised the both of them up over his head like maybe they would get unwet and would get unsaturated of a sudden and with so much to do all at once and so much to think about and so considerable much to be sorry for Mr. Russell Newberry kind of neglected the ocean temporarily and turned around to face the beach which was how what snuck up on him snuck up on him and it slapped him full across his raw pink shoulders and full across his upraised arms and full across the back of his head and the blow downward on his upperparts in combination with the tug outward on his lower parts sort of turned him upside down and kind of caused him to get dragged along the seabottom on his face for a spell which struck Mr. Russell Newberry as kind of another stupid thing and so as to compensate straightaway he commenced to beat and flail his arms underwater and thereby managed to get shed of his keyring entirely which impressed itself upon him almost instantaneously as the height and culmination of his idiocy and Daddy said he was already swearing near about before he could get upright and bring his mouth into the air to swear with.

Naturally he commenced to feel around for the thing with his toes straightaway but he could not tell was he feeling around where he needed to be feeling around as he did not know was he upright where he had just shortly before been upside down and he attempted to calculate just how far it was he'd got jerked and washed and thrown to so to go back to where he'd got knocked over in the first place but Daddy said your general calculating was not anything Mr. Russell

Newberry had much of a talent for and so he just sort of felt with his toes along the ocean floor wherever it was he guessed he might ought to feel and he did in fact find a few items including a sizeable bluecrab that took ahold of Mr. Russell Newberry's great toe for a spell and held to it with tenacity and resolve until Mr. Russell Newberry kicked his leg like he kicked it and thereby transported the creature up out of the water and through the air in a kind of gentle southerly arc. Otherwise he did not feel with his toes anything that even seemed for the first instant of feeling it like keys on a ring and after the bluecrab that he kicked and that he flung Mr. Russell Newberry lost some of his enthusiasm for doing with his toes what he was doing with them and he waded out of the water in a direct line with a light-pole in the dunes so that he might know where he had been when the tide went out and made what was seabottom just beach instead.

Daddy said of course the worse part of the whole business for Mr. Russell Newberry was telling Mrs. Russell Newberry, not because she would grow violent or even extraordinarily peevish but just because she would say what he knew she would say which was not hardly the sort of thing that needed saying as it was not hardly the sort of thing that served any purpose in the telling or any purpose in the hearing either but was just the sort of thing she had to say as she was the type that had to say it, so he stepped onto the screenporch where Mrs. Russell Newberry was stretched out on the chaise lounge reading the magazine she'd carried with her all the way from Neely just to stretch out on the chaise lounge and read and he kind of hunched himself up at the shoulders and kind of puckered his face so as to seem partly incensed and partly just sorrowful and pathetic and he kind of let out a little at the time just what had happened and how and Mrs. Russell Newberry shut her magazine and slapped it down atop her thighs and told him how he shouldn't have carried his keys into the water in the first place which was what he'd known he'd get told and which was surely not anything he needed to hear so he told her back a hard thing, Daddy said, which was not directed truly at her but got aired out anyhow so as to indicate Mr. Russell Newberry's opinion in the matter which Mrs. Russell Newberry did not appear to pay much mind to as she went direct ahead and said to Mr. Russell Newberry what he had known she'd say to him after she'd said what she'd already said to him which was how she guessed he hadn't remembered to bring the spare keys out from the endtable drawer that Daddy said she already knew the answer to even before she said it as there were not any spare keys in the endtable drawer on account of Mr. Russell Newberry had lost the original keys previously and so was driving on the spare keys and had been for a considerable while which Mr. Russell Newberry knew she knew and so did not feel moved to respond to except to say again the same hard thing he had said before and then he took his folding money out from his wallet along with his social security card and the tape receipt from the Sears and Roebuck for the hair dryer he'd given Mrs. Russell Newberry the past Christmas and he wrung them onto the porch floor and Mrs. Russell Newberry watched it puddle up and then watched it spread and run across the concrete afterwhich she told Mr. Russell Newberry how he shouldn't have carried his wallet into the water in the first place.

Daddy said he sat atop a dune amongst the seaoats in his wet checkered swim trunks and with the rest of himself naked and exposed otherwise and primarily pink and primarily raw and not getting but pinker and rawer and he waited for the tide to go out which it did not seem to him it ever would do even once it had started to do it and when it appeared to him he could walk out just on sand where he'd walked out in water previously he lined himself up with the lightpole and strode on down off the dunes and direct across the beach to where he figured maybe he had been but was not at all sure he had been on account of once he'd got there and once he'd commenced to cast around it did not seem to him but that maybe he had been out farther or maybe not out so far, so he set into looking near about everywhere and walked all stooped and bent over which allowed the sun to get at a little piece of his rearend that no sunlight had hardly ever fell on before, especially not for the considerable duration that sunlight got to fall on it this time and so he grew pink and raw in a new place and discovered just where when he stood up to stretch himself.

Now Daddy said that there was truly not much for Mr. Russell Newberry to see no matter how far he bent and how much he stooped, not much to see in the way of keys on a ring anyhow and not hardly much to see in the way of shells and your general tidal refuse either on account of the turbulence and on account of the undertow that had fairly much swept the beach smooth and clean but for some little grainy pieces of shells and every now and again one of those spinal cord things with the seeds in it that nobody seems to know what they are along with a considerable assortment of sandfiddler holes that continued to burp and sputter long after the water had drawn back off them. So Mr. Russell Newberry just kind of poked his index finger wherever it seemed to him that some keys could possibly be which was just about everywhere and while he stooped and poked Mr. Russell Newberry tried to establish in his own mind just what it was he had lost which aside from the roundheaded Pontiac key that opened the trunk and opened the doors and the squareheaded Pontiac key that started the motor was the goldcolored key that opened the side door to their house in Neely and the silvercolored key that opened the front door and the old browncolored key that opened the louvered door leaning against the garage wall that had been the back door once but was not the back door any longer and the new yellowcolored key that opened the new actual back door and the little silvery key that opened the padlock on the basement door and the long black skeleton key that threw the basement door bolt and the tiny clovershaped key that did not open anything anymore on account of what it had opened once had got thrown out and done away with so long before that Mr. Russell Newberry could not even remember what it was exactly but maybe just some sort of box he figured, some sort of case maybe for some one sort of thing or another, and then there was the item that was not even a key but was a kind of a screwdriver on one end and a kind of a wrench on the other but not so much of a screwdriver the one way and not so much of a wrench the other that either end was ever truly of much use for anything and as he bent over there with his tender strip of rearend exposed to the sunlight Mr. Russell Newberry attempted to recollect just precisely the last time his combination screwdriver/wrench had been of any particular use and utility to him and as an instance did not come to mind straightaway he continued to ponder and continued to consider and continued to search for an episode and so did not directly notice the big yellow dog that came up on him from his backside and did not notice just what it was that animal was doing with his nose, just where it was that animal was sniffing exactly until the actual black shiny leathery bulk of it got laid square up against the underside of Mr. Russell Newberry's dangling privates which caused Mr. Russell Newberry what Daddy called immediate dismay.

He said it was an altogether extraordinary sensation, said it for the benefit of Momma and Aunt Sister mostly who together did not seem much interested in getting enlightened about just what sort of sensation it might be but got enlightened anyhow on account of Daddy felt obliged to explain it and felt obliged to describe it as it did not seem to him that dogs tended to lay their noses on women where they tended to lay their noses on men. He said it was bad enough when you could see the dog coming, when you were in somebody's foyer being pleasant and being civil and maybe shaking hands roundabout with one arm and fending off the housepet with the other, but he said it was worse somehow when you were just standing somewhere trying to be plain human and maybe even a little dignified and of a sudden you found yourself leaping and jumping and otherwise attempting to hover so as to dodge and escape whatever it was had touched itself on your personal parts which you would discover to be just the black shiny leathery bulk of a nose when you had finally lighted and had finally come back to your usual senses which Daddy said Mr. Russell Newberry eventually lighted and did after he'd yelped and after he'd leaped and after he'd kind of hopped around for a spell.

It was a yellow dog, Daddy said, a big yellow dog, some kind of big yellow retriever-type dog and Aunt Sister told him, "Laberdor," told him, "Laberdor retriever," and added how they were big and how they were yellow, but Daddy said it was not fully one thing or another which was part of the circumstances anyhow and Momma wanted to know what circumstances exactly and Daddy said it was the strange ones and was the wondrous ones he was getting at and Momma said she could not tell was he getting at anywhere truly and Aunt Sister said it certainly could have been a Laberdor retriever if it was big and if it was yellow and couldn't Daddy know positively otherwise on account of Mr. Russell Newberry did not himself know a chihuahua from a baboon and if it was Mr. Russell Newberry that all of it was coming from couldn't anybody know but that it probably was a Laberdor retriever, likely was, Aunt Sister said, but Daddy insisted it wasn't fully one thing or another which Daddy said was part of the circumstances and Aunt Sister and Momma together asked him, "Which?" and Daddy said, "These," all firm and sharp.

He said it was a Tyson that owned it, a Scotland Neck Tyson that was a ways behind the dog up the beach, far enough anyhow not to see dear just where the dog put his nose and what effect he produced with it which Daddy said probably did not matter anyhow as it is most always the sorts of people that can't control dogs that own dogs that need controlling which Daddy believes is simply in keeping with the basic governing principles of earthly existence as your suitable things do not hardly ever get matched up together, not dogs and people and not children and people and not hardly people and people either which Daddy cannot ever say but with his lips laid wide as Momma will not allow it otherwise. And Daddy said the Tyson did not arrive at where his dog was with Mr. Russell Newberry until well after Mr. Russell Newberry had full well come to himself again and was not leaping and jumping and bouncing about or even palpitating in his chest like he had been for an appreciable spell but was just pressing against the big yellow dog's head with his open hand so as to keep the shiny black leathery nose off from what it had laid up against previously, and naturally like people will that own dogs like the Scotland Neck Tyson owned, the Scotland Neck Tyson just grinned once he got up even with Mr. Russell Newberry and saw what it was Mr. Russell Newberry was pressing against and why and Mr. Russell Newberry kind of grinned back at him as he felt a little too silly for any manner of serious expression, and Daddy said eventually the Scotland Neck Tyson did call his dog, or said Prince anyhow but without much enthusiasm or resolve and of a sudden the dog left off trying to put its nose where it was trying to put its nose which Daddy said was purely coincidental and did not stem at all from the Prince that had got called out by the Scotland Neck Tyson but was instead almost solely on account of a sandfiddler hole hard by that had set in to burping and sputtering in a highly animated sort of way and so attracted the animal after a fashion that Mr. Russell Newberry's dangling privates could not manage.

Of course, Daddy said, Mr. Russell Newberry observed how Prince was certainly a friendly sort of animal which is for some reason or another what people that get sniffed and probed like Mr. Russell Newberry had got sniffed and probed tend to say about whatever creature it was that sniffed and probed them and Daddy said the Scotland Neck Tyson agreed straightaway and then set in to telling Mr. Russell Newberry how it was he had come to own the big yellow dog that he said he'd got from his brother-in-law whose genuine retriever had come in heat and then had got let out the back gate by the garbage man and had caroused for a spell, Daddy called it, had caroused sufficiently anyhow to come home fertilized when at last she did come home and not hardly fertilized by the beast of anybody's choice but her own which Daddy said was probably not in any way a comely beast as it is generally not but the handiest ones that get to partake of what stray carousing gets partook of and Daddy said it did not seem to him that the handy ones were hardly ever the comely ones too. So the Scotland Neck Tyson's brother-in-law's genuine retriever dropped a litter of puppies that were not purely anything much but were mostly just somewhat genuine and just somewhat everything otherwise, enough of everything otherwise to contaminate the certified and the genuine parts in a noticeable sort of way, so the puppies could not get registered and could not get sold as registered and could not hardly pass for even half of an actual type so they just got give up, Daddy said, got parceled out to whoever would have one and the Scotland Neck Tyson decided he would.

He said did not but everybody know how a mixed dog was always smarter than your thoroughbred variety, insisted to Mr. Russell Newberry that a mixed dog could think and reason and he raised his voice some and said, "Prince!" all sharp and sudden and Prince that had commenced to dig into the beach where all the burping and the sputtering had been lifted up his thick yellow head and canted it over sideways so as to study the Scotland Neck Tyson that way dogs do study people sometimes and the Scotland Neck Tyson said to him, "Sit!" all sharp again and all sudden and then repeated it, "Sit!" and while Prince did not truly sit exactly, did not even squat in any noticeable sort of way, he did ponder and did consider the Scotland Neck Tyson with what appeared to be care and what appeared to be intelligence and then seemed to just decide on his own that sitting did not fit well into the present scheme of things so he stuck his nose back into the hole he'd started in the sand and sniffed and snorted and dug some more while the Scotland Neck Tyson explained to Mr. Russell Newberry all about spirit in an animal, all about spunk and such as that, and told how he'd come to the beach in the first place so as to cut Prince loose to exercise his spirit and exercise his spunk which he would not have got to do but for his uncle that let him have his beach house for the weekend once it came vacant when the man that had reserved and had rented it dropped dead of a sudden and so could not take his vacation like he'd planned.

And then Daddy left off so as to light a Tareyton that he drew on with considerable flair and ceremony and he wondered at Momma and at Aunt Sister and somewhat at me too didn't we see how circumstances were collecting, didn't we see how pure coincidences were just piling up, and Aunt Sister told him, "Piling up alright," and then looked at Momma that said, "Kneedeep," and Aunt Sister told her back, "Rising evermore," and showed her teeth at Momma who showed her own teeth after and the two of them together said, "Piling up, Louis, piling up," and Daddy gave them an Alright and then blew smoke onto his shirtfront and gave them another one after it.

He said was not all of it but happenstance, Mr. Russell Newberry and the keyring and the big yellow dog and the Scotland Neck Tyson with the uncle with the beach house and the man that had dropped dead to vacate it, and he wondered didn't it look random and didn't it look ordinary, wondered hadn't we noticed how random and ordinary it looked and Momma that did not ever say Lord God Almighty said, "Lord God Almighty, Louis, yes we see it, we see all of it. Random," she said. "Ordinary. Now go on and get to the thing."

And Aunt Sister pulled at what slight whole piece of Kleenex she could find to pull at and said, "Rising," and said, "Evermore," and kind of smirked at her lap and Daddy sort of told himself out loud how he had not expected such from Christian women and this time Momma said, "Rising," and Momma said, "Evermore."

Down at least a foot and a half, Daddy said, maybe even a full twenty inches but not hardly the two feet Mr. Russell Newberry had told at first or the two feet and a quarter he'd told later or the two feet and a half he'd told after that but just eighteen, Daddy said, and maybe twenty and still no sandfiddler yet on account of the paws were still digging and the grit was still flying and maybe they'd have got covered over and lost yet again but for the big yellow dog that barked one time and the Scotland Neck Tyson that looked to see why and did not see why truly but saw instead atop the heap of loose sand at the dog's flank the metal ring and the Pontiac keys and the latch keys and the bolt keys and the solitary inexplicable clovershaped key too all of which he snatched up at once and said he'd purely be dipped in shit over which Daddy was quick to add was not hardly anything next to what Mr. Russell Newberry said behind it once he saw just precisely what manner of item it was the Scotland Neck Tyson was set to get dipped in shit on account of. And then Daddy left the big yellow dog scratching after the sandfiddler and left the Scotland Neck Tyson holding the keyring up between his thumb and his forefinger and left Mr. Russell Newberry all set to say what it was he was all set to say and Daddy told us Forces and Daddy told us Strange and Daddy told us Wondrous too and then whistled all low and quivery and Aunt Sister said, "Dumb luck," and Momma said, "Blind luck," her own self and Aunt Sister said, "Dumb blind luck," and Momma threw in with a "Just precisely" and did not seem even partly tempted to say God like Aunt Sister was not partly tempted to say Jesus but just luck instead, plain dumb blind random and ordinary which Daddy objected to with Strange and which Daddy objected to with Wondrous and which Daddy objected to with Forces followed by additional whistling all low and all quivery like wind down a chimney pipe.

But Aunt Sister said it did not compare, said it was not anything, and she wondered did we recollect the Brownes with an e that had come from Danbury and had lived in the Upton house out the old Elisboro road and Daddy wondered back at her what old Elisboro road and Aunt Sister told him the one that used to go to Elisboro and Daddy said it still went there but Aunt Sister told him did not anybody drive it like the new Elisboro road and Daddy explained to her how the new Elisboro road was the old Elisboro road just with asphalt and lines on it and Aunt Sister told him it wasn't but Daddy told her it was and Aunt Sister asked Momma was it and Momma told her it was too so Aunt Sister knew it had to be and wondered did we recollect the Brownes with an e that had come from Danbury and had lived in the Upton house out the just plain Elisboro road and Momma did and Daddy did but I couldn't place the first one of them and so got told by Momma how Mrs. Browne was the one that wore the hat with the bird on it and Aunt Sister said it was a hat alright but was not a bird, was not a bird at all, and was a butterfly instead but Momma told her back how it was the other Brown woman, the plain eless Brown woman that wore the hat with the butterfly on it and she asked Aunt Sister didn't she recall how it was the plain eless Brown woman that had the boy that joined the navy and would come home holidays in his white jacket and his white pants and his white shoes and his white hat and take his momma roundabout town on his arm and her in those dark paisley prints she favored so and with that hat, that blue hat with the daisies and with the butterfly, and Aunt Sister pondered what it was Momma was attempting to draw up for her and saw it clear at last which was all the white parts on him and the paisley parts on her and the butterfly at the topnotch of the whole of it and she told me it was a bird, was a kind of a carvedout painted bird and I asked her who on and she said the Browne, the Elisboro road Upton house Browne that was a little woman, she told me, with a mole right there at the crease where the rounded nosehole skin met her face and then I even saw her too, saw her at the vegetable bin in the Big Apple pinching a tomato and watching herself do it with me off a ways cooling my feet on the linoleum and watching her watch herself and getting watched in turn by that bird of hers that was in fact carvedout and was in fact painted.

So we all got her plain and held to what it was we had of her while Aunt Sister told the thing she had set out to tell that she insisted was in fact strange and was in fact wondrous and was in fact all charged with Jesus that meant God truly but did not ever get called God out from the lips of Aunt Sister anyhow who had it all down to Jesus and had it all down to Christ, and Aunt Sister said the Elisboro road Browne got up of a morning with an inkling, a dark murky inkling that weighed on her, Aunt Sister said, made her low and made her sorrowful and without particular cause and without particular reason and Aunt Sister laid the fingers of her one hand roundabout the bottom of her neck and partway onto her collarbone and told us, "Nameless," in a dramatic sort of way.

And Daddy asked her back, "Nameless what?" though not with much drama to speak of.

"Something," Aunt Sister told him. "Nameless something all dark and all murky and weighing heavy on her." And Aunt Sister said the Elisboro road Browne took up her Chronicle straightaway and turned to the obituaries of it as she feared there'd been a passing on and while there'd been a few was not any of them anybody she had not known was dead already before she got up all burdened with her inkling and so she stayed blue and stayed heavy-hearted, Aunt Sister said, and did not know purely how come until what Aunt Sister called the visitation that manifested itself in the globe of the overhead light and she said it was an image, an image all plain and clear of the Elis-boro road Browne's brother, John Edward Gunn of Danville, a bachelor that sold office supplies, and naturally the Elisboro road Browne could not but assume and anticipate the worst about him once she saw him like she did in the lightglobe as do not people show up in lightglobes for any good and pleasant reason hardly ever, and Aunt Sister said she called him at his house but did not anybody answer and called him at his office but could not get through on the line and so she fetched out from her refrigerator the dozen speckled eggs she'd bought the day previous, the dozen speckled eggs she'd been fairly much possessed to buy and so had gone ahead and paid for and carried home though she did not usually eat eggs, Aunt Sister said, on account of how Dr. Shackleford had warned her off them but she'd been urged and had been possessed and so had bought the dozen speckled ones that she laid in a pot and covered with water and commenced to boil so as to have something to devil and prepare and carry with her when the time came for her to go wherever it was she might end up which Aunt Sister said she had an inkling about all dark and murky.

Naturally she commenced to get agitated, Aunt Sister said, that way most people get agitated when things go heavy and go bleak and go vague all at once, and so the Elisboro road Browne that had seen her brother in the lightglobe called on the telephone Mrs. Semple from up the road that she most usually called in times of agitation and distress and she set herself to explain who it was she had seen and where it was she had seen him and what it was she'd figured it all added up to when of a sudden Mrs. Semple from up the road commenced to blubber and commenced to yowl and explained all roundabout her gasping and all roundabout her wheezing how her Momma's sister that had stroked from a nosebleed Easter of 1957 and had stayed all frozen and bedridden ever since had just that very morning succumbed, had just that very hour in fact passed on into the everlasting beyond and it struck Mrs. Semple as purely miraculous that the Elisboro road Browne should call up just when she did call up and with what story of her lightglobe she had to tell once she did in fact get a chance to tell it and the Elisboro road Browne said back how she had been low and how she had been sorrowful and explained somewhat of her inkling to Mrs. Semple from up the road that was the sort to appre-date an inkling as she was evermore plagued by them her own self and just plain talk of inklings all dark and murky reminded Mrs. Semple from up the road how she had got a twinge just minutes previous to the phone-call from the Elisboro road Browne and had, she recollected, seen across the backs of her eyes the cordovan purse with the brass catch that the Elisboro road Browne tended to carry more so than all of the rest of her purses, and Aunt Sister said together the Elisboro road Browne and Mrs. Semple from up the road agreed it was a wondrous thing that had transpired, agreed it was somehow the hand of Jesus acting somehow like the hand of Jesus tends to act most times, and she told how the Elisboro road Browne deviled her eggs and laid them out on her eggplate and dusted them over with paprika and then carried them on foot up the road to the Semple's house and so got there with food even before the most of the local Semples with a bloodrea-son right to know had found out just why it was the Elisboro road Browne would go where she went and take what she took. And then Aunt Sister grew all sniffy at the nose and a little seepy at the eyes like she usually did when Jesus got brought into things in a prominent sort of way and she looked kind of up towards the ceiling, kind of up at the light fixture in the direct middle of the ceiling and said to it, "The Lord He works in mysterious ways," which was just the kind of thing to get Daddy all squirmy and irritated and he commenced to jerk and slip and slide across his chairseat like maybe he'd sat on an anthill and Momma said to him, "Louis," and Daddy said just out loud mostly, "Christ," and Aunt Sister said just out loud after, "Him." "Now let me get this straight," Daddy said once he'd got civil which was what Momma insisted he had to get, "let me get this just right on the beam here. This Browne with an e woman sees her own brother in the kitchen lightglobe and straightaway figures some harm has come to him on account of it isn't but your afflicted people that show up in lightglobes anyway."

And Aunt Sister told him, "Not just precisely, Louis. It was the inkling first, the dark murky inkling."

"Nameless?" Daddy said.

"Nameless," Aunt Sister told him, "and murky and dark."

"And then the lightglobe?" Daddy said.

"The visitation," Aunt Sister told him.

"On the lightglobe," Daddy said.

"On the lightglobe," Aunt Sister told him.

"So she calls her neighbor the Semple," Daddy said.

"Just precisely," Aunt Sister told him.

"On account of she always calls her neighbor when she's dark and murky," Daddy said.

And Aunt Sister looked at Daddy that way she looks at Daddy when she knows what he's up to and wants him to know she knows.

"Troubled too," Daddy said. "The lightglobe, don't you know, with the brother on it."

"Visitation," Aunt Sister told him and then kind of veered off the subject proper for a moment so as to explain to Daddy how there are actually some people on God's earth that do in fact like other people on God's earth and feel the need to communicate with them from time to time so as to express some one thing or another and Daddy said he'd heard tell of such previously and wondered at Aunt Sister was a brother on a lightglobe the manner of thing people on God's earth might feel a need to communicate about and Aunt Sister told him, "Some people," told him, "faithful people," and Daddy said he'd guessed as much.

"So she gets a visitation," Daddy said, "and figures rightoff there's trouble with the visitor."

"Wouldn't you?" Aunt Sister asked him.

And Daddy said, "Well I guess if I saw a brother of mine in a lightglobe I'd have to figure there was trouble somewhere and maybe I'd start with him so as not to have to start with me."

"And wouldn't you communicate it?" Aunt Sister wanted to know. "I guess I might," Daddy said, "but here this Browne with an e woman calls down the street to tell her neighbor the Semple how she's been visitated and where and who by and near about gets it out before she's told her own self what lady has passed into the beyond and when and how come that does not any of it have anything at all to do with the Browne with an e's brother in the lightglobe and not hardly much to do with speckled eggs either but's still Jesus and still Christ," Daddy said, "and for damn certain mysterious. I mean at least with a big yellow dog it's only strange and only wondrous but this business with Jesus is downright peculiar."

"There's not a thing peculiar about Jesus Christ," Aunt Sister said with some considerable conviction and emphasis and Daddy told her back, "Nothing but from the halo out in every direction," and Aunt Sister shot up stiff in her seat like she'd been electrified and opened her mouth to tell Daddy something with a barb to it but could not get it out straightaway, could not get it out long enough anyhow for Momma to wonder just what it was he'd thrown his arm out at, just what it was he'd seen there a ways up the sidestreet that maybe was strange and that maybe was wondrous, that maybe was somehow just extraordinarily coincidental, and Aunt Sister that had not left off working to say what she wanted to say did finally get her lips and her mouth muscles sufficiently coordinated to produce between them a little piece of scripture which was one of your faithless and heathen pieces of scripture of the variety that Aunt Sister generally flung at Daddy when he stirred her up in a religious sort of way, and Daddy flung a thing back at her that was somewhat blasphemous and somewhat profane though somewhat inaudible too so as to let him deny whatever it might be he might want to deny about it when the time came for him to say it again which the time came for straightaway as Aunt Sister asked him, "What?" and Daddy decided was not any of it anything he might want to say again and so he told Aunt Sister, "Nothing," which was worse than blasphemous and worse than profane on account of that made what he'd said not just the one actual thing he'd said but instead most everything she could think of and she could think of most everything and had commenced to get so palpably worked up and frothy that Momma felt obliged to wedge herself into the business which she did not much like to do when it was whose business it was she had to wedge herself into and when it was at what pitch it had come to be at but as she felt obliged she went ahead and did it anyhow and said all aloud and plain so as to not go unheard and misunderstood, "Who? Why? Shitfire?" and even Daddy looked at her just like Aunt Sister looked at her and Momma told us, "Arkansas," and flung out her arm and told us, "Shitfire," and added behind it, "Who? Why?" and Aunt Sister said, "Alright, who then and why then?" once she'd got it straight in her own mind just precisely why it had come out like it came out and Daddy that was supposed to tell all of us who and was supposed to tell all of us why just kind of looked at Momma for a spell prior to it with his cheeks all raised up and his mouth all laid out.

"Him," Daddy said when at last he did say anything.

"Him who?" Aunt Sister asked back as there was just the one Him for her that could get talked about as plain him and then there was other regular humans that had to get named off and had to get signified.

"Indian," Daddy said.

"Which?" Aunt Sister asked him.

"The shot one," Daddy told her.

"In Arkansas?" Aunt Sister asked him.

"In Arkansas," Daddy told her.

"Well, I'd purely like to know the how of it," Aunt Sister said to him.

And Daddy drew out a Tareyton from his shirtpocket and tapped it filter foremost on his thumbnail like he usually did not bother to and then just sort of sprawled and just sort of languished for a time and did not even begin to tell Aunt Sister the how of it until he was set just like he wanted to get set which was after he'd sprawled and languished and after he'd lit up and after he'd dragged hard one time so as to say it with smoke mostly, "Forces strange and wondrous."

Daddy said it was him, plain him, him straightaway to Uncle Jack anyhow who could tell even from the distance he had to tell from just who it was precisely and not on account of the kerchief that held the arm up and not even on account of the clothes either that were of course the same clothes only worse off as people then were not so particular as they are now and indians were not even so particular as people then, but it was just something otherwise, Daddy said, "Nameless," he added, "Murky," something that a man recollects about another man once he's had his ear gnawed on and his cowlick bit off, something almost intimate, Daddy said, that let Uncle Jack know who it was he was looking at even from the considerable distance he was looking at him, and he did not start running straightoff, did not start running until he walked some, or anyhow had strode out from the crowd, Daddy said, with just two big steps there at first prior to the little ones that set him in his jogtrot that built to an actual run in as much as Uncle Jack could actually run, and Daddy said the indian just stood in the middle of the sidestreet where he'd stopped and where he'd turned and watched the solitary white man, that did not look to him but like any other white man there at first, walk at him and then trot at him and then actually run at him with the rest of the white men commencing to fall in behind him and still the indian did not know who he was running from exactly once he had set in to running his own self and did not figure out and decide who it was until he heard what he heard which was "Pilfering son-of-a-bitch" that kind of struck a chord with him and he figured that maybe he'd best ought to get cleanly away if it was in fact who he guessed it was as who he guessed it was had at least a bonehandled knife with a long silvery blade and no cowlick to get bit and not but an ear and a half to get gnawed on and two well and actual arms to grapple and tussle with while the indian himself had but the well arm on the one side and the bullethole on the other, so he considered the thing, Daddy said, and considered most all the ramifications of it as he ran and concluded that he would not but keep running and so came off the sidestreet onto the main one and turned up the westerly end of it and charged on by the bank and on by the jail and on by the government land agent's office and beyond it to the general drygoods with the little wiry pointy-nosed bonneted woman in the doorway of it that had her finger and thumb in her cheek and left them there while she watched who went by and watched how and still had not hardly moved much when who came after came after.

Daddy said a man just can't run with one arm like he can run with two arms and so even a man that can't generally run much with two arms can almost always catch a man that can run with two arms but doesn't have but the one arm to run with and consequently Uncle Jack commenced to gain on the indian, commenced to gain so that even he himself noticed how he was verifiably closing ground which he had not really anticipated and had not truly expected but was doing anyhow and so figured he would maybe come up behind him and maybe grab him at the knees and maybe pitch him over that way and then crawl up the length of him and sit full athwart him and draw out from his own boot the knife the indian had drawn out from his own boot previous and raise it up so as to let it glint and glisten in the sunlight like he knew it could and then maybe even plunge it, maybe even actually stab with it, and he thought on this entire series of events for a time as he ran and still had not decided just what he would do with the knife once he got it up where he wanted to get it to but he did make his head sufficiently clear and his concentration sufficiently directed so as to remind himself in a pointed sort of way how he should maybe keep his various loose and dangling items off and away from that part of the indian where the teeth were since it was not the part where the teeth were that had got shot and had got wounded, so as he ran he thought on just how he would grab the indian and where and just what part he might crawl up and sit on and just how he might raise up the knife so that it would glint and would glisten and just how he might lower it after, as well, of course, as just where he would keep his ears and just where he would keep his fingers so as to have them when he got done at least fairly much like they'd been when he started.

Daddy said Uncle Jack was in fact so caught up in thinking and so caught up in pondering that he fairly much lost sight of the indian in an actual sort of way and when he finally looked up ahead of himself to see where it was exactly the indian had come to be there was no indian anywhere, not anywhere in the road anyhow and Uncle Jack, that had outstripped the livery crowd considerably, pulled up some there in between the wagon ruts and looked on up the road to where it bent out of sight and while he spied some few people in it and along it did not any of them look much like an indian and did not any of them at all resemble the shot one and so he turned around and looked back down to where he'd come from and saw what people were closing in behind him and what people were watching them do it and then turned to his one side and saw what blank storefront there was to look at and finally turned to his other side where he expected maybe nothing much but got instead an actual wild and agitated indian face not even a full yard from his own and then not even a foot and then not even anything really as it was him and as it was the indian too pitching sideways into the street and Daddy said Uncle Jack's plan just kind of popped all fullblown into his head and fully occupied it for a time, which would be the plan where Uncle Jack grabbed onto the indian where he'd figured to grab onto him and knocked him over how he'd figured to do it and then sat on him where he'd guessed he would sit and raised up the knife how he'd planned to raise it up, but as the knocking over and the sitting had already got done and as Uncle Jack was not the one that had done them it did not do Uncle Jack much good whatsoever to ponder where he would grab and how he would sit and what he would raise up which was all he could manage to ponder somehow, all he could manage anyway until the indian got his incisors into the fleshiest portion of Uncle Jack's previously unbit ear which reminded Uncle Jack straightaway how he'd intended to watch for his various loose and dangling parts.

Daddy said it is just the nature of things not to go the way people plan and expect for them to go on account of how there are so many ways things can go anyhow that not hardly one man and not hardly two men and generally not hardly an entire committee together can be expected to anticipate the whole slew of them, so Daddy said it was not any wonder to his own self that a solitary man running up a road with his feet going like they did not usually go and his mind working like it did not usually work and his lungs swelling up and caving in like they had not in pure decades might just plain forget what it was indians were known for which Daddy said was wiles and which Daddy said was ways too and Aunt Sister threw in with "Savages," saying it again like she'd said it previously, but Daddy said Uncle Jack did in fact remember at last what it was he'd forgot near about the very moment the indian came from where he came from and bit what he bit which was of course a little late in the progress of things for Uncle Jack to be recollecting what he did recollect but was surely not so late as it could have been and circumstances straightaway impressed upon Uncle Jack just what he had to do and how he had to do it and he saw opportunity right under his noseholes in the form of a nutbrown earlobe that he took into his mouth and clamped down on.

Now Daddy says does not much seem to be going on between two men that each have in their mouths a piece of the ear of the other. Daddy says it just does not look much like a death struggle on account of cannot either man go anywhere hardly and expea to take the bulk of his bit ear with him and so does not either man usually opt to much beating and thrashing about which leaves just stillness mostly, tense stillness, Daddy says, but stillness anyhow and grunting too, grunting that is sometimes like actual words but is not truly ever aaual words really. So Daddy said they just laid in the road there with their jaws all tight and their faces all sweaty and the most of their entire selves all wrapped up and tangled roundabout each other and naturally a throng commenced to collea and circled full around them and was not anybody much pulling for the indian but was not everybody vocal and enthusiastic for Uncle Jack either as there was a faction that could not truly tell what was going on anyhow and so some folks screeched and hollered and some folks just plain looked and some folks did not even last at that on account of how earbiting is what it is and involves what it involves which would be your jawpressure and your molars and your incisors and sometimes your various teeth otherwise and Daddy said people grew just generally lulled after a bit which would be your people in the throng but would be your people on the road too, Uncle Jack that is and the indian as well who together had the most reason to grow lulled as earbiting is a strenuous sort of undertaking and taxes a man considerably. So they each kind of let off, Daddy said, each kind of let off in such a fashion that the other did not know he was getting less bit than he had been just previously and Daddy said Uncle Jack took what concentration and what energy he had been expending on earbiting and focused it exclusively on scheming for a time which would have been alright, Daddy said, if only he'd set aside some little piece of it to leave on the indian who was scheming some himself and of course was better at it in a native sort of way as it was more of a custom and more of an inclination with his sort than with Uncle Jack's that were not hardly born to it and so it was understandably the indian that freed up his good arm and reached down with it to Uncle Jack's boottop so as to take hold of the bonehandled knife that he had noticed was there to get took hold of and understandably it was Uncle Jack that got interrupted in the middle of his pondering and his planning and his wondering too by the sensation in his boot that he had not hardly anticipated and could not at first decipher but did figure out once he noticed in the vicinity of his vital organs a long slender glinting glistening sort of thing.

Of course his energy come back to him along about then like energy will in the face of death and mutilation and the indian tried to roll and wriggle up atop him and tried to raise overhead the bonehandled knife so as to have somewhere to bring it down from all of which Uncle Jack resisted in a lively sort of way but none of which he could truly seem to prevent altogether on account of the indian did manage to get up where he'd been trying to get up to and did manage to raise overhead what he'd set himself to raise and of a sudden Uncle Jack saw all spread out before him his own pure and lethal misfortune and naturally, Daddy said, he did about the only thing he could do in the face of it, he commenced to swear, drew off a breath and just let out with whatever struck him at the moment as the sort of thing he might ought to go ahead and let out which was a great variety of things truly but all of it bound up and bonded together by a general anti-indian flavor that was directed somewhat at the indian with the shot shoulder and the bonehandled knife but somewhat at all the rest of them too, all of the rest of them everywhere there were some, and Daddy said as far as swearing goes it was colorful and vivid and altogether pointed but ultimately ineffective in the way of bonehandled knife defense and so Uncle Jack that could not work his arms loose and could not work the bulk of himself free even any slight and little how and that had already swore and reviled not just the solitary indian atop him but all his kin and all his sort as well concluded and decided in his own mind that was not much left for him but to get skewered and surely was not much need for him to watch it and so he shut his eyes and consequently did not see it this time like he'd seen it the last time and did not ever know if he even heard it either as his ears had been more listening to things inside than things outside but he felt it well enough and thought straightoff how it did not hurt so much to be dead afterall, how it was almost like being alive, how it was actually just exactly like being alive, and he opened up his eyes so as to find out did it maybe look to be dead like it looked to be alive and straightoff he saw the blue sky overhead with the little wispy clouds in it and he raised up himself on his elbows and caught sight of the indian all sprawled and laid out where he'd pitched to and caught sight of what pantslegs and what boottops there were to see roundabout him and then for the first time in what seemed a great while he heard not just his roaring insides but actual people again, people making wondrous and appreciative noises in those loud voices they generally make them in.

And Daddy said he could have been a stomach tar bottle this time and still would have got what he got on account of where it went in on his back and where it came out on his stomach that Aunt Della did not see her own self as she sailed like she sailed and landed like she landed and that Uncle Jack did not see either for reasons purely otherwise and that a particular dirt farmer across the way, an Avery up from the lowlands, saw maybe a little too well as once the bullet cleared the indian it did not stop until it hit the Avery square in the beltbuckle relieving him of the majority of his wind and the bulk of his will to stand up. So the dirt farmer went the one way and Aunt

Della went the other and the indian just kind of hinged over backwards on his kneejoints and Uncle Jack raised up on his elbows and saw what he saw and heard what he heard and then laid himself back down again and listened to his own breathing that he had not expected to ever get to listen to anymore and so paid some considerable attention to until there was "Daddy" from across the way that his ears picked out from all there was to pick out, and then "Daddy" again and he caught his breath short and held it and heard "Daddy" one more time just like the two times before it and then he said a thing himself, said it out loud but not altogether plain and not hardly with much volume to speak of and a man near about next to him could tell that Uncle Jack had said a thing but could not tell just what exactly and so squatted on his heels jam up to Uncle Jack's person and said, "What's that now?" and Uncle Jack said again what he had just said previously but not hardly any clearer and not hardly any plainer and so got asked all over what words it was he was making anyhow and Uncle Jack told him a third time what it was he'd told him a first time and a second time too and this time appreciably louder and appreciably plainer but not so appreciably loud or plain either so as to get understood clear and he just got huhed? at, afterwhich the side of a head with a fleshy ear prominent upon it presented its entire self to him so hard by and close in as to eclipse everything otherwise and Uncle Jack took in air through his nose and ran his tongue two times roundabout his mouth. "Orb," he said, "like."

ii

And Granddaddy dragged his skinflap across his mustache the fourth time and then the fifth time after and said, "Spangles?" just out into the air mostly and Aunt Sister that was still jumpy and agitated and a little sweaty overtop her lip dabbed at herself and told him back, "Yes sir, lustrous diamond spangles."

"What on," Granddaddy wanted to know.

And Aunt Sister told him how they'd been sprinkled roundabout a brooch.

"Whose brooch?" Granddaddy wanted to know.

And Aunt Sister told him how they'd been sprinkled roundabout Mrs. Vernon Littlejohn's brooch.

And Granddaddy said, "Spangles?"

And Aunt Sister told him, "Spangles, Elsworth, lustrous diamond spangles." She said it was a commemorative springtime item, a dogwood blossom of pure plated silver and adorned roundabout the petals with your lustrous diamond spangles and she told how Mrs. Vernon Littlejohn had picked it out of the catalog back in the springtime itself when your springtime items usually got picked out, and was not just the silver brooch, she said, but was a plated gold pinky loop too which qualified Mrs. Vernon Littlejohn for the set of six pewter napkin rings at a reduced rate which Mrs. Vernon Littlejohn had been looking to get qualified for and had ordered the pinky ring on account of as she was not one to generally wear pinky rings and such but just the gold band Mr. Vernon Littlejohn had give her at the service and the tiny diamond setting he'd give her under a walnut tree the year before that, but it had seemed so pretty to her, had looked so dainty and elegant there in the catalog like things will look dainty and will look elegant in catalogs sometimes that she went ahead and wrote out the check that was for the pinky ring and was for the spangle-studded brooch and was for the discounted napkin rings too and Aunt Sister said like usual she took the order and took the money and set out roundabout the countryside so as to collect what additional orders and what additional money she could collect and she seemed to remember how Mrs. Luther Dixon out Sadler way had gone in for a bracelet with dangling charms along the length of it, dangling flowerbud charms mostly but a dangling Chrysler Building too on account of Mrs. Dixon had been up high in the actual one previously and had been much affected by the view, and Aunt Sister recalled how maybe there was a little silver Bible too, how maybe there was both the little silver Bibles which would be the little silver open one and the little silver shut one as well that hung kind of pretty and fitting there among the flowers and there among the Chrysler Building. And there was a Lynch she sold to, Aunt Sister said, two Lynches she believed out towards Oregon Hill that bought those big ugly rings with the colored glass in them like Lynches always bought and nail polish, Aunt Sister recollected, nail polish off the back inside cover, nail polish in jars bigger than nail polish usually comes in and at prices lower than nail polish usually brings, kind of purplish-red nail polish, she seemed to remember, the sort of nail polish a woman that would wear big ugly rings would wear. And Daddy said Aunt Sister told how naturally she stopped in at the cigarette plant and sold off an item or two at breaktime and dropped on by Mrs. Jules Henry Graham's house where Mr. Jules Henry Graham smoked his pipe at the kitchen table while Mrs. Jules Henry Graham turned over the catalog pages so as to see what Mr. Jules Henry Graham said was all muck anyhow, and then it was on into town proper, Aunt Sister said, where she called like usual on Grandmomma and on Mrs. Talton up a door as well as Mrs. Hayes and Mrs. Askew and Mrs. Estelle Singletary and her sister Bernice Fay Frazier and the Drumm twins too, May and Hailey Verna that lived side by side in little white frame houses with formosa bushes across the housefronts and clematis up the lightposts, and Aunt Sister said May Drumm was quite taken with the diamond-spangled dogwood blossom brooch but could not see clear to spend the money for it and instead ordered a goldplated neckchain and a goldplated Jesus on the cross to dangle from it and it seemed to Aunt Sister that Hailey Verna Drumm next door was in her turn quite taken with the diamond-spangled dogwood blossom brooch but could not see clear to spend the money for it and instead ordered for her own self the goldplated neckchain with the goldplated Jesus on the cross to dangle from it, and Daddy asked Aunt Sister wasn't Jesus on the cross a Catholic kind of an item and straightaway Aunt Sister shot back how Jesus was everybody's kind of an item, and then she said, "Everybody's," again like maybe it was a proper name, like maybe it was Louis W. Benfield sr.

Daddy said Mr. Clay Weathers had been a little jumpy for a spell and was not getting but jumpier by the minute on account of how it was not daytime anymore and not eveningtime either but full nighttime and with no pink and no orange in the sky but just stars and a piece of moon and thoroughgoing blackness otherwise that Mr. Clay Weathers did not much like to be out in even though he was not truly out in it sitting as he was at Grandmomma and Grandaddy's breakfast room table with them and Daddy and Momma and Aunt Sister for company but since he was not at home like was ordinary for him he figured he was out in it well enough and so commenced to grow towards a purely palpable twitchiness once he could not see in the breakfast room windowglass anything but his own face looking back at him. It was that time of night when he was generally in front of his Zenith eating mixed nuts and drinking Pepsi-Colas and watching something otherwise than himself in a windowglass and so he kind of squirmed and kind of jumped and jerked roundabout and began to look appreciably wan and appreciably anxious which Grandmomma and Momma noticed straightoff and indicated to Daddy that offered to drive Mr. Clay Weathers home to Stacy but got told, "No sir," all firm and resolute by Granddaddy that did not ordinarily need to get addressed to answer anyhow but especially did not need to get addressed this one time to answer on account of the predicament, Granddaddy called it, on account of the sorry nigger bastard, Granddaddy said after and even Aunt Sister that had got knocked down and robbed by him could not hardly stand for it and she set in with her mouth like she might say, "William Elsworth!" that way Grandmomma said it most times she put the William and the Elsworth together but Daddy said Granddaddy had on that face that did not anybody see much but everybody knew well enough, that face that could stop even Aunt Sister who did not get stopped hardly ever by anything, and so she did but set her mouth and did but draw her breath but could not hardly come out with what she'd full well intended to come out with on account of what she saw and on account of where she saw it.

It was Grandmomma that suggested supper, or actually it was Grandmomma that went into the kitchen and got out the skillet from the oven drawer and the sausage from the refrigerator without saying exactly how come but without needing to either and it was Momma that got up to help and then it was the two of them together banging pans and rattling dishes and jangling silverware along with the grease-smell and the biscuitsmell and the coffeesmell that all suggested supper together and served to ease Mr. Clay Weathers, served to ease him from the noseholes out in every direction in a way that Pepsi-Colas and mixed nuts never did and he grew untwitchy and unjumpy and just generally contented straightaway and as his stomach commenced to gnaw on what juices he sent down for it Grandmomma stepped out from the kitchen and asked him did he like his eggs scrambled or did he like his eggs fried and Mr. Clay Weathers told her, "Yes ma'm," and grinned at his own self in the windowglass.

There was peas too, Daddy said, garden peas left over from lunch that did not anybody want but Aunt Sister who pushed them all roundabout her plate with a piece of biscuit and every now and again got to eat some of and would wash down with a swallow of coffee that she took heavily creamed and heavily sugared out from a cup with red lipmarks on it like she most always left on cups and on glasses and on foreheads too sometimes, and after she had dabbed with her napkin like she customarily dabbed once she'd swallowed, she would talk again while she chased more peas roundabout her platerim. Aunt Sister said they were late, said they were not much late but later than normal anyhow and so purely did not come

when she'd said they would which made a liar of her, Aunt
Sister told it, but wasn't any of it hardly her fault on account of
they should have come and would have come but for
Independence Day as Aunt Sister figured it since on
Independence Day the mail all stopped and laid somewhere for
a time and then likely did not get took up straightaway when
work recommenced, or anyhow likely did not get took up just
precisely in the order it had got set down and so went off
schedule, she figured, got laid aside or got diverted somewhere
otherwise but just got slowed anyhow and so did not get to her
when she'd guessed it ought to and had announced it would
which meant she was late already the day it came, and she said
she would have got it out the very afternoon, said she would
have separated what she had to separate and bundled up
together what she had to bundle up and then carried all of it
roundabout where she had to carry it but for the poison and
Daddy said she turned her hands palm upwards so as to
display for Mr. Clay Weathers that had not seen it her weepy
ivy rash on either wrist and Mr. Clay Weathers let down his
fork so as to study the weepy rash on the one wrist and the
weepy rash on the other too and then he laid against his
chairback and did not eat for a time.

Aunt Sister told how it had been in with the periwinkle in the
side-yard and she had set out of a morning thinning and
clearing like she liked to sometimes and had managed to get in
amongst it before she even knew she was and naturally it was
just on her fingers there at the first but migrated off to every
part she touched with them and Aunt Sister admitted to having
laid her fingers in a great variety of places, admitted to having
laid her fingers most every bare place she could lay them and
even some covered places too, so it got a hold rightoff, she said,
and commenced to pop out all over and she told how she'd set
in with the Clorox straightaway and Mr. Clay Weathers from
against his chairback said to her, "The Clorox," like maybe he
did not know could his tongue make the noise of it and Aunt
Sister went ahead and explained to him how it would dry and

how it would heal and how it would tingle somewhat in addition to the drying and in addition to the healing and Mr. Clay Weathers from against his chair-back said to her, "Tingle," and Aunt Sister told how it would even burn somewhat sometimes which did not seem to strike Mr. Clay Weathers as in any way extraordinary.

She said it got all up roundabout her eyes and just plain shut them for a time which she could not help much as it did not seem to her that even the slightest little drop of bleach in the eyesocket would be at all a pleasant kind of a thing and from where he had been for a spell now Mr. Clay Weathers told her, "Tingle," and Aunt Sister told him back, "Just precisely," and then washed down more peas with more coffee and dabbed like was customary for her, and then she said how Dr. Shackleford had called in to the Rexall and got her the little blue pills for the itch and the white cream for the rash and she told how the cream would heal and how the cream would dry and how the cream would not burn and would not tingle either and so could get put everywhere near about and would work in conjunction with the little blue pills that did in fact stop the itch but also made Aunt Sister what she called woozy and what she called drunk which she said she guessed was like liquor woozy and liquor drunk though she could not say for certain as spirits had not ever passed her lips, and Mr. Clay Weathers leaned his frontside up against the table edge and took hold of his fork again but did not stick anything straightoff except the empty air and told Aunt Sister, "Passed my lips, some nights going both ways," that Daddy liked well enough and Momma and Grandmomma liked well enough too and even Aunt Sister liked it in a tolerable sort of way which was everybody but Granddaddy that would have liked it best himself if he'd been regular and if he'd been ordinary which he'd got agitated away from and did not seem anywhere near settling into again so it was him that said, "Go on then," when it got said as was not anybody else ready for things to proceed but for him that was anxious, that was irate, Daddy called it.

So she said it held her up, said it was the both of them that held her up which was the mail coming when it came and the poison spreading where it spread but she went out and delivered, Aunt Sister said, went out and delivered before she was cured and healed like she ought to have been and she turned her hands palm upwards and displayed what weepy rash remained to her which Mr. Clay Weathers saw coming far enough ahead to look somewhere else entirely and so she was not up to delivering truly, Aunt Sister said, but did take her orders round nonetheless on account of she was not ever one to shirk and dodge, and she asked Momma and asked Grandmomma too didn't they know for a fact she wasn't ever one to shirk and dodge and they said no not ever to Mr. Clay Weathers mostly that would be the one out of the bunch of them not to know it, and Aunt Sister said she was pained and she was irritated and maybe somewhat woozy and maybe somewhat drunk but went anyhow and called on the Drumms with their goldplated neckchains and their goldplated Jesuses on the crosses and dropped by at Mrs. Askew's and Mrs. Hayes's and Miss Bernice Fay Frazier's so as to leave off what baubles they'd got and stopped in at the cigarette plant and visited the Lynches who she said were ill and testy like usual and delivered Mrs. Luther Dixon her dangling charm bracelet with her flowerbuds and her Bibles and her Chrysler Building already hanging from it. So it was just Mrs. Vernon Littlejohn after, Aunt Sister said, Mrs. Vernon Littlejohn clear out 87 a good ways farther than Aunt Sister figured she needed to go being itchy and being afflicted like she was but she said she went anyhow with the pinky ring and the spangle-studded brooch so as not to give sloth a toehold which Aunt Sister said is all sloth needs mosttimes and then she looked hard at Mr. Clay Weathers until he came out with the Yes ma'm that she figured he'd come out with if she waited on him to do it.

Aunt Sister said she did not find Mrs. Vernon Littlejohn in a particularly good humor and while she could not say just precisely why not she guessed it was maybe partly the fact that she was coming when she was coming after she'd said she'd be there when she'd said she would which Mrs. Vernon Littlejohn seemed to recollect was considerably sooner than when she got there, in fact was considerably sooner than when she'd said she'd get there too, as best as Aunt Sister could remember herself, but she said she let it pass as Mrs. Vernon Littlejohn was suffering acutely just then with the phlebitis in both her legs, or anyhow was suffering somewhat just then with the phlebitis and equally somewhat with the treatment for it which would be the rubber stockings she wore when she was up and about and as Aunt Sister told it rubber stockings are not hardly the sort of items a woman would prefer to cover her legs with in July and she asked Mr. Clay Weathers wouldn't he like some rubber underwear just to lounge around in in the heat of the day and he told her back how he guessed he wouldn't like that much, how that did not appeal to him whatsoever. So Aunt Sister said Mrs. Vernon Littlejohn was ill and was agitated and just generally in a humor prior to and for reasons otherwise than the brooch and the pinky ring, but as she was predisposed like she was the jewelry did not but touch her off partly on account of it was late getting to her and partly on account of it was not hardly what she'd figured it would be, or at least half of it was not what she'd figured it would be anyhow as she'd given such scant money for the goldplated pinky ring that she could not in all honesty bring herself to expect it to be but what scant money would buy. The brooch, however, was another matter as she had given middling money for it, or anyhow what was actually middling money but was in the framework of the Littlejohn riches a fabulous price and so she had been wondering over and had been anticipating the silverplating and the lustrous diamond spangles like people will anticipate and will wonder over what they figure they've given a fabulous price for. So Aunt Sister guessed it was partly the phlebitis and partly the heat and the stockings, and partly the late delivery, and partly the misconstrued worth of the dogwood blossom brooch that Aunt Sister admitted her own self was just a middling item, not hardly the sort of thing worth anticipating and worth wondering over which Mrs. Vernon Littlejohn discovered straightaway once she had unboxed it and had unwrapped it and had studied it with some considerable attention afterwhich she asked Aunt Sister straightout just what was that little piddly mess round the petals anyhow.

"Spangles," Aunt Sister told. "Lustrous diamond spangles."

"This here?" Mrs. Vernon Littlejohn wanted to know and scratched at one grainy petal with her fingernail.

And Aunt Sister shook her head and told her, "Spangles," and then Daddy said she explained to all of them there in the breakfast room how there was your stones and how there was your chips and how there was your dust lastly which was what got sprinkled and which was what got glued and which was what got just generally span-gleized, Aunt Sister called it, and which seemed to her a fine thing in a broad and socio-economical sort of way since there is afterall your stone class of people and your chip class of people and your spangle class of people too which means some piece of a diamond for everybody but Daddy said she just guessed that, as was the trouble most times, Mrs. Vernon Littlejohn was a spangle that thought she was a chip, and she wondered at Momma and Grandmomma mostly didn't that seem the truth of it and Momma and Grandmomma together guessed it was.

Aunt Sister said of course Mrs. Vernon Littlejohn had not asked her if the border was spangles to find out if it was spangles since she knew it was spangles all along but simply had not expected spangles to be what they were and she called over Mr. Vernon Littlejohn to show him the petaledge and have him scratch it for himself but he did not find the spangles so disappointing and irritating as Mrs. Littlejohn since he had not anticipated that spangles were one particular thing or another so Mrs. Littlejohn got annoyed with Mr. Littlejohn on account of how the spangles did not appear to affect him much and she became just generally more agitated and put out and vented herself somewhat at Aunt Sister who got the brooch shook under her nose and got advised what was lustrous diamonds and what wasn't and got told how some things that were supposed to look like a plain dogwood blossom could not even do that with much effect and Aunt Sister guessed had she not been a Christian woman she might have done a thing and said a thing and been sorry for both but instead she excused herself politely, Aunt Sister told it, and stepped out into the gravel lot on her way to her two-tone Bel Air so as to fetch out from it the catalog with which she intended to illustrate to Mrs. Vernon Littlejohn how the item she held in her fingers was precisely the item she ordered, or maybe if not precisely exactly then undeniably precisely mostly anyhow which she figured she could convince Mrs. Vernon Littlejohn of if Mrs. Vernon Littlejohn was willing to concede the various shortcomings of photography and the play of light and such, if she was willing to concede how a picture of an item did not always capture the purest essence of it, which it seemed to Aunt Sister that any sensible woman would have to give in to and she guessed, as she walked across the gravel lot, that maybe with the catalog to look at on the one hand and the actual brooch itself to look at on the other she might be able to purely establish a resemblance between the two of them that she could build on and maybe complicate and such until it seemed like the one was the other which she felt things needed to end up seeming like.

Naturally, then, Aunt Sister was considerably distracted and preoccupied on her way to the Bel Air having the chore before her of passing off the item she was endeavoring to pass off and for what and so she was not truly listening to anything but her own calculating and was not truly watching anything but her own feet which was how come she did not hear the motor grinding like it was grinding and did not see the Gilliam hunched over the steering wheel like he was hunched over it, or anyhow did not hear the motor and did not see the Gilliam near about until the very moment she grabbed on to the doorlatch and flung open the door to discover how there was an item atop the seatcushion she had not hardly expected to find there and so she just gaped at it for a time, Daddy said, gaped at it like most folks will gape at a thing they come across when they aren't really looking to come across it and as Aunt Sister had not hardly expected a negro where she found one she fairly fell out on the gravel lot with sheer surprise but recovered herself straightaway, recovered herself enough anyhow if not to be flatout indignant then peevish somewhat and she watched the negro hunched like he was hunched with his left arm wrapped roundabout the steering wheel and his right index finger on the ignition button and she laid her own hands to her hips like was her habit when peevish was what she was coming to be and she said, "You!" one time all sharp and firm and got herself looked at by the Gilliam that kept his left arm wrapped like it was wrapped and his finger on what it was on but turned his head partway and so showed off the lye scars that Aunt Sister pondered prior to the green shirt and the brown pants and the black laceless sneakers and the brown pants and the green shirt and the lye scars again and she said to him, "Get on out from there. Get on," said it like she full well expected he would mostly on account of what he was and on account of where he was and on account of who it was telling him to do it but he did not get out, did not even move straightoff and just looked at Aunt Sister with what she said was those yellow eyes, with what she said was those yellow eyes that the most of them have got, and then he unwrapped his left arm from the steering wheel and reached out with it until he'd laid his hand fingers upwards and palm foremost square across Aunt Sister's face and he snapped his elbow joint straight of a sudden and knocked her full over on her backside.

And Granddaddy said, "Goddam," and stood up out of his chair and sat back down in it and stood up out of it again and said, "Goddam," that Aunt Sister and Grandmomma and

Momma too all tried to curb but could not and he grew squirmy, Daddy said, and grew twitchy, and grew just generally quivery all over like people will sometimes when a thing gets right up next to them and takes hold and Daddy said it took hold, said it all took hold, and Granddaddy said, "Goddam," and Granddaddy said, "Niggers," that Grandmomma and Momma too got fairly much all over him about but could not hardly make him unsay and he put "Sons-of-bitches" onto it and got told, "Elsworth!" like he did sometimes but could not unsay that either.

Aunt Sister said she did not feel but a numbness straightaway, a numbness full up her backside and all down her legs to her very toes and all down her arms to her very fingers and naturally she could not but think rightoff how maybe she was done in in the way of walking and in the way of general mobility and such and Aunt Sister told how she got a picture of herself in her mind, clear and lifelike, she said, a picture of herself at the Eastern Star Home in Greensboro where she'd been wheeled in a wicker chair up to a window and was looking out it for a visitor that did not ever come, and she recollected it was Christmas, Christmas at the Eastern Star Home and everybody had family in but for her that just sat at the window in her wicker chair and looked out it for her people that did not ever come, and in lieu of the usual Kleenex Aunt Sister dabbed at her noseholes and dabbed at her eyes with her napkin and wondered why it was she was by herself on Christmas at the Eastern Star Home in Greensboro, wondered was it a sign, wondered was it an omen, wondered was it a thing that would come to pass, and Granddaddy said, "Christ," not with any compassion much and him and Daddy looked at each other with their face muscles tight like they might have bit off the same persimmon while Grandmomma and Momma too assured Aunt Sister they were likely just before arriving, assured Aunt Sister they would not miss a Christmas at the Eastern Star Home, would not miss even a Sunday afternoon, and Mr. Clay Weathers announced how he would ride with them and Aunt Sister told him back he was a decent and kind man which Mr. Clay Weathers seemed grateful to hear but which did not affect Daddy and Granddaddy too hardly the same way and they looked at each other again all puckered roundabout the face and Granddaddy wondered couldn't they all just come on back from the Eastern Star Home for a time, couldn't they all just head on out 87 to Littlejohn's gravel lot where they'd been at before Christmas came like it did and Aunt Sister got stiff and upright of a sudden and said she'd had a numbness and had got a fright on account of it and figured maybe her own flesh and blood, figured maybe her very own brother would want to hear of it, and Granddaddy said back how he didn't mind a numbness and didn't mind a fright but didn't need the trip to Greensboro much, especially not in that Christmas traffic, Daddy added, and Momma said a thing to him just with her breath mostly and not hardly with her vocal cords.

So Aunt Sister said she was numb for a spell and could not seem to move any parts of herself but for the face parts, not any of the getting up parts anyhow, which meant she stayed where she'd got put and watched the nigger Gilliam that naturally she did not know but the nigger part of just then and was calling even that something otherwise, watched the nigger Gilliam press the ignition button with his right index finger and so grind and grind and grind the motor like Aunt Sister generally had to grind and grind and grind it herself on account of aside from the original tires and the original paint Aunt Sister's Chevrolet Bel Air still had the original sparkplugs too along with the original rotor button and the original contact points which altogether had not made for any sort of lively and expedient ignition since along about December of 1955, so the nigger Gilliam turned it over and over and over and mashed the accelerator and let off the accelerator and turned it over and over and over some more until it did not do anything much but click which was when he commenced to push it and Aunt Sister watched him from there on her back in the gravel lot, watched him guide the thing onto the highway heading north towards the Dan River valley, and while he did manage to roll he did not gather any momentum straightaway as the slope before him was not particularly steep and headlong but only barely downhill, so truly he just crawled until the weight and magnitude of the Bel Air in conjunction with your regular laws of gravity produced some noticeable velocity and momentum, enough velocity and momentum anyhow to turn the engine which sputtered some and popped some but caught nonetheless.

Mr. Vernon Littlejohn, that was standing up behind the counter with the heels of his hands planted firm on top of it, saw the Bel Air going where it went but not how truly and not who with and he pointed the vehicle out to Mrs. Vernon Littlejohn whose spangle agitation had been heightening and had been compounding in direct proportion to the length of Aunt Sister's absence and so naturally she figured she was getting run out on and grew irate precipitously, Daddy called it, and her and Mr. Littlejohn together rushed on out the doorway and into the lot where Mrs. Vernon Littlejohn shook her clenched hand and said a hard thing while Mr. Vernon Littlejohn walked on across the gravel to see just what manner of heap it was that had been left for him to haul off as Aunt Sister, the way she was sprawled and laid, looked to Mr. Vernon Littlejohn like some ordinary manner of heap until he got right up on her or near about it when he saw for himself just precisely what manner of heap it was and he crouched down beside her anxious to know was she dead which was what she looked to be as she was not moving her getting up parts, which she couldn't, or her face parts either, which she could but was resting, and to find out what it was he was anxious to know Mr. Vernon Littlejohn laid his ear to Aunt Sister's chest which seemed to have a sudden and emphatic effect on Aunt Sister who roused up out of her lull most directly and raised herself onto her elbows so as to pitch Mr. Vernon Littlejohn's ear off from where it had become entirely too nestled as best she could tell. She said she'd been beat and had been knocked down and had her car stole, and Mr. Vernon Littlejohn turned round towards his wife who'd come partway across the lot herself to see what manner of heap it was her husband had laid his ear to and he told her Aunt Sister had been beat and knocked down and had her car stole which Mrs. Littlejohn appeared to believe somewhat straightaway but just somewhat and she wanted to know what model of car exactly and got told two-tone Chevrolet Bel Air sedan by her husband who'd got told it by Aunt Sister, and she wanted to know did the catalog get stole along with it and got told, "Sadly, yes," by Mr. Vernon Littlejohn who had got told that too.

Granddaddy said there was one nigger going to wish he'd never got born onto God's green earth and he wiped at his mouth and threw down his napkin on the tabletop and Grandmomma told him she wished he wouldn't talk so and Momma told him she wished he'd pay more mind to Grandmomma and Aunt Sister said it was blessing and a miracle how the feeling had come back and she wiggled all of her fingers and thumbs together and said for everybody to look at them which everybody kind of did but not hardly to Aunt Sister's satisfaction on account of blessings and miracles deserved more attention than she felt like hers had got and she said again how everybody should look and she wiggled some more and everybody did look but for Granddaddy that picked his teeth and Aunt Sister told how it was a blessing and how it was a miracle and watched her thumbs and watched her fingers like she'd never seen thumbs or fingers before.

Daddy said Grandmomma and Momma cleared the table while Aunt Sister, that did not feel so miraculous from the waist down, went ahead and let them and Mr. Clay Weathers, that got offered, laid his chin in the cup of his hand and thought for an appreciable while before at last deciding that he would in fact have a piece of custard pie and would in fact take ice cream on top of it. Granddaddy was set to ride the roads, ride the roads in the dark but Daddy impressed upon him how riding the roads in the dark would not be their most effective strategy as they could not hardly hope to spot a two-tone Bel Air from a moving car in the pitch black, so Granddaddy said he was set to ride the roads at firstlight but Daddy impressed upon him how, as it would be Sunday, they might best wait until church school when the cars of the goodly people would be all parked and collected together which would leave just the cars of your marginal and outright sorry people on the roadways which Granddaddy decided was sound after he'd considered the thing, and Daddy stood up and stretched himself and said how he guessed he would haul Mr. Clay Weathers on home to Stacy and Granddaddy was just dropping his chin to come out with a No sir when Mr. Clay Weathers himself came out with a No sir for him and then picked up his pieplate and drank off the melted ice cream from it prior to laying against his chairback and wondering into the kitchen could he maybe have a sliver more of that egg custard and a dibble more of that ice cream.

Granddaddy put him in the room opposite the plank door so as to have him handy, Daddy said, and Aunt Sister that did not feel so extraordinarily miraculous and blessed as to go home alone shared the front room with Grandmomma which put Granddaddy upstairs with the sewing machine that he did not mind much on account of how he could spit direct out the window onto the hedgerow in the sideyard, and Daddy said he did not guess it was seven o'clock in the morning when Granddaddy called him to see was he up and did not guess it was even seven-thirty when Granddaddy called him again to see was he coming and he figured he was at the door by eight and guessed they would have left straightaway but for Mr. Clay Weathers that had not finished his pancakes, not the latest heap of them anyhow, so they were not gone until quarter past or after and Granddaddy, that was navigating from the front seat, figured east was how they wanted to head while Mr. Clay Weathers, that was navigating from the backseat, figured west would best suit their purposes so Daddy, that was driving anyhow, struck out kind of to the northeast there at first and then turned off to the northwest shortly afterwards and headed on up 87 towards Mr. Vernon Littlejohn's grocery that he stopped Momma's Buick in the lot of and him and Granddaddy and Mr. Clay Weathers too all got out and looked at the gravel and then walked across it to the roadside where they looked at the road for a time in the direction of the Dan River valley mostly but somewhat the other way also.

Daddy said he could not hardly recollect where they didn't go as it seemed to him they went most everywhere they could get to which did not truly leave anywhere they didn't go, not anywhere much anyway, and he guessed they saw Chevrolets enough, guessed they saw Bel Airs enough too, guessed him and Granddaddy did anyhow while Mr. Clay Weathers still did not show much of a knack for vehicles and so figured everything for one thing and figured the one thing for a Bel Air which most things usually weren't but some things were, enough anyhow to encourage him to keep on figuring like he had been, and Daddy said it was late in the morning when they got onto 29 going north, said it was near about actual churchtime, and was not hardly anybody on the road but for them, but for them and Teddy Gilchrist that was not on the road proper but on the sidewalk just shy of the Neely limits and did not seem to be going north and did not seem to be going south either but was just standing astraddle a seam looking at his shoetops and Daddy recollected it was Mr. Clay Weathers that suggested they stop and consult him on account of he'd taken Teddy Gilchrist for somebody with sense just like he'd taken what vehicles he'd seen for what he took them for, and so Daddy said he pulled over to the gutter and Granddaddy laid out the window and said, "Hey mister," to Teddy Gilchrist that he did not know was Teddy Gilchrist until Teddy Gilchrist lifted up his tiny pointy head with the brown corduroy duckhunting cap on it and asked Granddaddy did he know what it was exactly that went into concrete to make it hard and Granddaddy said, "Well hellfire," and Daddy kind of blew out a breath towards the front window glass and Mr. Clay Weathers set his chin and his forearms on the front seatback and told how he'd always figured it was an item in the mortar powder that gelled with water and not so much the sand and not so much the gravel either, and Teddy Gilchrist said he knew where gravel came from, said he'd been out to the rock quarry other side of Ruffin, the one with the water in it, and had seen what stone there was to see and had seen what water and had seen Mr. Singletary and Mrs. Montgomery that sewed quilts all stretched out and tangled up together in a grassy place, and Daddy took in enough air to talk with straightaway and asked him, "Mrs. Estelle Singletary's Mr. Singletary?" and Teddy Gilchrist said, "Him," back and then skidded the toe of his shoe across the sidewalk where it left a brown mark that Teddy Gilchrist got all rapturous over and dropped down onto his knees to study and wonder at.

Granddaddy figured there was not much use to any of it and said, "Go on, Louis," and flung his arm, and Mr. Clay Weathers, still with his chin and his forearms on the seatback, asked in a slow and rhetorical sort of way why it was Mr. Estelle Singletary stretched out and tangled up with the Montgomery that sewed quilts out of everybody he could have stretched out and tangled up with and he wanted to know wasn't that the Montgomery with the stomach and Daddy said it was in fact that Montgomery but then it was in fact that Singletary too, and Mr. Clay Weathers that had not considered which Singletary exactly stopped to consider which Singletary, that changed his opinion of the entire matter and he said he saw it like Daddy did and Daddy said he guessed he might and Granddaddy said, "Hellfire," one more time and flung his arm, and Teddy Gilchrist from on his knees on the sidewalk announced how there was some bugs that had six legs and some bugs that didn't.

"Go on, Louis," Granddaddy said and did not fling his arm this time but instead looked square at Daddy all firm and earnest and Daddy guessed he would have just dropped the Buick into gear and gone on but for Mr. Clay Weathers that had removed his chin and his forearms too from off the front seatback and had laid them as far out the sidewindow as he could manage and he asked Teddy Gilchrist had he maybe seen the Bel Air, had he maybe seen Miss Addie Yount's Bel Air and Teddy Gilchrist got up onto his feet and said back at Mr. Clay Weathers, "Car?" that Granddaddy said, "Jesus," and Daddy exhaled on account of while Mr. Clay Weathers answered with a plain, "Yes sir."

"Lightgreen and bluegreen?" Teddy Gilchrist said.

"Yes sir."

"Chevrolet?" Teddy Gilchrist said and the Yes sir back was near about three parts blended. "Colored man," Teddy Gilchrist said. "Lightgreen and bluegreen Chevrolet. Colored man," Teddy Gilchrist said.

"Christ yes," Granddaddy told him.

And Teddy Gilchrist skidded his shoetip across the sidewalk.

"Where?" Granddaddy wanted to know. "Which way?"

And Teddy Gilchrist skidded across the sidewalk the shoetip he had not just skidded previously.

"Where, Teddy. Which way?"

"Yonder," Teddy Gilchrist said and flung his own arm though not in any direction a car might travel but mostly up and behind himself.

"Yonder where?" Daddy asked him.

"Yonder," Teddy Gilchrist said and flung his arm the second time almost the way the road went.

"When?" Granddaddy wanted to know and got just looked at from the sidewalk. "Today?" he said.

"Today," Teddy Gilchrist told him.

"Lately?" he said.

"Lately," Teddy Gilchrist told him.

"Just lately?" Granddaddy wanted to know.

"Lately," Teddy Gilchrist told him.

"Just now?" Granddaddy wanted to know.

And Teddy Gilchrist dragged his shoebottom along the sidewalk seam. "Just lately now today," he said.

Daddy said he had not ever suspected tires could squeal on a fullsized Buick, had not ever guessed the motor possessed the wherewithal! to spin the wheels like it did and didn't figure he would have likely found out what wherewithall there was exactly if he had not tried to leave in neutral and then decided of a sudden how low gear might be altogether more effective and so as to fix things straightaway he jerked the gearshift indiscreetly, Daddy called it, which would be without much forethought and without much clutch either, and so he found out just what it was tires could do even on a fullsized Buick that he'd never before so much as suspected and Granddaddy hooted one time and held himself steady on the vent window while Mr. Clay Weathers kind of pitched about in the back of the car and cast round for something to latch on to. And Daddy said they were up with him before they even figured they possibly could be, before they had even commenced to look to get up with him which naturally was before they had set in to deciding what they would do once they did, and Daddy said he roared on up behind him and blinked his lights one time and sounded his horn twice and then wondered at Granddaddy was it in fact Aunt Sister's Bel Air which he guessed was the sort of thing he needed to be purely certain of considering the circumstances and such and Granddaddy assured him it was and Daddy asked him how could he tell and Granddaddy said he just could which was not near as substantial as Daddy would have liked but he got convinced directly once Granddaddy laid the most of himself out the sidewindow, cupped his hands around his mouth, and hollered, "Pull over you sorry bastard," which the nigger Gilliam heard plain enough along with Daddy and along with Mr. Clay Weathers and along with the bulk of the congregation of the Wolf Island Primitive Baptist Church that was loitering outside in the fresh air prior to entering the sanctuary for the service, so the one nigger Gilliam in the Bel Air and the several dozen primitive Baptists on the roadside all looked at Granddaddy with near about the same degree of outright shock truly but it was only the nigger Gilliam that accelerated on account of it and Granddaddy drew himself full inside the car and told Daddy, "Get him."

"Get him how?" Daddy wanted to know.

"Just get him," Granddaddy said and flung his arm apd Daddy accelerated his own self and pulled up flush behind the Bel Air all over again with his lights blinking and his horn blowing which he did not figure would stop the Bel Air but might prove an annoyance anyhow and he was still just blinking and still just blowing and still just crowding Aunt Sister's Chevrolet as close as he dared to when Granddaddy spied the first dent on the right fender and then the dent on the left fender and then the scratchmarks on the bumper where that nigger had backed into whatever he'd backed into and Granddaddy hollered, "Ram the son-of-a-bitch!"

"No Chief," Daddy said out the side of his mouth and blinked his lights and blew his horn.

"Look it," Granddaddy told him back, "just look it," and he pointed all about the rear of the Bel Air until Daddy had focused in on the one fender and then the other and finally the bumper too, and Granddaddy said, "Run that shitass off this highway," which Daddy figured was along about when Mr. Clay Weathers migrated to the floorboard on account of it was surely along about when he felt in his kidneys and various other of his organs Mr. Clay Weather's pointy joints through the seatback.

"How?" Daddy wanted to know as it was a matter of some particular interest to him.

And Granddaddy flung his arm again. "Get up alongside him," he said, "and ease him off the road."

"But Chief, that lane ain't my lane to ride in," Daddy told him.

"Ride in it anyhow," Granddaddy said.

"But Chief."

"Go on," Granddaddy said and flung his arm one last time for Daddy that spied as far as he could spy up the road with his nose near about against the steering wheel and then eased on around the Bel Air once he had the dotted line and pulled up just dead even with it, and Daddy said Granddaddy laid himself partway out the side window and said to that Gilliam with his face not even a full foot off from him, "Nigger, get off this road," and he waited for the braking and the easing over that he figured had to follow which Daddy said he figured his own self had to follow too but did not any braking or easing over ensue exactly and instead that Gilliam turned his face round to Granddaddy's face and purely spat one time across the margin which was not so wide as to let the wind take all of it and Daddy said Granddaddy drew back into the car like he'd been scalded and wiped at himself with his bandana while Daddy backed off for a Dodge pickup heading south and then pulled out again and drew up even and Granddaddy that did not move to lay out the window this time said to Daddy, "Ram him, Louis, ram the son-of-a-bitch."

"But Chief," Daddy said back at him as it was Momma's Buick and as it was Aunt Sister's Bel Air and as he was not himself but an actuary anyhow and so had not hardly studied your controlled wreck with much attention until just lately and he did not feel prepared to cause one and did not figure he would no matter what manner of fit Granddaddy pitched, or anyhow did not figure he would until that Gilliam bumped him one time with the Bel Air front fender and then bumped him another time after and Daddy said, "Goddam," and yanked his own wheel with both hands together sending the Buick and the Bel Air and the Gilliam and Granddaddy and Daddy and Mr. Clay Weathers too off the pavement and over the shoulder and down through a patch of dog fennel and milkweed into a red claybank that the Bel Air and the Buick too just plain stuck in like darts.

Granddaddy was out first, Daddy said, was out even before they stopped, it seemed like, on account of that Gilliam was out sooner and Daddy said he watched the two of them through the windshield with the Gilliam in the front scampering as best he could and Granddaddy behind him scampering even better and Daddy said he figured straightoff Granddaddy would catch him right there in the loose dirt as his shoes were laced up tight and so weren't hardly filling like the Gilliam's sneakers that anymore had more clods in them than feet but just when it looked like Granddaddy might latch

on to him the Gilliam freed up his one foot and braced with his
other and kicked Granddaddy one time catching enough of his
shoulder to topple him over backwards and send him sliding
down the claybank but Daddy said he still almost caught him
anyhow and that Gilliam didn't clamor up over the lip and
disappear into the trees but with two steps on Granddaddy
that clamored up and disappeared right behind him, and
Daddy figured he would have been up with them himself but
for Mr. Clay Weathers that he couldn't hardly hoist up off the
back floorboard alone and couldn't get any help with from Mr.
Clay Weathers who could not decide was it his leg that was
broken or was it his arm or was it the bulk of his fingers and
then he wondered at Daddy just exactly what did a concussion
feel like and wanted to know could a man sprain the most of
himself, maybe a full two thirds. He said he felt at least two-
thirds sprained. So they fell behind, Daddy said, him and Mr.
Clay Weathers that finally did get off the floorboard and finally
did get outside on the ground, but still they did not make much
progress straightoff, Daddy told it, since Mr. Clay Weathers
did not care to take his sprained self up the daybank and
insisted instead that him and Daddy go roundabout the thing
which they did, Daddy said, roundabout it and direct into a
briar thicket that Mr. Clay Weathers got the most of his person
tangled up in while Daddy caught his trousers every time he
took a step.

Naturally they were long out of sight, Daddy said, Granddaddy
and the Gilliam that had not got sprained and hindered
otherwise and he did not suppose him and Mr. Clay Weathers
would have found out where they'd made off to but for
Granddaddy that had the wind to run full out and holler as
well, holler at the Gilliam mostly that Granddaddy called a
thing with near about every breath he could muster, so they
followed the swearing, Daddy said, and came up on a rise
where the brush and the trees thinned some and from it they
could see down across a gulley and into a stand of yellow pine
where they could make out somewhat the green shirt and

somewhat the brown pants too and just behind them
Granddaddy's white hair and Granddaddy's boiled white shirt
and Granddaddy's poplin trousers, and Daddy said he wasn't
two yards off the Gilliam even then and still swearing every
breath and hooting and yelping and gaining mostly and Daddy
guessed Granddaddy had already caught him outright by the
time him and Mr. Clay Weathers got so far as the gulley-
bottom on account of he had him down and had him beat some
when they made the pines and commenced to close in
themselves on that Gilliam that was stretched out on the
pinestraw with Granddaddy standing overtop him whipping
his fist in the air and instructing that Gilliam in just what
manner of son-of-a-bitch he was.

His legs were stretched out before him, Daddy said, and he
held himself up with one arm and with the hand of the other
he touched at his nose and then looked at the blood on his
fingertips and touched at his nose again and Granddaddy that
was standing astraddle him reached down with the hand he
wasn't whipping in the air and took hold of the Gilliam by his
green shirtfront and said to him, "Who are you?" and the
Gilliam touched his nose and looked at his fingers and touched
his nose again and then dropped his lower lip ever so slightly
like he might even speak but did not speak straightaway and
Granddaddy, with his grip on the green shirtfront, shook that
Gilliam hard one time and said to him, "Answer me," but could
not any English have got spoke between when Granddaddy
insisted on it and when he hit the Gilliam again which was not
hardly any time really and was not quite square on the nose
and not quite square on the mouth either but caught partly lips
and partly nose and partly fingers too that were up to touch
blood and draw it away.

"What you want with Sister's car?" Granddaddy wanted to
know and he took up in his fingers all the additional shirtfront
he could get them around and if that Gilliam had a reason and
had a reply he did not express it nearly soon enough to keep

from getting popped again and this time no nose and no fingers but just pure lips entirely and with quite sufficient force to lay the bottom one wide open and the Gilliam reached up straightaway to touch it and drew off his fingers to look. "She ain't but an old woman," Granddaddy hollered and whipped his fist overhead. "Can't you but plague old women? Can't you?" And Daddy said that Gilliam that had not looked square at Granddaddy even once yet rolled up his eyes and pondered him, big yellow eyes, Daddy said, brown in the middle but yellow everywhere otherwise and not the sort of eyes you could learn much from, Daddy said, not the sort of eyes that told you meanness or told you the contrary either like eyes will sometimes, but just big yellow empty eyes, Daddy said, eyes without expression, without evil, without fear, without hate, and mostly without regret that was near about exclusively what Granddaddy looked to see in them when at last he did get looked at himself and so looked squarely back and saw what he saw that was not anything he knew, Daddy said, not anything he could know truly on account of it was only the yellow parts and only the brown parts and only the pure emptiness otherwise and just not remorse on the one end, Daddy said, and just not malevolence on the other but only nothing mostly and Granddaddy said, "Goddam you," and brought his face down into the Gilliam's face and said it again while with the hand empty of shirtfront he felt around in the pinestraw until he laid his fingers on the knot he'd seen there and took it up and raised it overhead which Daddy said was when they caught hold of him, caught hold of him at either arm and held him and Daddy told him, "No Chief," and Mr. Clay Weathers said just, "Mr. Buck," two times and Granddaddy fought against the both of them but could not work loose and could not see the prospect of it either and so quit and just stood with Daddy on the one side of him and Mr. Clay Weathers on the other and with that Gilliam direct before the three of them, that Gilliam that still just sat, Daddy said, and still just touched himself with his fingers and did not for a time look but at his own blood and did not for a time take in air but to breathe with

until at last he lifted his head and looked full at just
Granddaddy and commenced to talk at him, commenced to
talk in a voice so thick and low that were not the words plain
and decipherable straightaway but came to be clear soon
enough, and it was swearing, Daddy said, was swearing pure
and absolute not like any swearing he'd ever heard before or
ever hoped to hear again on account of it was not your wild
and was not your agitated profanity like most profanity is but
was just plain talking that happened to be vile and mean and
evil, so plain and so vile and mean and evil that they did not
know what it was they were hearing until well after they'd
commenced to hear it, until well after they'd commenced to
decipher it even on account of did not any of it suit and mesh,
not the eyes to the words and not the words to the voice as it
all called for heat and as it all called for passion but did not get
any of either which Daddy said made it worse somehow, the
swearing that was not spat and hollered but just said, said
against Granddaddy and against Daddy and against Mr. Clay
Weathers, and against Aunt Sister and against all their kin and
against all their kin before them, against just everything they
were and everything they ever had been and not spat and not
hollered but just plain said, just plain told outright which
Daddy guessed was why they did not know what it was
straightoff as they had not ever been told outright before but
listened like they did and heard what they heard and knew
directly what it was which Daddy figured was when they let
loose of him, let loose of him even before he jerked and
strained to get loose that he did not need to jerk and strain to
do as he was free already and Daddy said he brought it down
almost before he could draw it back, brought it down quick and
savage and hit that Gilliam flush across the forehead with it
and then hit him again near about the same place and laid him
full out on the pinestraw maybe killed already, Daddy said, but
hit him again anyway and with such considerable force and
zeal that Granddaddy could not keep his own feet and so fell
onto the pinestraw himself partly and fell onto the Gilliam
somewhat too, the Gilliam that was purely dead by then,

Daddy said, but got shook anyhow by Granddaddy who took up as much green shirt as each hand could manage and brought that dead Gilliam's face up to his own face and said to it, "Goddam you," and then just let loose with his fingers and watched that Gilliam fall back like he fell back and hit like he hit which Daddy said him and Mr. Clay Weathers watched too, just stood by and looked at not like it was death and murder, Daddy said, but something entirely otherwise, something bigger and grander and altogether more significant and satisfying like maybe Granddaddy was all of us and like maybe that Gilliam was all of them and like maybe those blows to the forehead did not just do in a man but maybe the old troubles too and the old woes and the old friction and only a man also and a man as well, but Daddy said they had the carcass too and the bloody pineknot and the hollow stomachs that told them maybe it was just death and maybe it was just murder.

And they didn't hold him but with the door not even shut and locked, Daddy said, not their door anyhow, not the iron one, which Daddy said they did not need to shut and lock as he was where he was already, and it was just questions, Daddy said, and just facts and just circumstances and not hardly charges, Daddy said, not hardly charges at all on account of who it was and on account of when it was and on account of why it was in the first place. So Grandmomma insisted they turn him out and they did turn him out and would not even judge him which Daddy said was likely the worst part of all since if they wouldn't tell him was it the right thing or was it the wrong thing that left just him to tell himself and not hardly the one time with the judge and the gavel and the solitary verdict but evermore, evermore to ponder it and weigh it out so as to come down on the one side or come down on the other until the next time it got pondered and got weighed. Daddy said did not but Sheriff Browner look all roundabout the corridor everywhere people weren't and say a thing in that voice he generally said things in that could not anybody hear and understand, and then did not Deputy Burton, that did not anybody anywhere ever want advice from, open his mouth but to give advice and Daddy said he patted the buttend of his service revolver with his fleshy palm and said to Granddaddy, "Don't fret, Mr. Buck. There's some folks need killing," and he winked one time and lifted up his gunpatting hand to Granddaddy's shoulder where he laid it for a spell, raised it, and laid it for a spell again.

Five

Weren't but five to get back, Daddy said, weren't but five to get back all the way on account of the one that cracked its leg in a hole and had to get shot dead and on account of the two that run off, run off before Uncle Jack could take up the tether that he hadn't but just laid down which he wouldn't have laid down anyway but for what sort of creatures they were anyhow which did not Uncle Jack figure for your bolting variety as outright running seemed beyond them somehow, seemed beyond them somehow even while Uncle Jack watched the two that did bolt and run outright which he had not expected or anticipated on account of what breeding and cultivation he'd observed up till then and which he could not believe he was seeing even while he looked at it, even while he watched the flanks and the hooves and the roaddust rising and boiling behind them until it was just the dust mostly he could see and not the mules anymore at all, and Daddy told Momma and told Aunt Sister and told me too how you might figure a man that had watched the flanks and the hooves and the roaddust until it was just roaddust anymore might be feverish and might be irate on account of how what he'd give money for had gone where it went but Daddy said those loose mules had disappeared with such uncharacteristic vitality and such considerable speed that to watch them go was not so much for Uncle Jack like losing two mules as it was like finding five more which would be the five he had left after the shot one and after the loose ones and he wrapped the tether roundabout the hookeye two times further along than he had wrapped it previously and communicated to the remaining mules that way he had of communicating with mules and such how he knew a thing now that he had not before but suspected and then he ran roundabout to the frontend of the wagon and communicated to Aunt Della that way he had of communicating with her which was partly with his mouth and partly with his arms too that he waved and whipped all through the air while he told her about what mules had got loose and where they'd made off to and how, that Aunt Della understood the words of well enough but could not quite comprehend all the enthusiasm on account of and she said to Uncle Jack, "Run off?"

"Yes ma'm," Uncle Jack told her and clapped his hands together one time.

"Two mules?" Aunt Della said.

"That's right," Uncle Jack told her and grinned so that all the pine tar roundabout his face muscles cracked and separated.

And Daddy said Aunt Della just looked at him, looked at his mouth all laid open like it was and his pine tar all laid open like it was and at his hands and arms twitching and jerking about like they were and wondered to herself could she manage a crazed man across the length of Tennessee and up over the mountains at the border of it and she said to Uncle Jack, "Two mules."

"That's right," Uncle Jack told her.

"Run off," Aunt Della said.

"That's right," Uncle Jack told her.

"Gone," Aunt Della said.

"That's right," Uncle Jack told her and kind of beat himself across his chest with his open hand prior to hooting one time, afterwhich he added, "Spunk," that Aunt Della dropped her lip over and said again behind him. "They run off," Uncle Jack said. "R-u-n."

"Alright," Aunt Della said, "they run off."

"Flew near about it," Uncle Jack told her. "Flew, Della," Uncle Jack said, "like you might figure a hybrid cultivated mule could fly."

"Flew," Aunt Della said, "like bandits."

"But it's in there," Uncle Jack told her, "down in there somewhere and don't need but the bringing out," and he said, "Come back here," and fairly yanked Aunt Della down off the wagonseat and on around to the hookeye where Uncle Jack himself and Aunt Della herself looked at the five remaining mules and Daddy said Aunt Della saw fairly much what there was to see which was the slightness and the scrawniness and just the general unmulish qualities of the entire bunch together while Uncle Jack that turned his face full on them his own self and gaped just as hard as he was able could not see an item otherwise but for flanks and hooves and boiling roaddust and he slapped himself again and hooted again and said to Aunt Della, "What beasts."

And Daddy said Aunt Della spat one time and told him back purely the same thing.

He just got taken with it, Daddy said, as he was the sort to get taken and to get possessed and Momma said it was the Yount temperament that did it, said it was the passion and it was the fiery blood that Aunt Sister laid foolishness overtop of, and Momma told her, "Passion, Sister, temperament," and it was Daddy that gave out the foolishness this time and only Aunt Sister that added the just precisely behind it. He said it just got away with Uncle Jack like things tended to get away with him sometimes or anyhow like things tended to get away with him in the pondering and the speculating and wondering stages but not hardly in the actual doing and accomplishing stages as Uncle Jack could plan and could anticipate in an extraordinary sort of way what he could not hardly ever manage to do even passably, so throughout Tennessee and over the Smokies and down across the foothills towards home he held to the boiling roaddust and the flanks and hooves too and manufactured a market for hybrid cultivated mules unrivaled by any commodity anywhere ever and he figured how him and Aunt Della would fetch back the next few batches and then hire on crews to do it in their stead while they themselves operated on what little property remained to them a kind of jackass clearinghouse from which they would ship the creatures all across the Southeast and anywhere there might be a need to ship them otherwise which could be most places, Uncle Jack figured, and likely for uses he hadn't even thought of yet as these were not your plain regular mulesized mules but were hybrid and cultivated and slight of frame, which Uncle Jack found he preferred to scrawny of a sudden, and he guessed maybe they could do things regular mulesized mules couldn't do and guessed maybe they could fit places regular mulesized mules couldn't fit and he told Aunt Della how he foresaw the day when every laboring man on the face of the earth would need a hybrid cultivated mule near about like he needed trousers or shoebottoms, and Daddy said Aunt Della, that had heard out the whole business in silence, commented on it with a dibble of snuffbrown saliva that she blew out the side of her mouth in a dramatic and purposeful sort of way and which she figured was comment enough but was not hardly comment enough truly on account of Uncle Jack was already pretty well gone with clearinghouse management and such and was looking out along the road with his mouth all set that way that told Aunt Della how he was not actually seeing the road at all but just mules, or not even mules truly but just flanks and hooves and boiling roaddust and maybe fabulous wealth too in as much as Uncle Jack could know what it might look like, and then he said a thing that could not Aunt Della make out straightaway and so she asked him, "What is it?" but he was saying it again already before she could get done with that as it was not for her anyhow but for him and when he'd finished it the second time he opened his mouth directly so as to set in a third time and he told himself, "Mulebaron," all slow and deliberate like maybe it was a new hat and he wanted to see would it sit down on his head.

So Daddy said it was not Uncle Jack that got himself and Aunt Della and the wagon with the sides and the roof to it and the five remaining hybrid and cultivated mules across the length of Tennessee and up over the Appalachians and down through the foothills towards home but was little Spud mostly that just went where the road did and most anywhere else he pleased as well since Uncle Jack could not seem to plan and speculate and ponder and rein a mule all at the same time, so little Spud went where he wanted to go about as fast as he cared to get there while Aunt Della dipped and spat and Uncle Jack schemed and wondered and even spoke every now and again, sometimes to Aunt Della but just into the air mostly, and Daddy said of an evening while Aunt Della was frying the saltpork and cooking the dried beans Uncle Jack would pass around behind the wagon and admire his purchase with his chin in one hand and his elbow in the other and Daddy did not know what he saw exactly while he stood where he stood and looked where he looked, maybe riches and roaddust and just solid spunk somehow but surely not mules, surely not those mules anyway that did not seem to thrive on travel and were commencing to show off their ribcages in a prominent kind of way.

But he got them home, Daddy said, got them back out 29 that was not even 29 then but was just dirt when it was not just mud which it was mostly and tied them all up together to a walnut tree in the side-yard as he did not have any place else to put them on account of the barn, that had been woodpile when him and Aunt Della departed, was still woodpile now that they were back and the chickencoop and the pigpen, that had been actually a chickencoop and a pigpen at least somewhat, were both woodpile now too which left just the house that was still house mostly but had been occupied in their absence by a multitude of gray squirrels that had gnawed their way in under the front door and then run all roundabout the place biting off little pieces of everything but for the bedstead which they had fairly much eaten up entirely. So Uncle Jack tied up the mules to the walnut tree in the side-yard which was the only item on his property sturdy and stout enough to tie them up to and him and Aunt Della unloaded the wagon with the sides and the roof to it and set in to evicting squirrels which Uncle Jack did the most of once he had fetched his shotgun out from the corner by the cookstove while Aunt Della swept clean the planking that was covered up in processed bedstead primarily, and they tidied all they could tidy and repaired and patched all they could repair and patch and as Aunt Della took down a jar of tomatoes from off the cupboard shelf Uncle Jack carried himself off to the walnut tree where he held his chin and held his elbow and got all distracted and absorbed, so distracted and absorbed in fact that he had not noticed what Aunt Della indicated to him he should notice once she had stepped outside to tell him how she had finished doing to the tomatoes whatever it was she had set out to do to them and only then did he look off from the mules and out to the fringes of his property where he discovered, like Aunt Della had just discovered for her own self, that Mr. Nunnely had cultivated what land he'd got deeded to him and had planted it all over in what looked to Uncle Jack like wheat, or anyhow did not look to Uncle Jack like weeds unless it was all the same weed which even Uncle Jack did not figure it could be mostly on account of his extensive experience with weeds as a crop. Anyhow it was a border, Daddy said, a near about knee-high border around three sides of the yard and Uncle Jack studied where it ran off to the east and then down to the south and then out to the west where it met the road and it all sort of suggested a thing to him and Uncle Jack said, "Yes, yes," that way he'd said mulebaron previously and Aunt Della that heard in the yes yes just exactly what she'd heard in the mulebaron asked Uncle Jack, "Yes what? Yes what?" and Daddy said Uncle Jack turned his face to her and turned his eyes on her and seemed to even look at her full on and told Aunt Della, "Yes, yes," all over again which actually he was not telling to her at all but just observing to himself almost exclusively.

Daddy said Uncle Jack designed and built the fence on his own, actually designed the fence as he was building the fence which Daddy said was Uncle Jack's way as a builder since he did not hardly ever start a thing but with just a notion of what he wanted it to turn out to be, like a house or a barn or a shed or, in this case, a mule corral, so he would fetch out his hammer and his nails and round up what planks he could manage to round up and set in in a general sort of way on something he figured to be houselike or barnlike or shedlike or mule corrallike until maybe he stepped back from it one time so as to assess and so as to observe and so as to decide just what changes he might set in on and whereabouts exactly, and Daddy said consequently Uncle Jack did not usually so much build a thing as he caused it to propagate and sprawl, and it was fairly much the same with the mule corral as it had been with the house and the shed and the barn and the chickencoop and the pigpen too since Uncle Jack knew he wanted a fence and knew fairly much where he wanted it but did not know what manner of fence exactly until he built the first section of it across the front of the lot and then stood back to admire what it was he had done which he found he did not much admire really and so he set in on the second run with a mind to adjust the posts and rearrange the rails and then stepped back from that for a spell of admiration which he could not generate on account of it either as it did not look anywhere near exactly like the picture in his own mind of what it should look like which Daddy said was truly Uncle Jack's chief trouble as he was ever carrying around in his head the pyramids and the

Greek temples and the Great Wall of China and such and was ever building outhouses and mule corrals and so should not hardly have hoped for the one to be the other but could not keep himself from it somehow which Daddy guessed was why he did like he did and was like he was that Momma called passion and that Aunt Sister called foolishness but that Daddy said was just the wanting on the one hand and the getting on the other and the appreciable difference in between.

So Daddy said it was a fence and it was a mule corral when Uncle Jack did at last get around the lot with it but he said it was purely Uncle Jack's variety of item and so looked to have been laid out and constructed by a dozen blind and crosseyed onearmed old ladies, maybe two dozen, Daddy said, as did not any one section look much at all like any other section as the whole business together was too tall most places except where it was too short and was not plumb anywhere but leaned out and leaned in and seemed ripe all around to get laid over by a wind, and Uncle Jack climbed up on a knoll alongside his lot in

Mr. Nunnely's wheatfield and he looked down on what it was he'd done and it seemed pretty much like a fence to him from there, seemed pretty much like the sort of fence he'd set out to build, especially if he wrinkled up his face and brought down his eyelids a ways, so he was near about as satisfied with it as he ever was with anything and came down out of the wheatfield and set in to touring the borders of his lot so as to find out did it strike him pretty much like a fence up close too, and it did, Daddy said, even seemed a little too much like a fence in the place where the gate was supposed to be since it was just a fence there and not a gate whatsoever until Uncle Jack made it a gate with his bootheel.

And he turned loose the mules, Daddy said, turned loose the mules in their new mule corral which had been his own yard one time but was to be a mule run anymore as far as Uncle Jack could figure it, a mule run with a house in the middle of it

maybe but a mule run nonetheless, and Uncle Jack stood
outside it with his arms draped over a piece of fence and with
the rest of his own self not hardly leaning forward and not
hardly pulling back either and he watched his five hybrid and
cultivated Oklahoma mules stand on the packed dirt with their
heads hung and their ears twitching every now and again and
he saw what he saw which Daddy said was still hooves and
flanks and roaddust, and he reached down into his boot,
Daddy said, just so as to have a thing to do with his hand and
drew out from it the bonehandled knife that he held the
bonehandle of in the palm of his one hand and felt the pointy
blade of with the fingers of his other which did not Uncle Jack
know he was doing with either hand truly until he blinked one
time like people will and saw ahead of him there in the yard
not hooves and flanks and roaddust but actual mules and saw
down against his own fingerends the glinty glistening
bonehandled knifeblade and he got a notion of a sudden and
looked from the knife to the mules and back from the mules to
the knife and then told himself, "Yes yes," in near about
precisely his mulebaron tone of voice.

So he got done up in some raiments of his own, Daddy said,
some muletrading raiments as best as Daddy could figure
which was a fuzzy shirt and broadcloth trousers and boots and
a Sunday jacket and even a hat, a hat somewhat for the style
and flair that your general hatwear-ing makes for, Daddy
supposed, but maybe mostly to cover the plughole his cowlick
had come out of until such time as he figured the plughole was
what he wanted to display, and Daddy said he hitched little
Spud up to the wagon with the sides and the roof to it and then
struck out south down 29 that was dirt and mud and not 29
anyway, not just then, and he rolled on into Neely proper
where the road was packed mostly and strawed over some
places and he climbed the hill up by where the icehouse would
be when it got built and up around where the Confederate
soldier would stand when it got erected and then he leveled off
on the boulevard that was not even the boulevard just then but

was the Greensboro road towards Greensboro and the Danville road towards Danville and only the main road otherwise that would come to be the boulevard when it was not packed and was not strawed anymore and he proceeded on up it square into the middle of what was town then and he stopped his wagon direct in front of Eaton's which Daddy said was not where Eaton's is now and was not then hardware like it has come to be hardware but was mostly everything instead on account of back in those days, Daddy said, there was not so much of everything as there's come to be so you could pretty much put it all in one place and manage to make it fit there, which the Eatons had fairly much managed to do but for what spilled out the front door and but for what spilled out the side door and but for what stayed piled and stacked and just generally heaped up on the pier out back and Aunt Sister said how she recollected that particular Eaton's back when it wasn't just hardware but was hardware and purely everything else too and she asked Daddy did he recollect Jackson P. Eaton that ran the business and Daddy asked her did she mean Jackson P. Eaton the one that rubbed his head like he did or his daddy and Aunt Sister said it was his daddy she meant and told how his daddy rubbed his own head himself which she guessed was where Jackson P. Eaton jr. got it from and she wondered didn't that seem likely which Daddy said he had no quarrel with as far as he could tell.

Aunt Sister recollected how her own daddy, Great-granddaddy Yount, would carry her with him into town some days and they would evermore end up in Eaton's on account of it was the place after all that had everything and could not hardly anybody after something help but end up there somehow, and Aunt Sister said Great-granddaddy would set her down on the front counter and would tell Mr. Jackson P. Eaton, "A cracker for this young lady, please sir," and Mr. Jackson P. Eaton would tell Great-granddaddy back, "Surenough," and

Aunt Sister wondered was that a thing that carried over like the head-rubbing but Daddy could not recall that Jackson P. Eaton the second had distinguished himself except with the headrubbing mostly and Aunt Sister herself could not remember either but his daddy's surenough which she said she could still near about hear in her ears and Aunt Sister left off talking for a time and shut her eyelids and tilted her head in a general listening attitude and seemed to actually hear a thing which me and Momma and Daddy sat quiet so as to listen at ourselves but did not seem to me there was anything much on the air to pick up except for briefly when Mr. Tiny Aaron passed by the housefront in his stark white Impala with the wheelbearings that clicked like they did. And Aunt Sister said it was always so low and always so deep that it did not but vibrate in her head and would still be rattling roundabout her insides when Mr. Jackson P. Eaton in his mostly white apron with the grime and the stains midway down his stomach would step out from behind the counter and remove with both hands the barrel lid so as to reveal for Aunt Sister what crackers she had to select from and she said she would study every whole one and every little piece and portion of all the rest she could see and then would select whichever might look a little bigger and might look a little browner than all the rest as browner especially was what she wanted in a cracker and just bigger only somewhat, and then she would point, Aunt Sister said, and Mr. Jackson P. Eaton would take up crackers one at the time and lay crackers back down until he had at last taken up the proper cracker which he would hold between his big knobby first finger and his near about flat thumb and present to Aunt Sister who said she would study it all roundabout from the edges inwards and then commence to eat on it at the corners like always and work it, like always, into a circle until she had made of a square cracker a round cracker that she would hold up for Mr. Jackson P. Eaton to rub his head on account of which he did not ever fail to do. And Aunt Sister said she would keep eating the edges off until there was just a little crumb left that she would finally put in her mouth and savor there while she looked for Great-granddaddy back in the reaches of the store which was purely cavernous, Aunt Sister said, and dim all around if not outright dark in places and with merchandise all over and just little pieces of plank floor to walk on by it and between it and around it and sometimes she would spy Great-granddaddy, she said, but mostly she couldn't and so would just call to him to see was he in there somewhere and he would call back like he always did, would call back, "Here, sugar," Aunt Sister told it, which would ease her and which would soothe her, and she said sometimes while she waited there on the countertop Jackson P. Eaton jr. that helped his daddy would get sent up the wall on the ladder with the wheels at the top and the wheels at the bottom too so as to fetch an item he could not hope to reach otherwise and mostly he would just go up and just come down again but sometimes he would push himself and roll the length of the wall and Aunt Sister said the whole place would fill just slam up with the noise that the wheels made and it seemed to her she could still near about hear it in her ears and she left off talking for a time and tilted her head like before.

Daddy said it was a place for a crowd, which was the thing, Daddy said it was a place for a bunch of people on account of how anybody that wanted anything could just go to Eaton's as they had everything anyway, or most everything anyhow as far as Daddy knew, certainly everything anybody else had and all of it in once place which was right for a crowd and right for a bunch of people which Uncle Jack figured was near about all he required and he climbed down off his wagonseat and struck out up the steps that was fairly littered with squatting and sitting men and standing men too and all of them together dipping and chewing men which Daddy explained to Momma he added just so as to keep the atmosphere intact, and Daddy said Uncle Jack stopped once he'd gained the plank porch and laid his hands to his hips and exhaled one time and looked all roundabout himself at the few men in the road and the more men on the steps and the most men laying all across the porch on feedsacks and propped atop crates and such and he said, "Well," Daddy told it, just plain Well and stretched himself after and what men knew him, which was the bulk of them, acknowledged him back, some with his actual name and some with just necknoises and some with not but a look to see who'd Welled at them in the first place, and once Uncle Jack was near about as stretched and unkinked as he could get he laid his hands back to his hips and said again, "Well," and then added behind it, "I been gone but I'm back."

Daddy said did not anybody seem inclined to argue the matter with him, not those that knew he'd been gone and not those that didn't since all of them together could see he was back anyhow, and Daddy said did not anybody even comment at all on the fact that he'd been gone or on the fact that he was back until a Holleman down on the first step asked a Shipp up on the third step, "Back from where?" that the Shipp made a face at like he was not privy to where exactly and did not much care either but up on the porch Uncle Jack that had waited for it to get asked and had heard it when it did told not just the Holleman but everybody otherwise as well, "I been out west, gentlemen, and have seen a thing or two," and Daddy said a Judd up on a grainsack opened his mouth and said, "I ain't gone nowhere, and I've seen a thing or two," which was the kind of thing Judds were generally given to saying, Daddy told it, and Aunt Sister wondered wasn't that the truth, that Momma nodded at, and Daddy figured maybe all of them there on the porch and there on the steps and there in the street too would have yelped and hooted like some of them did anyhow which Daddy said would be the ones that did not see Uncle Jack reach up with his fingers and lift from his head the hat he'd put there somewhat for the style and the flair your hatwearing produces but somewhat to cover the cowlick which got uncovered of a sudden and brought into the day where Daddy said it could not be but noticed straightoff as it was tarred over somewhat and scabbed over somewhat and just evil and angry-looking in a general sort of way, or anyhow more evil and more angry-looking than your regular cowlick which those men that had seen it before likely were figuring to see again and which those men that maybe hadn't seen it at all would not have been much surprised and astounded by as a regular cowlick is more of your ordinary item to see on a head than maybe the hole one got wrenched from and Daddy supposed it was likely the Holleman that opened his mouth and wanted to know a thing, wanted to know a thing of Uncle Jack truly but did not ask Uncle Jack outright which Daddy said is the way your Hollemans operate when they are that quizzical sort of local Holleman, and instead asked the Shipp that was closer but asked loud enough so as to get heard purely all over, "What's wrong with his head?" and Daddy said the Shipp made his usual face while Uncle Jack, that looked to have been waiting to get asked what was wrong with his head, did not say anything but just stood where he'd been standing and watched his fingers do what it was they were doing on his hatbrim and he did not drop his chin and did not being to reply until he'd got asked it again and not by a quizzical Holleman this time but by an Utley instead, an Utley up on the very porch planking that had been laying back on a grainsack but raised himself up on his elbows and said, "Where's your lick, buddy?"

And Daddy said Uncle Jack let out with an "Oh!" and shot one hand towards his plughole like maybe it was his open fly he was reaching for and he touched with his fingertips at the scabby parts and at the pinetarred parts too and then brought his hand back down to his hatbrim where it had started out from and said to the Utley, "It's gone."

"Well how's that?" And it was not the Holleman again and not even the Utley this time but was instead a Stewart off to the other end of the porch, an actual upright Stewart not sitting or leaning on anything but just standing with his hands plunged down into his back-pockets and Aunt Sister tried to recall when she'd ever seen a Stewart sit and look comfortable at it and Daddy told her they were simply not your lounging variety of creature on account of they'd come up poor here and come up poor in Scotland before it and so had not ever had the leisure to lounge much and Aunt Sister wondered did they have regular chairs in Scotland, the sorts of chairs that would provide a person with proper lower back support like people need to get from a chair or did they sit on rocks and such, and Daddy said he'd heard they were pretty well caught up with us furniturewise which struck Aunt Sister as sinister somehow and she let out an "Oh!" her own self.

So Daddy said this actual upright Stewart that had asked what he'd asked stepped forward like Stewarts tended to when they were waiting to learn a thing from somebody and he canted his head around so as to present an ear in the proper direction and Uncle Jack that was still touching his hatbrim and still watching his fingers do it said at last pretty much at the side of the Stewart's head, "I had a sort of a set-to."

"A what?" And Daddy said it would not serve well to tell who had said A what? exactly on account of near about everybody had said it.

"A set-to," Uncle Jack said back. "A run-in."

"What sort of run-in?" which the Holleman got out first as he was customarily quizzical anyway and so had the jump on the bulk of the crowd.

"Well," Uncle Jack said and Daddy left off so as to fetch out a

Tareyton and so as to fetch out a match and while he lit the one with the other he commenced to tell us through the smoke and the sulfur smell how there was some people that had a natural talent for pauses and for your general drama, how there was some people that knew how not talking sometimes said more than talking and said it better than talking ever could, how there was some people that could take just a plain and usual word like Well and put it to actual work the way most people didn't and couldn't, how there was some people that could render it up into a thing otherwise than just to spend breath on, how there was people like Uncle Jack that could say just "Well" and leave it at just Well for longer than most everybody else can stand not to talk, and Daddy said it just lingered there in the air and held everybody firm like a pure incantation while Uncle Jack, that had been standing where he'd stood all along, stepped across the porch towards a stoppered upended nail keg which Daddy said a Littlejohn just got up off of before Uncle Jack even had to ask him would he and Uncle Jack set himself down on it and laid his hat bottom upwards on the planking beside him and then reached over with his hatlaying hand and removed from his boot the bonehandled knife that he took hold of midway up the blade and commenced to clean under his fingernails with. "What I had me was," Uncle Jack said and wiped some grit off of the bladetip onto his pantsfront prior to setting in on a new finger altogether, "what I had me was a lethal sort of a run-in."

And Daddy said the Holleman that had his mouth set anyhow went ahead and repeated, "Lethal," as it was a word he was not entirely acquainted with and so could stand to hear again and the Stewart, who Daddy said had come from a people that was pretty much up with us wordwise as well, asked Uncle Jack, "Who to?" and turned and canted his head in a preparatory sort of way.

"This fella," Uncle Jack told him. "This fella," Uncle Jack told all of them and then reapplied himself to his fingernails that he had left off with for the sake of talking.

"Killed?" and it was the Holleman again that had got hold of lethal once he'd recollected where he'd heard it and how.

"Killed I guess," Uncle Jack told him and wiped more grit on his pantsfront prior to raising up the bonehandled knife so that what light it could catch glinted and glistened off the blade, and Daddy said he did not guess the knights themselves of the actual roundtable could have beheld the genuine holy grail with more plain flatout wonder and awe than your Hollemans and your Shipps and your Utleys and your Stewarts and your Sapps and your Littlejohns and your Judds and your Askews pondered that glinty glistening blade and that white bonehandle and those fingers wrapped roundabout it which all three together seemed to purely mean lethal in a way no word could really, and Daddy said they fairly much all rose up as one— your Hollemans and your Shipps and your Utleys and your Stewarts and your Sapps and your Littlejohns and your Judds and your Askews—and pressed in roundabout Uncle Jack so as to see up close the actual blade and the actual bonehandle and the actual fingers roundabout it and so as to hear where and so as to hear who but so as to hear how mostly which they figured they knew at least some of from what it was they could look at plain and clear.

"Tell it." And Daddy said it was the Stewart that had not got up from sitting to move a length and sit again and had not got up from squatting to squat all over but had just stepped one time, had just strode forward half across the porch and had arrived where he'd aimed to arrive at with his mouth part open and his head part cocked and his hands jammed and plunged like always. "Go on," he said. "Tell it."

And Daddy said Uncle Jack got to looking like he wouldn't, got to looking like he didn't aim to which Daddy said was part of the art and part of the flair and part of the pure and natural talent and did not but everybody insist he go on and insist he tell it, even the Shipp that was not generally much good but for faces, and so Uncle Jack breathed out that way he could that meant alright he guessed and Daddy said he flung the knife forward where it stuck between his boots in the planking and he rared himself back on his nail keg and worked first his one shoulder muscle and then his other prior to grabbing on to each knee with a thumb on one side and four fingers on the other and then drawing off a breath so as to say with it, "Gentlemen, there's danger in every bend of the road," and the whole crowd together made a noise like a hillslide and thereby suggested their agreement and approval.

Daddy said it was kind of the story Uncle Jack had been telling but was not the story exactly, was the indian anyhow and was the Williford and was himself and was Aunt Della too but was a mule mostly and not hardly little Spud that got put out from the thing entirely but one of your hybrids instead, one of your cultivated Oklahoma hybrids and Daddy said it got spoke extraordinarily well of, not like most mules anyhow which tend to get spoke of often enough but not hardly ever with much affection and regard, and not just plain and only spoke well of but even coveted too, Daddy said, coveted by real and actual indians, real and actual Cherokee indians, Uncle Jack told it, and then he wondered was there anybody amongst the crowd that had been to Oklahoma his own self and so maybe could throw in with and verify what it was Uncle Jack was insisting about indians and mules and such and while the Holleman and the Utley had traveled throughout Tennessee and the Shipp had himself been in the fat part of Florida which he thought maybe butted up against Oklahoma somewhere or another until he got corrected, Daddy called it, by the Stewart initially and everybody else after, was not there a soul among the crowd that had truly been into the very state itself and so was not there a soul among the crowd that could throw in with and verify or even refute either what Uncle Jack commenced to insist the indians in Oklahoma rode which was mules, of course, hybrid cultivated mules, and Uncle Jack kind of shut his eyes and laid back his head and recollected for the benefit of everybody present how stirring and moving and near about thoroughly inspiring it was to look out across the prairie and flatland at your various throngs of indians charging about on their jackasses.

"Can't nobody judge a mount like an indian," Uncle Jack said, "can't nobody ever hope to," and Daddy said everybody, even the Stewart, grunted and nodded and told each other how it was the very thing they were fixing their own mouths to say and Uncle Jack wondered in an idle sort of way had maybe any of those fellows there ever laid eyes on an actual indian which the Holleman and the Utley too said they'd laid eyes on when they crossed the Blue Ridge through the gap and so had run up on what Cherokees had hid and had lingered and had not been driven away, and Uncle Jack said how he guessed they knew that was the frail and scrawny variety that had got left, and the Holleman and the Utley said they knew that well enough, said they had not been clear to Oklahoma maybe, but there were some things they did know anyhow and the frail and the scrawny was one of them, and the Holleman told how he would have said it himself if he'd had half the chance to open his mouth and get the words out, and Daddy said straightoff Uncle Jack apologized and made himself so earnest and remorseful at it that even the Holleman grew a little shameful at having snapped like he'd snapped and so bit off what it was he had started in on and yielded entirely to Uncle Jack that just sat holding his knees looking stricken and then breathed in and then breathed out and set back in on indians in a general sort of way, conferring from time to time with the Holleman and the Utley so as to benefit from their experience and their advice, and Daddy said Uncle Jack talked about the red skin and talked about the black hair and talked about the white teeth and the courage and the muscle and the savagery and then commenced to localize in the direction of your Oklahoma Cherokees which were not the frail ones and were not the scrawny ones and, according to Uncle Jack, were not the regular peoplesized ones either, but were kind of your mammoth indians, Uncle Jack told it, kind of your broad towering hulking indians, and Daddy left off to draw a breath where maybe he figured it'd best make for some drama or where maybe he figured he'd best take in some oxygen and Aunt Sister, that had been attempting to say a thing for an appreciable spell judging from how she'd been holding her mouth just precisely open enough to get words out it, did in fact get words out it at last and asked Daddy and asked Momma too didn't they recollect when them and her and me and Granddaddy as well went up into the mountains that fall and drove through the Ashville tunnel and along the ridge and down into Maggie Valley and then up by the reservation and on into Cherokeetown itself where she remembered how her and Granddaddy and she thought Momma and me too had our pictures took with the indian chief out front of that place with the tepee on the roof, that place that sold the leather shoes and the beads and the spears and such, and Momma said she did recollect the very spot and I said I did recollect the very spot too, but Momma and Aunt Sister together told me how I didn't and held their hands apart so as to indicate why, and Daddy said did not anybody have their pictures took with an indian chief, and Aunt Sister got indignant straightaway like she's able to and suggested to Daddy how she knew what she knew and what she knew just precisely was the indian chief and the store with the tepee on the roof and the snapshot that got took out front of it, and Momma said, "Yes ma'm," just after, and Daddy went ahead and allowed for the store with the tepee on the roof and allowed for the snapshot too but drew up short at the indian chief that he said wasn't, and Aunt Sister said, "A chief?"

"Not that," Daddy told her.

And Aunt Sister said, "An indian?"

And Daddy told her, "Not that either," and he wondered why it was that her and that Momma who recalled the tepee well enough and recalled the posing and the picturetaking could not seem to recollect the indian chief that Daddy said was not just not a chief but was not an indian either, was not even an American but was instead a full-blooded Greek, a full-blooded Greek with feathers on his head but nowhere near an indian, and Momma and Aunt Sister looked at each other with their chins hanging some and said together, "Oh."

"Brown, don't you know," Daddy said, "nut brown, not hardly red but then not hardly white either so good enough to suit while the usual indian was down in the back."

"That's right, down in the back," Aunt Sister said, and she remembered of a sudden how it was that Greek indian chief that told Momma how to make the spaghetti sauce with the green peppers and the eggplant in it and Momma said, "Oh," again and admitted how she'd forgotten all about that spaghetti sauce with the green peppers and the eggplant and wondered why it was she'd left off making it in the first place as it was so tasty, she recalled, and Aunt Sister figured it was maybe how the garlic had affected Granddaddy and Momma guessed maybe she was right and said it did the same to her every now and again that Aunt Sister guessed was maybe just the way with garlic and Momma said she supposed that was the truth of it.

Then Daddy put in with his alright like he does sometimes, which was not his alright that means alright exactly and was not his alright that means the opposite of it but was instead his purely grammatical alright that he uses in a punctuational sort of way so as to put the brakes on whatever sort of thing seems to him needs the brakes put on it, like spaghetti with eggplant and green peppers which Daddy figured was a ways from indians and a ways from mules and purely a considerable ways from Oklahoma, so Daddy said, "Alright," like he can and drew out filter foremost with his thumb and his forefinger a solitary Tareyton from the pack in his shirtpocket that he lit off the one he was finishing up which was just the sort of thing to thoroughly arrest Momma in the middle of whatever she might be in the middle of which was still garlic at least somewhat and digestion at least partly and she looked at Daddy that way she looks at him sometimes like maybe he'd just sacrificed a virgin or something near about as unwholesome anyhow and she watched him crush out his butt in his scallop shell ashtray and then snatched it off the chairarm and carried it on into the kitchen so as to dump it and rinse it and clean it like she does sometimes.

Daddy said Uncle Jack fairly much laid out Oklahoma so as to let your Hollemans and your Shipps and your Utleys and your Stewarts and your Sapps and your Littlejohns and your Judds and your Askews get a notion of what places were where and situated how and on which terrain exactly afterwhich he fairly well filled in what civilized parts he'd give out with your basic Oklahoma white settler that Uncle Jack let on was your fairly regular variety of human though likely measurably inferior to the local product which the Holleman said was another one of those items he did know for his own self as he had met a man from Oklahoma once and had not been especially taken with him. Then it was more indians, Daddy said, with some considerable breath expended on the broad parts and the towering parts and the hulking parts too that Uncle Jack attempted to illustrate and approximate with his arms that he stretched up and stretched out and stretched most every way otherwise as well but eventually left off working and raising and flinging altogether once he had told how there was some things a man just had to see with his own eyes to truly get a grip on that the Holleman straightaway threw in with on account of some things he'd seen that he could not hardly speak of. And then it was mules, Daddy said, was mules after places and settlers and indians and was mules for an appreciable while too as Uncle Jack had more interest in the mule end of the thing than the place end or the settler end or the indian end either and had more reason to carry on like he carried on and Daddy said he did carry on like maybe he was not so much set to describe a creature as he was to redefine a species which Daddy said he fairly much did redefine on account of what inspiration he worked from that was flanks and hooves and roaddust mostly and not much of your actual muleparts otherwise, so what got formed, Daddy said, and what got created and described was kind of in the way of a mule, Daddy guessed, like maybe a dinosaur is kind of in the way of a lizard. It did not hardly seem Oklahoma was big enough to hold more than a dozen, fifteen at the outside, but seemed like maybe fifteen would be enough as they could do near about every mulework anybody had ever heard tell of and could likely manage what people hadn't even thought to do yet but would which was mostly your pulling and your toting and just your generally burdensome sorts of endeavors, and they were sleek, Uncle Jack said, sleek for speed, he said, and sleek for elegance, and sleek as well, he added, for wind resistance and he paused to explain how the wind came down from the northwest across the fruited plain and was not any breaks much in the way of your cedars and your spruce pines as it did not seem a habit with your fruited plain people to plant breaks and the Holleman made a noise in his head that signified how he knew as much himself. So Uncle Jack said the wind just came pouring on through on the way to wherever it was on the way to and most times stiff and steady so that a mule could stand to be sleek if he had to plow into it, could stand to be thin and spiny, but not too thin, Uncle Jack said, and not too spiny, on account of did not these mules just plow and tote and labor in a mulish sort of way but got rid too, got rid everywhere by everybody as it was not too thin a back and not too spiny a back to lay even the broadest rearend across with comfort and ease, and they could prance and canter, Uncle Jack said, and evermore geed and hawed like most mules never would.

"Horse mostly," the Holleman volunteered.

"Mule, sir," Uncle Jack told him. "Mule entirely. Oklahoma hybrid cultivated mule."

Uncle Jack said he bought five, said he wanted ten, said he wanted twenty, but said he bought five with what money he carried that he said would likely have bought ten and would likely have bought twenty places otherwise but not where he was and not for what he gave it for which Uncle Jack said he did not regret the least penny of since it was not just extravagant money but was extravagant beasts too and he asked everybody couldn't they see the sense of it which the Holleman made his headnoise at firstoff that got followed all roundabout him by noises likewise, and Daddy said Uncle Jack bent himself over and reached down with both his hands together to work loose the bonehandled knife that had stuck firm in the planking and he raised it up holding the bonehandle with one set of fingers and feeling the blade edge with the other and he said, "Now," and then wiped at his mouth with his coatsleeve and said, "Gentlemen, I'm gone tell you a thing about mules and a thing about indians and lord I guess a thing about that wife of mine and it ain't none of it like nothing you've ever heard."

And the Holleman said, "Aw," on account of he did not figure anything was like nothing he'd ever heard as he guessed he'd heard most everything or near about it, and the Shipp made his usual face as Shipps are pretty much Hollemans, Daddy said, every way but in the vocabulary, and then nobody else said anything and nobody else did anything but for Uncle Jack touching again at the blade edge and when words got spoke at last it was the Stewart that said, "Tell it," which Daddy said the Stewart had a way of coming out with that would just make a man commence to narrating regardless of whether or not he had a thing at all to tell which Uncle Jack did, Daddy said, and which Uncle Jack commenced to narrate, commenced to narrate with just the general atmosphere straightaway like Daddy said your best narrators will and he told how it was a fair midday outside Harts-horne Oklahoma, no clouds much, no breeze much, no shade anywhere, and just mules against the grass and against the blue sky and against the sunshine,

Oklahoma hybrid cultivated mules in a sprawling corral and him outside it looking in and Della outside it and Mr. J. T. London outside it too and Uncle Jack slapped the flat of the knifeblade into his palm two times. "Mr. J. T. London," he said, "mulebaron."

"Extravagant," Daddy said which Momma liked to lay at him most times she bothered to lay anything at him so Daddy gave it back to her. "A purely extravagant production," he said and naturally figured it was somewhat on account of the size of the mules and somewhat on account of the size of the indians that both served to swell the whole business considerably but Daddy said it was Uncle Jack too that had told it and refined it and so knew just where to leave off and for how long and knew just where to dally and why and when to talk loud and when to talk low and when to shake his head slow back and forth that way he could shake his head that meant everything at once. Daddy allowed how the most of it was bent and stretched beyond your usual bounds but did not figure there was much in the way of outright falsehood except maybe for the mule that got rode where it did which would be the mule that got took and the mule that got fought over that had been little Spud but was not little Spud anymore and got to be hybrid and got to be cultivated instead and got to be coveted on account of it by your particular broad towering hulking indian that ended up coveting the thing he coveted as it was just what he required to charge roundabout the prairie on. So Daddy said you had your motive and you had your forces and you had your good and your evil and your frail woman somewhere amidst it and of course you had your kind of native animosity, Daddy called it, your red man and your white man and the solitary item that can't but one of them possess truly and then you had your narrator too who could pause and who could linger but who could tell a thing flatout when flatout was what it needed.

So it was an item to hear, Daddy guessed, and Momma and Aunt Sister that had heard it all before not just from Daddy but from relations otherwise that sometimes even knew what it was they were speaking of guessed that it was likely an item to hear from Uncle Jack himself though your coveting and your brawling and your shooting and your killing was not hardly in their line, not near so much in their line as it was in Daddy's who seemed to see a thing in coveting and brawling and shooting and killing that could not Momma or Aunt Sister seem to spy out for themselves or even seem to want to really, but they all agreed it was likely a thing to hear anyhow and I figured my own self maybe it was even if I had just heard it like I just had, so we all did not doubt he had them like Daddy said he had them, had them collected roundabout him and had them still and silent even down to the Holleman that watched the blade glint and glisten and sat quiet through the pauses and sat quiet through the Della parts and the indian parts and the mule parts and the Uncle Jack parts too until all the parts commenced to rise and surge and come together when Uncle Jack left off of a sudden and adjusted himself on his nail keg and wiped his mouth with his coatsleeve and did not set back in hardly soon enough to suit the Holleman that said, "Well, well?" like maybe there actually was a thing he didn't know and needed to.

So he did get to the tangling and the tussling and the rolling around in the street and it was the thing he did best truly as he had armscabs and facescabs to show off somewhat and scars various places to point at and indicate and uncover when it was seemly to do it but mostly he had the pure absence of cowlick that had started it all anyhow and so took prominence, Daddy said, and became most extraordinarily significant or anyway the plug it got yanked from and the pine tar on it and the scab on it too, and of course there was some elaborate earbite talk as well, Daddy said, a regular earbite panegyric, Daddy called it, with a part about your teeth and a part about your earflesh and a part about the mating of the one to the other, and Daddy said the earbite talk was so extraordinarily vivid and descriptive that could not anybody help but reach up

with his fingers and feel his lobes and be grateful that they
hung like they hung all whole and ungnawed on. And Daddy
said naturally there was a loose approximation of the actual
swearing that had gone on during the tussling and the rolling
around in the street, which would be somewhat of the swearing
that had gone on and somewhat of the swearing that should
have or could have, and Daddy said it was all lively and fitting
and a piece of it come out from the indian that Uncle Jack gave
reason to swear but the bulk of it come out from Uncle Jack
himself who did not have his mouth full of various indian parts
and so was free to use it anyhow he figured best which Daddy
said was swearing there for a spell and he guessed the spirit of
it caught hold of your Hollemans and your Shipps and your
Utleys and your Stewarts and your Sapps and your Littlejohns
and your Judds and your Askews as they commenced to throw
in with Uncle Jack when it seemed to them they had a thing
vile and profane enough to throw in with and the whole gang
of them there on the porch decking kept the air fairly much
crowded with obscenities for an appreciable stretch and they
all said some hard things against savages in general and
against indian savages in particular, especially your variety of
indian savage that would bite earflesh and would bite cowlicks
and would just mostly close his teeth on anything that
happened to end up between them, and Daddy said the more
your Hollemans and your Shipps and your Utleys and your
Stewarts and your Sapps and your Littlejohns and your Judds
and your Askews considered just what items exactly might end
up between an indian's teeth the uneasier they grew and the
madder and the hotter and the viler and the profaner until it
seemed to Uncle Jack that they were purely ripe for the gun
part of the business and so he said, "Sharps," and so he said, ".
50 caliber buffalo rifle," and it was like he had pointed the
thing, Daddy said, and like he had pulled the very trigger and
they were soothed of a sudden not by the actual gun but by the
notion of it and not by the actual bullet in the actual shot
indian but by the pure and proper anticipation of that.

Daddy said there was appreciable talk of stomach tar bottles straightaway, not just shot-at stomach tar bottles but hit ones mostly, hit ones spoke of by Uncle Jack somewhat that had used a rock but did not mention it, and hit ones spoke of by the Holleman somewhat too who let on how he'd broke likely a caseworth from near about miraculous distances that did not anybody begin to believe but for the Holleman that did not hardly insist on it himself until he got told what palpable horseshit it was when he grew insulted and irate and swore on his dead mother's grave, swore how it was not just stomach tar bottles at miraculous distances but was stomach tar battles at miraculous distances in the dusk of the day in a wind, and your Utleys and your Stewarts and your Sapps and your Littlejohns and your Judds and your Askews and even your Shipps too used up on the Holleman what hard talk they had not used up on the indian previously. And then there was talk of holes after, Daddy said, holes in people mostly that had not any of them not seen but at least one of as it was when it was, Daddy said, which was then and so meant lawyers sometimes and judges sometimes and juries and verdicts sometimes but then just bul-letholes sometimes too and they all knew which made what, Daddy said, and how and so did not anybody quarrel with Uncle Jack when he butted the tipend of his first finger against the tipend of his thumb so as to make a loop and laid it on himself at his shoulder socket and said, "Here."

And it was the Utley that said back, "Where now?" on account of he could not see clear just exactly what piece of Uncle Jack's self he had laid his loop on.

"Here," Uncle Jack told him and reared up at the shoulder.

"'Who on?" the Holleman wanted to know and Daddy said did not but everybody tell him, "Indian."

"Well, who by then?" the Holleman wondered and Daddy said they all got set to tell him who by exactly when they realized all at once and of a sudden how they did not truly know who by and so could not tell it and instead looked to Uncle Jack to tell it for them, looked to Uncle Jack on his nail keg where he felt the blade edge of the bonehandled knife with his fingertips and spat one time and wiped himself with his coatsleeve and then set in with some legitimate pausing so as to inflate the drama like he could.

And Daddy said he did not start back in until the Stewart suggested how he should, or anyhow until the Stewart said, 'Tell it," which set Uncle Jack to narrating on the inhale straightoff as he had not been quite fixed to narrate and he started in with a brief comment on women just as a form of native life and then commenced to narrow his view in a regular sort of way until it got clean down to Della herself that Daddy said came out kind of like Della but kind of like something otherwise or anyhow what seemed something otherwise to your Hollemans and your Shipps and your Utleys and your Stewarts and your Sapps and your Littlejohns and your Judds and your Askews on account of how they were expecting the hooked nose and the bangs and the general wiriness which was what they knew best of Aunt Della as it was what they could see of her but got instead essences mostly, Daddy called them, that could not any of them see and did not any of them know and recognize as they were not near so well acquainted with Della as Uncle Jack was and so could not but look roundabout at each other while Uncle Jack waxed, Daddy called it, connubial, that Aunt Sister just developed a passion for rightoff and had to hear three times directly and one time thereafter before she could get the hang of it her own self and so say it to her satisfaction like she managed to twice before the connubial got altered like it was bound to and came out upside down.

So Uncle Jack carried on, Daddy called it, and had a word to say about matrimony and love and devotion and just most all the sorts of things that men don't generally speak of in front of men, not ever, but the sorts of things Uncle Jack could get away with on account of what verbosity he had and what story he was telling anyhow that needed matrimony and love and devotion so as to make it work like it had to and consequently did not anybody but the Holleman make a noise and did not anybody but the Shipp make a face and Uncle Jack told Essences and Ties and Vows and lastly told Orblike that nobody much seemed to grasp and comprehend but for the Stewart that seemed to grasp and comprehend it near about. You had your forces then, Daddy told it, and Momma threw in with the strange and the wondrous that Daddy said did not suit, that Daddy said Momma knew did not suit, and Momma said she did not know but the strange and wondrous sort as she had not been instructed in forces otherwise and Daddy said his Alright like he was bound to and fished after a fresh Tareyton so as to have it set to light off his spent one and he said not strange and he said not wondrous and he said just forces, forces surging and swelling and running all together like they had to which would be your savage covetous indian forces and your indignant vengeful white man forces which Daddy said was your two prime forces there for a time until things commenced to look like they commenced to when your matrimonial forces, that Daddy said was somewhat your love and somewhat your devotion and somewhat your essences and your ties and your vows and maybe even your orblike too, got brought in and applied, Daddy called it, steel and wood and brass and lead and powder load. "Applied," Daddy said.

And Uncle Jack scratched his face with the blunted knifespine and said, "We was rolling, boys, we was rolling in that dusty road and the both of us just a grunting and a straining against each other, and didn't I have it on him and didn't he have it on me but we was just rolling and him working with his teeth mostly and me working with my knuckles best I could and he'd get up and I'd get under and then I'd get up and he'd get under and we was rolling and biting and hitting in that dusty road and just agrunting and just astraining and then I seen this,"

Uncle Jack said and he stuck the bonehandled knife blade-first into his own boot and drew it out with appreciable stealth and slyness. "I seen this," he said. "Didn't see him reach truly and didn't see him take hold but I seen this," and he raised up the blade so that what light there was hit on it. "I seen it shine," Uncle Jack said, "I seen it shine in the sun and just along about then I feel him let loose of whatever piece of me he was biting, I don't even recollect which piece it was'but I feel him let loose of it, and before I know what it is that's all shiny and glinty and silvery in his hand he's got it raised over his head as raised up as his arm can raise it and I don't need to see it but just the one time there to know what it is and what it's for and where it's going to end up and I tell you boys, I figured that was purely the last of me." And Daddy said Uncle Jack raised up the knife himself and held it like the indian held it and then brought it down, Daddy said, plunged it like the indian never got to, plunged it clean into the plank flooring, and Uncle Jack said he'd seen things, things otherwise than what his eyes were trained on which was the glinty knifeblade and the indian attached to it, things like bright light, bright yellow light, he said, and faces, not indian faces and bystander faces but holy faces, and the Holleman wondered how he could tell which faces were holy and which faces weren't, and Uncle Jack said when he's about to get skewered a man can just tell some things and the Holleman allowed it as he had not ever been close to death as best as he could recall. And Uncle Jack said he heard things, said he heard singing, kind of highpitched singing, not squeaky highpitched but just plain airy highpitched singing and Aunt Sister said, "Praise, praise," through her fingers that she was dabbing with at the time, and Daddy told how Uncle Jack figured it was heaven and figured he was on his way there, figured maybe he was dead already, figured maybe he was done in and likely would not know it until Jesus told him as it seemed to him that maybe that was how things worked, that Jesus would say to him, "Are you Cyrus Barnard Yount?" and he would say back, "Yes, Jesus." And Jesus would say to him, "Welcome to heaven," and he would say back, "Thank you, Jesus, it's nice to be here," or something like it Daddy figured as Uncle Jack was not ever the sort to get all stiff and formal even with his savior.

So he said he saw lights, bright yellow lights, and heard singing, airy highpitched singing, and guessed it was all up with him and as he was flatout on his back and sat atop of and as his eyes were not working much anyhow he could not see Aunt Della standing where she was standing and bringing to bear on that indian what she was bringing to bear on him which of course was the Sharps .50 caliber, Uncle Jack told it, that she aimed as best as she could aim and held as best as she could hold and then shot as best as she could shoot and Uncle Jack butted the tipend of his first finger against the tipend of this thumb and laid the loop on his own shoulder. "Just here," he said, "and the bones acrunching."

"Acrunching," the Holleman said behind him and the Shipp made one of his faces.

And Uncle Jack told how his eyes focused of a sudden, focused on the shoulder hole and focused on the indian as a general item and focused on the knife in particular that dropped onto the road just as that indian commenced to pitch over like Uncle Jack guessed a .50 caliber slug might make a man pitch over, even your broad hulking towering sort of man, and Uncle Jack said they both set to scratching and scrabbling roundabout in the dirt straightaway and Uncle Jack took up the knife himself while the indian got upright and laid his fingers on his bullethole and struck out running, Uncle Jack told it, struck out running down the road with Uncle Jack behind him that said he was beat and bit and gnawed on and near about spent entirely but wasn't hardly shot like that indian was shot and so closed in, Uncle Jack said, closed in tighter and tighter behind him until he threw himself, Daddy said, threw himself just straight out in the air and grabbed hold of that indian at the knees and brought him down.

"What's this now?" Aunt Sister said.

"Brought him down," Daddy said, "grabbed him roundabout the knees and brought him down."

"Whereabouts?" Aunt Sister wanted to know.

"Square in the road," Daddy told her.

"What road where?" Momma said just before Aunt Sister could manage to.

"Hartshorne," Daddy told her, "Oklahoma."

"Arkansas," Momma told him back, "Osceola."

And Daddy said, "No ma'm."

"No ma'm what?" Momma wanted to know and Aunt Sister got out a What her own self.

"No ma'm not Arkansas, not Osceola," Daddy said and Momma looked at Aunt Sister that looked at Momma and then the two of them together looked at me that looked at them back and so I guess it was the three of us that looked at Daddy when we all stopped looking at each other and Daddy said, "Listen. There's how it got done and then there's how it got told and it isn't but sometimes that a thing gets done like it needs to get told."

And Aunt Sister looked at Momma that looked at Aunt Sister that looked at me that looked at both of them back.

"License," Daddy said.

And Aunt Sister wanted to know, "Which?"

"License," Daddy said. "The poetical variety."

"The what?" Momma asked him.

"The poetical license," Daddy said.

And Momma told him, "Alright," a way he was familiar with though from lips otherwise.

"It means," Daddy said, "that what got shot and done in in Arkansas can get shot and done in in Oklahoma if it suits."

"Suits who?" Aunt Sister wanted to know and said it in such a way so as to indicate straightoff it was not her it suited at all.

"Not who," Daddy said. "Suits what."

"Alright," Momma told him. "Suits what then?"

"The drama of the thing," Daddy said back. "I mean you got this ponderous covetous indian on the one hand and you got goodly Uncle Jack on the other and his mule between them that's got stole and plundered, what we call the conflict that sets things to rising to what we call the crisis."

"The crisis," Aunt Sister said.

"The crisis," Daddy told her. "The knife raised up and set to plunge and the indian ready to plunge it."

"Alright," Momma told him. "Then what after?"

"Why then it's your basic complication," Daddy said. "You got your rising action on the one side with Uncle Jack and the indian and you got Aunt Della on the other, essences and vows and ties and such, don't you know, and so you throw her into it, her and the buffalo rifle, and well things just get complicated on account of it's Uncle Jack after the indian for the mule and Aunt Della after the indian for Uncle Jack.

"Complicated," Momma said.

"That's it," Daddy told her, "and then don't you see how what action's been rising stops rising and new action commences to rise instead."

"New action," Aunt Sister said.

"That's right," Daddy told her, "as it's not anymore the indian with the raised knife but is instead the indian with the shot shoulder and not atop Uncle Jack but in front of him and Uncle Jack not under him but behind him and himself with what knife the indian had raised and set to plunge and Aunt Della and the buffalo rifle behind him."

"So it rises all over?" Aunt Sister said.

"Yes ma'm," Daddy told her. "Rises all over."

"Then why is it things can't rise all over in Arkansas like they did actually rise all over?" Aunt Sister wanted to know.

"Because," Daddy said and moved his posterior somewhat on the chairbottom, "you got your conflict and you got your crisis and you got your complication but then you got your pacing too, you got your poetical velocity," which was just the sort of thing to inspire some earnest looking between Momma and Aunt Sister and then me as well. "Don't you see," Daddy said, "it all has to happen in a hurry on account of it's drama and high adventure."

"It's a lie," Aunt Sister said.

"Near about always," Daddy told her. "Drama," he said. "High adventure," and raised his left hand palm upwards like they were perched upon it. "Real actual life," he said and raised his right hand palm upwards too.

So we figured we'd let Uncle Jack tackle that indian where he didn't for the sake of art which Daddy told us we would be letting him tackle the indian for the sake of and so we did and he did right square in the road back of Hartshorne and Daddy told how Uncle Jack from atop his nail keg reached forward with both his arms so as to illustrate how he lunged and how he grabbed and he said does not anything truly fall so hard as a broad towering hulking indian on account of how they are not a graceful sort even unshot and unchased and untackled and so shot and chased and tackled are something even less than that and he pitched over directly, Uncle Jack told it, and bounced one time and said an indian thing, a thing partly for Uncle Jack but mostly for the bullethole, he guessed, mostly for the bullethole and the general agony of it, and then they were tangled up and rolling and both getting bled on and Uncle Jack said how he stabbed at that indian with his own bonehandled knife, but could not stick him anywhere proper which he guessed the indian had a thing or two to do with but which he guessed he had as much to do with himself on account of how stabbing a man with a knife is not hardly at all like shooting a man with a gun since with a gun it's just the finger that pulls the trigger that looses the hammer that strikes the pin that fires the bullet while with a knife it's the very hand that drives it home and Uncle Jack said how he simply could not bring himself to drive it much of anywhere, could not find what fierceness and savagery he needed to find if he was to stab and if he was to kill, and so they rolled and tussled and both got bled on and Uncle Jack said he swore and punched and hit and got bit and got beat and then straightaway got sat on again, sat on by the indian that even with one good arm was still too broad and too towering and too hulking to be managed by just a regular human and so he got up where he had been and sat like he'd sat and wrested loose from Uncle Jack's fingers the bonehandled knife that the indian did not seem to lack the fierceness and the savagery to drive like it needed driving and he raised it, Uncle Jack said, and set to plunge it, Uncle Jack said, which was when it hit him, Uncle Jack said, and he could not even recollect the gunshot, did not even hear it as far as he knew, but saw the hole straightoff and he laid his fingerloop on his own chest. "Here," he said.

"Dead I bet," the Holleman said, "dead I bet in a hurry."

"Dead," Uncle Jack told him. "Purely quick." And Uncle Jack said Essences and Ties and Vows and said even Orblike all over again and then he added Mules behind it so as to remind your Hollemans and your Shipps and your Utleys and your Stewarts and your Sapps and your Littlejohns and your Judds and your Askews just precisely what it was an entire indian had got shot up on account of, which was mules, special mules, Uncle Jack told it, hybrid cultivated Oklahoma mules, and Daddy said Uncle Jack cleaned under the last of his fingernails with the bladetip of the bonehandled knife and then breathed in deep and breathed out hard and loud and took hold of his kneejoints and pushed himself upright off them and then bent over to stick the knifeblade in his boottop and then stood up again and stretched himself and said how he guessed he would go put out some oats and put out some hay, how he guessed he would feed those mules and tend to them like they rated and deserved until somebody come along to snatch them up from him which he didn't guess would be awful far off, which he didn't guess could be awful far off seeing as how those mules were hybrid like they were and cultivated like they were too and seeing as how mule buyers roundabout could generally tell a prime item when they saw one, and Uncle Jack stretched himself one more time and dropped his chin to yawn with it and said kind of up towards the porch ceiling, "Ya'll stop on by when you're able," that your Hollemans and your Shipps and your Utleys and your Stewarts and your Sapps and your

Littlejohns and your Judds and your Askews all made necknoises at as they watched Uncle Jack climb up onto his wagon and gee his regular mule on around in the road so as to head it back the way it had come from.

And Daddy said they did go and did stop by even though it did not seem to look at them that they would ever rise up off their sacks and their heels and their stairtreads but for the Stewart that did not lay and lounge like the bulk of men but stood like a Stewart always, and Daddy said it was not even just them but was them that had heard it firsthand and then them that had got told it by them that had heard it firsthand and them that had got told it by them that had only just heard it themselves and they rode draft horses and plain geldings and wagons and mules too up 29 that wasn't even 29 yet and all the way out to Uncle Jack's just so as to see it, just so as to lay their own eyes on the very thing, and Uncle Jack spied them coming way up the road and knew just what it was they were coming for, he figured, and so got agitated and generally worked up that way he could get agitated and worked up and he fixed his mouth and told himself, "Mule-baron," while he watched approach what was approaching, and Daddy said like men will sometimes did not anybody say just what it was they'd come to see and come to look at and did not Uncle Jack ask either but just stood and just talked about everything otherwise like he got talked at and then excused himself and circled round the corral towards the backside of it while the men that were down off their horses and their mules and out from their wagons pressed up against the ramshackle fence at the lotfront and the men that had not got down and had not got out did at last and pressed up against what they could press up against themselves and Uncle Jack climbed over the back fence where the mules were, the hybrid cultivated Oklahoma mules, and slipped on up behind three of them and then hooted and yelped and slapped his hands together and stomped near about all at once and so it was flanks and so it was hooves and so it was yarddust and the three mules together shot around the side of the house and out across the front of the lot towards the far fence that was topped the full length with dangling arms and shoulders and necks and heads above them and the three scrawny puny hybrid cultivated mules together angled off across the yard and then up along the other side of the house towards the back again, and Daddy said Aunt Della that had heard all the galloping about, which was not hardly anything she'd come to expect and be accustomed to considering what animals it was closed up in her yard anyhow, flung open the front door and stepped out onto the stoop and Daddy said near about precisely half the dangling arms rose up of a sudden so as to point and indicate and he guessed maybe the bulk of the men said together, "There she is," though it was only the Stewart that Aunt Della heard at it on account of how it was the Stewart could say a thing most times.

And Daddy said Uncle Jack came trotting around the side of the house the mules had come round prior to him and him still seeing flanks and hooves and yarddust and telling himself nothing but mule-baron anymore and when at last he did gain the frontyard he did not even see straightoff how it was empty of mules entirely, how it was empty of every trace of mules really but for your dung, Daddy called it, here and yonder, and Momma and Aunt Sister said how they were both obliged and Daddy waved his hand like the pope does. Weren't mules anywhere at all, he said, but still they were looking and still they were gaping from the corral fence and indicating with their arms and pointing with their fingers and Uncle Jack could not figure what at directly as there was only the house and only the front stoop of it and only Aunt Della atop that and the Stewart said, "There she is," all by himself this time, said, "There she is that shot him."

"Dead in a hurry," the Holleman said, "purely quick," and three or four at once wanted to know what sort, wanted to know what sort exactly that the Stewart said was an Apache as Apaches were somehow on his mind just then but the Askew

insisted it was not an Apache though he could not himself
remember what it was exactly only that it was not an Apache,
he was sure of it, and somebody otherwise guessed a Saura,
somebody otherwise that had not heard it firsthand anyhow
and he got scoffed soundly by what men had heard it firsthand
who did not know what it was either but for the Stewart that
only thought he knew what it was but who altogether figured
they knew fairly well what it wasn't and it wasn't a Saura. So
there was suggestions all around, Daddy said, Croatans and
Sioux and Black-foots and even Iroquois that couldn't anybody
say anyhow and of course still Apache that the Stewart was
growing adamant about and finally it was the Shipp himself
that did not usually but make faces who asked Uncle Jack,
"Which?" hollered it to him across the yard where Uncle Jack
was looking from fingers and arms to the house-front and then
back again and when he did not get told, the Shipp that did not
usually but make faces even hollered it again, "Which?" And
Daddy said Uncle Jack found him out from the crowd and
looked square at him and asked him back, "Which what?"

"Sort," the Shipp told him, and it was the Holleman that added
"Indian," that added "Indian sort."

And Daddy said Uncle Jack that did not know anything but
hybrid and but cultivated and but mulebaron had to stop his
processes like people do sometimes and had to ponder sort
and had to ponder indian before he could come out with just
"Cherokee" that sent into some genuine palpitations and
outright flinching the Stewart who said how he meant
Cherokee, said how that was the one in his head that he just
did not get out plain and clear, said he knew that's what it was,
said he knew that's what it had to be and then he said it
himself, "Cherokee," in that voice he could say things in, and
so it was set and it was established and the arms that had
pointed and that had indicated dangled down again and the
faces that had been all twisted up and creased with thinking
laid out plain and regular and turned to Aunt Della again that

just stood on the stoop like she'd been standing with just her bangs and her nose and her wiry self along with the floor-sweep she'd happened to bring with her that was nothing but broom-straw tied to a stick. So they watched her and studied her, Daddy said, but did not see her really, not the woman, not the little wiry woman with the floorsweep but just the item, just the instrument, just the thing that had done what it did which was hardly the rifle and hardly the finger that shot it and hardly even plain Aunt Della truly but just what they saw of her, just what she'd come to be which was near about purely what she'd done and near about purely what she'd done it to. An indian, Daddy said, shot and killed and finished forever and maybe on account of mule thieving as that was convenient as a reason and a cause but was not hardly necessary, Daddy said, was not hardly necessary for what men had lined the corral fence to see her since it was an indian after all, savage and strange and evil and blackhearted and not hardly civilized like they were civilized and not hardly lawful like they were lawful and not hardly plain and decent like they were plain and decent but exotic and terrible and threatening mostly, threatening to everything they had and everything they figured they wanted, so they commenced to celebrate how there was one less anymore, one less on account of a tiny wiry hooknosed woman with a floorsweep and Daddy said it was the Holleman first like it was the Holleman first most everywhere. "Red heathen son-of-a-bitch," he hollered. "Cherokee bastard."

"Goddam savage," the Stewart yelled behind him like only the Stewart could yell it and the Shipp made his face and said a thing after, a harder viler thing than Shipps are usually known for, Daddy said, and it set off the Utley and the Littlejohn and the Askew and the Judd who had all got it firsthand and so were allowed to do their swearing and their reviling before the crush and the bulk that followed from what people that had not heard it direct and had not heard it firsthand but wanted to say a thing anyway, a thing against indians and against savagery and meanness, and Daddy guessed from the front stoop Aunt Della could not but hear most of it anyhow and could not but see faces above the corral fence, faces all red and twitching, mouthholes open, arms outflung, and Daddy said she just stood and just listened at what she heard and just looked at what she saw and did not do anything for a time aside from just the standing and the looking and the hearing that was not anything truly, not anything to see anyway until she raised up the floorsweep like she raised it up which was straight into the air in her one hand and she held it there until the arms dropped and the mouthholes closed and the eyes all focused in on her which was the ones at the fence and the pair in the yard too and when there was not any noise but for treeleaves up high and mulesnorting off back of the house Aunt Della opened her own mouthhole, Daddy said, and told them, "A man. A man," and then she spun round on her shoebottoms and carried herself back into the house, her slight wiry self, Daddy said, and her makeshift floorsweep that was not but broomstraw tied to a stick.

And Daddy guessed that was the whole point of it, guessed that was what it all came to after it had been things otherwise, was what it all arrived at when at last it stopped and settled. A man, he said. And he recollected how Granddaddy insisted not just on the eggs but on the eggplate too, the eggplate with the handpainted pear in the middle of it which had been Grandmomma's momma's eggplate before it was Grandmomma's and which Daddy said even Grandmomma herself was reluctant to let loose of, but Granddaddy insisted how it was the proper thing, how it was the thing that she would do for regular peo-pie like Granddaddy was trying to figure these people were, Daddy said, and it was Grandmomma that made the chicken on her own, made the chicken like she made it sometimes with the black olives and the nuts in the buttery sauce and Aunt Sister remembered the taste of it of a sudden and made a noise in her mouth and said could not anybody else do it like Grandmomma could, not even with the actual recipe to do it with, said could not anybody else make it come out like Grandmomma always did, and Momma threw in with how that had been the case pretty much with most things and not just chicken only and Aunt Sister said she guessed that was the truth of it and together they looked weepy for a time and did not either one but swallow.

And Daddy said he carried the chicken his own self, the chicken that was on Grandmomma's turkey platter with plastic wrap overtop of it and Granddaddy carried the eggs on the handpainted eggplate and they got into the Buick, Daddy said, Momma's Buick with the ding on the right front fender and the broken headlamp and the scratches and dents across the hoodfront and even red dirt still caught up in the grillgaps, and Daddy said Granddaddy set the eggplate on his kneejoint and held it there and took the chicken from Daddy and set the turkey platter on his other kneejoint and balanced it too and Daddy eased the Buick like he normally did not ease it off the driveway runners and back into the street and then stopped and shifted like he normally did not shift and they headed out towards the boulevard and then north past the square and the monument and down by the icehouse and out 29 towards Pelham which they knew it was close to somewhere though not hardly where exactly, and Granddaddy that had torn out the column himself took it from his shirtpocket and read off to Daddy, "Mrs. Luther Gilliam," like he had read it near about every mile, Daddy guessed, like he had said it near about every time he parted his lips to say anything, and Daddy told him back, "Alright, Chief. Mrs. Luther Gilliam," and Granddaddy folded the paper and stuck it back in his shirtpocket and again laid his fingers on the eggplate rim that he had let loose of, and Daddy said they asked, asked whatever people they could find, said Granddaddy would stoop his shoulders and lower down his head so as to see whoever it was out the driver's window and so as to say to him, "Mrs. Luther Gilliam," that did not but seem the only thing he could manage to say, but

Daddy said did not anybody know where for a spell, did not anybody even know who as they were all white, Daddy said, and so were not acquainted somehow, and they left Pelham proper, Daddy said, and drove roundabout through the countryside to the east and roundabout through the countryside to the west but did not happen onto Mrs. Luther Gilliam anywhere and did not happen onto anybody that knew of her until they came back to Pelham and rode down to the colored part of it that was not but one street behind a lumberyard, one oiled street between two paved ones and Daddy said they found a man in his yard in a metal yardchair, a slight bony little man, Daddy said, all dressed and done up like most folks did not get for yardsitting with creased trousers and shiny shoes and a shirt buttoned clean up to the collar and a hat too, a lacquered straw fedora with a striped band around it, and Daddy said Granddaddy stooped and Granddaddy looked and Granddaddy said, "Mrs. Luther Gilliam," and that bony little colored man took hold of his chairarms and resituated himself somewhat, resituated himself back farther on the chairseat and up higher on the chairback, and lifted one finger and pointed off behind himself with it, off behind himself over his shoulder and then said a thing, Daddy told it, said a thing in a voice all broken and slight and tiny like maybe he had not talked for a considerable spell, and then he lowered his finger and laid back his hand on the chairarm and Daddy said Granddaddy that was still stooped and still looking opened his own mouth and said, "Mrs. Luther Gilliam," that way that Daddy guessed was the only way he could manage to say it and the bony little colored man in the metal yardchair told him back, "Yes sir," all clear and plain.

Daddy said he got the directions himself, shut off the car, climbed out from it, and stepped on into the yard proper where he watched some pointing and heard some slight broken talking and gathered what it was he needed to gather from it and shook the hand, Daddy said, the hand that had pointed and indicated and Daddy said that little bony colored man asked him did he know Mrs. Luther Gilliam had lost a boy and Daddy told him, "Yes sir," back and the little bony colored man wondered wasn't it a sad thing and Daddy told him yes sir it was a sad thing indeed and Granddaddy, that could not seem to begin to unstoop and unlower himself, said "Mrs. Luther Gilliam" one last time and that little bony colored man raised up his finger and pointed behind himself with it again and said something broken, Daddy told it, something slight and tiny.

And they went, Daddy said, went the way he'd said to go that was out the oiled road to the end of it and south on the paved road and west on another one and north on another one still and then off east down a road that commenced paved at the tongue of it and then went to gravel and then went to ruts mostly, Daddy said, deep ruts side to side across the road that the Buick bounced and skidded on and then loose dirt after, that the rearend would hardly stay straight in, and then just plain road like road ought to be, Daddy said, packed and firm and straight and then down through creekbottom and up again and straight some more with near about a dozen acres in tobacco on the lefthand side and near about as many in soybeans on the right and a house every now and again and a trailer every now and again too and another turn, Daddy said, down another road and no gravel this time and not ruts or silt either but just plain hardpan all over and some cultivation off to the one way and to the other too and scrub woods and rye grass cover every now and again and then the house, Daddy said, back from the road a stretch but not so far as to get missed and passed up, and Daddy said he slowed while Granddaddy held to the turkey platter and held to the eggplate, and Daddy said he turned and brought Momma's Buick into the driveway that was dirt for the wheels and a grassy hump between and it was washed and dug out here and again, Daddy said, so they did not but barely go forward, did not but inch and crawl and dropped down into places the dirt had given way and rose back up out of them again and just eased along slower than a walk even and Granddaddy watched the platter and watched the eggplate that he had his fingers closed on rhe rims of and every now and again when he felt like he could he would look at the house too that Daddy said it did not hardly seem they were getting any closer to until the driveway spilled out in the frontyard and of a sudden they were right up on it. Daddy said there were cars near about everywhere a car could be, all variety of cars but your basic sedans primarily, your basic long lowslung sorts of sedans and all of them well tended to, Daddy said, and seen after and shiny and lustrous and parked in the frontyard, that was not but packed dirt, and parked in the sideyard, that had some little bit of grass in it, and parked, from what Daddy could see, in the backyard too where the driveway finally gave out at the porch door. And Daddy said there was just weeds everywhere elsewise, weeds everywhere the yard quit, belt-high fennel and nettle and yellow wildflower and a smokehouse in the midst of it off to the side Daddy stopped the Buick at and beyond that a Dodge pickup that Daddy said he could not see but the cab of and some little bit of the bed or some little bit of what was piled in the bed anyhow which Daddy said was trash and rubbish and every manner of refuse, and there was little bantam hens that ran into the weeds, Daddy said, and ran out from them, and dogs too, Daddy said, three spotted wiry-haired dogs that looked like they'd been bred from goats at least partly, and then negroes, Daddy said, what sounded to him a great passel of negroes in the backyard that he could not see on account of the house, or that he could not see clear and complete anyway though every now and again one would step into view and look at him.

Granddaddy would not give up the eggplate and would not give up the chickenplate either not even so long as to free his hands to grab on to the doorframe with the one and prize against the seatcushion with the other and thereby raise himself up like usual, and Daddy said instead he balanced the eggs and balanced the chicken so as not to spill the buttery sauce and he swung his feet out onto the ground and just stood up and closed the door with his posterior and Daddy said he could not but follow him up between the cars to the housefront and could not but offer to carry a thing or do a thing otherwise which Granddaddy did not seem to even hear as he was walking that way he walked, Daddy told it, that way he walked all quick and pitched forward when he was feeling singular, Daddy said, and purely caught up and he did not stop until he'd reached the front steps where he turned roundabout and spied out Daddy wherever it was Daddy had gotten to which was not nearly so far as Granddaddy himself and Daddy said Granddaddy told him, "Come on here," like he was some manner of loitering child.

Daddy said it was not any considerable and sprawling sort of a house but not your cramped tiny sort either and was fairly middling actually with a wide part across the front and a long part down the back and a kind of a wing off of it to one side that somebody or another had decided was as good a place as any for a wing and so had put one on there. Daddy said the whole business looked to have been painted once, maybe white, but was not hardly painted anywhere anymore and so was just gray wood mostly, gray hand-beveled clapboard and gray window casings and window sash and gray pickets across the front and gray railings and gray columns and little gray carved wooden florets up at the columntops, lacey florets like maybe it had all been something once, like maybe it had all once truly been a place, and Daddy said even the front door was elegant in its own way with one long narrow graceful glasspane on the doorknob side and a piece of naked plywood opposite it where the other long narrow graceful glasspane had got broken out from, and Daddy said Granddaddy was already knocking even before Daddy had gained the front steps, said he had caught up the eggplate in the crook of his chickenholding arm and was tapping at the doorlight with one of his knuckles, was still tapping at the doorlight when Daddy got up with him and tried to take hold of the eggplate that Granddaddy would not let him take hold of so he just stood

and watched Granddaddy tap like he'd been tapping and
looked around at the clutter on the porch decking that was
mostly just pieces of things but for an oil burner that was the
entire item, and then the doorglass rattled on its own as
another door somewhere inside got drawn open and sucked air
and they heard footsteps on the hall floor, slow, ponderous,
heavy footsteps, and heard the latch rattle and watched the
knob jerk and twitch and then drew themselves upright like
people do when a door is set to be opened on them and they
looked out level to see who it was that had actually opened the
thing anyway but was not anybody level to see and so they
looked down a ways like they had to to find Uncle Deal, round
squat Uncle Deal Meacham that worked at the slaughterhouse
and walked everywhere with his bloody apron turned down at
the bib and tied roundabout his waist, round squat Uncle Deal
with the freckles across his cheeks and the bald place that ran
clean up the length of his head and was shaped like a footprint
or a peanut or some such as it kind of bulged out and then
drew in and then bulged out again and got noticed and
observed by near about everybody since it was what most
people saw of Uncle Deal Meacham primarily him being squat
like he was and nearly everybody else being regular and so was
what people knew and recognized aside from the freckles and
the bloody apron and the laugh too that was near about a
cackle and came out from Uncle Deal most anytime he smiled
which he did not ever do but clean up to his gums. And Daddy
said he had on a blue suit like Daddy had not ever seen him in
and a stiff white shirt and a spotted tie and shiny black shoes
and he did not hardly grin, did not hardly smile, did not hardly
move his face, Daddy said, but only so much as to make his lips
come out with a Louis and come out with a Mr. Buck, and he
just cleared a way for them, Daddy said, just stepped off to the
side and cleared a way so as to let Granddaddy pass with his
deviled eggs and his chicken in a buttery sauce and so as to let
Daddy pass too with just his hands in his pockets, and
Granddaddy said, "Where?" and Uncle Deal pointed direct
down the hallway to the kitchen at the end of it that Daddy

said he followed Granddaddy into where was not anybody but a little colored girl in a frock with a piece of whitebread in her hands that she held up to her face and commenced to eat from the center outwards and Granddaddy set down his turkey platter and his eggplate on a little round eating table in the corner and laid his hand atop that little colored girl's head and told her, "Hey, sugar," which did not get him anything back but for the eyes that she rolled up and looked with. And Daddy said Uncle Deal that had followed them down the hallway to the kitchen door made his lips come out with Louis and come out with Mr. Buck once more and he motioned at Daddy and at Granddaddy too with one entire hand and led them partly back up the hall to the door he'd come out of firstoff that he turned the knob on and pushed open and then stepped aside from so as to let Granddaddy pass and Daddy pass behind him and Daddy said it was a kind of a sitting room they ended up in, maybe even a regular-sized sitting room though it did not seem so as it was crowded with mourners, Daddy said, and was close and stifling and even in the middle of the day was near about dark too that way old houses can be dark no matter what manner of light you bring to them, and Daddy said it smelled like people, not bad like people but rich like people and almost sweet and was not but everybody colored but for him and but for Granddaddy that just got so far as inside the doorway before they stopped and before they stood and Daddy said Granddaddy set in with his skinflap straightaway as Uncle Deal Meacham eased his squat round self on by and crossed over to the farthest corner where he talked into a woman's ear without hardly stooping to do it, an old small purely inky black woman, Daddy said, in an upholstered chair that was losing its insides out the arms and out the cushion too and Daddy said she told Uncle Deal a thing back and got told another thing her own self which she nodded at, Daddy said, and then wiped at her nose after, wiped at her nose, Daddy recollected, with a lacey linen handkerchief, and as Daddy told it him and Granddaddy got motioned at again with an entire hand and together they crossed the room where a way had been made for them and naturally everybody looked, Daddy said, and everybody watched as they were white men where they were and doing what they were doing and Daddy said Uncle Deal, in a way that was almost regal and stately and so was not hardly ordinary, not for him, announced to Granddaddy, "Mrs. Luther Gilliam," and then indicated with his own hand how Granddaddy should extend his and so take up Mrs. Luther Gilliam's fingers which Granddaddy extended his own hand and did and he set in to saying how he was sorry and saddened and pained that what had happened had happened and Mrs. Luther Gilliam listened at him with appreciable attention and let him get through and full well done before she talked herself and she did not say much, Daddy said, but was plainly grateful for what visit she was getting and what sentiments she'd heard and then she got her fingers took up by Daddy that told her near about precisely what she'd just got told and she talked back all low and quiet and kindly and wiped at her eyes and dabbed at her nose and then sat with her hands in her lap, and Daddy said Uncle Deal showed them out the sitting room and up the hallway and onto the front porch just like he'd showed them in and Granddaddy struck out directly down the steps and across the yard to the Buick while Daddy said he lingered for a time on the decking and got told a thing by Uncle Deal Meacham who stuck out his own hand and let it get shook after, and Daddy said he did not start the car straightaway but just held the key in his fingers and turned partway around so as to face Granddaddy that Daddy said was seeming almost regular, was seeming almost changed and improved, and Granddaddy said, "You know," near about light, Daddy said, near about airy, and Daddy laid his own hand on Granddaddy's forearm so as to stop him and he said, "Chief, Uncle Deal told her we were Dunleavys from where he'd worked at. She didn't know it was you, didn't know it was me," and Granddaddy reached up with his skinflap like he would stroke and groom but did not, Daddy said, and instead left his whole hand across his mouth and looked anywhere he could find that Daddy wasn't.

And Aunt Sister that had been trying to talk and had been trying to speak for a spell but had got kept from it by Daddy who would not yield to her finally did get to talk and finally did get to speak and told how she'd been to a colored funeral once for her neighbor Mrs. Burleson's cleaning woman's husband that had died of complications, Aunt Sister said, and she recollected how there was considerable screeching and carrying on and how a woman, she thought it was maybe the sister of the deceased, a big thick woman in a hat with a full veil on it of a sudden shrieked one time and pitched herself out of her pew into the aisle where she laid on the runner in a faint until all six of the pallbearers together came to snatch her up and revive her, and Aunt Sister said she did not hope to ever again see anything like it, not ever again, she said and pulled at her Kleenex and moved on her chairbottom and then looked at Momma that looked at her back with her mouth turned up ever so slightly that way Momma turns up her mouth sometimes and together the two of them looked at Daddy that had fetched out a cigarette and was hunting a match and he eyed Momma and eyed Aunt Sister with the filterend stuck on his lips and the white part hanging like Momma finds so irritating most times and he brought out a matchpack from under his chaircush-ion and opened it and laid his finger on a matchhead and then stopped himself so as to draw a breath and so as to blow it directly back out again.

ii

And then it was Granddaddy, was still Chief and Mr. Buck and William Elsworth but was Granddaddy too on account of there was me then which was after all of it, not awful long after all of it but after all of it anyhow, past when anybody spoke of it much or thought of it much or wondered about it hardly at all except maybe for Granddaddy that did not speak of it either but likely still thought and likely still wondered, and first it was just his trousers, the feel of them on the backsides of my legs as they were stiff from what starch Grandmomma used on them and made for considerable friction with my legskin sometimes when I'd get bucked and bounced around like Granddaddy used to buck and bounce me with his one hand covering the whole of my stomach and his other covering the whole of my back, not that I was so slight and tiny but that they were so sizeable, so long and so broad too and with that waxy veiny skin on the backs of them that I would pinch up in my fingers sometimes prior to pulling with both hands together on Granddaddy's masonic ring that I could not ever get past the knuckle. And he carried two knives deep in his pockets, a Treebrand on his left hip with three blades to it, one of them a screwdriver that couldn't Granddaddy open but with another screwdriver to prize it up, and on his right hip a little silvery Sunkist Cola knife with a tiny slender useless blade but a place on the spine of the casing to open bottles and they rattled around in his pocketbottoms with what change he carried and what keys he carried and with what watch he carried too that Great-granddaddy had bought his own self in Knoxville and it was bronze and near about as big around as a coaster and Granddaddy fetched it out from his own pocket with the same leather thong that Great-granddaddy had fetched it out from his pocket with and told the hour much like Great-granddaddy had told the hour too which was just with the short hand exclusively as the long one had dropped off early on and slid all about the watchface but did not seem to hinder the works, so it was not ever any time in particular with Granddaddy but was always just past something or going on something else.

It was him that put me in the boat when Daddy said no and it was him that insisted when Daddy insisted too and it was him that got his way as it was always him that got his way and Daddy paddled out into the very middle of Tadlock's pond like he had not wanted to, like he had said outright he wouldn't on account of it was deep and far off from anything to cling to and clutch at and Granddaddy wondered when in the hell was it that Louis W. Benfield had come to be an old woman and Daddy said he wasn't and Granddaddy said he was and Daddy said was nothing to cling to and Daddy said was nothing to clutch at and Granddaddy told him, "Louis, let loose of this child," and so Daddy paddled out into the very middle of the pond and moved every time I moved and jerked every time I jerked and did not breathe but in spurts and sighs and Granddaddy himself held to my britchesbottoms and baited my hook and threw out my line on account of Daddy was in a state, Granddaddy called it, which he explained to me was how adults got sometimes and I turned roundabout to look at Daddy and he moved and jerked and raised his arms like he would catch onto me and then he heaved some and spurted a breath and sighed. A state, Granddaddy told me, purely a state. And so I held to my pole with both my hands and Granddaddy held to my britchesbottoms with one of his and held to his pole with the other and I watched my cork and he watched my cork and his cork too and Daddy watched how Granddaddy's hand held my britchesbottoms and watched how my hands held my pole, and every now and again Granddaddy would let loose of my parts altogether and would take from me my pole and give to me his and say, "Hold this, son," and straightaway I'd have a fish on the line that I did not even guess he'd give along with the pole and the cork and the sinkers and it was a bream mostly as Tadlock's was not full of much but bream but it was an actual bass once too, an actual bass that breached and leapt hard by the gunwale and I laid and rolled back like anybody would and thereby set Daddy to jerking and scrambling and clutching and clinging so as to almost put himself into the water.

We evermore took Sunday dinner with Granddaddy and Grandmomma as Grandmomma would not hear of anything otherwise and she always cooked it herself and always laid it out and would not let Momma carry down even so much as a bean salad, and everybody said Momma could truly make a bean salad, but it was Grandmomma's house and it was

Grandmomma's dinner, chicken mostly, sometimes with the buttery sauce but fried more often than not, and garden peas and onions and potatoes always and greens of some ilk and biscuits and beets for Aunt Sister when Aunt Sister came that did not anybody but Aunt Sister eat though she was ever pushing them off on the rest of us but for Daddy who had told her early on how he'd rather sit down to a spadeful of backyard. So we would settle in at the table with the linen tablecloth and the linen napkins and the real silver and the actual china and Grandmomma would look to see was there a spoon in everything that needed a spoon in it and a fork in everything otherwise and Granddaddy would tell her, "Sit," and she would sit if there were spoons and if there were forks and she would sit sometimes if there weren't so as to let Granddaddy lay his chin on his shirtfront like he did and pray the grace he always prayed in that voice he always prayed with which was not like any of his other voices as it was deep and loud and purely inarticulate but for the Our Father at the outset and the Amen at the end. What fell between was not ever but buzzing and droning but did not anybody seem to mind as it was always the same buzzing and droning let out just precisely the same way it always got let out and punctuated with a truly comprehensible Amen that seemed to sanctify the bulk of it and then we would all breathe once more and set about to pick up our forks but would have cause to stop at it every now and again when Aunt Sister would throw in behind the Amen like she did sometimes so as maybe to bless an afflicted somebody she knew though if she could not land on anybody straightaway she'd thank Jesus for something or another, family communion mostly but weather sometimes and health too when she felt something coming on. And then we would actually eat, me and Momma and Daddy and Grandmomma with our forks and with our knives and Granddaddy and Aunt Sister with their biscuits mostly like they'd been raised, and Momma talked some and Grandmomma talked some back and Aunt Sister put in every now and again and I even got asked a thing sometimes while

Daddy and Granddaddy did not but make necknoises usually as they were the sort that figured you ate what you were going to eat and then you said what you were going to say and did not ever mix the one with the other.

There was custard pie afterwards, one for Granddaddy all burnt up on the top like he liked it and another one cooked regular for the rest of us and we'd all have a piece but for Aunt Sister who did not ever want but a taste of Grandmomma's rightoff and then would figure she might just have a little sliver herself and would go into the kitchen and cut herself one little sliver to eat there and one little sliver to carry back on her plate, and there was coffee too that Granddaddy made himself on account of would not Grandmomma go nearly so heavy on the grounds and so light on the water as he wanted but could not anybody drink it but him and Daddy and Daddy cut his fairly well with milk but Granddaddy took his like it came from the pot and drank it from his saucer mostly that way Grandmomma said was like a cowhand might and Granddaddy would blow like he blew and would slurp like he slurped and would tell Grandmomma, "Yee ha," all flat and plain.

It was Grandmomma that cooked the turkey at Thanksgiving with the sausage dressing that Granddaddy could not ever taste enough sage in to suit him and it was Grandmomma that cooked the lamb-shank at Easter and the beefribs on Independence Day and did not a holiday pass but that we spent down the road in the house Granddaddy had built his own self as that was the only way they would have us do it and Christmas eve we even slept over and got up in the dark or anyhow I got up in the dark and they got up after due to what racket I'd make to get them up and I'd show off what it was had got left under the tree for me and they would admire it all like maybe they had not guessed and had not figured just what would get left exactly and Grandmomma would cook eggs and would cook slab bacon and would make doughnuts and oatmeal and Aunt Sister would show up on the front porch and commence to sing "Deck the Halls" like always and we would look at her through the doorlight until she quit and said her Yoo hoo and waved her fingers when she got let in with whatever she'd brought for us which was generally socks for Daddy and some manner of face powder for Momma and most often a pullover sweater for me but one time an entire checked suit from Mr. Hooper's downtown. For Granddaddy she would usually bring just a Merry Christmas and Granddaddy would give her one back as that was all they had ever exchanged with any regularity while Momma and Daddy and me would have wrapped up a box of chocolate-dipped cherries that Aunt Sister would rip the paper off of and then would rip the plastic off of and then would take the lid off of and then would lift the liner out from so as to have just one and she would have just one and would put back the liner and would put back the boxlid and would suck from the recesses of her mouth what sweetness she could find there and then she would guess maybe she would have just one more and off would come the lid and out would come the liner and in would go the cherry so as to get chewed and savored and swallowed and sucked away.

Summertime we took a house in Kitty Hawk for two weeks, a long low stucco house on the ocean side of the road and it was painted a kind of a green that does not anybody ever paint a house except at the beach and it had an actual garage on the one end and an actual lawn out front planted in some sort of exotic curly grass that felt like shredded wheat underfoot. The inside was all paneled in knotty pine and so was not ever but dark in the daytime and dark in the nighttime too and was not any television to look at but just a radio and it shortwave so was not truly any radio to listen to but for Spanish mostly that did not any of us understand and but for English every now and again that could not any of us decipher. There was a bookcase in the main room with old magazines in it and a whole shelfful of Reader's Digest hardbacks and one ponderous dictionary that was what got looked in the most on account of the Scrabble game in the cabinet with the doors on it which was near about the only game to get played as were not any of the card decks full and complete and as the Ouija board in the cabinet with the Scrabble game had suffered considerably in the sea air and had lost enough of its lacquer to keep the little pointer from slipping and sliding like it needed to. So we played teams with me and Granddaddy and Daddy on the one side and Momma and Grandmomma and Aunt Sister on the other and they made words like ladies knew how to make and we made words like men knew how to make and Granddaddy was evermore challenging what it was they'd lay down and Aunt Sister was evermore challenging what it was we'd lay down and Momma was the one of us that would use the dictionary on account of Momma was the one of us that could spell worth a piddlysquat but she did not hardly ever find what she was after as they were not hardly ever words anyhow except for sometimes but even then they were not ever the sorts of words that would hardly suit everybody like when Aunt Sister found an A off ARGYLE sitting free and clear at the top of the board and she spelt DAM across it as they did not have but consonants, Momma said, and so could not do better just then and Aunt Sister hadn't hardly lifted her fingers off the board when Granddaddy commenced to butt letters up against her DAM so as to make it into DAMNATION which Aunt Sister challenged and objected to and just grew instantly peevish on account of and Granddaddy's triple word score did not soothe her much and she said it was slang, not to mention profane and tasteless, but Momma found it in the dictionary straightaway and so allowed it but Aunt Sister took up the boxlid and commenced to read through the rules in search of one she might bend and apply and she tried a few but did not any of them stick and Granddaddy announced our point total just along about then which prompted Aunt Sister to raise up the boxlid and smack him on the top of the head with it and Granddaddy touched himself on the topnotch with his fingers and said to Aunt Sister, "Damnation."

But then that was just the way with them as friction and strife and such between Granddaddy and Aunt Sister was as natural as regular talking between most people and they did not hardly ever open their mouths to each other but to be quarrelsome and irritating and was not any of it annoying but to everybody otherwise as the bickering and the aggravating was fairly much a hobby with Granddaddy and with Aunt Sister and did not either one of them ever get all heated and irate and done in like Grandmomma did sometimes just from listening to them, so late of an afternoon at the beach when Grandmomma had already had an earful and was trying to get supper on she would send me out over the dunes with the hinged shovel out from the garage and I would dig two rectangular holes side by side and then call to Granddaddy and call to Aunt Sister back on the screen porch and they would come over the dunes themselves and sit in what holes I'd dug while I covered their legs over with hot sand that tended to soothe their joints, and they would just sit there side by side buried from the waist down and look out over the beach and out over the ocean and Granddaddy would see a little speck of something on the horizon and point at it and Aunt Sister would look down his arm and down his finger but would not see any speck herself and so would conclude there wasn't one truly and Granddaddy would say how there was too and would say it was a ship and would tell her what kind of ship it was exactly and then would squint and then would point and Aunt Sister would look down his arm and down his finger and say to him, "Water, William. Nothing but water," and Granddaddy would send me to fetch Daddy's binoculars but usually by the time I got back they were on to something else already, people ordinarily, whatever sort there might be walking the beach which was not ever but scant people and them not doing anything in particular but maybe just walking mostly and just taking up shells every now and again which was enough for Granddaddy and enough for Aunt Sister as they did not need to see somebody but walk and but bend to get ahold of them as best as they wanted to and Aunt Sister thought it was scandalous how people went near about naked at the seashore, people that likely would not think to step out from their own houses but fully dressed, and she wondered where it was modesty had gone to but could not Granddaddy ever tell her, could not Granddaddy ever tell her to suit her anyhow, but did not Granddaddy ever care truly except for every now and again when Mr. Ransom of Lexington that generally stayed two doors up when we stayed two doors down would bring himself and his little fuzzy dog with the bows on it and his own extraordinary stomach out for an airing and then Granddaddy would commence to wonder where modesty had gone to a little and would commence to wonder as well how it was a man could stand upright with such an item to bend and burden him but Aunt Sister did not ever wish to speculate on it or discuss it whatsoever.

Generally, it was just me and just Grandmomma and Granddaddy and Aunt Sister and just Momma and Daddy too but the last summer we ever went, which was the summer Grandmomma was sick but did not know it, Momma got a wild hair, Daddy called it, and invited Mr. and Mrs. Phillip J. King to come along as they had not ever been but to Moorehead City and that in 1949 so Momma figured it would be a fine thing to carry Mr. and Mrs. Phillip J. King down to Kitty Hawk for a couple of weeks and let them take the air and see the sights and such and it does in fact seem like it would have been a fine thing when you ponder it in terms of taking air and seeing sights and leave out the Mr. and Mrs. Phillip J. King part which is mostly just the Mrs. Phillip J. King part really as she is the one that says what gets said and he is just the one that hears it. So we took two cars and Momma and Grandmomma rode with Mr. and Mrs. Phillip J. King in their Pontiac and me and Aunt Sister rode in the backseat of Momma's Buick with Daddy driving and Granddaddy map reading like he was given to which did not have much at all to do with turnoffs and highways and directions in general but just with places mostly, places all over that Granddaddy would see the names of and read out to me and to Daddy and to Aunt Sister to find out had any of us ever been there and sometimes we had and said so but most times we hadn't and said so too and pretty regularly Aunt Sister would say how she'd been to a place and Granddaddy would tell her she hadn't or Granddaddy would say how he hadn't been to a place and Aunt Sister would insist he had.

We stopped for lunch roundabout Parmele in the churchyard we always stopped at which Mrs. Phillip J. King did not much care for on account of it was buggy and Daddy and Mr. Phillip J. King had parked under cedar trees anyhow and Mrs. Phillip J. King said you could not ever know what manner of thing would drop out of a cedar tree so she took her lunch in the Pontiac with the door shut and the window partway up and she had some of Grandmomma's fried chicken and some of Grandmomma's potato salad and a half of one of Grandmomma's pimento cheese sandwiches and she ate everything but the breadcrust and the bones and got out from the Pontiac long enough to throw her plate away and announce after a general fashion how the chicken had not been near so greasy as it had looked and then she got back into the Pontiac again and sat quiet for a spell after-which she commenced to fidget some and breathe heavy and then she rolled down her window near about halfway and said out into the air how it did not sit well with her to stop and loiter on the way to a place, how she was the sort that liked to get where she was going and Daddy set himself to say a thing back but Momma prevented him from it and we carried what we had not eaten with us and ate it on the highway with Mr. Phillip J. King ahead and us behind for a spell anyhow until he went straight where he shouldn't have and so put us out front and we led on across the Alligator River and through Man-teo and over the sound and then north to Kitty Hawk and our long low green stucco house with the garage and the wiry grass that always looked just like we'd left it the summer before, and Mrs. Phillip J. King said it was comely for a beach house, said it was not near so offensive as most and she walked roundabout the garage side and looked out towards the ocean that she could not see but a little piece of on account of the dunes and the sea oats and she said she had figured there would be more to sit on the porch and look at than sand and than weeds sprouting out from it and she slapped at a greenheaded fly on her forearm and wondered at Granddaddy was it always so buggy roundabout and Granddaddy explained to her about your seabreezes and about your landbreezes too and how the first one blows salt one way and the second one blows bugs the other and Mrs. Phillip J. King made a kind of a face like she can make and Daddy set himself to say a thing but Momma prevented him from it.

They slept in the room Momma and Daddy usually slept in on account of Mrs. Phillip J. King did not much like how the afternoon light came into the one they'd been put in first and she wondered straightaway was there a vacuum handy as the floor seemed a little gritty to her and Momma fetched out the Hoover from the utility room and Mrs. Phillip J. King plugged it in and went over her bedroom with it and then up the hallway and all across the main room before she cut it off so as to tell Aunt Sister how some people could put up with grit on a floor but she was just not one of them. Like always on our first night, Daddy drove down to the fishmarket at Nags Head and bought shrimp and bought scallops and oysters for supper and carried them on into the kitchen for Grandmomma to tend to like she always did and Mrs. Phillip J. King, that found herself idle after her vacuuming, offered to help and Grandmomma set her to washing scallops and set her to washing oysters too while Grandmomma herself commenced to vein the shrimp as Mrs. Phillip J. King watched her do it and then took up what individual creatures she was not entirely pleased with and reveined them her own self explaining to Grandmomma as she did it how there was some people that could put up with grit and how there was some people that couldn't. And Grandmomma dredged the scallops in egg and corn meal and dredged the oysters too and fried them together in her iron skillet notwithstanding how Mrs. Phillip J. King wondered wouldn't the scallops come out tasting like oysters and wouldn't the oysters come out tasting like scallops which she said she wouldn't mind much truly as she did not care for oysters herself on account of how they tasted rank and spoiled most all the time though there was people that didn't seem to mind it, and Grandmomma started the water to boiling for the shrimp and got advised by Mrs. Phillip J. King how she'd best salt it and how she'd best keep it medium to medium high and not purely high entirely unless she wanted her shrimp to get all rubbery and overdone and she guessed there was not anything worse than rubbery shrimp as far as she could tell and Grandmomma said, "Maybe not," and then excused herself to the main room and shortly returned to the kitchen with Momma that had discovered how she needed Mrs. Phillip J. King for a thing, how she could not do without her.

Mrs. Phillip J. King did not play Scrabble and did not think awful much of people who did and so she sat on the sofa turning the pages of a Life magazine from 1954 while me and Daddy and Granddaddy and Mr. Phillip J. King faced off against Momma and Grandmomma and Aunt Sister but Mr. Phillip J. King was truly not much advantage as he did not have a mind for letters and words and such and was evermore rearranging our squares on the rack so as to alternate the vowels and the consonants afterwhich he would study what he had made and ask Daddy and Granddaddy and even me too was that a thing or not and it was not ever a thing truly and did not hardly ever even suggest a thing but it was Mr. Phillip J. King that spelled FLAPJACK there near the end which pretty much cinched the match and we all congratulated him and he told us how it was not anything really, how it had just kind of come into his head. He could not say from where. And we listened to the shortwave some too and got a weather report from somewhere, we did not find out where exactly but it wasn't hardly where we were as they weren't hardly having what weather we were having which was just stars and which was just breezes, breezes blowing salt instead of bugs like we all discovered when we went out in the dunes like we did sometimes so as to stretch and gape and all eight of us laid back our heads and looked at the sky that there is so considerably much of at the beach with the ocean to the one side and the sound to the other and Granddaddy pointed out what constellations he knew which was just the two dippers mostly and he raised up his arm and indicated with his finger a spot of light he insisted was Mars and Aunt Sister looked up along his arm and along his finger and said how it wasn't Mars at all, how it wasn't but a star way off somewhere and she raised up her own arm and pointed off another way entirely and said, "Mars," but Granddaddy could not hardly hold with it and expressed as much and then did not anybody but breathe and but look and but wonder too, I guess, and nobody pointed and nobody indicated and did not even Mrs. Phillip J. King have a thing to say.

We stayed our usual two weeks that we did not know was our last two weeks ever and me and Daddy and Granddaddy took Mr. Phillip J. King up to the pier after flounder and bluefish and Granddaddy advised him on a shirt with sleeves to the wrists and trousers clear to the ankles but Mr. Phillip J. King wore bermudas and a t-shirt instead on account of how he wanted to take the sun and he did take the sun, an appreciable dose of it concentrated mostly on the backs of his kneejoints and full across his neck between where the hair stopped and the collar had started and he was in some pain and some discomfort for a day or two after, chiefly behind the kneejoints and on the neck but somewhat in the ears too as that was where he took in what it was Mrs. Phillip J. King had to say about his stunt, she called it, and she seemed near about inexhaustible on the topic. Mrs. Phillip J. King was not much of a basker herself and did not ever go out but with her sunbonnet and her dark glasses and her blouse with full sleeves and her white trousers that stopped at the shins and she did not see why it was people subjected themselves to your ultraviolets and your rays otherwise on account of they did to the skin what Mrs. Phillip J. King explained to Grandmomma they did to the skin that Grandmomma had not truly been altogether curious about but found out anyhow, so Grandmomma sat on the porch with Mrs. Phillip J. King and got told all manner of things and Daddy and Granddaddy fished off the pier and fished in the surf and Mr. Phillip J. King wrapped himself from the toes up and fished with them every now and again like I did too sometimes, and Momma walked up the beach and down the beach picking up shells and watching the gulls light in the water and bob there, and in the afternoons late Granddaddy and Aunt Sister would sit half under the sand and half out of it and would tell each other whatever Mrs. Phillip J. King stories they could think of to tell.

And then we did not go back ever again as Grandmomma, that was sick even then and did not know it or would not tell it, got sicker and they tested her and poked at her and cut into her even but could not seem to improve her any and could not seem to say why not and so just watched how she went which was down, not down quick really but down steady and sure like Daddy said people go down every now and again when it is time to though it did not hardly seem time as there was still Granddaddy and still us and still Thanksgiving and Christmas and Easter and Independence Day and two weeks at Kitty Hawk and everything otherwise that maybe had not seemed but just usual and just ordinary until after they stopped and after they weren't anymore and so she went down and we watched her, watched her from the green vinyl chair next to the hospital bed with Granddaddy in the mornings and Momma in the afternoons and Daddy in the evenings and me whenever they could slip me up to the room since I was not then of an age to go up regular and so had to be snuck by the guard in the lobby and had to be slipped past the nurses in the hall who were fearful I might carry an ailment or maybe leave with one, and since I did not see her near so often as they did I guess I could always tell how she was purely worse when it just seemed to them that she simply was not better and she would lay on her back with her arms across herself and would every now and again take water out from a clear plastic jointed straw and then lick her lips that the nurses kept balm on due to how they dried and how they cracked and she did not ever say much but only laid her head sideways and looked mostly and sometimes she would reach out with her near arm and me or Granddaddy or Momma or Daddy would take up her fingers and hold them in our own as that was what she seemed to want and need and then she went down and went down and went down until she left us that we all had got set and had got primed for, or anyhow that we all figured we'd got set and primed for until there wasn't Grandmomma anymore and it was like she'd dropped dead on the sidewalk, like she'd just fell over stone cold.

Momma washed dishes, all our dishes everywhere she could hunt them up, and looked out the little window over the sink through the limbs of our apricot tree and past the carshed roof to something farther on and then she drained the sink and scoured it and filled it again and washed everything all over while she pondered whatever it was she'd found to ponder out the little window past the carshed roof. There was much talk of what would become of Granddaddy, much talk at the viewing, much talk at the burial, considerable talk after both, talk on the part of Momma and on the part of Daddy and on the part of Aunt Sister too but talk primarily on the part of the widowwomen roundabout that seemed worried and troubled on Granddaddy's behalf, worried and troubled in an altogether zealous sort of way, so everybody seemed to have an opinion about who should come in to tend to him or where he should go to get tended to, everybody but for Granddaddy that tolerated what people came to visit with him and what people carried him food and then ate it off his plates and sat in his chair and smoked in the very room he could not ever so much as spit in afterwhich they wandered freely all throughout his house poking and nosing most everywhere and ultimately always wanting to know just what was that hinged plank in the hall that did not go anyplace or open onto anything and Granddaddy figured if they were the sort that had to ask then they were not hardly the sort that needed to get told, so he was gracious for a spell and then he was just civil and then he was ill and put out and took himself off to the sewing room upstairs to pick his guitar while Aunt Sister sat in the front room with what ladies still came and what men got brought with them and they told stories on Grandmomma and said earnest decent things after and drank coffee and ate chicken and bean salad and gelatin and whitecake and sometimes when there was more chewing and regular breathing than talking of a sudden they could hear what little bit of Granddaddy's guitar picking came through the ceiling and Aunt Sister dabbed at her nose and told how it was angelic, she called it, purely angelic, and did not anybody else seem to think but that angelic suited and fitted as best as anything could.

He had not ever kept house and had not ever cooked but for coffee which had the body of most stews but was still only coffee anyhow, so he could not truly do for himself like would suit Momma that would not let him eat just potted meat on crackers the way he wanted and onion sandwiches and those little powder-dipped doughnuts but insisted on something hot and something hearty which was not hardly in the way of potted meat or onions or doughnuts and so was purely out of Granddaddy's depth as far as your cuisine went, so Aunt Sister stayed with him for a spell and cooked his breakfast and cooked his lunch and cooked his supper but did not Granddaddy much care for Aunt Sister's way with food on account of she left the salt off it due to blood pressure and the fatback out from it due to cholesterol in combination with her own personal low opinion of animal fat and she made iced tea that Granddaddy said looked like creekwater and she could not even begin to bake a biscuit, not one that would hardly hold up under pushing and sopping and such anyway which Granddaddy said didn't matter much as there was not hardly ever anything worth pushing or worth sopping either and he figured he'd just as soon sit down to a bowl of wet postage stamps than anything Aunt Sister could whip up otherwise. Consequently, then, they did not get on so well, or anyhow got on like normal which meant Granddaddy always up and told Aunt Sister exactly what he thought and Aunt Sister always up and told him back exactly what she thought herself and somehow they did not ever manage to up and say the same thing, not but your opposite sorts of things usually, and to worsen the predicament considerably Aunt Sister had a habit of pointing her fork when she talked and Granddaddy had a habit of swatting at forks when they were pointed at him so things would go along badly enough for a spell and then Granddaddy would say a thing and get told a thing back which would prompt him to say another thing and Aunt Sister would hear him at least partway out before she set in to raising her fork and set in to jabbing with it as a means of emphasis and punctuation and Granddaddy would free his fingers from his own fork or spoon or knife or biscuit crust and raise up and slap with his hand in a motion so quick and agile that could not Aunt Sister ever but drop open her mouth and gape at the empty air where her fork had been while the actual item clattered against the far wall and fell to the floor. Daddy figured this was just the sort of thing to do in what gentility and good will might have arrived at the table with the two of them.

So Aunt Sister went back home, called Granddaddy a goat first and explained to him why he was one which seemed agreeable enough to Granddaddy who did not but open the door for her and indicate with his forkslapping hand the way outside and he managed two days' worth of potted meat and onion sandwiches and powder-dipped doughnuts before Momma left off inviting him up for meals and set in to insisting on it and he came for breakfast and he came for lunch and he came for supper and he would linger sometimes and would chew of an evening on the porch glider while Daddy smoked and I sat and every now and again he would play for us and every now and again he would get joined at it by Mr. Wyatt Benbow and Mr. Emmet Dabb and Mr. Wiley Gant and Mr. Phillip J. King and they would pick and blow and strum and then leave off for a spell and Mr. Emmet Dabb would remark how they could have stood a snatch of fiddle music over the melody and they would all throw in and agree with him and think for a moment on Mr. Emory Boyette that had passed on with a stroke and Mr. Wyatt Benbow would recollect how he could saw on that thing and make it moan and he would get all weepy and set in to wishing for Mr. Emory Boyette, set in to longing for just one of his fiddle notes, and Granddaddy would say, "He's gone, Wyatt," and Mr. Emmet Dabb would say, "He's gone," and they would tune and pick at some aimless something until Mr. Wyatt Benbow had come back to himself like he always did and then Granddaddy would play one string at a time with just his fingertips and Mr. Phillip J. King would blow a note and bend it into another and bend that one after and Mr. Wyatt Benbow would set in with his own fingertips so as to hit what strings he hit while Granddaddy was between his and Mr. Emmet Dabb would lay in overtop of it with some fingerwork otherwise and they would all go round a time or two with the melody while Mr. Wiley Gant worked up his spit and took in his breath and then came out with that voice of his, that voice so rare and wondrous that even me who did not know much at all about anything heard enough in it to know beauty for a while. And then they would quit and bust it up for the night and Mr. Wyatt Benbow would pack up his guitar in his black case with the brass latches on it while Mr. Emmet Dabb did not but slip his banjo, that had hung and dangled in front of him, around to his backside where it hung and dangled behind him, and Mr. Wiley Gant and Mr. Phillip J. King would drop their harmonicas in their shirtpockets and everybody would stand up together which was me and Daddy too that were not going anywhere really but had to stretch and had to say our goodnights with everybody else, and then they would be off all four of them down the front steps and across the yard and up the walk towards town and Mr. Phillip J. King would leave off from them next door and say his own goodnight and cross his own yard and climb his own steps and we would watch Mr. Wyatt Benbow and Mr. Emmet Dabb and Mr. Wiley Gant proceed on up the road passing in and out of the blue mercury light and disappearing in the darkness between.

Then like always Granddaddy would just say, "Well," that meant everything for him and meant enough for us too and he would take up his own guitar by the neck and lay it across his shoulder bigend hindmost and knock on my topnotch with his knuckles prior to striking out himself down the steps and across the yard and down the walk two doors to his own house that was purely dark throughout as he would not ever leave a light burning in it since that seemed to him a squanderous thing to do, so we would listen at him rattling his keys and listen at him shut the door behind himself and watch the front-room light come on and then go off and then the breakfast room light come on and go off and then the upstairs sewing room light come on and stay on for a spell and me and Daddy would sit back down on the glider with our feet on the rail and most times Momma would step outside once she did not hear music and once she did not hear voices and she would suggest how it was a rail had not been made for feet to be put on and then she would turn full around and look down the road herself at her daddy's house and she would study the solitary light in the peak of it and then let out a breath and then suggest to me and suggest to Daddy how it was a rail had not been made for feet to be put on.

So it was one of those things that's almost already done even before it gets mentioned or suggested, one of those things that had been so absolutely decided upon and determined that it has as good as happened before it ever even commences, and of course Granddaddy said, "No!" and meant it and insisted on it but was not a no hardly enough to stop what had as good as happened anyway and so we emptied it out and Aunt Sister took what pieces she could make room for which was the maple table from the dining room and the front bedroom suite and two endtables she said she'd admired for a considerable while and a share of the bedlinen and a share of the china and the silver and a chair she did not particularly want or care for though she figured she might possibly grow to be fond of it and Momma got some things too though not awful much as Daddy did not care for a cramped house himself and was fairly emphatic about it to Momma that took a phone table for the hall and a bedstead for Granddaddy and what pictures she had room for and her share of linen and her share of china and silver and odds and ends otherwise and then called in Mrs. J. Randolph Sykes, Grandmomma's niece from Draper, who picked over what was left and hauled off a thing or two herself and Momma gave Mrs. Phillip J. King Grandmomma's sideboard that Mrs. Phillip J. King went into raptures on account of that way only Mrs. Phillip J. King can and the most of the rest of it got carried off by the rescue mission which would be some few sticks of furniture and several boxes' worth of kitchen utensils and such and most all of Grandmomma's clothes and the bulk of Granddaddy's clothes too since anymore he did not wear but the white shirts and the poplin trousers and so had no call for what suits he'd accumulated which Daddy did not guess anybody else would have much call for either since you could have taken the bunch of them and reupholstered a sofa with the lapels alone.

They put him in with me since there was not anywhere else to put him but in with me though Momma had a notion he could move upstairs if Daddy would insulate proper and run a duct and paint but

Granddaddy did not seem altogether anxious about it so we turned my bed around from crossways to longways and moved my dresser and moved my nightstand and set up Granddaddy's bed other side of the window from me and cleaned out a half of the closet for him and two full drawers at the dresser bottom and but for my watch that glowed and my dish with the pennies in it the bulk of the nightstand went to him too and he settled in straightaway so that it almost did not seem he had ever lived away from us and he had his place at the table and his coat on the rack by the door and his chair next to Daddy's in the sitting room where they would exchange with each other what piece of the Chronicle they'd read for what piece they hadn't and he would walk with us in the mornings and would rap me on the topnotch with his knuckles before I could get away across the road and up Darden Street to school and then him and Daddy would keep on to town where they would part company at Daddy's office door and Granddaddy would stop in at the bank and stop by at the barber shop and loiter roundabout the trainyard for a time before heading to the square and on up the post office steps into the lobby where he kept a box as Granddaddy was always a little skeptical of home delivery and he would see what he had and see what he wanted of it and carry it with him back out the lobby and down the steps and across the square to the benches in front of the town hall where everybody with the leisure to sit did and they chewed and they smoked and they laid their legs out before them and lied to each other about things they'd seen and things they'd heard and things they'd just thought up and did not anybody care that wasn't hardly a scrap of any of it true since hadn't but everybody heard all of what true things there were to hear already and anyhow could not any of their actual circumstances hardly compare with what it was they could manufacture and render up, so the talk did not ever give out truly but just quit at the noon whistle, which was the noon whistle at the cotton mill and the noon whistle at the cigarette plant out 29 and the siren at the Omega firehouse that did not ever all set in at the same time and did not ever all leave off at the same time either but always wailed together for a spell there and everybody would get up from the benches and would stretch themselves and would work their joints and them that were taking lunch at Mr. Castleberry's Dinette would head off towards it and them that were taking lunch at the counter in the drugstore would strike out that way and them that were taking lunch at home would set out otherwise and Granddaddy would stop in to fetch Daddy whenever Daddy was able and they would walk back home the way they had come and sit down in the breakfast room to whatever Momma had set out for them which tended to be something healthful and balanced most always that Daddy would go ahead and eat straightaway but that Granddaddy would usually complain on for a time as he did not ever want but the potted meat and but the crackers to spread it on.

Anymore Momma cooked the turkey at Thanksgiving and the ham at Christmas and the lambshank at Easter and the beef ribs on Independence Day and so it was almost like always sometimes if you didn't think on it hard and would not ever but Aunt Sister be the one to say a word on Grandmomma that everybody was working so at not thinking of and not saying a word on since Aunt Sister was the one that always up and said the things nobody else wanted said, and did not Granddaddy seem but happy enough and content in our house with us, and him and Daddy got on like brothers and him and Momma got on like always though it was a little backwards anymore since mostly she'd been his child up until he'd come to be hers and him and me got on some too and afternoons we'd fish at Tadlock's or walk out past the icehouse to the old rolling mill that Momma would not let me go in but with Granddaddy and we'd circle back through the woods and come into town alongside Mr. Demitt's house and stop in at Eaton's to poke around for a spell and then cross the boulevard towards the square and up into the post office lobby where Granddaddy would check his box for what the afternoon had brought and then it was by to fetch Daddy who walked with us home where him and Granddaddy would sit in their chairs reading their pieces of the Chronicle while I lay on the carpet watching television and Momma cooked supper in the kitchen and sang to herself like she tended to. And after we had eaten, and after Momma and Daddy and Granddaddy had taken their coffee and had told what things it was they had to tell, Momma would clear off the table and would set in to washing and me and Daddy and Granddaddy would fetch our jackets off the rack by the door and walk off our meal down the road and then back up it again and it was all I could do to stay abreast of them with them striding like they could, like they did, and not hardly ever stopping for anything or even slowing down truly except for Granddaddy sometimes that would leave off from us in front of the house he had built and would just look at it all lit up like it mostly was and occupied anymore by people otherwise than him and otherwise than Grandmomma, Palmers from Greenville with a wife and a little girl and a short-haired dog and a mister come to town in the hire of the bottling plant and were not any of us hardly acquainted with them at all as they did not seem the sort eager to be acquainted with and had not Granddaddy himself exchanged talk with any of them but for the day they came with the truck and the furniture and the colored men to haul and carry it, and me and Granddaddy sat on our porch steps and watched what passed down the ramp from the truck and across the yard and up into the house and after Mr. Palmer had gone in and had come back out any number of times he spied me and spied Granddaddy and came on up as far as the front walk so as to ask and so as to inquire just what exactly was that board in the hall that did not go anywhere or open onto anything.

Of course we didn't vacation at Kitty Hawk anymore after Grandmomma but went to the beach sometimes and took a house elsewhere though it was not hardly the same, and we did not go back to Gatlin-burg like we had been with Grandmomma but still drove up into the mountains mid October or thereabouts so as to see the leaves and me and Momma and Daddy and Granddaddy and Aunt Sister rode down to Charleston once for the weekend and Momma and Aunt Sister went into every historical place they could manage to hunt up while me and Daddy and Granddaddy just wandered some and just sat around mostly and decided how South Carolina was not hardly a state we much cared for.

Otherwise we stayed close in to home and rode roundabout the countryside judging tobacco crops and soybeans and corn and cattle too and we picked strawberries for Momma out of Mr. Cosgrove's patch when they came in and went back for wild grapes later on off the vines that grew up Mr. Cosgrove's yellow pine trees and one November we watched Mr. Othell Lucas and his middle boy, Mason, slaughter a hog out back of their smokehouse and bleed it and scald it and butcher it into hams and loins and bacon and everything otherwise, but when dead winter set in was not anywhere much we could go on account of Granddaddy's joints did not but ache and stiffen in cold weather so it was only me and Daddy that walked after supper while Granddaddy took to his chair and took to his hotpad and watched the news on the Greensboro station which he would tell us about when we came back and it was better to hear the news from Granddaddy since he did not ever clutter it up with particulars and would just tell us, "Somebody got killed."

And Daddy would want to know, "Who?"

And Granddaddy would tell him back, "I can't 'call his name but I've seen him."

"Seen him where?" Daddy would say.

And Granddaddy would scratch his cheek with his fingertips and finally tell Daddy, "Somewhere or another."

And Daddy would say, "Killed how?"

And Granddaddy would tell him, "Shot, I guess," and then would call out towards the kitchen, "Inez, how was it that man got killed?" And Momma would call back, "Which man, Daddy?"

"That man that got killed on the tv," Granddaddy would tell her. And Momma would fairly shriek, "Who?" and rush out from the kitchen wiping her hands on a rag and she would look at the tv screen that would be all filled up with Ripcord by then and then she would look at Daddy and would look at me and we would all look at Granddaddy that would usually set back in with his fingertips and look nowhere much really.

Spring we took to the woods, me and Granddaddy, and sometimes fished the Haw when we could catch a ride to it and Granddaddy would fix up the bait dough and I would tie the hooks like he'd taught me and we would go after catfish and go after carp and they were mostly sizeable fish and good for a tussle and we would draw them up on the bank and admire them for a time but did not ever carry them home as Momma would not cook carp and would not cook catfish on account of they were foul, she said, and rank and so we gave them all to a little colored boy that lived with his aunt by the low-water bridge and she would barbecue them on a rack and most times they did not smell so awful foul or rank either.

Come summer we always drove to Winston-Salem at least one time for a Red Sox doubleheader at Ernie Shore Field. It was triple A and so right fair mostly, near about like real baseball, and generally just me and just Daddy and just Granddaddy went but there was the one time we took Mr. Russell Newberry with us as Mr. Russell Newberry did not have anything else to do otherwise and liked baseball well enough himself. I do recollect it was along about mid August and the Red Sox were playing the team from Kinston and wasn't neither one in contention for anything but to finish so the crowd was not considerable really but was more considerable than it would have been on account of how it was fan appreciation night and the club was giving away a black-and-white Motorola and a set of Ben Hogan golf clubs and a sailboat along about the size of a bathtub and an actual and authentic warm-up jacket down from Boston and six cotton jerseys, three with the red sleeves and three with the blue. Between the games they were to draw numbers out from a bucket that would match up with the numbers on the programs and Daddy said it would be a fine thing to win a Motorola as far as he could tell or maybe even some golf clubs too but Granddaddy and Mr. Russell Newberry agreed how they'd come to see baseball and did not want it all mucked up with televisions and golf clubs and sailboats and such since most everything elsewise was mucked up already and didn't seem they needed to drag baseball into it and that fairly much set the two of them on a jag about what was wrong with everything and as there was so much wrong with so many things Granddaddy and Mr. Russell Newberry could not hardly manage to ease off the topic until the bottom of the first inning when they both recollected how they had intended to keep the line score and so asked me and so asked Daddy what had got done exactly that top half and who by.

Mr. Russell Newberry was already feeble-sighted with glaucoma by then and wore glasses not any less thick and purplish than the ones he wears anymore and he would slip them up onto his forehead to look at the program and slip them back down on his nose to look at the field and could not see much of either really and he would hear the bat crack on the ball and hear the ball slap against gloveleather and hear folks all roundabout him hoot and cheer and yelp but would not have much clue himself as to what had happened exactly though he suspected something had and so he would ask Granddaddy, "What was that, Mr. Buck?" and Granddaddy would tell him what man had hit what sort of pitch where and to whom and how he'd fared by it and Mr. Russell Newberry would repeat it all back to him and Granddaddy would say, "That's it," and so Mr. Russell Newberry would commence to putting the numbers in the little boxes but he could not ever remember what position was which number exactly and so he would set in to counting on his fingers but could not always recollect which direction to count in and so was ever wanting to know from Granddaddy was it the pitcher that was number one or the catcher and whichever it was who was number two. But he managed to keep it all and managed to put it all down, up until the top of the eighth inning when the Kinston right fielder lined a sluggish fastball back through the box and the pitcher threw out his glove so as to swat at the thing and did actually hit it, or hit some little piece of it anyhow, enough of it to send it skidding towards the shortstop that was running after where it was going and so kicked it when it got where it went instead and it sort of spun around on the infield for a time before the third baseman could get at it and then snatch it up with his bare hand and then drop it and snatch it up again and the Kinston right fielder had near about stretched the thing into a double by that time and so the third baseman fired the ball sidearmed towards second and the second baseman caught the thing at his shoetops and made the putout, and couldn't Granddaddy hardly explain any of it to Mr. Russell Newberry though he tried to give it out like it happened and couldn't Mr. Russell Newberry hardly get the numbers all marshaled and lined up like he needed though he tried to put it down like he heard it, put it down and erased it and put it down again and scratched it out one more time so as to put it down all over and would lift up his glasses off his nose and read what he had to Granddaddy who would say just, "No sir," and shake his head. So Granddaddy took the book from him and filled in the boxes himself and read the numbers back out to Mr. Russell Newberry that pondered on them for a time and then wondered at Granddaddy was it the pitcher that was number one or the catcher and whichever it was who was number two.

The game was tight right up to the end of it when the Red Sox catcher beat a ball into the dirt and made first before the bounce gave out and the right fielder bunted him to second and the shortstop fouled off two pitches and got called out on the third that Granddaddy said was a spitball and he stood up out of his seat and hollered, "Spitball!" and a lady down a row from us twisted around and glared at Granddaddy with a face

Aunt Sister would have endorsed herself, and so with two runs and two outs and the game even and a man on second the first baseman stepped in and took a ball low and away and took another one high and inside and looked hard at a curve that got called on him and then fairly much uncurled on a fastball and drove it deep into right center where it bounced off the Timex advertisement on the ballpark wall and the run scored and the game was over and we all hooted and yelped and Mr. Russell Newberry tugged at Granddaddy's shirtsleeve and asked for the particulars of the thing.

We ate hotdogs and drank Pepsi-Colas and watched a man in coveralls drag the infield with a tractor and a portion of chainmesh and Mr. Russell Newberry bought french fries in a cone and sprinkled them all over with vinegar on account of he'd seen the man ahead of him do it and we all sampled and tasted the french fries with the vinegar on them and me and Daddy and Mr. Russell Newberry liked them well enough that way but Granddaddy insisted as how vinegar was for greens and ketchup was for french fries and he was not much taken with finding the one on the other.

The man in the coveralls and a policeman and some fellow otherwise in a nylon jacket all three together toted a long folding table out towards the pitcher's mound and set it up and then commenced to carry out the fan appreciation prizes to put atop it and we all admired the Motorola and the Ben Hogan golf clubs and the sailboat that got set in the grass with the sail up and the authentic warm-up jacket and the jerseys too, or anyhow the box that they were in, and then a man somewhere struck in to telling us over the speaker what was set to happen and why and who for and then he got to who by, which had not any of us given much thought to until the man on the speaker introduced the reigning Gold Leaf Queen, Miss Pamela Louise Spain-hour of Lexington and out she came from the visiting dugout on the arm of a blackheaded man in a blazer and the sight of her just purely got away with near about everybody. Of course mostly it was the stretchy blue bathing suit which was not hardly indecent but snug enough everywhere and surely unforeseen considering how it was a ballpark we were in and how it was baseball we'd come to watch and instead were seeing what looked to be two of the longest naked legs a human could possibly be possessed of and naturally all the men drew breath and naturally all the women watched them do it. Of course there was the tiara too that glittered and sparkled in the floodlights and there was the silk ribbon across her chest with Gold Leaf Queen spelled out along it in shiny letters, but aside from the bathing suit, though maybe mostly in conjunction with it, the thing that truly struck and stunned us altogether was the highheeled shoes with the slender ankle straps and the pointy toes. Did not many women in Neely wear but flats and pumps and did not many women in Neely wear bathing suits either except at the Optimist park and then only the kind with the little skirts, and did not any women in Neely ever put the one on their feet and the other elsewhere at the same time, so it was rare to us and exotic, Daddy said, which was how come we tended to watch it with what attention we watched it with as far as he could tell and she walked on out across the baseline on the arm of the blackheaded man in the blazer and up onto the pitcher's mound which she got deposited at the very peak of and once she'd got herself set and steady she waved at the bunch of us that way beauty queens wave with their elbows going one way and their fingertips going the other, and we studied her from where we were, mostly that part between the thighbone and the ankle knob, which Daddy said it would be wise to give some attention to since did not any of us know if we'd ever see such again, and so we did give some attention to it and Mr. Russell Newberry tried his own self to give what attention he could and for a time kept his glasses flying up and down from his nose to his forehead and back to his nose again like maybe he was fanning his eyeballs.

They had put all the numbers in a bucket and the blackheaded man mixed them and tossed them and jumbled them up and they figured to start with the Motorola and then go to a jersey and then back to the golf clubs and then another jersey after and then maybe the sailboat and the authentic warm-up jacket with a jersey or two in between and finally cap it off with whatever jerseys were left, and the blackheaded man stepped up onto the pitcher's mound and held the bucket out in reach of Miss Pamela Louise Spainhour who stuck her arm full well into it and drew out a paperslip between her fingers that she gave over to the blackheaded man who rared back so as to fill up his lungs as best he might and then read off what numbers he'd been handed with nothing to amplify or further the sound but his own vocal cords which were more than up to it and he read it the once and then read it a second time and a third time after and a woman on the third baseline, what Daddy calls your thick sort, commenced to flap her hands in the air and screech and then she stood up and then she sat down again and then she stood up all over and tried to climb the rail and get herself onto the field somehow but as she was thick she could not quite get her leg up to where she needed to get it and she was bound a little too by her green knit slacks that she'd used up all the give in just by putting them on and so she kind of crawled under the rail instead, and without looking to see where she laid her hand exactly she reached back behind herself and grabbed onto her husband that did not have much bulk to him and she yanked him one time and near about landed him in fair territory and then crossed over the foulline with him in tow and she screeched and she waved her free hand and made direct for the Motorola that she laid both her arms roundabout once she'd got to it and hugged to her breast as best she could while her husband, that had hold of the program, got taken up by the blackheaded man who guided him to the pitcher's mound where they set in to comparing numbers and Granddaddy made some considerable nosewind down across his mustache and said how he'd come for baseball, how he'd come for sport and such and did not hardly need it put off and cluttered up like it had got and he made his Iampurelydisgusted sort of exhale through his mouth and crossed his arms over himself and Mr. Russell Newberry set in to agreeing with him and was in the midst of some hard words against clutter and such when the Motorola number got verified by the blackheaded man and of a sudden Miss Pamela Louise Spainhour, the Gold Leaf Queen, bent some at the waist, laid both her arms across the thick greenpantsed woman's husband's shoul-dertops, and kissed him square on the mouth and Granddaddy said, "Christalmighty," and Daddy said, "Jesus," himself and looked overtop my head at Granddaddy that looked overtop my head back at him and Mr. Russell Newberry left off with his tirade on account of what it was he had heard in the Christalmighty and what it was he had heard in the Jesus too which had not either one seemed much directed at clutter and Motorolas and paperslips in buckets and so he eyed the field with his glasses up and with his glasses down but could not see but his usual blurs and his usual shapes and shadows which left him just to look at Granddaddy beside him and just to look overtop my head at Daddy beside me and just to say to the both of them, "What?" which got him told Jesus and which got him told Christalmighty back, and Daddy unrolled his program and found his number on the inside cover of it and then unrolled my program and found my number on the inside cover for me and he held his and let me hold mine and Granddaddy turned his program back to his own front cover and found his own number and then snatched Mr. Russell Newberry's program from Mr. Russell Newberry's lap and found the number on it too and Mr. Russell Newberry said, "What is it, Buck?" and Granddaddy raked at his mustache with his skinflap and looked to be formulating some manner of sensible reply but when he opened his mouth to tell Mr. Russell Newberry what it was exactly he could not manage but a Christalmighty that prompted a Jesus from Daddy and together brought from Mr. Russell Newberry another What? and some additional eyeball fanning behind it.

We guessed we didn't want a sailboat much as it was not hardly the sort of item we could tote off in the Buick but we figured we'd be grateful for anything otherwise and while I was myself anxious for the authentic warm-up jacket down from Boston, Daddy and Granddaddy and Mr. Russell Newberry too, when the Jesus and the Christ-almighty as well had finally got explained to him, did not show much preference for any item in particular but took a near about excruciating interest in the number calling and since Mr. Russell Newberry could not quite make out his number, as they were such tiny little sons-of-bitches, he said, Granddaddy took charge of his program for him and checked it against whatever it was the blackheaded man rared back and called out but did not any of ours match up with the jersey after the Motorola or the golf clubs after the jersey or the other jersey after the golf clubs or the sailboat after that or even the authentic warm-up jacket which I had only four of the numbers on myself and them backwards, so we listened to what got called and studied what we had to judge it against and watched other people hoot and holler and run down the bleacher steps and out onto the field and Daddy and Granddaddy watched with particular interest how they got greeted at the pitcher's mound and Mr. Russell Newberry, that could not quite make any of it out, would say, "Well?"

"Square on the mouth," Granddaddy would tell him.

"Right flush?" Mr. Newberry would want to know.

"Flush," Granddaddy would say and Daddy would throw in with a Jesus sometimes or just a meaningful exhale otherwise.

And it did not look like we would get but more baseball as there weren't but jerseys left and only two of them when the blackheaded man finally laid back and called out the six and the three and the two and the seven and the nine and the six again and I did not hardly have it and Daddy did not hardly have it either and Granddaddy did not hardly have it on the

one of his programs that he discarded straightaway onto the
concrete under his seat once he saw how his other program did
have sixes and threes and twos and sevens and nines and
seemed pretty much the sort of thing the blackheaded man was
calling for though he could not be certain straightaway as he'd
forgotten what it was he'd heard near about as soon as he'd
heard it and so he asked Mr. Russell Newberry what it had
been and as Mr. Russell Newberry was blessed with some
considerable recall he set in to repeating the string of numbers
just prior to when the blackheaded man rared back and set
into repeating it his own self so Granddaddy got them all twice
and slam up one behind the other which did not but muddle
things up a little and so he still had not concluded if he had
what he needed until the blackheaded man rattled off the
numbers one last time and Granddaddy read along with him
the six and the three and the two and the seven and the nine
and the six again and he stood straight up out of his chair and
waved his program over his head and hollered one time and
commenced to sidle his way by Mr. Russell Newberry who
wanted to know wasn't it his program, who wanted to know
wasn't it the one he'd got handed when he come in through the
gate, who wanted to hear from Granddaddy how if it wasn't the
one he'd got handed at the gate it could have been if he hadn't
been so kind and courteous as to let Daddy and as to let me
and as to let Granddaddy too on in front of him, but
Granddaddy just sidled and just slipped and just made the
bleacher steps that he set about descending altogether
recklessly and Mr. Russell Newberry picked up his glasses off
his nose and then laid them back down on it and took himself
up out from his own seat and struck out down the bleachers
too and at a considerable velocity himself which prompted
Daddy to get up and prompted Daddy to sidle and prompted
Daddy to slip and prompted Daddy to tell me how I should
keep the seats and then he set out after Mr. Russell Newberry
who had set out after Granddaddy who had made the playing
field and was waving his rolled-up program over his head like a
war club.

I do believe the blackheaded man thought things were pretty well up with him the way he got swamped and overrun with Granddaddy straightoff and soon after Daddy that had passed up Mr. Russell Newberry on the railing on account of how Mr. Russell Newberry had dropped his hat and in stooping over to retrieve it had lost his ink pen out from his shirtpocket, but he came along directly himself and so finished out what circle had formed roundabout the blackheaded man that was reading numbers and saying numbers and attempting to verify numbers while Granddaddy watched and Daddy watched and Mr. Russell Newberry watched too as best he could and when at last it was determined that Granddaddy's number was what number had got fetched from the bucket and what number had got called out the blackheaded man presented Granddaddy with a red-sleeved jersey that was the last red-sleeved jersey and Granddaddy closed his hand on it without paying much mind to the thing as he was instead occupied with Miss Pamela Louise Spainhour up high on the pitcher's mound, and her tiara glistened in the white electric light and her silky ribbon and stretchy bathing suit both shimmered a little and her legs did not hardly seem to quit from the hip sockets after and she stood all tall and glorious and elevated and looked purely a princess while Granddaddy and Daddy and Mr. Russell Newberry too fell in line before her like holy men come to the temple to pray, and it was square on the mouth, was all square on the mouth even for Mr. Russell Newberry that could not see everything but could surely see some things well enough.

They got a sizeable ovation when they cleared the rail and gained the bleachers again and Mr. Russell Newberry lifted his hat off his head and swept it before himself as he bowed down which fired the uproar a little and Daddy and Granddaddy, that did not possess much trace of Mr. Russell Newberry's theatrical disposition, watched their feet carry them on up the bleacher steps, Daddy with his hands deep down in his trouser pockets and Granddaddy with the red-sleeved jersey hanging out either end of his fist and his free skinflap working at an appreciable pace and did not any of them have much at all to tell me about where they'd been and what they'd done and how it was things had looked from down there that maybe they did not look at all from up in the seats and it was only Granddaddy that said a thing to me and that just, "Here, son," as he handed me the red-sleeved jersey that was crushed and damp in the middle where he'd closed his hand around it.

Did not anybody keep the line score for the second game but me as the programs had all got gone somehow but for mine and I quit along about the middle of the fourth because would not anybody help me much except for Granddaddy that tried to every now and again but it was always 632 with him and 796 and would not those numbers hardly work on the field ever since the Gold Leaf Queen had left it for the dugout, so we did not any of us but watch and did not all of us do that with much focus and attention and Daddy let me have a Pepsi-Cola and let me have my own french fries in a cone with vinegar sprinkled overtop them and Mr. Russell Newberry called for hot nuts from a vendor across the way and the vendor threw the bag at him and hit him in the nose with it. We left in the middle of the eighth with Kinston out front six to one and playing like they meant to stay there and Daddy let me take off what shirt I'd worn and put on my new jersey in the parking lot and the sleeves hung down over my fingertips and the tails left off about midthigh but Daddy and Granddaddy and Mr. Russell Newberry too all said it was a fine thing, all said I looked like the splendid splinter himself, and did not anybody talk hardly all the way home but we just sat and just breathed heavy every now and again with me and Mr. Russell Newberry in the full dark of the backseat and Granddaddy and Daddy up front with the green dashboard light on their faces.

Did not the Gold Leaf Queen come up with much prominence when me and Daddy and Granddaddy told Momma what we'd done and what we'd seen and what manner of thing we'd had to eat and then we all went pretty much direct to bed and Momma let me wear my jersey under the topsheet and I laid on my side like usual and watched Granddaddy that came in from the bathroom in his pajamas and sat on the edge of the mattress with his feet flat on the floor and the heels of his hands pressed down beside himself and he just looked direct and level across the room where there was not anything to look at truly and he stayed like that for a time, stayed like that until he drew off that last hard breath that straightened him up and then commenced to let it out in bits and spurts down to the very end of it which he spent in "lordy lordy lordy" like always and then just sort of tipped over onto the pillow and brought his feet in under the covers that he drew up clean to his jawbone and I shut off the lamp myself and pitched over to face the wall which was how I stayed all throughout most nights while Granddaddy commenced to shift and roll and blew through his mouth what was almost whistles sometimes and most nights it would seem he would not ever light and lie still and most nights I guess I was long asleep before he ever did but sometimes not and I would notice how the shifting dwindled and how the rolling dwindled and how the whistles finally left off altogether and maybe he would snort a time or two but he did not snore awful much and generally just sank and settled into a sleep that was as near about death as sleep can get, always near about death itself until at last it was death finally which was November, I do recall, on a Saturday, and I was up to rake out the crepe myrtles along the back border and I touched Granddaddy on the shoulder and said to him, "Granddaddy," loud and plain which even when I said it I knew there was no call to say on account of how he felt underneath my fingers that was not cold and that was not stiff but that just was not Granddaddy anymore.

And even then I didn't know it and for a time after didn't know it either and when it finally got said and told to me it was not hardly from Daddy or from Momma or even from Aunt Sister that would generally say and tell a thing firstoff, was not even

any of my people at all but was instead Bill Ed Myrick jr. that
had got it from his own daddy that had known it a spell on
account of everybody knew it, Bill Ed said, on account of
everybody knew it but me, and so he opened his mouth and let
it out again. "A nigger," he told me. "With a log," he told me.
And Jack Vestal said it was right, said he'd heard as much
himself and said it was right, and I said no back in my throat
so that could not anybody hear it really but me, and Bill Ed
Myrick jr. told me, "A nigger," and told me, "With a log," and it
sounded low and it sounded evil and he grinned after and I
said, "No," full out this time and he would not leave off
grinning and I said, "No!" shouting it anymore and Bill Ed
Myrick jr. fairly smirked and so I hit him, hit him across the
chest and hit him alongside the head and threw my whole self
at him and knocked him down and crawled up all overtop him
and hit him everywhere I could hit him and told him NO! with
every breath I could get to tell it to him with until Jack Vestal
rolled me off him and sat on my one arm while Bill Ed Myrick
jr. got his knees atop my other and I kicked and swore and spat
until I was just done in with all of it and they tried to lift me
and tried to hoist me but I would not let them get me up and
just laid in the grass until they had gone on up the road and
left me and even then I did not go home straightoff but walked
west to the boulevard and down the alleyway behind the Big
Apple and roundabout the square and out past the Heavenly
Rest and then east again and along our street and up our steps
and into our house and down our back hallway to my room
that did not have but the one bed in it anymore and that back
crosswise again and I sat on the edge of it and looked out level
across the room to the far wall which was how Momma came
through the doorway and found me and which was why
Momma wondered on my account like she did as I was not
hardly the sort for wallstaring in the usual way of things and so
I told her what I'd heard and I told her what I figured it meant
and Momma said how there were just some people that would
find out everything and how there were just some people that
would tell everything they found out and how it just happened

most times to be the same people and then she quit talking altogether and looked at me like maybe she had answered the business entirely and I looked at her back like surely she hadn't and she said, "Louis," still looking at me, and then said it again and louder this time, "Louis," and I heard Daddy's chairsprings groan and heard the floorjoists pop and creak beneath him as he crossed the living room.

"A nigger," I said. "With a log," I said, and Daddy leaned against the doorframe that Momma had vacated for him and he did not say no back and he did not say yes back either but just nodded at me up and down and just pondered for a time and when he guessed he knew how he'd get at it he said to me, "Come on," and we went together through the bredkfast room to fetch Momma and to fetch Aunt Sister that had come by for a cake sliver and Daddy took his chair and Momma took hers and Aunt Sister got the one with the pillow in it and I brought in the straight hard one from the living room that mostly did not get sat in at all and it was Daddy that commenced with just who'd got stabbed and how come and whereabouts and it was Aunt Sister that said blood thing and Aunt Sister that said foolishness and it was Momma that wanted passion and wanted temperament and it was Daddy that said it for her but got told No sir back by Aunt Sister that said blood thing and that said foolishness and with two fingers Daddy drew out a Tareyton from his shirtpocket and laid the filter on his lip and with the same two fingers Daddy brought out a matchpack from alongside his chaircushion and he looked at Momma and he looked at me and he looked at Aunt Sister that had not quite got still and had not quite got quiet but commenced to directly and he tore out a match and struck it and used it and shook it out and looked again at Momma and again at me and again at Aunt Sister and he let out a portion of smoky breath through his nose and with the rest of it he told us, "Alright," that way he does sometimes.

Fuquay-Varina

1984

Made in the USA
Coppell, TX
24 October 2023